MW01593438

NEXT

BY HENSEN MARCH

Published by Starry Night Publishing.Com
Rochester, New York

Copyright 2022 Hensen March

To Susan from Jim aka: Hensen March

Hensen March

Acknowledgement

Andie Highlands, thank you so very much for your encouragement, suggestions, and efforts. Your expertise as an editor made this a better book. It was a shared effort; thank you for agreeing to help.

Contents

Hensen March

1 – Family of One

This story is inspired by actual events.

The sunlight from the windows of the bus was bright against the pole that steadied the riders as they filed down the steps. It was summertime. The bus was hot as he pointed at the hospital and said to the riders seated nearby, "That's where my mother works."

His father mumbled something.

It was the summer of 1951 in the biggest city he had seen. He knew his mother didn't work in the hospital...he had seen her for the last time in the bed, thin and pale. She hugged him. "They cut a nerve in my neck, and it doesn't hurt anymore." All of it lasted less than a minute, and he was back on the bus with the shining pole.

The windows were open in the hotel room where he sat on the end of the bed. His feet did not touch the floor. To his right, the black phone rang and his father picked up the receiver, and he saw where the light in the ceiling reflected off the oil in his father's hair. His father put down the receiver and said, "Your mother is dead." He looked at his father's face. He looked at the top of his feet; he stopped thinking or feeling.

It may have been shock. He remembered nothing until he arrived at the edge of the plank bridge that crossed the forty-yard ditch that led to the shack with the dirt yard. It was the shack of his father's drinking buddy, Sonny. He found out later that he was named after this short, ignorantly violent man. He followed his father across the plank bridge, holding onto the one handrail. The rail was above his head, and the plank was narrow.

Ahead, Sonny was standing outside the doorway with children appearing to his left and right. He counted six. A thin woman with long, unkempt hair that looked like vines on an old tree and two dark oval eyes peering from deep within her skull had appeared in the doorway and moved to the far-right side of the porch. By the darkness in her eyes, he felt he was not welcome.

"Sonny, here he is." He saw his father place the suitcase on the porch. Inside were the picture of his mother when she was eighteen years old and a coin collection with various pennies and dimes placed in holes set in cardboard. The suitcase was an odd shape, taller than wide and blond in color. It had been his only true companion for some time.

He followed one of the children through the screen door into the first room. To the left was a mustard-colored couch, one chair to the right, a tall black stove in the corner with a pipe that passed through the ceiling. He looked back through the screen door when he heard Sonny say, "Want a nip," and he saw him pass a short, flat bottle of brown liquid to his father. His father turned it up, and he saw the dark liquid appear in the neck and shoulders of the bottle. Then Sonny turned quickly, with the screen door slamming behind him. "Boy, let me show ya the place." He said nothing.

As Sonny passed by, he smelled like the brown liquid, and the boy saw the same kind of bottle in the right back pocket of Sonny's faded overalls...he wore no shirt. He followed Sonny into the next room. Along the wall to the left were six narrow beds crammed together like one wide bed; there were no sheets like the hotel room had in the big city. To the right was a bed that was wider than the others. Behind the headboard, he could see the corner of the room. This was where Sonny slept with the woman.

They went through the kitchen to the back porch where three poles held up the roof and a fabric couch was pushed up against the outside wall of the house; there lay two hound dogs with frightened eyes. Sonny said, "You'll sleep here" and laughed. He knew this was not a joke. He could count...six kids, six beds.

"It's Saturday; we're goin' to town." Sonny went into the room with the beds and turned left to get the keys to the old truck. Then, through the front screen door, he saw the back of his father's body with the shiny hair. His father stepped off the other side of the plank bridge and disappeared into the trees. He ran to the front porch as he heard the car drive away. He said nothing. He felt the familiar wind pass by his heart. Now he was a family of one...

2 – Man With the Kind and Gentle Face

He was in the back of the truck with the six children while it moved down the dirt road. He sat with his back against Sonny's side of the truck, with his right hand holding onto the top of the tailgate. He knew it would be dusk soon. Through the back window of the cab, he could see that the woman had put her hair up in a bun with a faded pink ribbon that moved in the breeze from the open window next to her. The oldest boy was sitting with the back of his head close to the cab, looking at him. "He's gonna' do it!" He saw the arm with the hair on it and the fist that struck the woman three times above her ear. The ribbon went out the window and up and across above his head and rolled two times before settling in the dirt of the road. The woman did not have a bun. He could see the tips of her hair as it was pulled out of the window and wrapped around the outside of the cab, moving up and down as the truck was nearing the town. "Told ya' so."

The sign went by fast, "pop. 924." He heard the brakes grind as the truck slowed and stopped at the curb. The big children jumped out of the bed. The small ones put one leg over while the older ones put their hands under the little ones' arms and turned, placing them on the sidewalk. He didn't know why they were excited. He climbed over the tailgate, placing one foot and then the other on the bumper and taking a long jump to the street. As he rounded the back of the truck, he heard Sonny yell, "Come on, boy!"

The group walked down the sidewalk—the older ones up front, little ones in the middle, and the woman close behind, touching her left temple. He and Sonny were walking side by side; he stayed out of Sonny's reach. He quickened his pace to blend in with the little ones just in front of the woman. He noticed he was no taller than the ones in the middle, but he knew how to disappear in front of the eyes of the men who drank brown liquid from the flat bottle.

It was those last moments before dusk when there was violet in the sky, and then he saw it—a tiny plastic gold frame lying on edge in the dark, purple-looking grass. It was irresistible! He stepped off the sidewalk and squatted down, turning the frame to see a picture of Gene Autry with his ten-gallon hat. It was a true prize! He turned his feet in the damp grass and rested the frame on his right knee with his thumb and forefinger. It was truly a thing of beauty. He smelled sweat and saw the boots behind the cowboy picture. The toes of the boots were pointed at him. It was Sonny. "Boy, that ain't yours. Put it down!"

He looked up; Sonny didn't look short anymore. He dropped Gene Autry and ran to the group that was rounding the corner two buildings down. He was no longer invisible.

Be careful! You can be a child sometime later. Not here. Not now. He turned the corner as the plate glass door closed behind the woman with no bun. Her hand was still rubbing the side of her head. He looked up quickly at the sign; it read "Franklin's." No time to look anymore—Sonny would turn the corner at any moment. He placed his thumb on the handle and pushed down hard and shoved the door wide enough to put his foot in the opening. He heard the bell above the door ring as the door closed behind him. Sonny's face was on the other side of the glass.

"Sonny, hey Sonny, you old son of bitch come have a drink!" There were five men across the street standing under a red neon sign, "BAR." He heard one of the men yell, "You got a lot of damn kids." The man sitting on the bench hollered, "You gonna fuck that woman to death."

Sonny was listening. His face was still in the glass. He grinned, and his nose flared and his eyes narrowed; he was deciding what would happen next. Then he turned and crossed the street.

He realized that he had been holding his breath when he heard in his skull the sound of air coming out of his nose and mouth, making a round cloudy spot on the glass of the door. He knew he had a few moments to look around the store. He had heard about these stores—*it was a dime store!* He had never been in one. Even when he was in the big city, he only saw the hotel room, the bus with the shining pole, and the hospital room where his mother had been. *Can't think about that now!*

This store was different than the general store near where he had lived with his parents. The general store was on ten-foot-high stilts next to a wide river. Thirty-two steps led to the door. He always counted them when he went with his mother to "get supplies." His mother told him he was born in that store, near where the boots were displayed. The owner and his wife laid a tarp on the floor, and his mother took her underwear off, got on the tarp, and squeezed him out between her legs. The husband called the doctor on the wall phone behind the counter. The doctor came and cut the cord and wrote, on the flap torn off of an envelope, that he was there for the live birth of... Then he realized that he had been standing in the same spot in the dime store, seeing everything in his mind the way his mother had described.

He saw the children with their hands in a row of double wooden bins that were back-to-back and on six legs. He was standing at the end of the handmade, wooden structure. He looked in the bins and saw colorful toys in each of them. The bins were painted a chocolate brown color that made the contents seem brighter and more desirable. He understood why the children were excited before and why the woman looked the way she did and why he hadn't heard her speak a word. He hadn't said anything himself. He saw her beyond the bins, sitting on a stool looking at the slats in the floor. The boys were looking in one bin that had cork popguns made of two pieces of tin soldered together to look like tiny rifles that were painted on both sides. They had a string with a small cork on the end and a round plunger that, when pulled back and the tin trigger squeezed, pushed air through the barrel causing the cork to pop out of the barrel. They were impressive! One on the top of the pile had double barrels, double corks. There was only one double barrel—the other twenty or so were single barrel with only one cork.

He was closely examining the toy when he heard the bell above the door ring once and then twice, followed by footsteps. He continued to look at the toy. The smell had returned and the boots. He looked down at his feet; *the boots looked huge!* They were touching the side of his shoe. This time he didn't hold his breath.

"Boy, get the double barrel!" He knew if he got the double barrel the other three boys would have to choose one of the other twenty or so. But, that would mean the man with the smell, the man with the flat bottle, the man who hit the silent woman three times in the head, the man with the flaring nostrils and narrowed eyes staring at him through the plate glass door...*what would this man do?* He chose the boys, whose names he did not know, over the fear. At that moment, Sonny was not as tall as when he had dropped his hero, Gene Autry, into the purple grass of dusk.

With the single-barrel toy rifle in his hand, he turned toward the man. His eyes were on the same level as the bulging waistband of

Sonny's overalls. From the weight of the man's large belly, the center of the waistband pointed down toward his boots. Sonny had sensed the change in the boy. Sonny kicked the center leg of the structure, and the toys in both sides of the bins rose and then fell making a rattling tin sound. The double barrel was no longer on top of the pile of rifles. He could feel Sonny's eyes on the top of his head, burning through his hair down to his scalp.

The store became silent. The woman on the stool continued to look at the floor; the children did not move. The other customers moved back, clearing a straight path to the door, and the men slowly moved in front of their women. Sonny quickly turned, moving his left boot in front of the large belly; he staggered briefly, catching his balance. He stomped toward the door, slamming something down on the counter next to the gold-colored cash register. The store clerk jumped when Sonny's open hand hit the surface of the counter.

The children waited until the door closed then filed out the way they had been on the sidewalk earlier. The store was still silent. There was a tiny sound of tin rattling...it was the single-shot popgun in his trembling hand. He passed the counter where seven dimes lay in front of the clerk who still had his back to the wall. He walked fast to the door.

A man with a kind and gentle face stepped away from his woman and opened the door for him. The man leaned over and whispered, "Better hurry, son...the missus and I will pray for you."

He ran through the door, turning left and left again around the building until he slowed and passed the woman; his hand with the toy lightly brushed the woman's dress. As he moved toward the truck, he could see the round front of the truck with the two dim headlights and the looming figure behind the steering wheel. The shadow figure was pounding the metal dash of the truck with both fists. He carefully stayed in the long shadows cast by the headlights shining on the front of the group. All heads were down, not daring to look through the windshield at the face of the man who kicked the leg of the toy bins.

He thought he had made the right decision in the dime store. Now he realized the children and the silent woman would pay dearly for his decision. He planned to hide in the deep woods when the shadow figure came for him...he thought about the hound dogs. *Would they be able to track me? I would keep moving—fast!* He

10

managed to stay in the long shadows of the group, but the shadows were getting shorter as the group approached the dim lights of the truck.

The older ones helped the little ones over the side of the bed. He jumped to grab the side of the truck bed. He held on tightly with both hands, placing his left foot on the small hubcap just above the faded red letters "GMC" Condensation had formed on the hubcap from the cool night air on the warm metal. His foot slipped, and his chest hit the back fender; the air rushed out of his lungs. He was gasping, with his legs dangling in air. The oldest boy grabbed his right foot with both hands and lifted. He slid his body over the side like a snake over a log. He looked back at the oldest boy still standing next to the truck, with a silent message exchanged between both pairs of eyes. The boy vaulted into the bed like a deer. All seven children settled into their previous spots. Everyone in the bed of the truck had slid down below the view from the back window of the cab. The oldest boy's head was below the back window, too. He knew the oldest boy was a "watcher" like him. He could see two things in the oldest boy's eyes: resignation and something else that was opposite and quietly more powerful. Another sense.

Sonny pushed down on the floor starter of the truck. The starter turned twice, and the engine began running. Through the window he could see Sonny's head momentarily disappear when his foot pushed down on the clutch and reappear when he pulled the lever down on the steering column. The truck lurched forward and the engine died. Sonny adjusted the small rear-view mirror, and the boy could see Sonny's eyes searching for the seventh child. Sonny stared, once again, through the glass at his namesake, now reflected through a mirror...this time he stared back...pupil to pupil. He felt an anger rise up in his chest, and he sat up straight above the other children's heads. Sonny started the truck again and turned around in the street, grazing the light pole, which violently swayed from the impact, briefly shining light on the oldest boy's face and eyes. He heard the voice "Don't do that again!" He knew it came from the oldest boy, but the oldest boy had not opened his mouth.

The little ones began to cry. The woman was looking through the back window with her finger up across her lips. Her finger and the tip of her nose suddenly were pushed against the glass as Sonny pressed the accelerator to the floor. The bed of the truck moved to the left and right and settled in the center of the dirt road as the truck slowed a bit. Some of the little ones were quietly sobbing, then began to stop as the night air flowed through their hair in the darkness.

Deep woods lined both sides of the road. The trees stood tall, straight, and strong as the front lights of the truck illuminated the canopy of branches and leaves. He looked over the top of the tailgate at the pink glow cast by the truck's one red taillight. The moon was new as he saw the low hanging clouds drift in front of it.

He looked around the bed at the little ones sitting close together, quietly showing each other their choices of toys from the store. The older ones kept their treasures hidden in their shirt pockets and the pockets in the folds of their summer dresses. There was no money for store bought clothes...they were all originals, handmade by the woman who never spoke. He didn't know this for sure, but he could see it in the oldest boy's eyes. Everyone was still sitting as low as they could below the back window of the truck's cab. He began to have the sense that the trip to the dime store was a rare event. He remembered seeing no toys in the shack during his tour with the driver of the truck. He also knew things would be unpredictable when the truck reached its destination. Until then, he would enjoy the wind, trees, and the moon.

Everyone leaned forward toward the center of the bed, away from the sides, as the truck slowed and turned left onto a narrow lane through ten-foot-high Johnson grass with razor sharp blades. The oldest girl looked at him and said, "When the truck stops, get out on this side, fast!"

The truck stopped in a clearing; the older children grabbed the little ones in their arms and jumped. He put his foot on the side of the bed and jumped, hitting the dirt and rolling on his right shoulder. Now he was on his back as the truck backed up fast, with the front of the truck swinging to the left as the back tire made a half moon close to his feet. The woman had stepped out of the truck, running with the passenger door still open. The truck sped forward with the accelerator pushed to the floor; the back tire spun, kicking up dirt and small rocks as Sonny drove through the Johnson grass with the door banging against the cab of the truck. He heard the door finally slam shut as Sonny made a hard right turn, heading back to town.

Next

He sat up and spit the dirt out of his mouth and saw the ruts from the tire. *Next time jump faster and farther!* Even the little ones were standing. It was his first time but not theirs. Everyone stood for a few moments in silence to see if the lights of the truck would return. They did not...this time.

Hensen March

3 – Blue and Daisy

After Sonny left, there was a break in the clouds as they began to cross the plank bridge. The new moon was silver on top of the water and a shiny, pale, white on the bridge. The group was in a different order than before—the woman was first, with the youngest girl holding the back of the woman's dress just below the waist and her right hand holding the handrail above her head. Next came the oldest girl, the one that warned him about what to do when the truck stopped, big one, small one, with the oldest boy next to last. The oldest boy motioned for the seventh child, the last one, to curl his left index finger around the belt loop in the center of his waist. It looked like the oldest was to fish anyone out of the water before the water moccasins, banded water snakes, and snapping turtles could reach any of the children. He was near the middle of the bridge when he began to see the heads popping out of the ditch water, moving toward the bridge. The heat from the bodies of the crossers and the vibration of the bridge brought more heads to the surface. *This was a looking ditch, a fishing ditch—not a wading ditch!*

The silent woman watched until everyone had crossed. He reached the front of the dirt yard as the woman pulled the chain to turn on the light on the porch. As he walked under the light, the chain looked like a long line of BB's connected together with a tiny lampshade on the end. The bulb was bare; above it two cloth-covered wires twisted around each other connected to a round white receptacle nailed to one of the porch rafters.

He walked through the two rooms to the kitchen. The woman had put three large iron skillets on the three-burner stove and lit the burners with a long wooden match. He had not seen food prepared for some time. The woman was peeling and slicing potatoes from a webbed, orange sack that hung on a large nail. She turned and pointed to the back door. He could see the children washing their hands, while the oldest boy moved the pump's cast-iron handle up and down. The oldest girl checked everyone's hands before they went to the porch, through the kitchen, and to their beds to sit and play with their new treasures. The dogs did not like the sound of the corks popping out of the toy rifles. It was his turn at the pump.

He did what the others did, but before the oldest girl checked his hands, the oldest boy said, "When you finish using the pump, fill this can up to the top and hang it on that post. If you don't, thar be hell to pay!" His hands were checked. He entered the kitchen, where sliced potatoes were frying in one skillet, sowbelly in another. The silent woman was slicing tomatoes and had lettuce torn and ready to prepare wilted lettuce with hot bacon grease.

The oldest boy came through the kitchen after filling the can as he had warned. He continued through the two rooms and sat on the edge of the front porch. The oldest boy was the lookout for Sonny's return. If Sonny returned before the woman finished and the children had eaten, there would be no supper for anyone but Sonny. Once again, he saw it in the oldest boy's eyes—he was the "watcher." The seventh child had decided hours ago that he would be a "watcher" of the "watcher." The oldest boy had survived the longest, second only to the silent woman. He could see what years of living in a three-room shack, closed up in a truck cab, and being humiliated at every turn by a violent animal predator living inside a human form—as disgusting in appearance as the behavior itself—had done to the silent woman. She had no voice, no name; even the children did not call her "Mother." He knew that sometime in the past she had spoken, was someone's daughter, laughed, and had friends. Someone loved her...that was long ago.

The smells brought him back as the woman pulled a tray of biscuits out of the small oven below the sizzling skillets. She poured the hot bacon grease on the pile of lettuce as the children brought their plates. As each child was given a portion, he waited until last. As he stepped forward, the oldest girl gave him a plate containing more than expected. Every child sat at the table on long benches, little ones on one bench, older ones on the opposite bench. There were no forks or knives; each plate had a large spoon placed to the right. He waited, because the others waited. The woman fixed a large plate with a metal cover and placed it on a cloth on the open oven door and brought her plate to the end of the table facing the back screen door. She sat on a low stool. She nodded, and the spoons began to move rapidly. He had not had such a meal before him since his mother had become ill. He felt urgency at the table as each, including the woman, ate quickly. The oldest boy finished first and returned to the front porch.

He felt the energy from the food as he finished eating, wiping the plate with the remains of the biscuit. He saw the other children bring their plates to the woman who scraped the food remains onto her plate. The woman went through the screen door to the back yard and emptied from her plate into a metal pan with sides for the dogs.

He was standing in the kitchen when he heard the whistle from the front porch. The silent woman was at the stove before the screen door slammed behind her. All of the children were in bed with a thin blanket pulled to their necks facing him, their backs to the front porch. He saw the dogs stop eating as tall, thin, and dim vertical shafts of light followed by bands of darkness moved from right to left on the trees surrounding the back yard. The silent woman pointed at the back screen door. He grabbed three biscuits off the stove, sticking one in the pocket of his shirt and one in each hand to introduce himself to his new sleeping partners.

He opened the door slowly and quietly as the dogs raised their heads. He could see white teeth in the light from the kitchen. He knew dogs were like people—some friendly, some not so friendly. There was a chance that one had an attitude, but they both had teeth. He did not intend to sleep in the woods where larger things lived. Moving slowly, he positioned himself near the center of the couch and sat down gently, placing a biscuit in front of each dog. He could hear, in the rib cages of both dogs, a distant rumble that moved up into their throats. They sat facing him; their heads were taller than his, and he could feel their hot breath on both sides of his face. They were not interested in the biscuits—he was in their bed. He heard the oven door close. He sat quietly with his legs straight and his feet barely beyond the center edge of the couch. Instantly, the dogs cowered, grabbing their biscuits and eating them in two gulps. The dogs were curled up tight and trembling.

He began to hear a faint creaking of the plank bridge. Then he knew that he and the dogs had suddenly become bedfellows beyond sharing the couch. *It was Sonny!* He knew part of what would happen next...the sound from the bridge would get louder and there would be boot sounds on the front porch and then the front screen door would slam; beyond that would be up to Sonny.

He heard the unsteady boot sounds pass through the room with the beds; he curled up low against one of the hounds, with his eyes on the back door. The door swung open hard and stuck against the back of the outside wall. Sonny wrapped the fingers of his right hand on the frame and slammed it shut. "You sass me again, I'll whoop ya hard." He pulled the bottle out and threw the cap at the boy. Sonny turned the bottle up and the boy saw the brown liquid make a thin straight and then crooked brown line as the liquid moved along the bottom edge of the side, rising up to the neck of the glass and disappearing. Sonny threw the bottle into the darkness, and the glass broke against a distant tree.

Sonny was in the kitchen making grunting sounds, and soon the boy could hear the spoon rapidly scraping across the plate of food. The sound of his eating was not much different than the dogs eating from the flat metal pan with the sides that was now turned upside down in the back yard. The dogs had stopped trembling, but their muscles were tight. The boy's head was resting on the dog behind him. His head felt like it was against a breathing stone.

"Ain't feedin' no seven kids." He heard the plate slide the length of the table, skid on the floor, and twirl briefly. The only chair at the table scraped against the floor. He heard the springs of the bed, followed by one boot and another dropping to the floor.

The silent woman's shadow was moving across the trees and pump. The screen door opened, and the woman set the low stool on the porch. Stacked on top were the three skillets, dishes, spoons, and a dirty dish towel. One clean towel was draped across her right shoulder as she threw a long strip of fried sowbelly to the boy. He caught it like a greasy stick and tore it along the wide strips of fat making three strips—one for him and one for each of his couch partners. He made sure he got more meat than fat.

As the three finished their second entrée of the evening, the woman set the stool next to the pump. She took the can off the post and poured the water into the top part of the pump while moving the handle up and down. The water began flowing. She put the stack on top of the can, placed them on the stool and began washing the dirty towel. She kept the water flowing by moving her right elbow up and down, freeing both hands. The woman started with the spoons, drying them with the towel from her shoulder, then plates, tucking each clean item underneath the previous one. She pulled a bar of lye soap from her apron and made diagonal lines in the skillets. She scrubbed them with steel wool, rinsed them carefully and placed something shiny on the inside, sides, and handles of the iron skillets.

The boy and the dogs watched the woman walk from the pump to the porch. He got up from the couch and opened the door for her. She looked at him with the dark eyes and motionless face; he quietly closed the door behind her. Through the outside wall, he heard the woman pass behind the couch and return the items to their proper places. He could hear Sonny snoring, and then darkness fell when she pulled the chain connected to the bulb. He closed his eyes to adjust to the darkness, opened them, and closed them again. Now he was outside in the darkness. No sides or screens between him and the woods, only the dogs breathing. The breathing stone was softer now as his head moved slightly with the dog's breath. His eyes remained closed as he thought of secret names for the four-legged creatures that shared their bed with him. The male would be "Blue" and the one under his head would be "Daisy."

The insects and the aromas of the couch were thick as he slowly opened his eyes. The new moon that had been behind the truck as it came from town was now above the roof of the shack, bathing the left sides of the trees with a dim, pastel white. The sounds of the woods became louder than the snoring from the room with beds. Things scurried with reflections of eyes close to the ground; some moved slowly and others fast. The ones higher above the ground with two eyes that did not move invited him to think Blue and Daisy would let him know if true danger lay behind the twin reflections. He closed his eyes and tried to remember his mother's face.

He was resting with his eyes closed in that place between awake and asleep when he felt Daisy's head move. The spring on the back door made a slow, metallic, stretching sound. He could see the hem of the three nightshirts flow through the opening, off the porch, and down the short path to the left leading to the outhouse. The oldest girl held the little ones' hands and let go and walked in front as the path narrowed. Blue jumped off the couch into the yard and sat where the yard ended and the path began. Daisy was on the porch, looking at the center and right of the tree line.

The girls emerged from the small structure with the little ones in front, half running, half skipping. The warm ground and the night air had created a low-hanging, foggy mist. The little ones spread their arms, moving them up and down with the flow of their nightshirts through the mist like fairies in a picture book. He smiled in the darkness. They drifted by him and the door closed quietly. The couch creatures settled back in their places, and he fell into a deep sleep.

The air rushed into his lungs along with a flying bug of some sort. Instantly, he was awake but not alert. He coughed, spitting out the insect while Blue and Daisy sat erect and focused on the woods. He could see six to seven sets of eyes reflecting through the trees, moving left and right, stopping, and moving closer to the ground and freezing in place. When he saw pairs of eyes, they were looking directly at the porch; when he saw one only one eye, they were moving.

Several things happened at once: The shaft of moonlight hit medium-length, light gray fur; eyes lit up like flash lights; electrical shock shot from his tailbone to the opening at the base of his skull, standing the neck hairs straight out like sticks; Blue and Daisy leaped half the length of the back yard, disappearing into the trees; and the scream in his head came out like a windy whisper. "Coyotes!"

There were death screams from the distant woods. He was sitting on top of the couch with knees under his chin as the back door flew open, and Sonny fired both barrels of the shotgun and shouted, "Getonoutaheer." Sonny looked at the boy and said, "Yer 'n the contray now—better lern howda thro' rocks good an' swing a stick fast. Are ya stupid, boy?" Sonny pulled the spent shells out of both barrels and dropped them on the porch.

Within moments he could hear the snoring again. The woods were silent.

He didn't care about the ignorant man. *Where were Blue and Daisy? Were they lying in the woods hurt or dead? What would Gene Autry do? He wouldn't be sitting on the back of the couch with his chin between his knees.* His legs and feet were tingling from sitting in the same curled-up position. He straightened out his legs and stretched them. He stared into the woods at two sets of eyes moving slowly. He stood up on the porch behind the middle pole.

Blue and Daisy cleared the last tree and the yard and lay hard on the porch. There were blood and gray hair around their mouths, wounds on Daisy's right hindquarters, and a wound on Blue's belly. He ran to the outhouse and tore pages from the Sears catalog and used both hands to take the can of water off the post. He put the can on the porch and dipped two pages into the water. Blue nipped at his hand as he touched the wound but let him wipe the blood from around the wound. He dipped two more pages into the can and placed them on top of the bite marks, leaving them there to stick to the blood. He did the same for Daisy and wrapped the wet paper around the upper part of her leg. He put the can by the door and lay down on the porch between his friends...his only friends.

The woods had come alive again, making a constant ringing in his ears as he watched over Blue and Daisy. There were some moans at first, but their breathing was steady as they rested. He dozed off and on until the birds became active. He dipped his hand in the can and dripped water on both of their tongues, then turned the can at an angle so they both could drink. All three put their heads down on the boards of the porch for a bit longer, resting.

The back door swung open and hit the dogs, knocking the can off the side of the porch. Blue and Daisy yelped and hobbled behind the far end of the couch to hide. The boy stood up and rammed his right shoulder into Sonny's bare belly between the horizontal folds of fat that made giant lips hiding a cavernous, mouth-like navel. Sonny placed his boot in the boy's chest and pushed fast and hard, sailing him off the porch into the dirt near the pump. Sonny reached for the can and threw it at the boy. "Best be gettin' some primin' water before I come back from dumpin' some shit." The beast in the dirty underwear headed down the path to the outhouse.

He had seen some of the heads of the creatures that lived in the deep and wide ditch. Now it was the only water source to prime the pump to pull the fresh water from below the ground. He picked up the can and headed toward the water, thick with reptiles with teeth that could kill and maim. The banks were steep, covered in roots exposed from floods and time. He put his left arm through the wire handle, resting it in the crook of his arm. Using both hands, he climbed down the ten-foot bank using the tree roots as ropes. The can banged against the roots, bringing the heads to the surface. They were coming fast as he dipped the can deep into the ditch. It was heavy. He turned and began to grasp the roots with his left hand while pushing the bottom of the can up the slope with his right. The heads in the water had lost interest and had sunk below the surface, while the smaller snakes headed for larger limbs to bathe in the morning sun.

He was halfway before he saw the open mouth with the cotton-white interior and the dripping fangs. It looked to be almost four feet long, with thickness in the center of the jet-black body. He moved sideways slowly, keeping the can between him and the deadly snake. He moved up the bank at an angle.

"I'm comin' for ya, boy!" He heard Sonny on the bridge, moving faster than his usual lumbering gate. He was watching the snake's head as the black body moved under and over the roots. Still coming at him.

"Get down, boy!" He dropped low between the roots, holding the can just above his head. He saw the hole appear in the word "lard" just between the "a" and "r," followed instantly by the sound from the barrel. The chunky, green liquid shot out of the hole into his face and down his shirt. The snake's head was pushing the mud under the can forward toward his face. He slammed the bottom of the lard can on top of the bulge of mud and went straight up the root where the bullet had struck the can. He looked back as the can rose, tilted and rolled down the bank into the ditch.

He was at the top of the bank looking at Sonny on the bridge continuing to shoot, laughing between aims and trigger pulls. The flat bottle rested on the handrail, and none of the shots hit their mark. The water moccasin had backed away from the can before it rolled into the water and was moving slowly over and under the roots to the ditch, with tufts of mud spitting up from the poor marksman's bullets. He realized that if he hadn't lain flat, the back of his head would have been in line with the pencil-sized hole in the lard can. As the thought rolled around in his brain, he saw Sonny drop another can into the water secured by a rope. "No wonder ya don't say nothin'; ya stupid...brain can't push words out...stupid, stupid. Come get this here can, stupid."

Sonny untied the rope from the can, put the bottle in his back pocket and carried the rifle with his left hand up the plank bridge toward the shack. They met at the end of the last plank. The boy was standing to Sonny's left as the man turned toward him. The barrel of the rifle was pointed at the buckle of the boy's belt. The boy moved to the side, with the barrel following him.

He had wondered, before, if Sonny was shooting at the can or the snake or him. He saw in the man's face that it was not a decision that was pondered or even considered—it made no difference because Sonny did not care either way. Then the boy realized that if Blue or Daisy stood between him and Sonny, they would be shot. They had been kicked enough to know their lives were of no consequence. That's why they were dogs with no names and the children did not play with or pet them. They were collateral against anyone who cared for them. But they did have names...secret names the boy whispered to them in the darkness.

Sonny and the rifle barrel had not moved; he and Sonny were standing still. He could see a clear film of puzzlement seep out of the pores of the man's face. It was like two very different minds studying each other...two different species...creatures of a different stripe.

Sonny turned toward the shack. "Told ya get tha can, boy!" He was glad he didn't move before Sonny. As Sonny walked toward the porch, the boy watched as the vertical brown streak on the back of the creature's underwear contorted between two narrow cheeks, dwarfed by the rolling flesh above.

He walked a third of the planks, coiled the rope, picked up both the can and rope and headed around the side of the shack to the back yard. Green, slimy tassels hung from both the rope and can as he neared the pump.

The silent woman was waiting at the pump to prime it and start the first meal of the day. The boy knew he would not be sitting at the table for this meal or any other. He also knew that the woman was not helping him but protecting herself by preparing the meal as quickly as possible. She poured the green water into the pump, moving the handle several times before the green turned to clear, filling a large jar. She filled the can and pumped more water that hit the V-shaped tin that filled the water trough for the dogs with no names.

He grabbed the handle and swung down, moving quickly to cup his hands at the end of the open spout and drink deeply. He looked down and to the left and saw Blue and Daisy lapping water out of a metal tank that had been cut in half lengthwise, with two metal bars welded at each end to keep the trough upright. He wet the catalog pages still stuck to Blue's belly wound and jerked them off fast. Blue yelped quietly. Daisy's bandages had dried from the morning sun and had fallen off. Both wounds were no longer bleeding, and both dogs were walking a bit easier; all three returned to the couch.

He could hear the children playing in the front yard. He rested on the couch, with the early smells of breakfast drifting through the screen door. A new smell of the ditch was now added to the couch—green slime on his pants and shirt. He closed his eyes and thought of his mother. She loved to fish, and he would lie on the bank next to her. "Momma, when I close my eyes and look at the sky, why is it always red?" She would answer softly, and he would put his head on her lap and feel her breathing. This memory would never fade. As long as his brain was alive, the image and softness of her voice would live on.

The children came through the door to wash their hands at the pump and the smells of cooking food were stronger now. Hands were checked. Each passed by the couch, looking briefly then down, on their way to breakfast. He heard the voice: "I'll get you somethin' soon." It was the voice of the oldest boy, the same as the night before in the truck when he heard "Don't do that again!"—but the oldest boy's mouth didn't open. No one was outside this time when he heard the same voice: "I'll get you somethin' soon."

He began to see that not only did the dogs have no names, no one had called him by his name since he had arrived. Just as with the dogs, the children did not play with him. He guessed they were told not to by Sonny, who obviously had developed a deep-seated disliking for him. He believed Sonny was a coward and a bully and Sonny knew that the boy knew this.

Hearing the spoons moving across the plates at the table intensified the hunger in his stomach. He had felt the pain before in the hotel room in the big city. Most of his father's calories came from the flat bottle, with seldom a thought of food or the fact he had a son to care for...he had been a family of one since his mother had become ill. The man he rode with on the bus had the title of father. He had honed the skill of disappearing before the eyes of the men who drank from the flat bottle with this man called father. The same man that stepped off the plank bridge and disappeared into the trees without saying a word to him. The boy was no different than the suitcase that was set on the front porch and now resided under Sonny's bed.

He heard the scraping of the plates, and shortly after, the woman with the stool appeared. She did not throw sowbelly this time but instead walked directly to the dogs' bowl, scraping the contents into their metal pan. He watched the ritual of cleaning as the dogs ate. She returned to the kitchen without a glance.

Once she was out of sight, both Blue and Daisy stopped eating and walked to the couch, placing a biscuit and a piece of sausage on either side of the boy. They looked into his eyes and returned to the metal pan. He felt the tears on his cheeks, and he quietly sobbed. Daisy and Blue returned to the couch, sitting closer and using their noses to push the food toward him. He ate the food, with the two dogs resting their heads in his lap. He was no longer a family of one...*now there are three of us!* This new family had no status or public names and was intermittently in danger, but they shared love and respect.

The dogs jumped off the couch and sat low behind the end of the couch as Sonny passed through the door, heading for the outhouse. The boy did not look as Sonny began taking the straps off his overalls. He was relieved that he did not have to see the crusty underwear again. The outhouse door shut, and all three were off the porch, stepping into the woods just out of sight. He followed Blue and Daisy through the trees to a small clearing some hundred yards from the house. The two dogs carefully smelled the perimeter and settled down in the grass. The indentations in the grass had been worn; this was their secret place away from the violence and chaos of the shack.

He was looking for a proper walking stick that could be used as a weapon, and he was looking for proper throwing rocks. This is where he would develop his skills at throwing and handling a long stick and be with his new family, undisturbed.

Hensen March

4 - Practicing

The rocks were easier to find than a strong stick. He gathered the rocks in a pile, some ten yards from a rotted tree with a large knothole. A large opening traveled from the base of the tree up to the knothole. Good target without losing throwing rocks. He lost many rocks and gathered more. Hit the tree seldom, missed the knothole always...this was the first day, with a sore arm. He gathered more rocks for the next day. He walked the perimeter, looking for the right stick—none to be found of the proper length and hardness. But, there were blackberries just outside the clearing. He ate many and brought back some for Blue and Daisy. They were not impressed with the flavor, so he ate theirs without protest. He needed an ax to select the right stick. *This would have to be a secret Gene Autry mission!*

He petted Blue and Daisy and thanked them for sharing their secret place. It could be the family's "cabin," without the cabin. He lay down with his head next to Blue and Daisy's heads and looked at the small opening of the sky and the silver bottoms of the leaves. This place was cooler and smelled better than the couch—a most proper place for relaxing and training.

It was late afternoon as the three headed through the woods. He noticed crispness in the air, and some of the sugar maples were beginning to have a hint of color in their leaves. He stopped to pee against a tree. He noticed that the foreskin of his penis was stuck to the head with a white adhesive substance that was impossible to remove, and there were bites on his groan, and then he saw that his arms were covered in mosquito bites. He must have scratched them in the night; dried streaks of blood circled both arms. He felt the fear rise from his stomach and flow down from his jaws. *Will I make it?* He was facing just the second night on the couch. *Last night there were coyotes; will they come back?* Blue and Daisy smelled the fear and stopped to look back at him. They walked by his side to the back porch and all returned to the couch. It would be noticeably cooler tonight.

The silent woman and the oldest boy had finished the supper chores, and there was food in the dog pan. The oldest boy stepped out onto the porch to check the priming can. He looked at the boy and pointed to the back corner of the shack. "It's hanging on the limb." Once again, the boy heard it in his head, and then the oldest boy was through the door, inside. He got off the couch and looked around the corner where he found a small pail with a lid and wire handle hanging on a low, short limb. He waited until he heard the creaks of the planks and the truck pull away...Sonny was gone.

He grabbed the pail and returned to the couch. The lid, which had a long handle attached, was thick and slid tightly into the top of the pail. He pulled and twisted and could hear the swish sound. Inside were identical, but smaller containers...three in all. The first had mashed potatoes with brown gravy, the next carrots with peas, and the third sowbelly. One large spoon. Blue and Daisy had eaten their supper and were not interested in the metal-covered swish-sounding feast...he was! The food helped with the fear and the tight stomach. He ate everything except two strips of sowbelly for his couch mates. He returned the pail to the tree and settled in for what he hoped would be a quieter night.

He thought of the stick and the ax needed to free it from an unsuspecting hardwood tree—not maple but walnut. He didn't know what a walnut tree looked like, but he knew what walnuts looked like. He also knew a proper stick when he saw one. There was still some light as he looked under the porch, and there it was, an ax. Like most things around the shack, it was in poor shape from lack of use. He dragged the rusty ax from underneath the porch and went down the outhouse path, placing it carefully behind the aromatic structure. *OK, have a pile of rocks for practicing and an ax of questionable condition; tomorrow will be a busy day!*

All three were on the couch. He closed his eyes and tried to picture finding the right tree with a limb the right size and low enough to reach. "Needs to be one foot taller than you." He wished the oldest boy wouldn't talk when it was dark outside. "The size of a dried walnut...make a spear and burn the end."

He whispered, "OK."

"No coyotes tonight."

He noticed Blue and Daisy had been looking at him before he said, "OK." They were picking up his leaky head. They did not speak human, but their senses were keen; they heard or felt some of the voice. He closed his eyes, and the dogs settled in; he fell into a deep sleep.

He heard the birds and opened his eyes to the orange ball of light low through the trees. It was morning, cool with fewer insects, and there were sounds from the kitchen. The silent woman opened the door; he slipped into the kitchen while she was heading for the post with the priming can. He opened the long box of matches, removing three, and was on the couch before the woman had primed the pump. *Gene Autry would have been proud!*

He pretended to be asleep when the woman returned to the porch with the heavy jug of water—another breakfast ritual. Soon the kids would file to the pump, hands checked, followed by breakfast for the silent woman and six kids—not seven.

"Sonny's not here. He'll be gone till dark." It was the oldest boy. He knew Blue and Daisy heard the voice. The dogs looked up at him from the drinking trough.

His plan was to wait until the kids finished hand washing at the pump and all were at the table before he checked the limb on the side of the shack for food. He could not wait. Slipping off the couch and looking around the corner of the shack, he saw a small cloth sack on the limb and a tin drinking cup, with a flat rock covering the top, balanced on a larger limb.

He was back on the couch before the children came through the screen door. Hands washed and checked. They glanced at him without moving their heads. The door closed. He could hear the sound of spoons, and he moved quick and low to the limb. Inside the sack were fourteen saltine crackers, making seven little peanut butter sandwiches. He took the rock off the cup and there was milk. He sat on the ground with his back against the outside wall of the shack and ate fast, only stopping for sips of milk from the tin cup. He finished quickly. He decided to keep the sack; it might be useful. He placed the cup with the flat rock on top next to the tree and returned to the couch. Now he had to wait until the woman went to the pump with the low stool and dirty dishes.

The children were playing in the front yard again, and the woman had finished at the pump. As she approached the porch, he opened the door for her. She turned her face to his, and he could see only a shell of a spirit left, just enough to stand upright, moving her arms and legs. Each day she silently performed repetitive movements to tend to the basic needs of the children. She had left long ago. He could not give up his spirit to such a place, but he knew his body would suffer if he remained. *Best get on with the day.*

He and the dogs left quietly and entered the woods. They circled around to the outhouse for the ax and headed in search of a walnut tree. On the way to the clearing, he realized he could carry a selection of rocks in the small cloth sack, but he needed to learn how to throw them better than good—*but first, the walnut tree for a proper walking stick/spear.*

The dogs settled into their grass beds as he walked the perimeter just outside the clearing. The plan was to look for walnuts on the ground and a limb low enough to reach. He passed the blackberries and continued around the clearing. He stepped on them before he saw them. *Walnuts.* The lowest limb was curved like a bow, but the one just above and to the left was straight. Both limbs were beyond his reach. He leaned against the adjacent tree and studied the situation. He picked up the ax and looked at the handle for rot, especially where the wood entered the metal. Thinking he could make a metal step from the head of the ax, he practiced swinging the ax with the handle angling up, pointing at the low curved branch. He swung. The ax bounced off the trunk and out of his hand.

Again, he leaned against the same tree as before. He needed height. He found large, flat stones, pulled them up on edge and rolled them under the branch. He used a large fallen branch to slide two flat stones on top of the first, placing smaller stones under the edges to steady the pile. The ax was leaning against the pile as he climbed up on the top stone and hooked the metal end of the ax on the bottom branch...hand over hand up the handle until his feet were off the top stone.

Now he felt his full weight and struggled, grabbing the branch with his right hand. He pulled hard on the handle with his left hand and turned his face away from the rusty edge of the ax while wrapping his right arm around the branch. He moved the ax slowly along the branch and away from his body. With both arms around the branch, he pulled his chest onto the branch and lifted his left leg high over the ax blade, straddling the branch. He faced the trunk and began to move the ax closer. His legs were tight around the branch.

With small swings he made a notch in the branch. The wood was hard and the ax rusty. He knew he couldn't repeat the climb—at least not today. He continued with small swings making the notch deeper until the branch began to pivot downward. Almost there and then it fell into the leaves and walnuts below. He threw the ax away from the tree and hung by his arms and let go, falling away from the rock platform.

Blue and Daisy were watching from behind a nearby tree and came to inspect the fallen limb. The center section of the limb was the size the oldest boy recommended. He sat next to the limb and stretched his legs out and used the edge of a rock to make a mark on the grayish bark. He lay flat and made another mark where his head met the branch. The limb began to curve just shy of a foot beyond the head mark. He got the ax and, with his right foot on the limb, began chopping. Now he had one end prepared and began on the other. He stood the new stick upright and could just barely touch the tip. He headed for the clearing, stopping briefly for blackberries. He could feel the sugar and energy.

There were no trunk shadows on the ground, just gently moving leaf shadows; it was noon with the sun directly overhead. He inspected the stick and found it to be straight and covered with a grayish bark with deep, uneven ridges. He cut the bark off the stick, before it dried and became loose. He worked with the ax to make a long sharp point on one end and a shorter point on the base of the stick. He gathered dry leaves and small twigs for the fire. He took one wooden match out of the small cloth sack and struck it on a rock near the leaves and twigs, and a flame appeared. He hoped for little smoke that might give away his location and activities. He slowly rotated the tip in the flame to harden the wood and prevent splitting. He put out the fire with dirt, and there was little smoke.

He practiced holding the stick/spear parallel to the ground, holding it with his right hand just above his shoulder. Finding the perfect place to hold, where the spear was perfectly balanced, was the first skill to learn. He needed the proper force to throw the spear any distance, but accuracy would be more important. After many unsuccessful tries he learned to start with his left foot, then right, and then plant his left foot, releasing the spear. If he did this quickly in a fluid motion, he got more thrust and distance, but the tip of the spear went left and the stick struck the target sideways. He made sure his toes were always pointed toward the target, but the sideways flight continued. He tried to repeat each of the movements the same way, changing only one part at a time.

The position of his elbow when he snapped his wrist was causing the sideways problem. He put the spear down and practiced keeping his elbow directly below his wrist, snapping his wrist in a direct line from his elbow to his wrist. He picked up the spear and stood in front of the knothole…three quick steps, elbow in and snapping his wrist correctly. The spear entered the knothole and one foot of the spear stuck out the back of the rotted tree. He repeated the throws, taking one step back after every three throws…they all hit their mark. Now he had a proper hardwood walking stick/spear and was learning how to use it. Practicing with the rocks came next.

The rocks in the pile were different sizes and shapes. Throwing rocks was different than throwing spears. The flat rocks with the sharp edges always curved to the left but were useful for their sharp edges. The larger round rocks flew straight and had weight…hopefully to stop an animal if hit in the head or rib cage.

After many attempts he learned to point his feet at an angle—slightly to the right of the target—lifting his upper left leg horizontal to the ground. Throwing rocks and spears had one thing in common: elbow directly under the hand with a snap of the wrist without turning the hand left or right. At ten yards nearly every rock passed through the knothole and rolled out the opening at the base of the tree. He had thrown each rock in the original pile at least three times at ten yards. He backed up two steps and continued practicing. The flat rocks with the edges tended to curve more at longer distances. He adjusted his aim. He planned to practice every day he could slip away from the couch without being detected.

He was thirsty and the angle of the trunk shadows suggested midafternoon. He knew Blue and Daisy were ready to go. He placed six stones of different shapes and sizes into the cloth bag and picked up the spear and walked behind the dogs to the shack. A few trees away from the back yard he began to circle to the left and stepped out of the tree line at the far end of the couch. He slowly slid the spear under the couch and placed the bag under the couch cushion.

He was thirsty and the dogs' water was low. He would try to prime the pump. On the way to the pole with the can, he turned and squatted down to see if the spear could be seen under the couch; he saw only a long shadow under the couch. He pushed the can up with his right hand and unhooked the wire handle with his left. He walked like a duck with the can between his feet. He tried to lift the can to the top of the pump but could not. He poured some into the water trough where Blue and Daisy quickly began lapping it up. He balanced the lip of the can on the top edge of the pump, moving under the can and pushing up the bottom of the can with his back against the pump facing the underside of the handle. He pulled the handle toward him with his right hand, pushing with the left and pulling with the right. The water flowed into the top of the pump, but the can rolled off the lip and fell into the dirt; he pushed the handle away from him and swung his body around the handle to pull it down again. Up and down.

The water began coming out in a thin, transparent ribbon. He pulled the handle down and grabbed the can and put it under the spout. The water stopped coming out of the pump but began again as he pushed the handle up. On the next downward pull, he slid the V-shaped tin beneath the spout and began pumping water down the tin into the water trough for Blue and Daisy. Next time he would find something to stand on, so he wasn't swinging on the handle like a monkey. He pulled down on the handle and rushed to cup both hands at the end of the spout and drank deeply.

The priming can was full. He remembered when it was knocked off the porch and emptied in the dirt...the water moccasin, the hole in the can from the rifle, the stare down, and the contorted brown streak. *If I am around, the priming can will always be full!* He looked in the edge of the woods for something to stand on so he could put the can back on the post. He saw the leg sticking out of the leaves. He pulled on the leg and a three-legged stool emerged. He had seen these for sale in the old general store. It was low and you sat on it to milk cows...a milking stool. It seemed sturdy enough to stand on. He placed it about a foot from the pole and then carried the full can (duck style) to the stool. Holding the can, he stepped on the stool and was able to hook the handle in the notch. He put the stool three to four trees deep into the woods just beyond the notched priming-can pole.

Blue and Daisy had been watching from the couch. He checked again to see if the spear was visible from the pump area...nothing but darkness under the couch. He sat down in the center of his family and rested. Blue and Daisy had seen a lot of secret activity today and were ready for a nap. He closed his eyes and saw the things he had done and, most importantly, the things he had learned about throwing. He had a sense they would become useful one day. He dozed off, with the sounds of the children playing on the front porch.

His eyes opened as the woman appeared with the low stool from the table. She walked to the couch and handed him two biscuits with meat in them. She did not speak or look at him on her way to the pump. Blue and Daisy were standing at their food pan and received the scraps from supper. He wondered how he had missed the sounds of supper and why the silent woman walked to the couch with the meat-filled biscuits. The meat was tough and salty—country ham biscuits. *Good, but they make you thirsty... more priming*. He would time it so he could drink from the silent woman's last handle pump, like last time. She finished and he moved quickly to drink and returned to open the screen door for the woman. No look from her. *She gave me biscuits and country ham. No conversation needed.*

Fall was approaching. Tonight, would be much cooler. Blue and Daisy had fur and were good snugglers. He had the spear and the small cloth sack with well-chosen rocks. Each night he planned to be more prepared and skilled for sleeping outside on the couch. Tomorrow would be a busy day of practice throwing the spear and various kinds of rocks. Each rock had its purpose and, if thrown well, could be a useful weapon. He knew he would sleep well from today's activities. The last conscious thought before drifting asleep.

5 – I'm Gonna Kill Ya, Boy

He was sleeping so hard that he didn't see the lights moving from right to left in the trees or hear the plank bridge creaking or the front screen door slamming. But he awoke suddenly from the vibration of the walls and the voice: "Hide."

He, Blue, and Daisy jumped off the side of the porch and disappeared into the woods. They circled around the trees to the center of the woods facing the back yard. He saw the children and nightshirts moving quickly off the front porch to his right. They moved beyond the reach of the light from the bulb hanging from the front porch rafter. The silent woman was screaming and making primitive moans and Sonny's yelling was full of rage; it sounded like a wild animal. The yelling and crashing stopped. The woman's quiet moans continued, and the dogs moaned from deep within their bodies.

The back door swung open; Sonny's shadow from the kitchen light bulb looked like a giant eggplant with legs. He was walking in the boy's direction. He knew the man could not see him in the darkness of the trees. Sonny was staggering badly and tried to steady himself by grabbing the pipe that came out of the ground with the pump on top. His left hand grasped the pipe, but the force of his motion spun his body around and down, falling on the V-shaped tin, his back in the dirt and his face toward the black sky. He rolled over toward the pipe and was on all fours like a hog at the trough. He used the pipe and the pump handle to pull himself up and then tilted his head up at the treetops… "I'm gonna kill ya, boy!" He fell backward, unconscious.

He saw the oldest boy quietly moving into the front porch light and, through the back door, saw him move into the room with the beds. He carried the thin woman and placed her in Sonny's chair and gently laid her head on the table. He came through the door with the glass jug and stepped off the porch. He stood over Sonny's bloated body, then stepped over it and began priming the pump and filling the jug. The oldest boy went back in the kitchen and placed a pan on the table, pouring water into it from the jug. He raised the woman's head and began wiping her face. Through the trees and through the back of the chair slats, the boy could see that her dress was torn off her shoulders. The oldest boy wiped the woman's neck and shoulders and draped a towel over her bare shoulders. He folded another towel and laid her right cheek on the towel. He came to the pump again and poured the water from the jug into the top of the pump and filled the jug and the priming can, returning it to the notched pole.

The oldest boy walked through the shack, and the children stepped onto the front porch and silently returned to their beds. The oldest boy picked up the woman and put her in the bed. He took Sonny's chair from the table and put it on the back porch and sat there looking at Sonny lying in the dirt. The boy in the woods stood up and walked into the back yard, making a wide path to the left of Sonny's body. Blue and Daisy walked up to Sonny and sniffed his butt and his crotch and returned to the couch. The seventh child and the oldest boy sat in silence. Both did not close their eyes but watched. Once again, the seventh child was a "watcher" of "the watcher" who was watching. Both sat motionless until dawn.

At first light, the dogs drank from the trough and stopped by Sonny to sniff the more fragrant parts of him; both sneezed and snorted. The boy's nostrils were deadened from days and nights on the couch.

The oldest boy started breakfast chores. The seventh child did not want to be on the couch when Sonny became conscious. He looked around the side of the shack and saw the tin pail, along with the tin cup, hanging from the branch. He sat with his back against the outside wall like before, but he knew he was less than three feet from the wide bed where the injured woman lay. There were two pieces of bread in the top inside container, bacon in the second, and the bottom had four slices of tomato. He put them together and ate while looking around the corner of the shack. The milk was still cold. *How could that be*—the oldest boy was within his line of sight all night, and he had heard him preparing breakfast from the moment the oldest boy entered the shack. The boy drank the milk and returned everything the way he'd found it.

He moved to the end of the couch, and without taking his eyes off Sonny he pulled out the spear and the bag of rocks. Blue and Daisy were ready to go; the three disappeared into the woods. They gave the back yard a wide berth and turned a bit to the southwest, heading to the clearing.

The spear had gone through the knothole so many times that he could see through the tree. He picked up dead limbs long enough to stick through the bottom opening to cover the back of the knothole. He would use this tree for rocks and find another rotten tree for the spear.

He began picking pieces of flint from the rock pile. He used larger stones to break the flint into rounded, razor-sharp edges. They were thin and light and could be thrown farther than the other rocks. He had four perfect ones. He backed up fifteen yards and aimed to the right. The curve to the left was significant but consistent. Three of the four went into the hole. He continued, pushing for four rounds of four perfect throws. He placed the flat stones in the cloth bag and began with the heavier round stones. He chose three perfectly round, heavy stones with rough surfaces. Once again, four rounds of four perfect throws. He placed the round stones in the cloth bag. Then he practiced pulling a stone of choice from the bag without looking and throwing quickly. Again, four rounds of four through the hole. And again, faster. And again.

The tree was a few yards behind and to the right of the knothole tree. He walked around the tree, looking carefully. He did not want to dull or break the tip of the spear on the wrong tree. Starting over was not an option. He backed up just beyond fifteen yards and practiced the steps and pretended to throw the spear: feet together with toes pointed at the target; left foot first and a quicker right step, digging in for greater thrust; elbow under the right hand; wrist in perfect line with the spear and target. Throw with left leg extended slightly, with left foot pointed at the target, and follow through. The spear hit the center of the tree and sunk deep. He pulled it out; the tip was intact. He threw again aiming for the same hole, hitting just to the right. He had turned his wrist slightly outward. Next throw had good follow through and hit the original hole. He threw twenty times, and each time the spear hit within eight to ten inches of the original hole. There was a noticeable indentation in the center of the trunk.

He stuck the base of the spear in the ground and walked through the trees to the blackberries. He ate several and picked more and returned to Blue and Daisy. They had grown accustomed to the spear hitting the rotten tree and had been dozing in their grass beds. He sat down between them and finished the blackberries.

He thought about the injured woman and the long night with his eyes open and the intense fear. *Is Sonny still lying in the dirt?* He felt the hairs on his neck rise. The bellowing, "I'm gonna kill ya, boy!" *Where did I leave the ax?* It was already getting chilly in the evenings. *What will I do when it is bitter cold and raining? Is Sonny going to kill me? Could I stay on the couch?*

He thought about the pail on the tree, the food. *The cold milk?* The first night at the supper table, there was only water in old jelly jars. The pail on the tree was a thankful mystery, and he knew it would unfold before him if he watched carefully. He also knew he had little control over the happenings in and around the shack. Even though he was small, he was cleverer than Sonny. He remembered Sonny saying he was in the country now and he needed to learn to throw and swing a stick fast. He liked the spear better.

He stood up, with many unanswered questions, and began throwing the spear...over and over. When he finished with the spear, he would start with the rocks again. That's what he could do. And he did it over and over until the two kinds of rocks and the spear were a part of his eyes, arms, and legs. He did not have to think. They left his hand and hit their mark.

He had many questions about returning to the shack. He did not want to go back, but he did not want to stay in the darkness of the woods. It was late afternoon, and the trunk shadows were long. He knew the dogs were hungry. He tried to remember the time when supper dishes were completed by the length of the shadows from the couch. He needed to wait longer, but he did not—the invitation to return was strong. He took the spear and looked for the ax around the remnants of the spear branch. *Did I put it behind the outhouse?*

He was not walking fast. He stopped twenty yards into the backyard tree line and crouched down in the same spot as last night. His heart was beating uncomfortably fast, looking for the spot where Sonny had fallen backward the night before.

The dogs flinched when his body jerked. His eyes adjusted, and his brain reevaluated. First, it looked like the back yard was surrounded by tall misshapen-people creatures. Clothes were draped over almost all of the low branches of the inside tree line. He felt the physical reaction when he saw Sonny's overalls hanging heavy on the branch.

Two number-two galvanized washtubs stood in the center of the back porch. One had the washboard sitting in it at an angle, with the silent woman's low stool to the left. The oldest boy and the oldest girl came from the kitchen and lifted the washtub, pouring the dark soapy water off the porch making an instant mud hole. The oldest boy took the washboard from the remaining tub; both used the hanging handles of the tub to tilt it, adding to the mud hole. The water was also dark, with little soap. The mud hole began to drain toward the pump, gathering in the spot where Sonny's head had hit the dirt and continuing along to fill the two boot-heel imprints. Traveling along the gouges in the dirt where he stumbled and the knee and handprints from when he was on all fours...a muddy-water portrait of drunken violence.

The oldest boy and girl took the washing equipment around the opposite side of the shack from the couch. Blue and Daisy were eating their supper from the metal dish with sides. The timing for his return was good. He thought of the silent woman and wondered whether she had made some kind of partial recovery. He quietly walked around the woods surrounding the back yard. He was seven trees behind the tree where the tin pail had been. He stayed low and approached the side of the shack; the branch was bare. No pail. No food. He walked a long half circle to the left through the trees, far from the front yard. The truck was there, beyond the plank bridge behind a thin strip of trees. It was late dusk, and the night was uncertain.

He did not want anything to happen tonight. But something needed to happen so he would know where to be and where not to be. All of it needed to be at the right time and place. He had little information to make a decision. But there was some information. The truck was on the other side of the plank bridge. Sonny was around somewhere, most likely in the shack.

There was no food, and it was not safe to go to the pump. It seemed summer had changed to fall in the span of days. The days were crisp, and the nights were hovering between very cool to slightly cold. He did not sweat when he was practicing, but he was still thirsty. The kind of thirst that comes with a headache and strange sensations in the jaw and limbs.

He made a decision. Probably two: best place to gather information is back against the wall of the shack facing the limb where the tin pail had been—there he could feel the vibrations from the walls and floor—and if he got thirsty enough, he would drink from Blue and Daisy's water trough. He had reached two decisions, one easier than the other.

He retraced his steps and leaned against the wall. He listened. He heard one of the dogs step off the couch. Daisy was looking at him with her neck stretched around the corner of the shack. Hound dogs were hard to sneak up on. She kept looking at him. He heard the bedsprings and the boots. He saw Daisy and Blue jump off the side of the porch and straight into the woods. When he heard the screen door open, he crawled sideways under the house. He knew the heavy sound of the boots as they stepped off the porch. He waited a few seconds, and with half his body under the house, he crawled low toward the back porch and around the post that held up the corner of the shack. He peered over the arm of the couch.

Sonny was walking away from him and then stood in front of his overalls hanging from the branch. He was wearing the brown-streaked underwear and his boots. He pulled the underwear down and over his boots. He wiped his butt with them and dropped them in the dirt. He yanked the clean pair off the branch next to the overalls, pulled them over his boots and up. They had a gray vertical streak—gray was better than brown, even in the dark.

He was already under the house when Sonny put on the overalls. From under the house, between the outside and middle post of the porch, he could see the tips of the soles of the boots. He slid out and put his back against the wall and heard and felt Sonny walk through the kitchen, room with the beds, and front room and then step off the front porch. The boy moved quickly around the corner and onto the couch before the truck lights had shown through the trees. Something did happen, and he was where he needed to be at the right time.

He heard the truck drive off, headed to town. He stepped to the side of the porch to look for Blue and Daisy and saw the tin pail on the limb with the flat rock on the tin cup. He had made no progress on the thankful mystery. He took the tin cup and removed the rock; there was cool water. He turned the cup up and felt the water move down the inside and into his stomach. He opened the pail quietly. The walls were thin, and he knew the silent woman was in the wide bed close to the wall. The top inside container had a small bottle of cold milk with a glass top and wire clasp. He set the bottle down and opened the second container, finding two slices of homemade bread. The bottom container had the thickest slice of meatloaf he had ever seen. He ate half the sandwich, opened the clasp and took sips of milk and then returned to the sandwich.

He thought of the silent woman… "She will be up tomorrow." A voice in your head is not always welcome, but this one had returned, and it was welcomed and missed. He would deal with the loneliness later. He had meatloaf and milk to finish.

He returned the tin pail and the cup where he found them. He slid the spear under the couch and the cloth bag with the seven rocks under the cushion. He sat on the couch and waited for Blue and Daisy. No sounds were coming from inside the shack. Since he had become a couch dweller, he had not heard one conversation. It was a place of whispers and caution. He had grown accustomed to the silence and the few and faint whispers that flowed through the screen door. At times he was unsure if it was the breeze passing from front to back screen. The voices of the children playing in the front yard were pleasant...midmorning after breakfast and late afternoon before supper. For days he had not heard them in the late afternoon because he was practicing and taking brief naps next to Blue and Daisy in their grassy beds.

He practiced in his mind what to do if Sonny were to make it through the back screen door and try to kill him. He practiced it in the day and before and after he closed his eyes at night. At first it made him afraid, but after the fiftieth time he was calm and knew every step and movement. There were two versions: Blue and Daisy on the couch and Blue and Daisy off the couch. The latter was more likely.

Blue and Daisy had not returned, and he was alone. He got up and stepped off the side of the porch, slid the spear from under the couch and walked to the right of the mud left from the wash water. He used the spear to lift the underwear by the waistband and throw it into the woods to the right. He wanted to spare himself from having to kneel down in his favorite spot for viewing the back of the shack from the woods and have the underwear next to or even near him. He turned around and saw Blue and Daisy sitting on the couch. He slid the spear behind the couch and sat down. He knew they had been hunting from the tuffs of rabbit fur stuck to the moist areas of their faces...a second supper. He had meatloaf and they, rabbit. *Meat all around—a fine evening after all.*

He knew it was smart to sleep now before any late night, run for your life into the woods happened, or didn't happen...not knowing was exhausting. The ever-present feel of whispering caution was thick in the air from learning to live around a violent predator. It was a weight that the non-predators carried, woven into their behaviors like heavy metal threads. The silent woman had mentally left to a faraway place. The oldest boy was the quiet protector who had developed an additional sense. The oldest girl had a practical mind that allowed her to move within the oldest boy's shadows while never being alone with Sonny. The little ones had learned to ask for nothing and played children's games in the front yard but rarely spoke inside...never to be a bother to the predator. They still had their invisibility. Something he had lost within an hour of his arrival.

He was alone because his spirit was intact. The surface of his spirit had been damaged by the claws of recent events, before and during his arrival. The loss of his mother was a grief that he would allow to brush by him for portions of a moment. His father's real son was the flat bottle. Long visits with the real son caused bruises to appear on his mother's face and bred invisibility and an absence of family. The absence of his father's body was of little consequence. His father and the silent woman lived in separate distant lands, arriving by different paths.

The boy's spirit had moved back into a central part of his brain and remained strong, intact, and well defended by reason. He closed his eyes and searched for a pleasant moving picture with color...

I was standing in a room divided in half by a low, carved railing with a small gate in the center that swung both ways and then swung back in line with the low railing supported by carved columns. Behind the railing were four desks with tall black typewriters. Two of the typewriters had people behind them, rapidly pressing the keys. There was a rhythm to the tapping sounds, occasionally interrupted by a sliding sound when they pushed the chrome lever to the left and the paper would rise. One person was writing with a pen, and the other desk had no one.

I turned around when the door opened, and my father knelt down and gave me a toy, a thick rubber motorcycle with a rider leaning forward. The rider's helmet was painted white, and the tires were black with silver paint in the center; the motorcycle was painted blue. It was a special toy. It was an I-have-to-leave-for-a-while toy. My father put on his white straw hat and left. I watched my father cross the street and turn the corner. I pretended to roll the wheels along the carved railing—they did not roll. The toy was a single piece of thick painted rubber. One of the women who had been typing stood up and commented on the fineness of the toy. I looked at it and agreed. It was a fine toy.

A few moments later Mother came in. She had on a large, blue, tightly woven straw hat with a wide, straight brim and a pretty blue dress. Her eyes were brown, and her face was beautiful, especially when she smiled. She loved me. I loved her. I looked into her eyes and understood part of what she said. Something about the big city and I would come to see her soon. She hugged and kissed me and went out the door. I moved to the front window and watched her, in her pretty blue dress, walk the same way my father had gone. I memorized the moments and the movements as she walked down the sidewalk. She turned the corner and disappeared; a sight never forgotten.

He stopped short of the grief and the bus with the shining pole. His head was resting on Daisy. She was his alarm system—when her body tightened like a stone, he would move fast. He drifted to sleep. One eye opened halfway as the door opened quietly and the night-shirted fairies floated to the outhouse and back like in a dream...he smiled for the second time.

The birds were awake, and he moved. Sonny was snoring in the room with the beds. There was movement in the kitchen, and the silent woman appeared on the porch with the oldest boy. She carried the large empty jug. Through the strands of her hair, he could see purple and black on her face. She moved slowly. The oldest boy took the jug and her arm; they walked to the pump. The oldest boy primed the pump and filled the can and the jug. The silent woman stood favoring her left side...Sonny was right-handed.

Once again, he pretended to be asleep. The silent woman and oldest boy returned to the kitchen. This was the difficult part of the morning. He had to wait until breakfast was finished and the dogs got the scraps. He was prepared to hide if Sonny went to the outhouse before breakfast or just peed off the porch like before. This morning he chose to stay on the couch with Blue and Daisy.

Once again, the sounds he'd grown tired of—the bedsprings, the boots, and the slamming open of the back door, where it stuck against the outside wall of the shack. He moved so he was sitting on the edge of the couch. Blue moved next to Daisy, directly behind him. Sonny stepped to the edge of the porch and began to pee in the dirt.

"I could kill them there dogs and ya'd have more room there." Sonny was looking straight ahead at the tree line. "Ya ain't lookin' too good." The stream looked like it was coming out of his hand way below the giant flesh of his stomach. He knew the man had not seen his own penis in years.

Sonny finished and turned to the boy. "Wanna come inside, boy? Get some food. Ya hungry, boy? Ya learnt to not sass me, boy?" Sonny took a step closer to the boy.

He didn't know if this was the time to do what he had practiced in his mind. *Is this the time Sonny would come the last four feet and kill me?*

The boy slid his feet to the floor and turned, facing Sonny. Looked like it would be the mentally practiced version where Blue and Daisy were on the couch.

Sonny stomped his left boot and jerked his arms. The boy jumped. Now it was the version with Blue and Daisy off the couch.

"Ya scared, boy? I'll hang them dogs and gut 'um in front of ya, and I'll bury all three of ya in the deep woods!" The boy knew the difference between predator talk and bully talk. One said less and did more. The other would keep talking.

A cold hard thought flashed past the boy's brain...*I could kill this man and sit on his chest and eat a sandwich and then take a nap!* The thought made his body shake.

"Ya scared, ain't ya, boy!"

Sonny would have been less confident if he knew the flash thought that raced past the boy's mind. The boy was more terrified of the thought than of the man. Still, he was frightened of Sonny. The mental practicing had contained the fear just outside reason and planning.

Sonny opened the door halfway and looked through the screen. "Be snowin' 'fore long. See how long ya last out here. I'll be havin' me some breakfast 'bout now." The door swung shut.

Have I come this far—from a rubber motorcycle and a mother with a blue hat to thinking of killing? He feared the infected sores on his limbs would seep silently into the tissues of his brain, and he would truly become the seventh child of the shack. The unwanted, outside creature that was there but not there. He knew this was how the silent woman's spirit had begun its slow journey away. Only her body was pulled into the darkness of the place where Sonny lived. His mind felt the pull.

Blue and Daisy returned to the couch, and the three waited for the two to have breakfast scraps. There was more practicing to do, more planning for winter to do…*another busy day*. The spoons were moving across the surface of the plates; the only other sound was Sonny's slop-jaw grunts. There was no tin pail on the limb. Today would be a long drink at the pump at the end of breakfast cleanup. And there were blackberries and the kindness of Blue and Daisy.

He began to plan for winter. The simplest place for warmth was inside the shack. The upper part of the wooden door had glass in it where he could see the kitchen and the long row of beds in the next room. *How noisy was the door when it opened?* He would find out about the door when the weather turned.

The scraping of the plates began, and the bedsprings were creaking—Sonny's nap after breakfast—and the children were playing in the front yard. The oldest boy was carried the low stool with the breakfast containers balanced on top. The oldest girl had the silent woman's arm. She needed help stepping off the porch, and then she moved to the pump unassisted. The woman was watching the food being scraped into the dogs' food tin. The oldest girl slowly backed up to the porch and motioned for the boy. She pulled three biscuits out of her apron and he took them. She returned to the stool and dishes while the oldest boy moved the pump handle. The silent woman supervised. She no longer favored her left side. He hid the biscuits as the three approached the door. He nodded to the girl. She did not look his way.

Blue and Daisy finished their breakfast and were drinking from the trough. He had been distracted by the gift of biscuits and had not gotten a drink from the pump. It would be a long day without water. He put the biscuits in the cloth bag with the rocks and put it back under the cushion. This would be the day to drink with Blue and

Daisy. It was unwise to prime the pump after the three had returned to the kitchen; he had not heard snoring.

He knelt down next to the trough. Blue and Daisy were still drinking, but they were looking. The surface of the water was moving with thin swirls of grease from the remnants of the fried breakfast scraps. A few of the swirls had dead gnats and others trying to escape the grease. He cupped his hands, pushing the gnats and grease away, and drank three times. He could tell his stomach was deciding what to do with the dog water. One partial heave and it stayed down. He returned to the couch and pulled a biscuit out of the cloth bag; it had fried potatoes piled inside—greasy dog water and greasy fried potatoes. He was thankful to have both. He put the bag on his belt and retrieved the spear and the three were off for a busy day.

There were more colored leaves on the ground; the leaves were crunchy, and the trees were bright. There had been no rain since he arrived. He wondered what a rainstorm would be like on the porch. Blue and Daisy settled in, and he sat with them, pulling the biscuits out of the bag. He pulled two slices of fried potatoes from the half-eaten biscuit and shared them. The second biscuit had a fried egg and the third, four pieces of bacon. He chose the egg for now; the bacon would make him thirsty too early in the day. He placed the third biscuit high in the fork of a sapling. He would start with the rocks. During breaks he would check the biscuit for insects; there were fewer now with the cooler air.

He began. It was difficult not to picture Sonny's face in the large knothole. He threw the four thin, round, flint rocks with the edges and the three heavy, round rocks with the rough surfaces until there were no trunk shadows. He gathered blackberries and sat with the dogs. They were masters of the art of napping. He took the biscuit from the sapling and shared one strip of bacon with Daisy—ladies first—and one with Blue. He took the top off the biscuit and ate the bottom with the two strips left. He piled blackberries on the top part of the biscuit and had a fine dessert. He lay down and petted his friends and dozed for a while. The afternoon would be focused on throwing the spear. There was only one chance with the spear. Seven rocks. One spear.

He added two parts to the spear-throwing routine: standing with the spear up and walking with the spear low and parallel to the ground. He learned to weave these two starting positions into the three steps and release. Before the throw, the spear needed to be slightly elevated to hit the mark at fifteen yards. He learned the proper speed to maintain consistent accuracy. He counted each throw. He was up to fifty-five by the time the trunk shadows were long.

Each day, the decision to return to the shack became more complex. He always returned for two reasons: Blue and Daisy needed their breakfast and supper and sleeping in the woods was too dangerous. Sonny had taught him much about coward bullies...they were unpredictable. The brown liquid made Sonny's preconceived plans less structured and more chaotic. Sonny's taunting had provided useful information to the boy; the information allowed the boy to plan for the immediate future. The three headed back to the shack.

Many of the low-lying branches had lost half their leaves. The tree trunks were becoming more critical in providing cover while moving in the woods close to the shack. He was mindful of approaching with as many tree trunks as possible between him and the shack. There was another concern—the fallen leaves concealed small dead branches that warned of an approach. He stepped lightly and stopped some ten yards short of his usual wooded spot for viewing the back porch.

Blue and Daisy saw Sonny on the back porch before he did. The dogs lay down low and he was on his stomach between them. Sonny took a white cloth pouch out of the center chest pocket of the overalls and pulled a thin package of rolling papers from the pouch. He handled the pouch with his left hand and rolled the cigarette with his right. He saw Sonny lick the adhesive strip with his tongue and pull the strings with his teeth. He put the pouch back in the bib pocket and pulled one of the wooden kitchen matches out of the same pocket. He placed the cigarette in his left hand and ran the match head up his right leg and lit the cigarette. His face looked distorted in the light from the match. Once again, Sonny was looking straight at the three. They were low in the dead leaves, not moving. Sonny blew out the smoke, and it hung low over the dirt of the back yard. He thought that was different, but he wasn't sure what it meant—something to do with the weather, most likely.

He could see that Blue and Daisy's food was in the metal pan with sides. He knew the dogs saw it and smelled it. They did not move. He did not move. Sonny continued to blow smoke, and it continued to hang low to the dirt. It moved over the dead leaves at the edge of the trees. He remembered seeing the smoke from chimneys roll over the roof singles of houses in the winter before a storm, *a storm...rain, maybe*. Sonny went inside. The screen door swung shut, and later the front screen door swung shut. They waited until the truck lights moved through the trees.

Blue and Daisy went straight through the trees and leaves to their supper. He moved to the left and stepped out of the trees and quietly slid the spear under the couch and the bag under the cushion. He looked down the side of the shack—the tin pail and the tin cup were there. *Once again, the thankful mystery!* He reached for the tin pail and the cup. He had lost count of how many times he had sat with his back to the outside wall and eaten from the pail and drunk from the tin cup. Each time he was thankful. He was thankful for the water in the cup and the milk and the pork chop and the mashed potatoes. He noticed, for the first time, a small, folded tarp beside the tree. He would examine it after he ate. This time he ate slowly and in peace. This time he wasn't hiding in the woods or under the house or looking at Sonny's boots. *This was the best supper of all!*

He unfolded the tarp. It was big enough to fit Blue, Daisy, and him under it. If folded twice lengthwise, it would fit under the cushions, undetected. That is what he did. He stepped back off the porch and the cushions looked no different.

He sat on the couch with the dogs and worked on the thankful mystery. First, not once had the food in the tin pail matched the scraps that Blue and Daisy had twice each day. There was just enough food to feed the eight people that lived in the shack. He saw no garden. He hadn't been in the front yard or on the front porch since the priming can, water moccasin, and rifle incident. He knew nothing about who or what came through the front of the shack. He only knew the loudness of Sonny's comings and goings—unlikely that the food in the tin pail came from the shack—the first clue of the thankful mystery. He would rather the thankful mystery continue than to know the answer about its origin.

Time to sleep. Daisy was a good pillow, and she did not seem to mind his head on her side. His mind wandered through the room with the typewriters and the blue hat, just short of the bus and the hospital. He stayed in the room with the motorcycle toy, looking out the window at his mother walking. He slowed the movement outside the window to make it last longer. He fell into a deep sleep.

Hensen March

6 – Winter's Coming

He opened his eyes during the last few seconds of night, before the air became orange and dawn began. The time when the outlines of objects remained undefined and the air gray. His arms looked bad. He stood and pulled his pants down. His legs looked bad. The insect bites had become infected from scratching them with his dirty fingernails. The ones without scabs varied in size and could hold one to three BBs inside them. He could see white tissue at the bottom of the wounds. His body shivered and his forehead was warm. Although connected, he was glad his body and spirit each stood alone. When his body was weak, he relied more on his mind and spirit. Knowing the difference was a gift he treasured.

He knew he was not drinking enough water. He would save the milk bottles from the tin pail until he had three: two for under the couch and one hidden in the clearing. The glass tops with the wire clasps would keep out insects and debris. He went back to the tin pail to retrieve the empty milk bottle. There was steam coming out of the tin cup, wrapping around the flat rock and disappearing. He removed the rock and smelled the tea-like substance. He saw a small pouch with holes that contained rolled up leaves. He trusted the cup and drank the liquid. The pail contained soup with large pieces of chicken. He sat in the familiar place and ate the soup with the spoon that always accompanied the pail. Blue and Daisy had their necks wrapped around the corner of the shack, wondering why he had breakfast before them.

He finished the soup, drinking the rest that the spoon couldn't reach. The two biggest pieces of chicken remained on the side where he drank. He put them on the flat rock and returned everything the way he found it. He took the chicken off the rock with his left hand and placed the rock on the cup. He moved to the back porch and gave Blue and Daisy their pre-breakfast snack.

All three sat on the couch and waited for breakfast to begin and finish. They closed their eyes and rested. The soup was still warm in his stomach. He tried to imagine that the rolled-up leaves and the liquid were helping and the soup with the chicken would give him more energy. He made no unnecessary movements.

He took a short nap until he heard sounds in the kitchen. The breakfast rituals had begun, and the dogs were ready for food to appear in the metal pan with sides. He knew the children would pass through the door one by one. Only two had spoken to him and each only once, with the exception of the oldest boy's thinking out loud. It was best to hear the oldest boy's voice in the daytime. The nighttime voice had foreshadowed a run-for-your-life event.

The back door opened, and the line passed through like moving posts with hanging garments, spaced evenly and never turning. Hand washing at the pump had become a no-looking silent ritual. He no longer pretended to be asleep or looked down; he watched each one to see if an eye turned. Their eyes stopped looking. He knew they were using more energy not looking than he was watching. At least he hoped this was true; if not, then he no longer existed in their minds.

Was the fear so great that they would not turn an eye even when Sonny was not there? They had looked before—glancing down quickly after a sideways peek—but not now. *Was the risk too high or the interest too low?* If he gave this mystery too much attention, he, too, might find his mind atop a post with hanging garments and never turning. Other mysteries were more pressing. Winter was coming fast, and he was not prepared.

The door mystery was first. *How squeaky was the door? Could it be opened without waking everyone in the shack?* This would be the morning he would seek an answer. The scraping of the plates had begun; he heard the sounds of the children playing in the front yard and the dishes being stacked on the low stool. The screen door opened, and the silent woman took the low stool to the pump. The dogs headed for their breakfast and he for the screen door. The woman's back was to him. She put the low stool down next to the dogs' pan and bent at the waist to scrape the scraps into the pan.

At that instant, he slipped silently inside and looked out through the screen. All he could see was the woman's rear end and the back of her calves where the dress had risen. It looked like she had lost the upper half of her body, with elbows protruding out the sides of her legs.

He moved the wooden door a fraction of an inch, and it made a screechy chirp. The woman's head rose and made a half turn to catch the sound with her right ear. He guessed that repeated blows from

Sonny's right fist had damaged her left. He was standing with his right shoulder pressed against the wall just outside the doorframe. He listened for the scraping to start again and for the sound of the plate being returned to the top of the stack balanced on the low stool. He kneeled down and looked through the bottom of the screen door with his left eye.

The silent woman's body had not moved. Her head was still cocked, with her ear pointing at the outside pole of the porch just beyond the far end of the couch. The children's voices sounded closer. The woman's head and shoulders disappeared, and her right elbow moved in and out of sight just above her right calf. He watched her stand and place the scraped dish on the stack. When she bent over to move the stool, he slipped through the screen door and quickly sat on the couch. She headed for the priming can. Her head was facing the priming-can post. Without turning her head, her dark pupils scanned the back porch—first the door and then the couch. He felt a shiver from the vacuum of her face.

He would wait for the last movement of the pump handle to drink as much as possible. He had learned to pass the woman on her way to the porch. Always passing to the right. He knew that if he waited until she returned to the kitchen, the pump often lost its prime. He had stopped opening the door for her when she returned from the pump. Trying to form any connection with the silent woman was like banging on the door of a vacant house—no one was there to respond. His connection with the children had been slowly unraveling for days. The oldest girl no longer backed up and handed him biscuits, and the oldest boy's voice in his head had remained silent. The only human connection left was the unwanted one...Sonny.

Strangely, this connection was the most important. He and Sonny pushed massive amounts of energy at each other. The energy had a fast pulse, and when directed at the other, the alternating current would surge and roll back over itself and return to its source. He had learned to store the returning current and convert it into useable energy. He had begun to capture waves of the current from Sonny before it returned to sizzle the surfaces of the drunkard's pickled organs.

The silent woman had finished, and he passed to the right of her and moved the pump handle and drank deeply. The woman was in the kitchen by the time he had finished. Blue and Daisy also had finished drinking. He preferred drinking from the pump to drinking from the trough with its swirls of grease.

The inside of Blue and Daisy's food container was shiny. He ran his finger around the inside of the metal pan. It was greasy. He ran his finger around again, capturing more of the greasy fat. He moved low to the porch, partially opened the screen door, and wiped his fingers over the outside hinges of the wooden door. He would come back in the late afternoon to see if the hinges were quieter when the parade of posts with hanging garments made its way to the pump for the no-looking, silent hand-washing ritual.

He gathered the rocks and the spear and stepped off the porch and into the woods with Blue and Daisy. Today, he would move slower to conserve his energy to allow his body to deal with the infected mosquito bites. There were more leaves on the ground. Some of the trees were like arms coming out of the ground with cupped hands and fingers that rose up and held the last of their colorful leaves. He hoped he would reach the clearing and feel well enough to practice.

Blue and Daisy ran ahead and stood in the center of the clearing. Their noses were in the air, and he could see the side flaps of their black nostrils folding in and flaring out. They smelled around the uneven line where the clearing met the trees. Both peed twice and went to their beds. He stood for a moment and listened, then stepped out of the clearing to gather some of the last blackberries of the season. He picked as many as he could and returned to the dogs. He sat down between them and ate. The sugar felt good.

The sun was at an angle and shone against the opposite sides of the trunks and bare limbs, casting thick and narrow dark broken lines across the leaves like lines of chocolate syrup over brightly colored candy. He stretched out and rested. He could see more of the sky; the clouds were flat and closely layered. Colder air was coming.

He had lost track of the days. He knew it was some time ago when he realized he didn't know if it was Tuesday or Saturday. It was as if his mother had taken the sense of time with her when she left. He knew she would never come back. *Was she some other place, or just unseen and unheard? Was she sitting on some other couch that was drifting past the stars?* He knew his couch sat on the porch of the shack surrounded by dirt. The couch faced away from the shack, and he ignored its whispered invitations to swim in its pool of nothingness. He planned each day to avoid dissolving and disappearing into the couch. He sat up. Stood. And began to practice.

He practiced until the shadows on the ground were round, dark suns connected by dark, webbed rays. It was noon; he gathered more blackberries and rested. He worked on his plan. The issue of cold weather was coming. He had Blue and Daisy for warmth, the tarp for protection from rain, snow, and wind. Freezing temperatures would require him to be inside the shack at night. Greasing the hinges of the wooden door was his only plan.

He heard it coming in his direction. The fallen leaves at the edge of the clearing began to shift and lose their color. He saw the darkness moving through the trees, swallowing the shadow designs and colors. The leaf blanket began to dance and then flatten. The clearing grass bent, and the drops hit his face. He ran behind the dogs, with the wind high in the trees. The rain was coming fast. The dry, colored leaves in front of him rose up in waves, meeting the falling leaves in swirls. He felt the rain nip at his back.

Blue and Daisy ran through the back yard and jumped on the couch. He circled around and slid the spear under the couch and lifted Daisy and her cushion to hide the pouch of rocks. He stepped off the porch into the trees and stayed low until he was even with the dogs' food tin. He moved low and fast out of the trees and ran his index and middle finger three times around the inside of the food tin, turned and entered the tree line. He stepped back on the end of the porch as the rain poured into the back yard.

The wind was banging the screen door against the frame. He heard the screeching chirps of the wooden door as it slammed shut. He knew that someone had slammed the door and was most likely still standing there looking through the glass at the rain. He looked at the glob of grease resting on the inside of his two fingers. It looked like enough. He folded in his fingers and held the fatty grease inside the palm of his hand. He knew if he left his hand open, Blue and Daisy would curl their tongues around it and throw it down their throats, and he would have to try again. He guessed the door slammer would grow bored of looking at the rain and turn away from the glass. He waited.

He was glad he had the grease and had out run the rain. There was another problem. The wooden door was closed, and the hinges were covered. He had forgotten the door opened into the shack; the door had to be open to grease the hinges. He felt a bit less clever. Now he would have to wait until the rain stopped and the door opened again. He might have to wait until dark. The grease was starting to liquefy from the warmth of his hand. He gathered leaves that had fallen and stuck to the porch. He slid them together to make a bottom, dumped the grease in the center, gathered more leaves to make a top and then slid the greasy leaf sandwich under the couch. The drop in temperature from hand to air would preserve it longer.

Large areas of water began forming in the low parts of the yard. The dirt and water made a creamy coffee color. The rain was coming off the tin roof in front of the couch in a thick, continuous sheet of water, cutting into the dirt just beyond the planks of the porch. Thinking about the hinges and grease and watching the rain distracted him; he was wet. It was still early afternoon, and he hoped the rain would pass. The dogs smelled like wet wool sweaters, and the moisture had awakened ancient smells rising up out of the fabric of the couch. Blue and Daisy moved to the center of the couch, and he curled up and made his body small, with the dogs wrapped around him. They hunkered down and waited for the rain to stop.

In front of them the waterfall continued, and the back yard became a pond. The lightning started; the thunder clapped, and the dogs trembled. He whispered, "Least it's not ice and snow." It was hard to doze with the dogs trembling...they stopped, and he slept.

The rain continued. He had planned to use the tarp after dark to avoid anyone knowing he had it. If the rain continued and the temperature dropped, he would use it. He dozed again. Later, his eyes opened to a different sound. The rain had slowed, and there were large drops falling from the tin roof. The drops hit the standing water, exploding into stems that were broad at the base and tapered up with perfectly balanced chocolate balls resting on top. They fell as quickly as they rose.

The wooden door screeched open; no one stepped out. There were sounds in the kitchen. The silent woman opened the screen door. This time it opened quietly—before he was able to open it just enough to pass through sideways without the hinges making noise. He and the dogs did not move. All three knew this was the initial gathering of pump water to begin the noon meal. He hadn't been around for the noon meal routine; he assumed it differed little from breakfast and supper.

The woman turned the dogs' trough, emptying the brown water. The trough began to float until filled with clear pump water. It settled with the edges less than two inches above the brown water. Blue and Daisy were there when she finished. The more they drank, the more the trough rose. They began to walk and drink, following the movement of the floating trough. He would wait to pass the woman to the right after she moved the pump handle for the last time as the large jug filled to the neck. He took his shoes off and left them on the couch. The standing water was above the silent woman's ankles. He waded out with the brown water at mid-calf and drank several large swallows.

He didn't like being around the shack so early in the afternoon. Too many things could go wrong. He was vulnerable to whatever came through the back door, and it was usually Sonny. On his way back to the porch, he stopped and moved his feet around to find the dogs' food tin. He brought it back and laid it upside down on the porch. The sun was breaking through, and he put his shoes on the edge of the porch to dry. He laid them sideways to catch the narrow band of light before the tin roof wrapped around it and reflected it back into the sky. He would try the grease tonight.

Another thought had been sitting quietly behind his eyes. *There is nothing here for me, so why stay here?* He would try the grease, and early in the morning, he would see if any tracks in the mud led away from the tin pail and cup. He could follow the tracks to find a person whose spirit still remained. He hoped the containers would appear later today or tonight.

The large muddy puddles reappeared as the water began to drain away from the back yard. He could see the water moving down the path to the outhouse. The smell was getting stronger as the hole in the middle of the structure began to fill. He hadn't known there was a smell more powerful than the couch. The steam rising from the couch fabric made the tree trunks look wavy and distorted. *This was truly a smelly place!* Waves of a third smell began rolling through the screen—greasy fried food. The couch, the outhouse, and frying grease made his stomach turn. Grease was the beginning of the journey, the outhouse the destination, and he sat in the steam between the two.

The rain and the steam had dissolved the crusted pond scum on his shirt and pants. He moved his hands down his shirt and pants to remove more of the green gunk. He was tired of being dirty, smelly, and alone. He knew if he let the emotions build, he would scream and cry, but no one would come. He swallowed the fear and focused on his plan: *hinges and tracks, hinges and tracks.*

There had been too much rain to practice in the clearing, and there was too much mud to step off the porch. Sonny had not been to the shack for nearly two days. The noon meal had finished; the woman brought the scrap plate and dumped the contents into the dogs' tin. Blue and Daisy ate on the porch in the early afternoon.

Hinges and tracks. The tin containers appeared just before dark, but there were no tracks in the mud. He placed the grease on the wooden door's hinges sometime after dark and before dawn, when all were asleep.

The days began to fold into themselves. Most were the same, with brief unexpected moments of terror. Most nights he used the tarp and occasionally slipped into the kitchen and hid behind the stove. On those nights in the kitchen, before sunrise he would walk backward to the door, wiping the moisture from his steps with the cloth pouch. He applied the grease daily before dawn. There were no screechy chirps from either door. He practiced each day when the weather allowed. The tin pail and cup had begun to appear in the time between dawn and the early sounds of the kitchen and again just before dusk. He always ate on the side of the shack—a reserved table for dining. He hadn't spoken to anyone in weeks.

He remembered the day when he was unsure if it was Tuesday or Saturday. Now he was unsure what month it was; he knew it was in the early part of winter. Frost on the planks of the porch at dawn made the porch sparkle. He opened his eyes one morning, and there was no sparkle—the air had less of a bite to it. As he sat on the side of the shack eating from the tin pail, he had a vague, undefined sense that the day would not be ordinary. It was now that the day began to change.

7 – Aunt Eunice Arrives

He heard the truck and the brakes; the movement on the plank bridge was faster than usual. He recognized the boot sounds. He replaced the top on the pail and slid the container under the house. He sat close to the wall with his knees on either side of his chin.

Sonny was in the room with the beds. "Boy, get your sister and unload the truck!" This time he was not the "boy." Then he heard Sonny next to the wall. "Get the hell up; she's comin'!" He heard the bedsprings move. "Come in here, now!"

Blue and Daisy were already twenty yards from the couch, low in the leaves. He moved down the wall toward the porch, next to the kitchen. The back wooden door slammed shut.

"Here read this...hurry, woman." He heard the sound of paper. "Bed and sheets are comin' from the truck. Get the washtub. Gotta get that damn kid cleaned up. She'll call the law on us. Damn kids get outta bed! Go play out front."

He sat on the couch. The back wooden door slammed against the wall, and the screen door made its usual collision with the outside wall. Sonny's fat fingers wrapped around the frame and slammed it shut. He knew exactly where the spear was and how to get to it quickly. He had practiced in his mind since he made it from the walnut tree. He was sitting on the edge of the couch.

Sonny was pulling the bottle out of his pocket; he stepped off the porch and stood in front of the couch. He put the middle of the sole of his right boot on the edge of the porch. The toe of the boot was pointed just above the boy's head. Sonny's right forearm was resting on his raised leg; the bottle, half full of brown liquid, rested between his thumb and first two fingers. He was swishing the liquid around inside the bottle. He unscrewed the cap and drank two large swallows. He put the cap in his bib pocket.

"We gonna get somethin' straight right now, boy. Your Aunt Eunice is comin' today. Ya best keep your mouth shut about how it is aroun' here. If ya don't, I'll kill both them worthless hounds, and ya won't be here when she comes. I'll say ya run off last night, and I'll bury ya under the shit in the outhouse. Nobody's gonna dig through shit to find the likes of you. I know ya simple minded and all—just move your head. Ya understand me, boy!"

He did not move his head. He had been watching the muscles in Sonny's leg to see if the man would lunge forward. He would roll over the arm of the couch, slide the spear out and throw it between the outside and middle poles of the porch into the man's neck.

Sonny screwed the cap back on the bottle and stood on both feet. "Know you understand some. How come ya don't say nothin'?" He continued to watch Sonny's movements; he had not looked at the man's face. Sonny went inside.

The woman and the oldest boy came around the other corner of the shack with the washtub. He could hear activity in the room with the beds. The two put the number-two washtub on the porch away from the couch, and the oldest boy headed for the pump. The silent woman went into the kitchen and brought out the low stool with two rags and a bar of lye soap. She returned to the pump, where the oldest boy had primed the pump and was filling the large jug and priming can. The woman took the priming can and poured it into the washtub and returned to the pump. The oldest boy brought the large jug and emptied it into the tub, while the woman filled the priming can. This rotation continued until the tub was half full.

The children were coming around the corner of the shack. The silent woman motioned for the boy to come to her.

He left the couch and stood in front of her. She was sitting on the low stool with her legs apart and her dress sunk low in the wide space between her knees. She took off his belt and his pants and motioned for him to take off his shirt. He unbuttoned his shirt and removed it. All the other children, including the oldest boy and oldest girl, moved onto the porch around the couch. His back was to them. The woman motioned for him to take off his underwear. It hurt. His penis was stuck to the underwear with the white adhesive film that he had seen before. There was more of it, and he knew the foreskin was completely glued to the head.

He stepped into the cold water, and the woman turned him around, facing the children. There was a collective sound from the children around the couch.

He was not looking at them, but as he looked down, he could see more white film on his legs. The open sores pushed up through the long white areas like miniature volcanoes rising up through snow. The dried blood streaked down like small lava flows. He knew this was the most singular humiliation he had experienced, and there were several to choose from since his arrival.

He stood as tall as he could until he looked down and to his left at the silent woman's face. The soul-sucking vacuum of her face was too close to him. He felt the pull to give up part of his life force to her, the children, and the humiliation. He replaced the stone face of disgust with his mother's face, and he did not flinch when the grit of the lye-soaked rag moved over his skin. He knew his stubbornness was a mixed blessing, but at this moment, it was a precious gift. His body was in the cold washtub, but his mind was with his mother on the riverbank looking at the sky with his eyes closed.

It was over. The towel was around him, and he walked toward the children and sat on the couch with his friends. The oldest girl gave him the dry, hand-me-down clothes. Now his skin was red from the soap and blue from the cold. He stood and put on the clothes then sat down again and petted his friends. The oldest boy and girl emptied the washtub. The water was blacker than the dirt it splashed onto. He knew the filth and the poverty of spirit in the place would not come as close to him again as it did when the silent woman's face was too near. *Never look directly at her face again!*

Blue and Daisy smelled him and the clothes. He heard the children in the front yard. He checked for the bag of rocks and stepped off the porch to look under the couch to check the spear. It was there. He walked down the side of the shack; the tin pail and the cup were no longer there where he'd put them. He did not like being too far away from the spear, but he ventured through the trees where he could see the plank bridge and the front yard. He hoped he would catch a glimpse of his father's sister when she arrived. He moved closer to the front yard and stood behind the last tree before the dirt.

The girls were playing jump rope and singing a jump rope song: "Lisa, Teresa. Girls next door are nice. How many hours did Lisa, Teresa sleep? One, two, three, four, five, six, seven, eight!" They switched places and started again. "Lisa, Teresa." He had moved into the edge of the yard, drawn by the song and the thought of the same girls being the night shirted fairies floating in the darkness down the outhouse path.

The front screen door flew open and Sonny ran out toward the girls. The door slammed shut before he saw what was between Sonny's legs. It looked like a large penis. Sonny was chasing the girls around the yard until the girls ran inside. He had seen this part of the drinking before—the playful part, before the mood changed to darkness. Sonny was grinning when he came to the boy, the thing still between his legs. Sonny smiled when he turned the thing around and showed the doll painted on the other side. Then he turned it over to the flesh-colored part saying, "It's a doll." The smile left quickly when the brown-liquid humor was not shared. Sonny shifted from one foot to the other swinging the fleshed-colored side from one leg to the other. "Ya don't like that, do ya?"

A large car pulled up next to the truck. Sonny walked to the porch and stood in front of the doorway. The children had been inside and began to appear to his left and right, and the silent woman moved to the far-right side of the porch. He did not look at her face. Many things had happened since he followed his father across the plank bridge and saw the people of the shack appear one by one on the porch. They had just now appeared in the very same way. It was the same but different, very different.

He slowly backed into the woods, making no fast movements to draw attention to himself. He moved quietly through the trees to the couch and kissed Daisy and Blue on their heads. He lifted the cushion for the cloth bag with the rocks and slid the spear out from under the couch. He walked down the outside wall of the shack and leaned the spear next to the corner and put the bag on the ground. He stepped back into the woods and made his way through the trees, where he could see the car, the bridge, and the front porch.

The car door opened, and a woman stepped out. She leaned over to close the door and stood up straight. She was tall with long, black, shiny hair. She wore a dress with wide vertical stripes of blue and a wide blue belt around her waist. She walked the plank bridge without using the handrail. Her back was straight, and her eyes were on Sonny. Sonny crossed his arms over his chest and sighed. As she neared the end of the planks, he could see she was beautiful, with dark olive skin. Her hair was the color of his father's. He remembered his father speak about her in a very kind manner. She looked at the silent woman. "Afternoon, Alice."

"Eunice." *The silent woman had spoken!*

"The children have grown!"

"Yes."

She said to the children, "My name is Eunice. I am the sister of your father's friend. Afternoon, Sonny."

"Eunice."

"I have come to see Jim."

Sonny pointed where the boy had been. "He's over there somewhere. He's simple, ya know."

"You are simple. He is not."

"This is my house, and I know he's simple!"

"Sonny, I will be pleased to sit with you and the sheriff and discuss intelligence and the treatment of your family! Would you like to begin now?"

"Boy, come out!"

"Jim, I would be pleased to meet you."

He wanted so dearly to go with her across the plank bridge. He wanted to leave this place. He stepped out of the woods and walked to her. He gently put his hand in hers.

"I am so very pleased to meet you, Aunt Eunice. It was so kind of you to come."

"I am so truly pleased to meet you, Jim." His aunt looked at the silent woman. "Alice, may we come in?"

The silent woman moved to the door. She tried to open it, but it hit the back of Sonny's boots.

His aunt took his hand and walked onto the porch. Her eyes were above Sonny's. "Alice, would you like to show me around?"

The silent woman pressed the door against Sonny's boot and spoke. "Sonny, will you move so Eunice can enter." He squeezed his aunt's hand. He was so proud to be blood kin to such a brave person. Sonny moved.

"This is your front room? The couch looks comfortable. And this is the bedroom. Which is your bed, Jim?" He squeezed her hand tightly.

"It's the second one, right here," Sonny said. All knew he was lying, and Aunt Eunice didn't believe him. He was squeezing his aunt's hand tighter.

"And this is your kitchen? Love those big iron skillets. Good for frying okra!" He was pulling his aunt's hand. "This is your back porch with a couch for sitting and watching the sunrise. Two fine blue tick hounds."

He sat down in his usual spot and whispered, "This is Daisy, and this is Blue."

As they stepped back inside Aunt Eunice said, "Alice, thank you so much for the tour. Sonny, I spoke to my attorney. He advises me that I can take Jim to visit his father. We'll be leaving shortly. Jim, where are your things?"

He looked at the suitcase under the wide bed. She slid it out and set it by the front room couch. "Sit here and check if you have everything."

He sat on the couch and opened the suitcase. There was the picture of his mother. He felt the tears well up. And the coin collection. He opened the cardboard books one by one. They were all empty. Then he remembered the first night at the dime store and the seven dimes slammed on the counter. *Those were my dimes!* All four books had been full of dimes and pennies his father had collected and given to him. It was as if Sonny had filled flat bottles with them and swallowed every coin.

There was anger. There was more—sadness for Sonny, sadness for a soul flailing, spitting out violence and chaos on its journey below the surface. He handed the suitcase to his aunt and walked through the front screen door. He moved to the corner of the shack and put the cloth sack with the seven rocks on his belt. He grabbed the spear and crossed the yard and waited for his aunt. He stood next to the first plank of the bridge and waited.

His father's sister stepped off the porch and passed by him with the suitcase. He looked at the shack one more time and turned. He was nearly across the bridge when Blue and Daisy caught up with him. He knelt down and hugged and kissed them. They had been faithful friends.

"You ain't takin' them hounds!"

He petted them one more time and told them to stay. He turned and walked toward his aunt. She stood at the far end of the bridge near the strip of trees; the car was in sight.

Sonny's soul had not yet reached the bottom of the abyss. The shotgun was in his hands. Blue and Daisy were headed back to the shack. Sonny rushed forward and kicked both dogs off the plank; they fell into the ditch and began swimming fast for the bank. Sonny fumbled putting the shells in the barrels. He planned to kill the dogs.

64

The spear was in the boy's left hand, and his right held the heavy round stone with the rough edges. His feet were at an angle. He lifted his left leg and threw the stone. It struck and broke Sonny's nose. Sonny's head spun to the right, and he fell onto his right knee. Both barrels went off, blowing a section of the handrail into the ditch. He threw the thin flint rock with the edges. It curved to the left and made a thin, bloody line on the back of Sonny's neck. Sonny got up and turned as the second the heavy round stone with the rough edges struck his left eye. His boot slipped off the plank. He grabbed the upright post on the way down. Sonny's arms were wrapped around the post; his boots were less than three feet above the water.

The boy walked the fifteen yards and stood where Sonny's arms were between him and the shack. The blood from Sonny's face, neck, and eye was dripping into the water, causing great interest.

"Jim, we have a long way to go to get home."

He looked at his aunt. He looked at the shack. Blue and Daisy were standing on the front porch with the children and the silent woman. They looked like a photograph; there was no movement. He walked away.

He heard the big splash before he reached the end of the last plank. Sonny was splashing his way to the bank and climbing the tree roots. He saw the water moccasin drop into the water from the post where Sonny had been. The photograph of the front porch remained the same, with Sonny lying in the foreground at the edge of the dirt yard.

He realized Sonny's thrashing soul and the darkness of the shack had pulled him below the surface for the edge of a moment.

"Jim, we have a long way to go to get home."

He stopped at the car. Put his feet together. Took the three steps and threw the spear fifteen yards. It sank deep into a rotten tree. He removed the seven rocks from the cloth pouch and threw them underhanded and together into the water. He kept the cloth pouch that once held the seven saltine sandwiches.

He rode in the front seat with his aunt through the Johnson grass, and they turned right. They headed to town..." pop. 924."

Hensen March

8 – Two Double Colas

He dug his fingers into his pants just above the knees..." pop. 924" passed by his window.

"Let's get you something for those mosquito bites. Franklin's has something, I'm sure."

The car passed by Gene Autry's resting place. His fingers had not moved. His aunt turned right and stopped in front of the dime store. There was more time to look at the sign, "Franklin's Five and Dime."

"Scoot over," his aunt said. "We'll get out on your side." He turned to his aunt and saw the red neon sign just to the right of her face. Under the sign two men were sitting on benches and three standing...all were drinking. He wondered if they were the same men from his first visit to Franklin's. He didn't want to stay in the car, and he didn't want to go in. His fingers dug in tighter.

"Honey, it will take just a minute." He knew if he did not open the door, he would forever be the seventh child of the shack. He relaxed his hands, and the color came back to his knuckles. He let go of his pants and got out of the car, holding the door for his Aunt Eunice. When they approached the door, men yelled vulgar things to his aunt. He pushed down hard on the handle and put his foot in the opening. His aunt used her left hand above his head and pushed the door wider; he waited for her to enter. He watched the door close. Sonny's face was not there.

Aunt Eunice took his hand, and they walked to the counter.

"Good afternoon, ma'am. May I help you?"

"Afternoon. Do you have penicillin salve?"

"Yes ma'am." The clerk turned and removed a tube from the shelf.

"How much?"

"Thirty-five cents, ma'am."

She placed the quarter and dime in the clerk's hand. "Thank you, sir. Jim, would you like a toy?"

"No thank you, Aunt Eunice." She smiled and they walked to the door.

A man with a kind and gentle face opened the door. His aunt nodded. He stopped for a moment, and the man handed him the tin pail and the tin cup. "This is for your journey. It will be long, but you will do well. The missus and I will pray for you."

He handed the man the cloth pouch and smiled. The door closed behind him. He knew he would add this man to the room with the typewriters and the window with the view of his mother walking. He opened the car door for his aunt, and she slid across the seat behind the steering wheel. He sat down and closed the door. They drove away from Franklin's, heading south. He looked through the back window..." pop. 924."

He watched the mirror through the open window for miles. The rolling reflection of the flying dust was hypnotic. The dust would fly up and curl under itself and fan out. And repeat, with half seconds of the imagined round front of Sonny's truck. The mirage faded, and he decided not to use the man's name in his thoughts. He looked at his aunt and she smiled. She was wearing shaded glasses and looked like someone in the movies.

He opened the tin pail. The first container had two small bottles of milk with glass tops and wire clasps. He opened one and gave it to his aunt. The second container had brownies. The brownies captured Aunt Eunice's attention. One was in her mouth before he could open the wire clasp. They raised the bottles in a smiling toast. He placed the container of brownies on the seat between them. He knew they would not last long so close to Aunt Eunice.

He opened the last container. There was a jar with a string tied just below the lid with a note: "Some extras from my collection. Wanted to pass them on to you." *A jar with pennies and dimes!* The smile was big, and the memory was good. He hoped, as time passed, that the room with the typewriters would always have the man with the kind and gentle face. It would be the memory room with wide, clear windows and lots of space for those who crossed his path with kindness.

"I have four boys; you are going to have fun!" *Fun would be no coyotes and sleeping inside.* "Who gave you the brownies and milk?"

"My friend. He helped me when I was there."

"When you were at Sonny's?"

"When I was there."

"We'll be home tomorrow before dark."

Before dark would be fine with him. More time went by without talking. He was not used to talking; his voice sounded strange to him. Talking was a crude substitute for thinking. Watching and thinking had served him well.

They drove south the rest of the day and stopped before dark at a single gas pump. A man with a white hat and shirt came out of a long, narrow building and walked to Aunt Eunice's window. "Evening, ma'am. Fill it up with Ethel?"

"Yes, sir. Do you have a restroom?"

"Yes ma'am; out back."

"Jim, will you come with me and watch the door?"

"Yes, ma'am." It was a nicer outhouse. His aunt finished, and he entered while she waited outside. He didn't need it, but there was toilet paper. They walked around the front and went into the narrow building.

"Jim, do you want an RC or a Double Cola?"

He knew he wanted a Double Cola; they were bigger than other soda bottles. "Double Cola."

"I'll have one, too." There was a white refrigerator with a rounded door. A handwritten sign was taped on the door: "sodas 5 cents." She took out the two bottles and placed them on the counter. The man with the white hat came in. "Ma'am, I washed your windows, checked the oil and tires."

"What do I owe you, sir?"

"Including the sodas, that would come to two dollars and thirty-five cents."

"Here you are, sir, and thank you for your kind service."

"You're welcome, ma'am. Drive safe and watch out for cows in the road next five miles or so."

"We will."

They pulled away with the headlights on and headed south, drinking Double Colas and watching for cows in the road. He didn't ask how long it would take to get to his aunt's house. He was drinking Double Cola, and each mile took him farther (and further) from the shack. He knew Aunt Eunice could smell the couch on him, but she said nothing about it. She knew where he had been and that was why she came for him. *Someone came for him!* He watched for cows in the road and felt so very fortunate.

He figured out why Double Colas came in bigger bottles than other sodas—they put more water in them. *Watered down soda that was bigger, not better. But it was fun drinking out of a big bottle!* If the occasion arose, he'd have another one someday.

There were no cows in the road so far. He finished the soda and closed his eyes. This time he was riding inside the vehicle, not bouncing around in the back of a pickup hitting light poles and jumping when it stopped. It was warmer going south, and he fell into a deep sleep without dreams.

9 – The Stone House

He felt the warmth on his face and his eyes opened slowly. Aunt Eunice was wearing her shaded glasses—the morning sun was coming through her window. The egg-yolk sun was coming up over the fields. He moved slightly to balance the orange ball on his aunt's nose. He smiled, bubble gum bubble out of Aunt Eunice's nose.

He had felt the gravel for some time. He knew dirt meant remote with very few people, and gravel meant more people. With the exception of the big city and its own heartache, he had lived mostly next to dirt and mud. He could see the town. There were several two-story brick buildings surrounded by framed houses with large porches; most were painted white.

The car turned left just before the smaller houses in the outer band of structures at the edge of town. The road ended into another road, and his aunt turned left again. Less than a mile down the road, she turned left into a drive that ran through a line of tall fir trees. The drive was to the left of a large stone house with wide stone steps that led up to a porch. The porch had chairs, and plants hung from the ceiling. The front yard was in two levels; the upper level where the house sat was supported by a stone wall. Grass that was cut short surrounded the house and lower yard.

"This is your home now!" Aunt Eunice had put her shaded glasses up on her head, and he could see her eyes; they were brown like his mother's. He knew they were not his mother's eyes. He would never see his mother's eyes again. The same blood nourished Aunt Eunice's eyes as his father's eyes. His eyes were the same color as his father's, his mother's, and Aunt Eunice's...*that is close enough for me!*

"Let's find the boys! Bet they're around back." They walked along the side of the house on a concrete sidewalk. The only dirt he could see was in the beds of flowers along the stone wall of the house and in the flat cropland that stretched to a distant line of trees. Steps on the side of the house led to the same level as the front. Around the corner of the house, stone pillars supported a roof over a large area of concrete. He stepped to the side of his aunt and saw four boys, in pairs, sword fighting with wooden tomato stakes.

71

"Boys, this is your cousin, Jim." Two more whacks of the pretend swords and they came over.

"Can you sword fight?" He wasn't a famous tomato stack sword fighter, but he was right handy with a spear.

"Yeah, I can fight."

"Boys, introduce yourselves to your cousin."

Each one said his name. He wasn't much for names. He paid attention to faces and eyes. Theirs were confident and prone to trouble. Innocent trouble, but there were four of them and they came up with stuff that Aunt Eunice knew about before they did it.

He was quiet, shy, observant, and had not learned the art of thoughtless free play. His moves were purposeful and cautious. These boys talked all the time and punched each other in the arms and dared each other— "Can you do this? Bet you can't do this!" They were used to playing and he was used to practicing, so he was more skilled at throwing and catching and anything that involved a chosen target.

He was challenged to a tomato-stake duel with each of the four. They decided he was all right after each of their pretend swords was on the ground at the end of each match. He showed them how to watch their opponent's eyes and the muscles in the chest closest to the arm that held the sword so they could predict their opponent's moves.

He heard the truck coming toward the house. Aunt Eunice came out of the house and kissed the large man getting out of the new looking truck. "Jim, this is your Uncle Bob."

He walked to the large man and shook his hand. "Pleased to meet you, sir."

"Least he has some manners, not like this wild bunch. Hear you're going to stay awhile."

Aunt Eunice responded, "No, he's going to live here."

He felt the slight breeze pass by his heart and the caution slowly rise in his chest. His luck with adult men had not been the best. This large man did not seem angry or violent. He could tell his uncle was a worker but was used to getting his way. The boy could tell the man had no interest in having a fifth boy in the house. He could see the great distance between the loving acceptance of Aunt Eunice and the distance of Uncle Bob, which may cause him to be on another long ride, looking in the mirror at the dust of another once-been place.

"Boys, put the sticks in the shed and come get washed up for supper."

The boys ran to the shed, and he looked for the pump.

"Come on," the boys called as they ran up the steps. "Got to wash our hands."

There were eight stone steps to the door. He followed the boys to a room that had a sink, a toilet, and a bathtub. He had seen a room like this before at the hotel in the big city; it was at the end of a hallway past the doors of other rooms. This one was in the house. There was running water in the house and grass in the yard. He looked at the bathtub. He had never been in a bathtub or taken a bath...he didn't know how to take a bath.

He did what the boys did, turning the knob on the sink and using the white soap that wasn't made of lye. The boys were using a knob with a "C" on it. The other knob had an "H" on it...he would figure out that one later. He dried his hands on a soft towel and followed the boys to the table.

He waited until Aunt Eunice told him where to sit. Everyone had a chair. His uncle sat at the end of the table facing the kitchen, the boys on the sides. He sat between the youngest two, to the left of his uncle. The oldest boy sat to the right of his father, and the second oldest next to the empty chair opposite his uncle. There was an empty chair facing him.

Aunt Eunice came out of the kitchen with an older woman. "This is Jim, the boys' cousin. Jim, this is Miss Betty. She helps me with the boys and the house."

"Nice to meet you, Miss Betty."

"My, you're a polite one. Need some more of that around here. You boys could learn some manners from your cousin, instead of taking after your father."

His uncle's eyes rolled. "Miss Betty, don't you have something to do in the kitchen?"

"No sir, I'm just enjoying the moment...just basking in a rare moment of politeness!" There was laughter. Miss Betty was laughing all the way to the kitchen.

There were knives and forks with no fast-moving spoons or fear. There was a white tablecloth. The names of some of the food on the table were the same, but everything else was different, very different. The food wasn't overpowered by the metallic taste of fear. It tasted better, much better! It was hot and felt warm moving down to a stomach at ease.

There were things he didn't know about white tablecloth living. He began to worry about the bathtub, the "H," and who to ask about things he did not know. He liked Miss Betty; *maybe I could ask her.* He could ask her about the "C" and the "H." He did not want to let anyone know that he didn't know about the bathtub and how to use it. It had a "C" and an "H" on it like the sink. He did not want to be embarrassed around the boys. They thought he was all right because he could sword fight.

Now he knew why he had chosen the single shot toy rifle at the dime store. He wasn't thinking of the other children—he was thinking of himself. He did not want anything different from the others because he wanted to blend in and not be different. He could feel tightness in his chest and heaviness in his stomach. His head moved.

"Hey, Jim." The boy next to him had punched him in the arm. "Can you throw rocks?"

"Yeah, I throw pretty good."

"Tomorrow, we'll put tin cans on a board and see who can hit 'em."

That familiar, dark visitor had turned and passed, and his chest loosened, and his stomach felt lighter. "Yeah, I'll throw some with you."

"Boys hug your father. Let's go upstairs and get those feet washed. Don't want my sheets ruined, again."

As Miss Betty was picking up dirty plates off the table, he leaned over. "Miss Betty, that sure was a good supper!"

"Thank you, young man. Tomorrow, we're going to have chicken fried steak, mashed potatoes and gravy, and the biggest bowl of fried okra you've ever seen!"

"Yes ma'am!" The last son had hugged his father. "Uncle Bob, thank you for letting me stay here tonight."

"You're welcome, son. Don't let them boys of mine run over ya."

"Yes, sir."

Aunt Eunice was waiting at the stairs. "Let's get your feet washed and some clean pajamas. Then we'll doctor those bites."

The stairs had carpet, and the upstairs had lots of rooms; all had carpet. He heard the boys and the water at the end of the hallway. He followed his aunt. The oldest two boys were sitting on the edge of the bathtub with their feet inside the tub. The water was coming out of the spout, and they were passing the white soap back and forth, washing their feet.

Aunt Eunice passed her hand in the stream. "Can't get those feet clean with cold water," and she turned the knob to the left—the one with the "H" on it—and passed her hand through the stream. "There, that's better." *One white-tablecloth-living mystery solved.*

The boys in the tub finished. The younger boys were drying their feet on what once was a white towel. His aunt intervened. "Get back in the tub and try soap this time."

He stepped closer to see how they did their feet. After a moment it was his turn. The water in the tub was getting brown, and his aunt pulled out the white rubber stopper and the water drained.

"Move closer and use the water from the spout." His feet began to return to their original color, or at least they matched his hands now. "We'll work on those fingernails tomorrow."

She opened a narrow door that had shelves and brought out pajamas. "Here, put these on, and we'll look at those mosquito bites." He turned and took off his clothes. "No need to be shy. I'm the mother of four boys."

He kept his back to her because he didn't want her to see how badly the foreskin of his penis had glued itself to the head. The opening to pee had slowly become smaller. He put on the bottoms and turned.

"Oh my, the bites are infected. You've been picking at them with those dirty fingernails."

"Yes ma'am, they itch something terrible."

She washed each bite and put the penicillin salve on each one. "Let's do your legs now." It seemed it took forever. The boys were running up and down the hallway, tackling each other.

The dark visitor passed and rested for a fraction of a second on his aunt's face. He knew the visitor. He had seen and felt him often. He floated past the trunks in the darkness of the woods and stood staring in the shadows next to the back porch couch. He lived in the heavy wool coat on the rusty hanger in the attic of a long-abandoned house on a dark, forgotten street. He traveled just outside the corner of one's eye and was invited in when the senses moved one's head to look. The soap was not lye, but it moved over the same sores that bled into the washtub below the vacuum of the silent woman's face. His senses did not turn his head, but the sores and the skin remembered. He would not scratch them again. Not this night.

"Jim. Honey, what's wrong?" His arms were around his stomach, and the tears were splashing on the tops of his feet. "Is it about where you were?"

"Yes, but I'm all right now."

"You're not going back there, ever."

"Am I staying here with you?"

"Yes, you are, for as long as you want! Want to see what the boys are up to?"

He put on the top of the pajamas, wiped his eyes and hoped the boys couldn't tell he had been crying. He was glad the pajamas hid the sores. The semi-famous wooden-tomato-stake fighter walked down the hall behind his Aunt Eunice. The older boys' room was on the right; they were on the floor arm wrestling. Comic books were spread across their beds. He guessed the next room was where he would sleep. The door was open at the end of the hallway, and the younger boys were sitting on the floor with their backs to the door. Aunt Eunice walked in the room and pointed to a bed in the right corner of the room. "Jim, this is your bed."

It had sheets, a pillow, and a small table with a lamp. The bedspread had wide blue and white stripes like the dress she wore when she came to get him. This had been another in a long series of very long days with indescribable changes, traveling by car from one planet to another.

The boys were throwing playing cards into two baseball caps. "Wanna play?"

"Yeah."

"When you run out of cards, whoever has the most in their hat wins. Here's your hat."

They gathered up the cards and dealt them out until only one was left. "If your card goes in somebody's hat, they get to count it for them. Got it?"

"Yep." They played several rounds. He hadn't noticed his aunt had left the room. He held the card at an angle and snapped his wrist. The cards would spin and arch to the left like the thin, flat, flint rocks from the clearing. His thoughts drifted. This was a planet that had carpet and sheets. He had traveled far and was among his people but still a stranger with different clothes and memories.

He heard Aunt Eunice in the hallway, talking to the older boys. "You got thirty minutes." She came in at the end of a round. "Time for bed. Put your things away and jump in bed."

"So, we can jump, Momma?"

"I stand corrected. Put your things away slowly, gently, and quietly get into bed."

Everybody laughed. Now everyone was in bed. His aunt kissed her boys on the cheek, and he got a kiss, too. He could see her hand on the doorknob and part of her arm with the bracelet closing the door part way.

"Hey, Momma!"

"Yes?"

A loud and long fart with two separate waves of sound pushed against the still air of the room and crashed against all four walls... "Sure do love that fried okra!" He could tell Aunt Eunice was laughing, too—her bracelet was jiggling.

"You're such fine gentlemen. Oh, my goodness, someone open a window!" Everybody was laughing; he was laughing.

"Gentlemen, good night and sleep well. See you in the morning."

He heard the muffled footsteps of his aunt going down the stairs. There were snorts and giggles...another not so impressive fart. The first one still lingered in the air.

"Hey, Jim."

"Yeah?"

"Can you fart?"

"Not like that. It still stinks!"

"Yeah, it was a good one; made Momma laugh."

"Does fried okra make you fart like that?"

"Nah, I just said that to make Momma laugh."

It was real funny—made him laugh, too. He was still grinning just thinking about it.

"Is your brother asleep?"

"Yeah, he gets in bed and he's out like a light. After breakfast, we'll throw some rocks."

"Sounds good."

"Good night."

"Good night." He knew the boy would be asleep way before he would be. He closed his eyes for a moment to adjust to the lower light. Even with the light off, it was much brighter than the back porch. The woods behind the shack seemed to suck up all the moonlight.

He wanted to memorize the room before he closed his eyes to sleep. The door swung in and away from him. He knew he was upstairs in the front of the house. The room was wider than deep. The fart master was slightly to his left, and sleeping beauty was more to his right. All three beds came out at angle from three corners of the room. The corner past the door had a tall chest with ten drawers with brass handles. It covered the corner like the beds. If something happened, he could run left through the doorway, down the hallway, left down the stairs to the landing, left down the last set of steps, a hard right down the hallway, left through the kitchen and through the narrow room with coats, out the side door, down the eight stone steps, across the side yard, across the drive to the far side of the fir trees to the road and hide in the ditch. All of the land was flat; the only cover would be the crop in the fields that hadn't been harvested. He couldn't remember which fields were harvested and which were not, but he would check in the morning.

He closed his eyes for a few moments to listen to the sounds of the house. He could hear a faint conversation downstairs but none of the words. The carpet in the house captured portions of the sound before it found its way along the walls to the doorways and hallways. The sounds fought their way over each ascending, carpeted step, causing the upstairs to approach silence. His ears started to ring from the absence of the sounds of insects, tree frogs, bullfrogs, and the four-legged beasts that traveled through the night woods. He did not miss the coyotes. He did not miss the insects. He did miss Blue and Daisy. They were on the couch now, and tomorrow, in the clearing napping in their grassy beds between breakfast and supper. He fell asleep.

He heard the heavy footsteps coming up the stairs and a door close at the other end of the hallway. There were softer steps coming. They stopped, then were coming to the room with the three beds. His right hand was across his chest holding onto the left side of the bed covers, ready to move quickly.

It was his Aunt Eunice. She pulled the covers up and tucked them around the fart master's neck and did the same with sleeping beauty. She turned and saw his arm and open eyes. He lifted his hand in a low, slow wave. She leaned over. "Time to sleep. I'm at the end of the hallway. No scratching. See you bright and early."

He returned his arm to his side and closed his eyes. He saw the woods. Opened them again and closed them to darkness and drifted off. Much later, his eyes opened wide and his body jerked...he was not on the couch. He closed his eyes and traveled around the room using the memorized picture in his mind. He slept, again.

Hensen March

10 – Harvest Season

The door closed at the far end of the hall, and he heard heavy steps down the stairs. He guessed it was his uncle. This was the middle of harvest season and farmers were up at dawn, and many ran their tractors and equipment through the night. Lights ran up and down the fields until dawn; they refueled and began again with a different driver. It was probably the same in his uncle's part of the country.

He discovered his bed faced east, with the dim sunrise of late autumn coming through the windows. He knew it would be in his face in less than an hour. He saw the tiny floaters drifting in the light from the windows. Each window had twelve panes of glass. He looked above his head. The light and the panes made a pattern on the wall, angled by the corner of the room and the slow movement of the light. He watched the top of the headboard post nearest the door and saw the light moving very slowly down and to his left. The light would soon pass through the partially open door and travel down the hallway. He had seen many dawns on the couch, and each was welcomed. The long cloudy nights with no moon brought a blackness that wrapped around the eyeballs and hung heavy in the air. The loss of a sense stirred pictures in the mind that caused the eyes to open wide and search for the familiar. Now he was surrounded by walls, ceiling, warm covers, and large windows. His pupils narrowed, his eyes closed, and his head turned. The sun had caught him daydreaming; its rays jumped through the window and pushed his face to the side.

He was on his right side looking at the base of the small lamp on the table next to the bed. This was how he slept on the couch with his head on Daisy just above her stomach. Her head would be on his arm, with her nose tucked close to his navel. This was the time after dawn that she and Blue would be waiting patiently for the breakfast scraps. They were far away but very close. Their grassy beds lay close to the clear, wide windows of the memory room with the typewriters, in the place where the sun lingered on the floor.

He heard the truck start, and he got up and looked through the windows at the front of the house. He could see the truck windows blinking through the fir trees as his uncle's truck moved down the drive. He watched the truck turn left in front of the house on the road next to the two levels of the front lawn.

His uncle was wearing a large-brimmed, tan hat that was the same color as his jacket and shirt. It was the uniform of a farmer. They wore tan pants with wide belt loops that came to a point at the bottom of the loop. Some farmers wore suspenders and some wide leather belts; most tied a blue bandana around their head to keep the sweat out of their eyes. The ones who drove the equipment had their bandanas around their necks to pull over their noses, especially when harvesting soybeans.

"Hey, Jim. What are you looking at?

"Saw your dad driving off."

"He's checking on the men."

"What men?"

"The ones that work the farm."

"Is he their boss?"

"Yeah, he owns the farm."

"Oh." *Must be a big farm if he needs men.* He looked beyond the line of fir trees for cover. Beyond the trees, unharvested corn ran so far along the road on both sides of the house that he couldn't see the end of the fields—excellent cover but not for long. The corn leaves had lost their moisture and color; the corn would be harvested in the next few days.

"Come on, Jim. I gotta pee!" The fart master ran down the hall and he followed. He didn't remember how the toilet worked, and he had more business to attend to than just pee.

"Remember, if you pee, always put the seat up. Momma said that she and Miss Betty do not like cleaning boy pee off the seat...it's not what civilized gentlemen do."

He was at the sink trying to get the dirt out from under his fingernails. His nails were long and had started to curl under. He dug his nails into the white soap, but the thick black lines remained. He looked in the mirror. The last time he had seen his reflection was at the hotel in the big city. His hair was long, and he looked older than he remembered. His cheeks were a bit sunken, and the skin under his eyes was darker.

The fart master pushed the chrome lever, and the pee went down, and the new water came up.

"Gotta wash my hands."

They changed places, and he put the seat down and sat. There was toilet paper—no curled-up Sears catalog.

"If you're pooping, have to close the door. Momma says people passing down the hallway don't need to see someone pooping. Everybody has to do it, but they don't need to see somebody else doing it."

The fart master was a wealth of information about white tablecloth living. Before, he would use the catalog pages. He did not use the outhouse. He didn't like the smell, and he did not like the possibility of being trapped in a small space and having to go past the drunken bully to escape. He dug holes in the woods then covered them. They were downwind and away from the practice clearing. Now he sat on a white poop receptacle that carried things away to another place.

He went down the hall and saw the fart master at the tall set of drawers.

"Here—underwear, blue jeans, and a long-sleeved shirt."

"Thanks." He sat on the bed next to the lamp and got dressed. He had made it through the first night without touching the bites. Some were less red and starting to close. He was wearing store-bought clothes for the first time; now he was fancy like the others who lived in the big stone house. It was important and not important, all at the same time. Somehow, he understood the difference and the sameness.

"Do you know how to make up the bed? Let me show you. First, fold up your pajamas and put them under your pillow."

He was standing on the side next to the lamp and the fart master on the side next to the door. The lesson continued. He knew the fart master liked him. He had been teaching him lessons that the fart master had most likely learned the hard way. He was bright, quick, and funny. He had a twinkle of the eye that meant mischief. He guessed Aunt Eunice knew about the sparkle and supervised his journey down the path, with real trouble lurking just beyond the ditches on either side. He, too, would try to stay away from the ditches. He would focus on the useful information provided by the fart master and listen carefully for the troublesome detours that were sure to come—those detours skillfully woven into the helpful but identified by the increased sparkle of the grand fart master's eye.

Strangely, daily life in the big stone house had a sameness just like daily life at the shack. The objects were different but tending to your things was the same. Folding the pajamas and placing them under the pillow was similar to placing the cloth pouch with the seven rocks under the cushion of the couch. Straightening the bed linens was similar to folding the tarp carefully so it lay undetected under the couch cushions. Placing the spear in the same place was like picking up things off the carpet and returning them to their designated spot. One major difference was basic hygiene. He knew he had not yet achieved the expected standard of cleanliness for white-tablecloth, big-stone-house living. It was easy to be cleaner if you had the stuff to do it but learning how to use the stuff fast enough could prove difficult. He was starting from way behind.

Sleeping beauty arose. He was swift footed and flashed past the fart master on the way to the toilet.

"Let's see what's for breakfast! Don't worry about brother toilet man; he'll go back to bed, and Momma will have to drag him out by his toes."

They walked down the stairs. His toes almost disappeared. *Aunt Eunice sure did like thick, deep carpet.* He liked it, too.

They walked down the hallway to the kitchen. It was bigger than he remembered. There was a round table to the left; he counted ten chairs around it. The two older boys were eating breakfast. He could see the yellow eggs in their mouths when they said, "Morning!" He smiled.

Aunt Eunice was across the kitchen, slightly to his right. The stove in front of her looked like one from a diner, with five flames going and a flat surface with piles of multicolored vegetables and the smell of onions. She turned and smiled. "Good morning, lads! Today's breakfast special is western omelets!"

He never heard of the "breakfast special," but it smelled good! His people of the stone house ate supper in one room and ate breakfast in another room. He knew some people ate three times a day. *Was there another room for that?* Like most things, he'd wait and see.

"Come get your plates." He followed the fart master to the stove. He waited his turn and received more than expected. The steam rose high on the plate.

He whispered to the fart master, "Where do I sit?"

"At breakfast, you sit anywhere you want." Of course, everyone knew that, except him. Some of the same focus was required at the stone house as was required at the couch behind the shack...to avoid the failure to adapt. The stakes were much higher with one than the other—so it appeared.

This was a household that believed in food and plenty of it! His belly had been full since his arrival yesterday. He worried that he moved slower and was less observant as a result. The tile on the kitchen floor had been cool on his feet. He sat on the corner of the chair with the toes of his right foot on the tile and let the steam from the plate cover his face and flow up his nose. The grits were white and hot, with melted butter in the center and a slight taste of sugar. He resisted the urge to hum. There was a sausage patty with a link—they looked like a cookie with a miniature hotdog—along with a large homemade biscuit broken in half and covered with white milk gravy. A portion of the vegetables with the onions from the flat part of the stove was tucked inside folded-over eggs along with diced ham and melted cheese.

The floor was cool; the food was hot; the boys were fun; Aunt Eunice was loving and beautiful; and grander surroundings could not be wished for...it was easier than sitting in the dirt in the darkness with his back against the outside wall of the shack and quietly from the tin pail and drinking liquid from the tin cup. *It was a most excellent moment.* He hoped his heart remained grateful for all the moments, regardless of place and time. Each was a moment when kindness quietly crossed his path and nodded with different faces. He would look forward and watch for its face again.

Miss Betty came through the side door into the kitchen and bowed and curtsied as sleeping beauty entered. The three boys stood and bowed as Aunt Eunice curtsied, and all said together, "His Royal Highness Has Emerged from His Chambers! Alert His Royal Subjects!" Aunt Eunice said, "Please come forward and receive thy plate of honor!" The people of the stone house had done this before, probably more times than they cared to. It was entertaining. Sleeping beauty was the youngest, and he knew it.

He put the last bite in his mouth; there was no room left for anything else. He did not know how these people ate so much. Miss Betty leaned over to get his plate and whispered, "Want some help with those fingernails?"

"Yes ma'am; started on them this morning."

"Follow me." They went past the stove, where Aunt Eunice winked at him, and through a doorway into a room with clay pots and two deep metal sinks.

"Jim, we probably need to clip these fingernails first. That's why you couldn't get 'um the way you wanted. Let's get over here by the sink where the light's better." Miss Betty cut the nails short. "Let's use a vegetable brush to finish them up." She used soap several times and brushed each finger. "Look at that—good as new!"

He hugged her. "Thank you, Miss Betty!" He felt like he had someone else's hands. He thought long and hard and couldn't remember the last time his fingernails were clean. He really knew when; it was before his mother became ill. He was not ready. He was not ready to be without her. He was not ready to feel all the painful loneliness. His mind knew he was alone, but it was not ready to tell his heart. He had made it through another night and part of a morning. Today, he would enjoy his new hands. And learn to keep them as new as possible.

He came back into the kitchen, and all the boys were gone. Aunt Eunice and Miss Betty were washing and drying breakfast dishes. "Boys are outside."

"Aunt Eunice, can I borrow some socks?"

"Sure can; follow me." They went upstairs to the tall chest of draws. "Here, these are good and warm. The socks were white, thick, and longer than he had seen before.

He looked at his feet. He hoped Miss Betty was up to another session of clipping and scrubbing. He knew his shoes were too tight, and they had pushed his toenails halfway under his toes. He hadn't had any socks for a long time, and the leather had made hard-looking bumps on his feet. He liked the socks; they felt good.

"Here, try these."

Wow, they were tennis shoes. They were tall. He put one on; it covered his ankle. "Is this, all right? Won't somebody need these?"

She laughed. "The boys have more shoes than they can count. They grow out of them in a matter of weeks! Did you sleep OK?"

"Pretty good. Not used to sleeping in a bed—it was nice! I didn't scratch anything."

"Good. We'll doctor them again tonight." He hoped it would not involve tears and leftover fear.

"Thank you for coming for me."

"You're welcome. You belong with your family."

"Don't know much about family."

"I know, but you're smart and polite. You're very much like your mother. I'll tell you more about her later. Saw you sword fighting. Are you as good at throwing rocks?"

"Yes ma'am, better!"

"Go show the boys how to do it right!"

"Yes ma'am!"

The soles of the shoes were thicker, but he ran anyway. He felt like he could run faster and probably jump higher. He ran through the kitchen. "Thank you, Miss Betty, for my new hands!"

This time he was going to play, not practice. Throwing rocks was something he knew about and was good at. It was going to be fun! He went down the eight stone steps at the side of the house. The boys were at the end of the fir trees, closest to the gate that led to the barnyard. They had buckets and were picking up rocks from a big pile at the end of the drive. "Where did all these rocks come from?"

"Dad dumped them here. He said he was tired of us getting rocks from the driveway. He said if we kept doing it, there would be nothing, but mud left."

"So, this is a giant pile of throwing rocks." He thought this must be what heaven would be like!

"Here's your bucket."

Wow, my own bucket!

He could tell the boys were grabbing rocks without looking carefully at each one. Most were smooth river rocks. The best throwing rocks from the river were oblong and two-and-a-half to three inches in length with no bumps on the flat sides—the thinner the better. The ends needed to be rounded, with no pieces missing. They were a good, all-around throwing rock. They had weight for stopping power, and they curved to the left much less than the thin flint rocks with the sharp edges so they could be thrown long distances with a predictable curve. If there was a tree between the thrower and a coyote and the coyote was some distance behind the tree, the rock would curve to the left around the tree and hit the coyote on the side in the ribs.

The boys' buckets were half full. He had fifteen carefully chosen rocks.

He knew it was important not to be bossy. So, he watched the boys haul their buckets to the back yard. They had put a ten-foot board on top of two fence posts that were eight feet apart. There were ten very large cans on the board—beans, juice, and tomato paste—the size that diners use...there were a lot of growing boys to feed.

He knew they would stand too close. And they did. They were playing, and he was thinking of the woods. If things were thinking about coming after you, it was best to change their minds before they got too close. *Hit them when they're deciding.* In his mind, that would be about fifteen yards. He stood back fifteen yards.

The rocks were flying, and some of the cans were falling. The cans the boys hit fell close to the fence. If you hit a can, it needed to fly backward at least four feet; otherwise, it was like you were pitching the rocks underhanded. The boys were so close to the targets that they were only using the muscles in their arms. He saw lots of side-arm throwing that made the rocks rise and curve, with glancing blows—not enough to change a larger animal's mind.

He helped put the cans back on the board and suggested they back up two or three feet. It was strange; he hadn't thrown one rock and wasn't sure if he wanted to. There were things they knew how to do that were difficult for him, like being excited when they hit one of the cans. He expected to hit every can, and if he did not, it was considered a mistake. They were freer. Their throwing forms were inconsistent, and their rocks poorly chosen. The more rocks they threw, the more fun they had. The cans would occasionally be in the way of a rock or two.

Sleeping beauty was losing interest; not enough cans were getting in the way of his poorly thrown rocks. He showed him a couple of things, and sleeping beauty hit two in a row. His brothers congratulated their royal sleeper king. He showed all four cousins his rocks and explained why he chose them. They took one each and went back to the rock pile and looked for ones that matched. He put the cans back on the board as the search for perfect rocks continued. They returned, and the time between setting up the cans and all the cans being knocked down became progressively shorter. Now he was having fun without throwing one rock. There was probably some great wisdom to be gained from his not throwing but helping. He decided to leave it less deep and call it "stuff they knew" and "stuff he knew." They learned something, and he learned something.

"Put the rocks back and the cans and board away...it's dinner time!" It was Miss Betty. The buckets were almost empty. He dumped the rocks in one bucket and headed for the rock pile. The boys knew where the rest of the stuff went.

So, they ate three times a day! He had serious doubts that he could keep up with the stone-house eaters. *There really couldn't be a third eating room!*

The oldest boy was holding the back door open, and Miss Betty and Aunt Eunice were carrying out a long table with folding legs. They straightened the legs and set it in the center of the large, covered concrete area and, of course, they put a white tablecloth on it. The older boys were carrying wooden folding chairs out the back door. The chefs came out carrying a large pot with a lid; there was a metal ladle. They put the pot in the center on a brass stand with four short legs. Big white bowls and an open glass container with large spoons that looked like a big metal bouquet appeared on the white tablecloth. Uncle Bob's truck was coming down through the fir trees. The door opened again and down came two trays with one glass pitcher of iced tea and one pitcher of milk, followed by cloth napkins and a tray of eight glasses. There was a large, white bowl that was deep with saltine crackers and an oblong platter of shredded cheese—*three large meals in three different places.*

He stood in line to wash his new hands in the deep metal sinks. The soap took all the dirt away, even under his shorter fingernails. Uncle Bob came in to wash his hands in the metal sink. "Jim, how'd you sleep last night?"

"Pretty good, sir. Saw you leave this morning."

"So, you're an early riser?"

"Yes, sir. Always have been."

"That's an admirable trait."

"Hope so, sir"

"Maybe you could teach my youngest to get up earlier."

"Doubt it...it's not in his nature; no offense meant."

"None taken. Let's see what Miss Eunice and Miss Betty cooked up."

"Yes, sir."

It was chili! And there was lots of it. And it was tasty. The beans, meat, and sauce were snuggled under melted cheese, surrounded by a big, thick, white bowl with a large shiny spoon that held more than was wise. The deep bowl of saltines traveled the table up and down and across...some crumbled, others dipped. He took a bite and chased it with the saltine from his left hand. It eased the spices and soothed the stomach. Once again, his stomach was asked to fit a watermelon into a cantaloupe.

The champion of the stone-house eaters was Uncle Bob. His skills were most impressive, and he was capable of achieving the structurally impossible. He knew his uncle would most likely disappear after eating; most farmers did after the noon meal. They would lie on the floor on one side and allow the blood to help with digestion. The stomach borrowed blood from the resting limbs to digest the food, before using them again in the fields. Most rested forty-five minutes.

The cleaning had started, and he carried things to the kitchen. All who ate helped move everything back to the kitchen. He sat on the bottom step that led to the back door. The covered concrete area had no sign that a grand feast had taken place. Although he had helped with the removal, every person, object, and edible had left the concrete area. They all came together for a time and, when it was over, then moved to occupy other spaces. The objects returned to their places, and the edibles resided in the stomachs of the ones who chose them.

He knew there would be more feasts—*would I be at the table for each, and when each ended, would I reside in the upstairs room at the front of the stone house? Or would time find me in another place?* He had chosen an answer to these mysteries. It was long ago. The answer had come to him slowly, without words, sometime between taking his first breath on the tarp among the boots in the general store and looking at the shinning pole on the bus in the big city. These were drifting daydreams. The drifting daydreams were a form of grayish entertainment that finely tuned his emotions for the unexpected.

"Jim!" It was the fart master. "Why you sitting there?"

Explaining the watermelon-cantaloupe deal and staying up with the stone-house eaters probably wasn't a good idea. He went with, "Full of chili!"

90

"Yeah, me too! Looked like you were thinking about something."

"Some."

"Momma said you were in a place that wasn't fit for a boy."

"It was different than here. How come you don't have a dog?"

"Had one, a good one! Got killed two months ago. Ran out in the road; got run over by a grain truck. Daddy said the road was too dangerous during harvest season. Said we'd talk about getting another dog after crops were in."

"Was it a boy or girl dog?"

"Boy."

"What was his name?"

"Sonny."

The watermelon went into the cantaloupe. He made it to the wire fence when the beans exploded through the tube at the top of his stomach and rolled up his throat and shot out of his mouth. The sour liquid and the beans went through the fence and made a funnel shape in the pasture grass. There were bean carcasses hanging from the barbed wire and the wire squares below. It was like a full-speed swarm of bumblebees smashed themselves into a screen door.

"Wow! Look at those bean skins and all that stuff dripping! Are you gonna do it again? If you ever do that again, I wanta be there! That was neat!"

He spit the rest of the sour liquid over the fence and looked around. *The fart master's sense of empathy was truly underdeveloped!* He had a special look, directed straight at the great compassionate one. The focused energy of disgust rushed across the yard. It passed by the fart master's turned head and through the partially opened door, losing speed as it was overtaken by, "Hey guys, come quick! You gotta see this before it's too late! It's something great!"

He was facing the back door with his back to the fence. He wiped his mouth again and heard the squeaking of tennis shoes running through the kitchen. They piled out the back door and down the steps with the fart master in the lead. All four stopped in front of him. "Can we see it?"

"Let 'um see it before it's too late!"

In a moment of graciousness, he stepped aside and made a half turn toward the fence, slowly moving his left arm away from his body with open hand and presented his creation. It was not in unison, but a collective "wow" came forth like echoes. The awesomeness of the sight drew them closer. "There's meat on the barbed wire!" They were very close now. "Look at that; there's meat inside that bean!"

Aunt Eunice and Miss Betty were standing just behind the boys, wiping their hands on their aprons. Miss Betty moved closer. "Can't say I've ever seen anything like that before."

Aunt Eunice said, "Jim ate a lot of beans."

Sleeping beauty said, "Dare ya to smell it!"

The fart master was not one to shy away from a challenge. "I'll do it!" He got closer and closer. "That smells really, really bad! Bet you won't do it!"

He walked back with Aunt Eunice and Miss Betty, while the three took their turns smelling the creation. He saw Uncle Bob in the upstairs window; he got a nod. What he wanted was to wash his hands and face and have several saltines. No one asked him how he was feeling after the great meteor shower of beans had struck the earth, leaving carnage on the fence. He guessed everyone was filled with such awe at the singular event that their minds were still processing what they had witnessed.

Miss Betty was filling a bucket with water from one of the deep metal sinks. He used the kitchen sink to wash his hands and face and rinse out his mouth. Miss Betty was talking with Aunt Eunice. "Better throw some water on the fence and grass before the buzzards come around."

He thought about the state fair. He could enter a picture of a buzzard on the fence eating dead meat and beans. He could put a brass plate on the bottom of the frame engraved with the words, "Hurled by Jim." It would be a blue-ribbon winner for sure. He could wear the ribbon on his shirt and get his picture in the newspaper, shaking hands with the governor.

"Jim, how does your stomach feel?"

"Better."

"Was it my chili?"

"Yes...I mean no. Found out your dog's name. Happened after that."

"Oh, I see. So, you threw up the name and the chili came along for the ride."

"I guess so."

Aunt Eunice was smart; she understood. "Boys are playing football out front."

"I really like your chili!"

"I know; I saw!" They both laughed.

He went through the front door and sat on one of the front porch chairs. He looked down on the yard. It was wide and long and had two levels. The boys were throwing the football on the upper level. They didn't see him, and he didn't say anything. The leaves of the oak trees along the left side of the grass were turning bright red and yellow. There were six on the upper level and five on the lower level. They looked to be eighty feet tall. There was twice the number of fir trees to the right of the yard, divided in two by the drive. The white gravel of the drive was bright as it wound through the low hanging, bluish-green limbs. He could tell the roots of the grass were hunkered down for the coming winter, with their blades turning brown in large patches across the lawn.

Around a quarter mile to the right, a corn picker had started moving through the field. The green machine had a grain truck moving next to it. The front of the machine had metal fingers that moved low to the ground and guided the stalks into the gears that stripped the corn. A steady stream of yellow shot out of a pipe just over the red side boards of the truck's bed. Behind the truck was another grain truck, moving slowly to replace the first when it was full. Soon a third truck would return from the grain elevator to replace the second truck. This mechanical relay would continue until it resembled a well-choreographed dance between truck and corn picker. The timing would become precise enough so that no machine stopped until the field was finished. It would continue through the night.

In weeks, the process would repeat with a different front connected to the same green machine. The new front of the machine would look like the back of a paddle wheel steamboat. The same trucks would do the same nonstop dance, and the stream out of the pipe would be light brown soybeans. He knew it, but he wasn't sure how. He had seen it, but he wasn't sure where.

"This is a good sitting porch." Aunt Eunice sat in the chair to his right.

"Yes ma'am, it is. Why do I know about the machines in the fields?"

"You've been around them all your life. Your mother and father were migrant farm workers. You've traveled across the country—north, south, east, and west."

"How come I don't remember?"

"You were a baby; they took you with them."

He wanted to ask more—like where was his father and why he wasn't around—but was afraid of the answers. The migrant farm worker and traveling information was enough to digest for now.

"Your new clothes came in yesterday. Want to try them on? I'll help you."

"Aunt Eunice."

"Yes."

"I've never been in a bathtub. I don't know how to take a bath, and I can smell myself...can you show me?"

"I would be pleased to...taught all four of my boys the same thing...some of them remember, some have to be reminded. Let's get started while everybody is busy outside."

He was proud that he asked but still a little embarrassed. He tried to think of it as learning a skill and a way to separate him from the odor that had accompanied him since shortly after his mother had become ill. He knew the smells of the couch would linger in his nose hairs for some time to come.

The lesson was helpful, especially learning how to wash his hair. He hoped that repeated warm baths would loosen the white stuff that had glued the foreskin to his penis. He had made no progress in that area but was too embarrassed to mention it to his aunt. *She was his aunt, but she was still a girl. Boys don't talk to girls about such things.*

She put more salve on the sores. Some were beginning to heal, while others were still open wounds. He had tried not to scratch them, but his pants and shirt pulled at them when he moved.

Now he had four new shirts and three new pairs of Tuf-Nut jeans that came with a Tuf-Nut pocketknife. It was his first knife. Aunt Eunice showed him how to open and close it. And she told him how to sharpen it with a special stone. He wished he'd had the knife back at the shack but was proud to have it now.

Aunt Eunice showed him the bottom drawer of the tall, ten-drawer dresser. "You can keep your clothes here. There are plenty of underwear and socks to have a clean pair each day for a week and a half. Change your underwear and socks each morning."

He had mixed feelings. He was thankful for the new things. Before, he had the suitcase, the picture of his mother, the coin collection...before each coin was plucked from its resting place, the clothes on his back, and later the tin pail and cup. Now he had more things. Would I be responsible enough to keep track and take care of all these possessions? "Aunt Eunice, where is my suitcase and the tin pail and cup?"

"I have a confession. I ate the rest of the brownies while you were asleep in the car. I washed the tin pail and cup, and everything is in your suitcase right up here on the closet shelf. Don't forget you have the jar of coins from your friend."

He smiled. Now he knew where each of the many items was; he wanted everything he owned always to fit into the suitcase, just in case. He had learned that life had a way of unfolding in unexpected ways.

"Jim, you look handsome after the bath and your new clothes!"

"Thanks." He went downstairs and out the front and threw the football. He didn't play hard; he liked smelling clean for a change.

The boys were talking about school. One of the older boys was talking about elementary and junior high school starting sometime between the end of corn picking and the beginning of soybean season. He had seen the corn picker today, and the beans across the road were gray and dry. School would start soon.

Children at the shack didn't go to school, but he knew his cousins would. *Would I?* He figured his mother had taught him enough to get by the first few days. He could print well and could read most words, but he had no sense of spelling. He had not been around a book of any kind since his mother left...died...went to the hospital. He needed to work on those last thoughts. He didn't want to cry every time he thought of his mother. He whispered to himself, "She went away...she's not here right now...she's on a trip...she left? That's it, she 'left.'" His mother left. That would have to do for now.

He would work out the details when the clumps of grief drifted forward into his thoughts...she left.

"Jim, wanta see the barn?"

"Yeah." His cousins ran hard around the left side of the house. He ran easy. He didn't know how much movement it would take for the body odor to return. He wasn't going to take any chances with that or with his new clothes. He caught up with them at the gate just behind the throwing-rock pile. There was a wooden peg for a handle. It stuck out of a board that slid to the right through the gate and out of a rectangular hole in the fence post to the left of the gate. There was no peg handle on the inside of the gate—probably to keep the cows from scratching themselves on it and opening the gate. *Cows on the road during harvest season with fast moving grain trucks...no peg handle on the inside of the gate was a good idea.*

The journey from the gate to the barn was thick with cow manure. The smell didn't bother him. Cows ate grass and grain; manure from humans and other meat eaters always smelled worse. The woods had taught him to step lightly and carefully. He moved through the crusty piles of manure.

The entrance to the barn was secured by an eight-foot high and twenty-foot-long gate that swung on ancient hinges. The large peg handle was above the reach of cattle and horses. The two oldest cousins pushed against the bottom of the gate and the fart master climbed up two rungs of horizontal gate boards and grabbed the peg handle with both hands and slid the latch board to the right. If left unattended, the gate would swing out wide and hit the front of the barn. Those on the ground held it while the fart master descended. Once inside the process repeated, with the ground crew pulling instead of pushing.

It was a giant barn with a tin roof that angled up some forty feet or more. It looked like it had been built a hundred years ago with twelve-by-twelve rectangular, upright posts of solid oak. There were no nails; every beam was joined together with wooden pegs, some as big as his arms.

There were several four-legged beings inside the dimly lit interior; all had white faces and looked like cows. No one moved from the gate. The floor was covered with deep manure the consistency of chocolate pudding. The oldest cousin pulled a metal scoop shovel off a wooden peg and began scooping manure and making a path like city folks did after a deep snow. The path led to a half door that opened to a concrete corridor that ran through the center of the barn and had feed troughs on either side. At the end of the corridor, steps led to the loft.

He reached the top of the steps; the loft area was massive. The inside peak of the roof ran from left to right. To the right were rectangular bales of hay held together by two wires, wrapped tightly lengthwise and spaced a third of the width from the edges of both sides of the bale. They were stacked twenty high. To the left was loose hay in a deep pile with a sagging rope connected at either end to twelve-by-twelve upright support beams...the rope spanned twenty feet or more. The middle of the sagging rope was fifteen feet above the hay.

He watched the fart master climb a series of wooden pegs in the right support beam and grab the rope and move hand over hand to the middle. He sat on the rope and began to swing and, at the highest point, let go and fell into the loose hay. *OK, now that looked like fun.* He went up the pegs, hand over hand to the middle...sitting was the tricky part...staying balanced enough to not fall backward. He let go and flew into the hay with a bit of a roll. He had a slight flash of a shiver of the jump out of the truck his first night at the shack. He knew the cure for a slight flash of a shiver...do it again until no flash, no shiver. Everyone took several turns.

The light in the loft was getting dimmer. It would be darker going down the stairs, and there were thousand-pound animals and lots of manure and no light bulbs. Nobody wanted to miss supper. They made it down the stairs and down the corridor, scoop shoveled their way to the gate, hung the shovel on the wooden peg, completed the hold-the-gate, climb-the-gate procedure twice and maneuvered their way around the crusty piles. They reached over the gate in the fence and moved the latching board with the wooden peg, shuffled their shoes in the grass to remove manure, made it across the yard and up the eight stone steps and through the hall of coats and lined up to wash their hands in the sink.

"Chicken fried steak, mashed potatoes and gravy with fried okra, boys!" *It was Miss Betty!*

Uncle Bob came in the back door and washed his hands and forearms in the deep metal sink in the room with pots. "Saw you boys coming from the barn. Did you close all the gates and hang the shovel up?" There were several "yes sirs."

Aunt Eunice was standing at the table. "Let me see all of your shoes. You're not bringing the barn to my supper table." Everyone had to stand on one foot and then the other to show the bottom of their shoes. "You too, Mister!" Uncle Bob stood on one foot and the other.

Miss Betty chuckled. Uncle Bill mumbled, "I heard that. I don't know why I pay you."

"That's because I'm the best cook in three counties! Besides, I'm here because of your lovely wife and your handsome boys. This new one here is the marrying kind. Ain't that right, Jim."

He grinned and looked sideways at his uncle. Uncle Bob rolled his eyes.

"If you finished talkin', let's see if the chicken fried steak is fit to eat."

Miss Betty was walking back to the kitchen. She mumbled, "Fit to eat."

Aunt Eunice said, "You two stop playing; you know you love each other. Let's have a nice supper." Both love birds grunted.

This was a supper where he felt confident. He had a proper bath for the first time in months. His fingernails were clean, and his clothes were new, and he had clean socks and underwear. He could feel the tightness of the holes in his skin and the tightness of the white stuff on his penis, but he had new hope that all would heal with time.

Bowls and platters of food were passing in two directions when Aunt Eunice announced, "The principal called today. Elementary and junior high will start on Monday and the high school after bean harvest."

There was a collective echoing of moans with many forks dropping on the china plates. Low murmurs rounded the table, rolling low under the passing bowls and platters. This was a time to listen and not speak. There were too many unknowns approaching fast. He had never asked what month or day it was...*how many days until Monday?* Uncertainty was his constant companion, moving with him where his body ended, and his shadow began. He stuck with the fundamentals: he was clean and there was food. Anything beyond that, he could learn to adapt. Lessons he had learned from long hours on the couch.

Aunt Eunice said, "After supper bring down your paper, pencils, and clipboards, and we'll practice writing and spelling. More groans. Everyone ate slower and in silence. Supper ended on a somber note.

The fart master lightened things a bit with a challenge. "Whoever is last bringing school stuff down is a rotten egg!" He followed the challenger up the stairs, hoping there were extra supplies for him.

The fart master grabbed two of everything and made it down first; he shared. Sleeping beauty was the rotten egg. Now all five were on their stomachs in the living room. Uncle Bob was sitting in his chair looking at wall-to-wall boys.

The fart master asked, "Jim, do you know how to write cursive?"

"No, but I can print anything."

"Let me show you some cursive letters...this is a small "e" ...keep writing it without lifting your pencil off the paper." He wrote four connected "e's" and the fifth dipped upside down.

"Try it again."

It was going well, and he was almost to the edge of the page...there was a slight puff of movement that brushed by his heart. Uncle Bob's newspaper was up and covered his face with the outside of his fingers showing on either side of the paper. He looked closer at the newsprint. The letters floated to the center: "Boy leaves stone house on Saturday." He pushed down the ancient feelings and leaned over and whispered to the fart master, "What day of the week is today?"

"Thursday."

He nodded and began to review the inventory of his current possessions. They should all fit in his suitcase. If he wore the same clothes until Saturday, then all of his clothes he put in the suitcase would be clean. He needed well-chosen river rocks and a sturdy stick. He could put a point on it with his new Tuf-Nut knife. Uncle Bob was turning the newspaper pages, the boys were talking, and Aunt Eunice was coming in and out of the kitchen...all he heard was silence, no sounds. He would pack his suitcase tonight while everyone was asleep.

"Time for bed, boys. Remember to wash your feet and take your things upstairs."

All four cousins hugged their father. He stepped forward and stuck out his hand; his uncle shook it. "Thank you for letting me stay here for a while." The look in his uncle's eyes told him that his uncle knew that he knew. It was the look of someone who knew their mind had passed too close to another's mind...uncomfortably close. His uncle watched him as he followed the boys upstairs.

He washed his feet and remembered that he wanted to ask Miss Betty to help him with his toenails. He'd do that tomorrow after breakfast. He would plan to take a bath on Friday night. He would be busy, and time was limited. He walked around his two-more-nights bed and took his new jeans off and folded them in half and smoothed the wrinkles; he did the same with his shirt and laid both on the carpet next to the nightstand. He lifted the pillow and put on the top of his pajamas, took off his underwear and put on the bottoms. He got into bed and looked at the ceiling.

"Jim, you thinking about stuff again?"

"Yeah." When the fart master wasn't messing with his brothers, he was a decent "watcher."

"Is it bad stuff?"

"Some, but it's going to be fine. Is your brother already asleep?"

"Yeah."

"Never seen that before."

"Me either."

He planned to sleep for a while and then pack his stuff. He heard Aunt Eunice coming down the hall. "Thirty minutes." She continued down the hall to their room. "Time for sleep, boys." She made the rounds. He wondered if she had ever kissed sleeping beauty goodnight when he wasn't asleep.

It was his turn, and he got a kiss. He looked into his aunt's eyes...*she didn't know about Saturday!* He already knew the reason she would be given for his departure, and it would be presented to her tonight. The reason he had to leave was a sound one, and no one could really blame his uncle for choosing it. He didn't blame him either, but he felt sadness for his aunt who would never have dreamed of making such a choice. It made no difference...in his eyes, Aunt Eunice had saved his life. It was as simple as that.

He knew, if he listened carefully, he could discover a clue as to where "next" would be. He waited for the fart master to fall asleep and the light to dim in the hallway after the older boys turned out their lights. It took longer than he wanted. He moved down the hallway with the ready-made excuse of needing to pee. He sat on the top step and listened.

The voices were not muffled or low. He heard each difficult word. The reason he had to leave was the one he knew when he first met his uncle next to the new-looking truck. The place was ten hours away and sounded north, with snow. At the moment, his other uncle didn't know he would have a third child living with him. He guessed Aunt Eunice would deliver the news to his other uncle. He heard hard things about his father that made his aunt cry. He had seen more of the hard things about his father than were included in the downstairs discussion. He didn't like hearing his aunt cry, and he wanted his uncle to stop talking.

Aunt Eunice ran up the stairs and he to his bed, but he could still hear her sobbing in the upstairs hallway. Her door closed and later he heard the side door close that led to the eight stone steps. He walked to the front windows. He saw a steady flickering of lights as the truck moved between the firs and away from the house.

He would wait until Aunt Eunice called her brother up north from the downstairs phone. It would have to be tonight for him to arrive by Saturday. He preferred it that way. He couldn't imagine riding with Aunt Eunice to yet another place. After he asked her if he could stay with her and she said he could for as long as he wanted...the pain to both driver and rider would be more than both deserved.

He waited for her door to open and her call to begin and end and for her to check on him a second time while he pretended to be asleep. He knew this would take some time, so he closed his eyes and lay down between Blue and Daisy in the room with typewriters, and all three enjoyed the warmth of the sun through the clear windows as it lingered on their faces. The man with the kind and gentle face stood at the door and watched over all that rested within.

Hensen March

11 – Ride This Horse to the End

The door opened and the sunlight was bright; one squinted eye saw the Friday morning sun spread out on his bed. The call had been made, and he had slept through the night. Unprepared and ready to pee, he walked down the hallway to the bathroom. He was relieved that he had slept and not stayed up for the darkness of the nighttime worry. He peed, washed his hands with attention to his fingernails, cupped his hands and splashed water on his face and dried with the towel.

He looked in the mirror and practiced his breakfast face. Aunt Eunice didn't know that he knew, and he didn't want to let her know that he knew. It was difficult to soften the angles of his face. He practiced smoothing the tension in his jaw and forehead. He knew his eyes would struggle to conceal the surfaces of thoughts that pushed and pulled the muscles of his face. He would close his eyes and look at the sun and ask his mother why the sky is always red. His eyes cleared, his face smoothed, and he decided to borrow clothes from the fart master—only for today. He would save the ones folded on the carpet for the trip to the northern snow. The place where next resided with other faces and different ways.

He returned to the room and the boys were still sleeping. He opened the fart master's drawer and borrowed (for one day) a shirt, pants, and underwear. He changed clothes and folded the pajamas and placed them under the pillow, smoothed the sheets, evened the covers and straightened the stripes on the spread. He quietly slid the suitcase from the closet shelf and laid it on its side. He packed his clothes from the bottom drawer, closed the suitcase and slid it under the bed. He sat on the carpet next to the bed and waited for sounds from the kitchen.

He counted the panes in the windows. They were the same each day that he counted. Six panes on the bottom, six panes on the top—twelve for each window and two windows made twenty-four. There were four horizontal rows with six panes in each row made twenty-four.

There was activity in the kitchen, and Aunt Eunice and Miss Betty were talking—muffled sounds with no words. He had practiced so he was less worried about his breakfast face. He wasn't leaving until tomorrow so he would enjoy the day...*the sky was always red when you looked at the sun with your eyes closed!*

He stood up and walked down the hallway and quietly down the stairs and slid out the front door. He went down the steps and turned left toward the line of oak trees, looking for a proper stick. He figured the limbs on the ground had fallen because of rot but hoped to find one that had been broken off before it rotted. He noticed that the corn picker had finished the field across the drive and was moving away from him just beyond the line of oaks. The truck was catching the steady stream of yellow. He walked along the trunks on the upper level of the yard. There were perfect limbs within reach, but he didn't want to cut one of Aunt Eunice's trees. He climbed down to the lower level of the lawn and continued his search. There were no good choices on the ground; he'd have to wait until he arrived in the North.

Time to choose some good throwing rocks from the throwing-rock pile. He walked across the lower level of the lawn to the drive. He knew walking along the drive between the fir trees was less obvious than walking past the kitchen window where Miss Betty and Aunt Eunice were preparing breakfast. He had no bag to carry the rocks, so he chose only six perfect river rocks. He'd carry them in his right pocket and his knife in his left. Most situations required a rock before a knife, so the rocks would be in the pocket closest to his throwing hand.

He walked down the drive and turned left on the upper part of the lawn and sat in one of the porch chairs. The corn picker had made it to the end of the field and was headed back toward the oaks. It was still a great distance away, just short of the horizon line. The first grain truck went past the end of the drive heading for the grain elevator, while the second truck was moving along side and to the left of the corn picker. He started to look back at the corn picker but saw the reflection of Aunt Eunice's car windows as her car went down the drive and turned right, headed in the same direction as the truck.

Uncle Bob's truck was not in the drive. He didn't know if Uncle Bob had returned after leaving or stayed away all night. Uncle Bob usually walked heavily on the stairs and would have woken him up if he'd left early in the morning. His guess was that his uncle didn't come home, and he wasn't sure how Aunt Eunice would have felt about that. He hoped she was all right.

He went in the front door and headed for the kitchen, thinking this might be a good time to ask Miss Betty for help with his toenails while everybody was still asleep. He saw her at the stove frying sausage patties.

"My you're up early, Jim. And dressed to boot."

"Miss Betty, you mind helping me with my toenails?"

"I'll turn the burner down, and we'll get right to it. How come you're up and dressed so early?"

"Slept well and woke up early."

"Well, nothing wrong with that." She was looking in the back of a kitchen drawer close to the stove. "You know we have several clippers here, and a polite gentleman like you needs his own set of toenail and fingernail clippers. Here, put these in your pocket." He put them in his left pocket with his new Tuf-Nut knife.

"I've got these here; let's go in at the metal sinks like before. Take your shoes and socks off and sit on this stool." He got along just fine with Miss Betty, and he didn't have to pay attention to his breakfast face. "Put one of your feet up here on the edge of the sink. My, my, they do need some attention! Watch carefully how I do this, and you can do it yourself next time, and it won't be so hard if you keep up with them."

"Yes ma'am."

"Where did you learn your manners?"

"Just took to it naturally, I guess."

"Most people don't."

"Yes ma'am, I've seen it before, more than once."

"Give me your other foot. So, what are your plans for today?"

"Well, if the boys are up to it, thought I'd teach them some more about proper rock throwing."

"Are you good at throwing rocks?"

"Yes ma'am, better than most. Of course, I practiced a lot, that's all. How'd you get so good at cooking?"

"Same as you—practiced a lot. My mother taught me a lot about cooking; then I learned the rest by just doing. Bet your momma taught you about manners."

"Probably, but she didn't have much time to teach me a lot, but some of it probably took some."

"I believe it took some, too. There you go, good as new!" He didn't say anything but hugged her tight around the apron. "Better get back to that sausage."

He put his socks and shoes back on and washed his hands in the metal sink. He remembered where things were in the kitchen and began getting out plates and silverware and putting them on the counter close to the round table. He was very alert during the first supper at the stone house and remembered how the plates and silverware were placed; he repeated the same on the round breakfast table. He wasn't sure why, but he didn't ask where Aunt Eunice had gone or if Uncle Bob had been home. Some things were better left unsaid. He and Miss Betty kept busy in the kitchen and didn't talk. He was putting the glasses on the table when three of the four cousins came in the kitchen.

"Morning, you handsome gentlemen."

"Morning, Miss Betty. Where's Momma?"

"She had some errands to run. She'll be back soon. Scrambled eggs, sausage, bacon, and toast; bring your plates." Sleeping beauty arrived without announcement or fanfare. He looked a little disappointed. Miss Betty did turn and give a small curtsy with her apron; that seemed to help. His cousins had a somber tone, and it had to be about school in three days.

He knew he needed to throw some rocks. That's what kept him sane in the insanity of the shack. He needed to push the tension and emotion of tomorrow to the side. He hoped his practiced face would perform well when Aunt Eunice returned, but he could feel the angular muscles tighten in his face.

To be prepared, he used to sit with his back to the outside wall of the shack and listen for information. He had little to no information about tomorrow: tomorrow, uncle, two children, north, and snow. He knew he would be uninvited and would be going because there was no place else available. He had not yet completed the journey to resentment, but he was angered that his father had made him an orphan and left him to grieve his mother alone. He sensed the dark visitor of fear floating just beyond the corner of his eye. He did not turn his head or his eye. Aunt Eunice would not allow him to go to another shack around another violent man.

Tomorrow would come and he would go. Once again, he would close his eyes and look at the sun and the sky would always be red, and he would remember the stone-house eaters and the laughter and the meteor shower of beans, leaving carnage on the fence. But that would be tomorrow; he was still here today.

He put his plate in the sink and gave an easy smile to Miss Betty and went out the back door to set up the cans. He had the ten-foot board on the fence posts, the ten cans lined up, and a selection of rocks in one bucket. The rest of the buckets were lined up in a row.

The fart master came down the steps. "You want to throw rocks?"

"Yeah, we're going to do it the real way this time." He stood fifteen yards out, with nine rocks in his left hand and one in his right. His left hand rapidly fed his right hand, and he threw all ten rocks in less than ten seconds. When his hands were empty, there were no cans left on the board. He felt warm and calm and good...not because there were echoes of "Wow" or because Miss Betty said, "You did it" ...it was because he had done it before for hours and days. It had provided structure, purpose, and did not allow him to accept the invitation to dissolve and disappear into the couch. "Go get some good rocks and we'll practice." He didn't need to throw anymore; he felt better. Up until the noon meal, many suggestions were made, many rocks were thrown, and many cans were hit.

The rest of the day went by quickly. Aunt Eunice had not returned; Uncle Bob was not there for the noon meal. He sat on the front porch and waited. Just before dusk, he saw Aunt Eunice's car turn left into the drive and come up through the fir trees. She got out of the car with bags, went into the back door and came out with Miss Betty. He went down the steps and around the side of the house and offered to help unload the car.

His cousins came out the back door. "Where you been, Momma?"

"I had to get all you boys school clothes and new coats for the winter. Miss Betty, I put names on each of the bags. Try to get the boys to try on everything. Jim and I will be back later. Can you stay late?"

"Yes, ma'am."

"We won't be too long. Jim, ready to go?" He wasn't ready, but he nodded.

He followed his aunt to the car. He sat up front in the familiar seat with the ancient, familiar feeling. He wondered how she was going to tell him. He thought he might tell her and save time. He decided to wait to hear her words instead. It all felt dishonest, fake, and nauseating. He didn't want to be in the car. He wished it could be tomorrow and he could just leave and deal with the next place.

They went through the town during the last few moments of dusk. It reminded him of the first trip to the dime store, with the failing light and the coming darkness.

The town was behind them, and they turned right onto a road that led to a slight hill. Just before the top, the ground disappeared from the windshield and came back with billboards and lights. The billboards went from the ground up to about twelve feet high.

Aunt Eunice pulled up to a line of cars that were stopping and giving money to a man with a silver coin changer hooked to his belt. The different-shaped red lights on the back of the cars would get brighter when the cars stopped at the man. Arms would come out of the left front windows, and sometimes the man would push levers hooked to the cylinders and coins would drop out of the bottom and go back to the arms; the lights would dim, and the cars would move forward. His aunt handed the man two dollars, and he pushed the lever on the largest cylinder once. A quarter fell into his hand and then dropped into his aunt's hand. She pulled forward. The cars had the billboards to their left and an open field to their right. A large arrow directed the cars left between the outside billboards and a second role of billboards to the right. The cars continued straight through the roofless tunnel.

The car just in front stopped, and three people got out of the trunk and jumped into the car. He started to ask, and Aunt Eunice said, "It's a dollar for adults and seventy-five cents for children; they hid in the trunk to get in free." *Get in free for what?*

The billboards on the right ended, and the cars fanned out in different directions. Now he could see what the free-trunk-people were up to…a free drive-in movie. The quick-before-dark car ride through town and out to a field through the billboards to see a movie all seemed a bit elaborate to tell someone they had to leave tomorrow. But he hadn't seen a movie in a field before. He would wait and see how everything unfolded.

He already knew the ending. He knew the beginning; he saw it on the outside of Uncle Bob's newspaper. He would wait for the part just before the ending. *Would the end come before the beginning of the movie, at intermission, or would the end come at the end of the movie?* Just like him, Aunt Eunice was probably waiting to see how things unfolded.

"Jim, how about something to eat and drink?"

"Sure." Looked like Aunt Eunice was going for the full humdinger, and he was right there with her. *Ride this horse to the end.*

They made their way to a low, flat concrete block building with bright lights inside. Inside the colors were bright and the smells rich. He could identify hamburgers, hotdogs, popcorn, and sugary syrup coming from the soda fountain. They stood in a winding line guided by velvet ropes hooked to chrome stands with wide bases.

"We're going to miss supper, so let's get everything we need for the movie. Tell me what you want."

He pretended it was the Christmas that he never had. "Hot dog with chili, French fries, Power House candy bar, and a cherry Coke, please. And popcorn." He waited for a reaction from his aunt. She didn't blink and ordered two of everything. *This was truly going out in style!*

They moved along the L-shaped counter to the cash register. Aunt Eunice paid, and the food and drinks came on two brown trays. There were thick stacks of paper napkins on the left side of the trays, with two hooks above the napkins and next to the silverware. He walked carefully with the feast balanced on the tray. He had been so distracted by the lights, colors, and smells that he had no idea where the car was in the coming darkness. He followed his aunt.

Aunt Eunice found the car and put her tray on the hood. She took his and he got in the seat. "Roll your window up to about here." She slid the tray hooks over the glass, so the tray hung on the window glass. The tray was outside the window where he could reach everything, but it wasn't in his way.

She turned to the pole next to his window and removed a metal box with a thick, black cord coming out of the back. She placed the box inside the window next to the tray hooks. The box had vertical ridges with slots between them and a black knob. Aunt Eunice repeated everything on her side of the car. He started with the chili dog, using plenty of napkins.

The bottom of the giant screen was just above the dashboard of the car. He sat up higher and saw little children playing on merry-go-rounds and swings next to the base of the screen. He wondered what the picture would look like standing that close to the screen.

He liked where he was sitting. He felt he was eating supper in the cockpit of a fast airplane. That's when he received a deeply disappointing answer to a question that he wished he had never asked. His middle name was the same as the last name of a famous family that was admired by all, and he had heard adults discuss their great contributions to the country. "Your first and middle names came from Sonny's formal name. Sonny and your father were good friends and served together in World War II, so he named you after his friend."

The disappointment and shame were so great that he felt like Aunt Eunice should have apologized for his father's choice. She did not. He ate the chili dog and decided, from then on, his name came from the famous family. Pictures of the food they were eating came on the screen, and it helped him to think of other things. He turned the knob to the right and the sound was louder and helped push the sides of his brain and popped the answer regarding his name out of the top of his head like a squeezed pimple. The departure of the thought was so vivid he touched the top of his head.

He finished the chili dog and worked on the remaining fries; most of the cherry Coke was left. He was looking forward to pacing himself with the popcorn. The movie began and something unusual happened. The sound became a hum, with the colors and movement calming his mind. He was using a different part of his brain that had little interest in language or story. He could see through the screen and saw his aunt in a situation involving her husband and his wishes, which the boy hoped differed from hers. She was left with the task of telling a boy that was the son of her dear brother—whom she had protected and tidied up behind since they were children—that his son was no longer welcome to live with her.

His mouth brought him back to the popcorn and the buttery grease on his hand. He used two of the napkins and went back to the place in his mind. *Would it be unkind to ask her when her other brother would arrive tomorrow before she started to tell him?*

He heard her laugh. She was watching the movie, and she realized he was not. "Your Uncle Bob doesn't want to raise five boys. He won't change his mind. Your Uncle Elbert is coming tomorrow, and you're going to live with him, your Aunt Sue, and their two kids."

"Why did you take me to the drive-in?"

"I thought you would enjoy it and it would be easier to tell you."

"Was it?"

"No."

There had been an elaborate build up, but the message was short, clear, and to the point. There was no need for Aunt Eunice to say she was sorry. They both were, and each knew it about the other.

"Thanks for taking me to the drive-in."

"You're welcome. Looks like the chili is staying down this time." They both laughed. "There's a lot of butter on the popcorn, so watch out—the chili may slide out the other end!"

His hand came out of the bag empty and didn't go back in. He opened up the Power House candy bar. *Chocolate and cherry Coke—a little better than wild blackberries and greasy dog water!* "Aunt Eunice, we got the hard stuff done. Can we go back to the house?"

"Let's throw our stuff in the trash, and we'll put the trays away." They pulled forward with the lights off and turned left toward the exit. They went down the hill and the lights of the drive-in disappeared. They turned left and headed toward town and later up the fir-tree drive. He felt relieved, and he hoped his aunt did, too.

He followed Aunt Eunice up the side steps to the kitchen, where Miss Betty was finishing the supper dishes. "Thought you would be late."

His aunt replied, "We left early." He smiled at Miss Betty, and she gave him a tight, sideways, shoulder hug.

"Did the boys give you a hard time trying on school clothes?"

"No more than usual. Looked like everything fit, and they all liked what they got. Do you think this fine gentleman will give us much trouble trying on his clothes?"

" Aunt Eunice, you already bought me clothes."

"You need more than you have. Got you some new boots and a winter coat."

He appreciated the new clothes, but he had made a promise to himself that he would limit his possessions to fit into his own suitcase. He knew that the new next would most likely not be the only next, and he didn't want to drag a lot of extra stuff around from place to place. He began trying on long-sleeved shirts and warm pants. The winter coat had a hood and would have come in handy on the couch. He liked the boots, and his aunt said they were waterproof and would be good in the snow.

When he returned to the kitchen, he heard Aunt Eunice whisper to Miss Betty, "Did Bob call?" Miss Betty shook her head.

The look on his aunt's face was adult and complicated, but he could guess part of it. He was a part of it not by design, but a participant in a matter of number and level of interest. The number was one too many and the interest was nonexistent. This was Uncle Bob's arithmetic and the sum equaled zero interest. The cyphering was done and nothing was the answer. An absence of numerical value equaled an absence of his presence, a formula he knew well. He wondered if all of the adult males he had encountered had the same math instructor.

He felt fortunate to have a healthy sense of self that allowed him the luxury of reason over accepting responsibility for situations that he did not initiate or promote. His primary connection had been severed by death. He had minimal connections with those who decided the length of his stay in any one location. Therefore, he was always at home with himself, regardless of location. He was his own mother. And would not allow the connection he had with himself to be severed.

He was going to need some help fitting all the newest new stuff in his one suitcase. Before he could ask, Aunt Eunice asked Miss Betty to get his suitcase from the upstairs closet and his clothes from the bottom drawer of the dresser.

"My suitcase is under the bed, and the clothes are in it." Both women looked at him. He had seen the look before; it was the look of "How did he know that?" He avoided an explanation by saying, "Don't know how all this is going to fit in one suitcase...thank you for helping." Miss Betty left for the upstairs, but his aunt was still looking at him. There was no emotion on her face; it was blank but receptive. Her face was ready to receive something more, so he offered, "Sometimes I know things and I don't know how.

Sometimes it's a feeling, or something seen, or both." That seemed to be enough for the moment.

Aunt Eunice went back to the task at hand. "You'll need your suitcase for clothes and a separate bag for your coins, coin books, and the tin containers. Something you can fasten or zip up to keep them safe. I may have one upstairs." As she headed upstairs, she passed Miss Betty in the dining room with his suitcase.

Miss Betty put the suitcase on the kitchen counter. "I'm going to wipe this down to get the dust off, and we'll open it up on the kitchen table and see what fits." The suitcase was wiped down and opened on the kitchen table kitchen when Aunt Eunice returned with another suitcase. He stood back and listened to the expert packers think out loud to each other while folding, transferring, and repacking every item. "He'll need one outfit for tomorrow."

"Clothes for tomorrow are folded next to the nightstand; borrowed these just for today." He knew they were looking at him again. He kept looking at the suitcase. "You're right; need a pair of underwear and clean socks for tomorrow." Miss Betty removed them from the suitcase, and Aunt Eunice resumed counting items to make sure there were enough combinations of clothes.

The new faces in the north may not accept present comments regarding future events—something to keep in mind.

The extra suitcase had a rigid top and bottom and was made of heavy canvas. It zipped up and had a flap that covered the top and the teeth of the zipper. It was a light color that was hard to describe but was not much different from his blond suitcase. Miss Betty took both suitcases and set them in the room with the metal sinks and the pots. Aunt Eunice hung his new coat in the narrow room with coats that led to the side steps.

"If I get up early, will I have time to take a bath before leaving?"

"Your Uncle Elbert should be here by ten."

"That's plenty of time—I get up early—and can I take the salve with me?"

"You sure can, and I got you a second tube. Just put it on once a day. Clean hands and fingernails, right?"

"Yes ma'am."

"It's late; time for bed. The boys are already asleep. Goodnight."

"Goodnight." He could see from the stairs that Aunt Eunice and Miss Betty had sat down at the breakfast table. He knew they had a lot to talk about.

He peed and washed his hands. He looked in the mirror and tried to have an encouraging look for his reflection. He whispered to himself, "You survived the couch and had fun at the stone house." He knew next was approaching fast, and he would look through the back window of another car at another once-been place. He was thankful for the mind and the temperament to manage the rolling change of faces and locations. The late autumn sun did not allow for oversleeping. Next would be at ten in the morning.

He closed his eyes and turned off the light in the bathroom and silently counted to five to allow his eyes to adjust to the dimness of the hallway. His one-more-night room was on the other side of the earth from the sun, but its light reflected off the moon onto the windowpanes. He put his one-day-borrowed clothes on the floor of the closet and got into the pajamas and into his one-more-night bed. He could tell the moon was up and to his right, and it made lighted capital "Ls" on each of the windowpanes. Twenty-four lighted capital "L's." He knew the earth would continue turning, and the sun would climb up his bed and into his face in a matter of hours. He counted the lighted capital "L's" one more time and fell into a deep sleep.

12 – Vanilla Acres

He slept and the earth turned his bed into the climbing sun. The sun had reached the end of his bed and made the wide stripes of the bedspread glow between his feet. The capital "Ls" were gone, and the windowpanes were orange.

He made the bed and grabbed his clothes and went down the hall to the bathroom. He left the door open a bit and turned on the light. He turned the "H" and "C" to the left and put the white rubber stopper in the drain. He peed, flushed and washed his hands. He got into the bathtub for his first solo bath. He washed everything he could reach. He pulled out the stopper and wrapped the chain around the spout. He got out of the tub, dried with a towel, put on the clean underwear. He washed his hands again and put the penicillin salve on each bite. He finished getting dressed and returned to the room and looked around for the last time.

He carried the salve in his hand on the way down the stairs and put it in the pocket of his new winter coat, along with the nail clippers in the other pocket. He checked his left pants pocket; the knife was there and in the other pocket, the six well-chosen river rocks. He sat at the kitchen table. Later, after the sun had warmed the air a bit, he would sit on the front porch. The house was silent, and the only sounds outside were harvesting machines in distant fields.

The stone house was on a hill and the porch was elevated; the view of the flat land was expansive. The front door opened quietly, and Aunt Eunice sat in the chair next to him. She had two egg sandwiches on two small plates and a glass of milk. "

"Breakfast on the porch." He smiled and nodded.

"Don't wake up the boys before I leave."

"OK. Are you doing all right?"

"Yes."

"Uncle Elbert understands more than you know."

"Understands what?"

"Your father, Uncle Elbert, and I were orphans and were separated about the age that you lost your mother. All three of us lived with different families."

"Did you move around a lot before getting a family?"

"No, we lived in an orphanage together."

He wanted to ask about his father but didn't. "Is Uncle Bob mad at you?"

"A little, and I am mad at him, a little. But we'll work it out; we always do."

"Tell him I'm not mad at him; I understand."

"I know and I will."

They ate the sandwiches, and he drank the milk. It was nice to have Aunt Eunice all to himself, just sitting and not talking.

"Can I get my suitcases and coat and wait on the porch? Uncle Elbert will be here in five minutes?"

"Jim, it's only six o'clock in the morning."

"Can I get them?"

"Of course. I'll help." They walked down the steps and around the side of the house, up the eight stone steps to the room with coats, and through the kitchen to the room with the metal sinks and pots. He took his original suitcase and Aunt Eunice the canvas suitcase, and he grabbed his coat and went back down the steps. His aunt followed him down the white gravel drive about halfway, they set the suitcases down, and he folded his winter coat on top. He stood there.

He could see the white film behind the tires and doors of the black car as it turned into the driveway. It stopped where they were standing. A short, thin man with a reddish complexion opened the car door and walked around the front of the car and said, "Eunice."

"Elbert."

"It's been five years; bet the boys are big now?"

"They are. This is your nephew, Jim."

"Pleased to meet you, Uncle Elbert."

"Likewise."

He could tell Uncle Elbert was a man of few words, and the trip would more than likely be filled with brief awkward conversation and hours of silence. His uncle had callouses on his hands, and his upper body was more developed than his lower body. He did manual work with his hands and shoulders. His eyes gave no clue as to violent outbursts but hinted at more of a quiet, guarded nature.

His uncle took the two suitcases and placed them in the trunk and closed the lid. "Eunice, I'll call you when we get there." He noticed his uncle and aunt did not touch each other, hug, or handshake. His uncle opened the front passenger door and motioned for him to get in.

He went to Aunt Eunice and hugged her tightly. "Thank you for coming to get me. I would have died there."

She smiled. "Elbert, go up the drive and turn around; there are too many fast-moving grain trucks on this road."

"Eunice."

"Elbert."

He and his uncle got in the car and turned around near the throwing-rock pile and headed down the drive past Aunt Eunice. He looked at her through his uncle's widow. The car passed her, and she stepped into the middle of the drive. He looked at her one last time through the back window before the car turned right and headed to town. The car reached the edge of town and turned right again and in a few miles turned left to the north for the long stretch without turns.

* * * * * *

It seemed more final when the car had turned north, and the sun was coming through his side of the car. Uncle Elbert and Aunt Eunice didn't seem that close. But here he was, riding in a car with a man he had never met, a quiet man who drove with purpose.

The car seats were covered with a woven, straw-like material, and he could feel the coiled springs underneath the woven straw. He felt four of them, two under his butt and two under the upper part of each leg. He wondered if Aunt Sue was a heavy woman or the car was older or both.

Uncle Elbert had a windshield, and he had one, too. Both windshields were joined together by a black metal strip that went from the top of the dashboard up to the roof. Both windshields had square corners where they joined, and the outside corners were rounded.

The dash was black metal with lots of chrome. There were three square gages in the dash just in front of the steering wheel. The center of the steering wheel had an emblem that looked like a crown and was covered with heavy, clear resin. The steering wheel was large, with the top even with the bottom of Uncle Elbert's nose. In the center of the dashboard was the word "DODGE" in raised chrome letters just above a large chrome rectangle containing the radio and horizontal slots for the speaker. The radio was off, and the only sounds came from the engine, rubber rolling on gravel, and the wind. Uncle Elbert wasn't a talker.

He looked at his uncle with sideways glances. The most prominent feature of his profile was his nose, narrow and longer than most with a slight hump just after it came out of his face. His right eye had dark skin below it. He guessed his uncle had driven ten hours through the night, said two words to his sister and headed north with a kid in tow…*probably not in a visiting mood.* He didn't want to find out.

He looked through his windshield, and his uncle looked through his. He looked at the clock on his side of the dashboard. It didn't move. So, he moved the hands in his mind, counting each time the minute hand passed twelve until there were nine more revolutions and he would be at the next.

If he imagined what next would be like, then he would have to undo his images when it was different than he imagined. These would be unnecessary steps that could interfere with spotting cues that could help him adapt more quickly. He would stick with the fundamentals: quiet, polite, and respectful.

The sun was higher so that he could look out the side window without squinting. The land had changed from flat to rolling but was primarily cropland that had been harvested. He could tell what had been in the fields from the stubble left by the machines. He began to wonder if his uncle ever peed, drank, or ate. He sure knew his uncle didn't talk. He and the springs in the seat were becoming way too familiar. There were seven imaginary hours left.

He had memorized the inside of the car and the right side of his uncle's face. He knew the car would eventually run low on gas and they'd have to stop. He had gotten accustomed to white-tablecloth living and the schedule of the stone-house eaters. He was thirsty, hungry, and needed to pee. He decided to let the sounds of the engine, rubber on gravel, and the wind lull him into a place between awake and asleep. He closed his eyes and drifted. He chose no images but occasionally looked at the inside of his eyelids. The frozen minute hand made one full turn past the twelve.

His eyes remained closed while his mind went down a checklist of sameness, searching for changes. There was warmth on the left side of his face and a different sound. One sound had left, replaced by another—a humming with a higher pitch than the engine. He peered through his eyelashes and could see his knees and the frozen clock. The shadow of the steering wheel made a dark rainbow across the dashboard and passed through the shadow of his uncle's right hand. The clock face winked when the hand shadow moved across. He knew his uncle's nose shadow would be impressive, but he could not find it through his eyelashes.

The car began to slow, and he opened his eyes. The car was on a concrete road with a white, broken line down the middle. His uncle slowed down more and began to turn right toward a white, one-story building. It had a porch-like structure supported by two square columns with two bright yellow gas pumps between the columns. A wide red stripe went around the building just above the tops of the columns. Attached to the red stripe were red letters, each with a yellow background, that spelled "SHELL."

His uncle drove the car under the porch-like structure and stopped with the back of his door even with the first of the two pumps. Two men wearing white caps came out; one started washing the windows, and the other said, "Fill it up?"

"Yep."

The "Fill it up" man pushed down a lever on one side of the pump and took the nozzle handle from the other side and started filling the tank. He held the handle until the tank was full. The man stepped past the other as he was cleaning the last window. "One dollar and ninety-eight cents, sir." His uncle gave him the exact amount.

He had missed his chance. This was a trip that had a beginning and, he hoped, an end—but nothing in between. The car pulled away from the yellow and red place of shells and continued down the road. He could see a town some two miles ahead. The seat springs, the woven straw covering, and his bladder were alarmingly close to the base of his brain. This was a trip without language or moderation. The sign ahead, "Population: 5,289." The car began to slow, with cars ahead and three- and four-story buildings rising up through the windows on both sides of the car.

His uncle pulled up to a curb and stopped, then looked at him and said, "You thirsty, hungry? Do you have to pee?"

He didn't say, "Oh, yes sir; thank you, sir." He looked his uncle straight in the eye and gave a sarcastic grin that only moved the right side of his mouth.

His uncle grinned back. "You know how to open that door?"

"Never had the call to, sir."

"Fair enough. Get your coat. You're from the south; it gets colder up here."

He was surprised when the door opened; he thought it was just a closing door.

"We're going across the street. Watch out for cars; you're not in the country anymore." He walked close to his uncle as they crossed the street in a brief break between cars moving in both directions. They walked between two parked cars on the other side of the street and under a red sign with big gold letters: "F.W. Woolworth CO." A striped awning went across the front just below the sign. Another sign on the glass door said, "Luncheonette Hours: 7 to 4:30."

He followed his uncle through the door and to the right. There were stools with red vinyl seats on top of chrome stands connected to the floor. The counter was black marble, and everything else was a combination of reds and chrome. Behind the counter was a large sign: "Fountain." His uncle sat on a stool, and he climbed up on the one next to him.

"Here's a menu; get anything you want." He had never seen a "menu."

One of the ladies behind the counter put a cup of coffee in front of his uncle. "What'll you have, gentlemen?"

"Ham salad and apple pie."

It was his turn. "Same thing, ma'am."

"What to drink?"

His uncle replied, "Coke."

He kept the menu and looked for his order. "Ham Salad Sandwich…30 cents; Apple Pie…Per Cut 15 cents" He couldn't find "Coke." There was "Extra Rich Ice Cream Soda with two dips."

"Make his an ice cream soda." Uncle Elbert had stepped up for a deluxe drink. He smiled and nodded to his uncle. He saw that it was 25 cents on the menu.

"The restroom is over there; better use it while you can." He was at the door before his coat had settled on the stool. Halfway through he decided to pee again after eating. *"Better use it while you can." No truer words had ever been spoken after riding in the car with the closing door and the frozen clock.* He washed his hands and returned to the stool.

The sandwich had toast and the drink was in a tall, fancy glass and there was pie! Uncle Elbert was a man of few words but a fast eater. He knew how to eat fast, too. This time it wasn't in the dark but eating the ice cream fast came with a cost. He ignored the headache and finished the pie. He went back to the bathroom and squeezed out as much as he could. Uncle Elbert came in on his way out of the bathroom. *So, the stone-statue driver does pee.*

He went back to the counter, put on his coat and waited next to the restroom. His uncle came out, and he followed him to the door and stood behind him between the parked cars. The air was cold, and he could see small amounts of steam coming off the back of his uncle's ears. Every few seconds larger amounts of steam would come out of his uncle's nose as he looked both ways for moving cars. He ran across the street next to his uncle.

He opened the door for the second time and sat down. He promised himself that if he rode in a car with his uncle again, he would bring supplies. The seat springs had been waiting for him...cold, hard, and indifferent. They snuggled into the same spots on his butt and legs. They sat until the heater stopped blowing cold air and the windshield began to clear. He thanked his uncle for the food and ice cream soda and got a nod in response.

Next was up the road in a distant, unimagined place. He hoped someone there used language as a form of communication, but it would be less of a priority once he was free of the confined space of the car. His uncle rolled down the window and stretched his neck out the opening looking back and to his left. He turned the front wheels left and pulled out on to the street just ahead of oncoming cars and behind the taillights of those in front.

This part of the trip was more interesting than the endless miles of open fields. There were connected buildings with large windows and people passing on the sidewalks. He could see people sitting at desks through the second story windows and single doors on corners of buildings with lighted stairways inside.

Women on the street wore scarves or hats with feathers and the men, dark, wide-brimmed hats. His uncle didn't wear a hat, and he wondered why. It seemed a hat was something you had to keep track of and was easy to leave somewhere. Women never seemed to forget their purses. The contents of women's purses had always been a mystery. They always had something for every occasion. Men had handkerchiefs that stayed in their right back pocket and were typically white and plain. Women had tissues and dainty handkerchiefs with lace on the corners.

Did his uncle wear a hat when it snowed? He would soon find out because there were patches of sprinkled snow on the small squares of grass in front of some of the buildings that had sidewalks leading to their front doors.

The car was leaving the area of town where the buildings were connected, but the buildings continued, unconnected, with cars parked in front of them. There were drive-in hamburger joints dropped in between motels with closed swimming pools. It was that time of the afternoon before the inside lights generated a warm glow and when the neon gas still slumbered in its tubes, yet to be awakened by current.

Whirling in the air were flakes of snow that seemed distant from the glass of the car windows but occasionally splashed on the windshield like translucent bugs on a summer evening. The burger joints and the motels trailed off, replaced by houses with small yards and front doors that waited by gravel drives. Each house had a name but not the name of its residents. The Smiths lived in the "old Jones house." If someone had built the house and lived in it still, it was built on the "old Philips farm." Each house had its story, and each man, woman, and child had a story. The stories were woven together as the residents moved through each room and in and out the front doors next to the gravel drives. Countless houses lined both sides of the road, with stories unfolding in each.

As each town approached, the houses changed from single file to deepening rows, with gravel drives joining roads off the concrete highway. The flakes were larger and touched the car more often. His uncle turned a knob on the dashboard, and the windshield wipers began to move the moisture to the side. The powdered roofs were six and seven deep, and three- and four-story buildings began to appear in the distance. Another town of connected buildings with another name, followed by burger joints and closed swimming pools.

There were more cars on the highway now, and the journey through the town was slower, with more people on the sidewalks wearing hats and scarves. The larger flakes whipped around corners of buildings and showered down from the roofs. He saw fewer people at their desks on the second floors, and the inside store lights had a warmer glow. Neon signs began to flicker and glow bright on both sides of the street, joined by headlights and taillights. The lights made the flakes look whiter and larger. The connected buildings began to be taller, and they lined both sides of the streets. More cars, more people, and more lights. Twelve-eyed stoplights swung on metal cables above the street, their three-eyed faces watching and ordering in four directions the movement of metal and flesh. The snow was heavier, and the cars moved slower, with the back right tire of each spinning faster than the other three. This was not a town—this was a city, a big city.

The cars moved by hotels with street-level glass fronts. Men in long black coats and hats with white gloves opened car doors and held umbrellas for travelers who entered glass panels that swung like tall merry-go-rounds trimmed in brass. Below ornate chandeliers, the hotel lobby floors were covered with Persian rugs. The travelers wore expensive clothes—the men in long overcoats with white scarves hanging down on either side of colorful ties resting on pressed white shirts. Women dressed in ankle-length fur coats with flashes of gold and diamonds.

The furs, colorful ties, and chandeliers were left behind when the car turned to the east along a cavernous trail of tall buildings with lighted interiors. People on the sidewalks moved faster, with umbrellas tilted at the same angle. The wind and blowing snow were rushing forward past the side windows of the car, and the umbrellas touched the backs of their owners. As the taillights ahead moved to the left and right, headlights lit up parked cars on both sides of the street. The street ran downhill, and the cars below formed a chaotic mix of angles and lights sliding under the distant string of red-eyed Cyclops, directing but unheeded.

Uncle Elbert slid the car around a corner heading south just before they reached the lighted pile of cars stacked up, door handle to door handle, at the bottom of the hill. As the car moved along the ridge of the city hill, his uncle glanced down each passing side street looking for fewer cars moving downhill. The car slowed and turned left down the slope.

Uncle Elbert drove very slowly, guiding the tires through the piles of snow and away from the shiny ice-covered tire tracks. Even so, the car slid, causing the suitcases in the trunk to move up even with the hood and the headlights to shine into the faces of people in the buildings. His uncle would use the side windows as windshields. The car would swing again, and the suitcases would come up the other side of the car, and he would lean back so his uncle could see past him.

He turned his head and looked out his side window and saw the intersection at the bottom of the hill moving fast toward his side window. The light changed to red, and the car spun and slid through the intersection. The car's front bumper just missed the rear bumper of a large dark blue box truck with orange wheels and gold letters on the side: "Ask the Man For...Ballantine Beer."

They slid in front of a northbound police car; he was looking through his windshield directly into the policeman's face. He stuck his hand up to wave just before the police car spun around until the door handles touched and he looked through his window and could see hair growing out of the policeman's left ear. The street leveled, and he looked through the back window and saw the police car sideways in the road with its white door, black body, and large red bubble light on top.

Uncle Elbert steadied the car, and they continued east without a word. He realized his butt muscles had clamped around the seat springs and prevented him from moving during the beer truck-police car performance. He wondered if his uncle would comment if a large asteroid struck the earth.

The buildings were shorter and unconnected, with businesses on each corner of the intersections..."True Value Hardware" and "Rexall Drugs." The car continued for some miles and turned south between "Twistee Treat"—a giant ice-cream-cone building with two feet of snow on the outside tables and no customers—and a giant root-beer-barrel building with awnings all around: "A&W Root Beer 5 cents."

One mile down the road his uncle turned left next to a sign: "Shady Oaks Estates." There were no trees but hundreds of small houses, all the same. Each was a story and a half, no porch, with three windows in the front and a front door between the second and third windows. The sides of the houses had three smaller windows on the ground floor and one upstairs. The window shutters were light gray and the shingles differing shades of blue. A giant milkshake had spilled on the earth and it was called "Vanilla Acres." He was thankful there were no plank bridges or dirt yards. There were dozens of kids playing in the snow; he was glad they were not dressed in identical clothing.

The snowflakes were large, heavy, and close together. His uncle pushed down on the accelerator, and the car sped toward a ridge of snow at the end of a driveway directly ahead at the bend of a curve in the street. The front tires went up the ridge and down. The front of the car rammed into the snow, and thick sheets of frozen snow came up the hood and covered the windshields; the motor choked, backfired and died. The car was pointed down, with the rear tires perched on the snow ridge at the end of the driveway.

His uncle turned the key to the left, and the lights went out on the dashboard. Uncle Elbert sat motionless looking at the no-see windshield. His hands dropped from the steering wheel and rested on his legs just above his knees. The top two buttons of his coat were wet from the two columns of warm air falling from his nose. The top of the columns moved fast then slowed and disappeared on the buttons. Uncle Elbert's coat looked tired, and teardrops were forming on the bottoms of the buttons. They sat there in silence. They were not riding in silence; they were sitting in it. Both did silence better than most.

The replica houses had disappeared, hidden by sheets of icy snow wrapped around the side windows. He looked at the rearview mirror and saw the upright trunk fade along with the flaky white sky, down to a small oval as snow closed the last eye to the sameness outside. His breathing was calm and slow; he waited in the metal and glass shell until it was time. Uncle Elbert's eyes had stopped looking at the no-see windshield; they were closed. He closed his eyes, too, and waited with his uncle.

Images flowed down the surface of his eyes…Aunt Eunice's breakfast table with her and Miss Betty visiting quietly over coffee. A plate of cookies sat precariously close to Blue and Daisy's wet noses. His eyelids moved the image up and back.

His uncle rolled down the window and pushed his open hands against the sheet of frozen snow. Some came in but most folded out and away from the packed snow against the door. His uncle cleared the last of the window snow and began to climb through the window. This was the first he had seen of the bottom of his uncle's boots. They had been pressed against the accelerator and resting on the floor of the car for more than twenty hours. The boots disappeared and his uncle rose up in snow that covered his knees. He watched his uncle punch his legs through the snow to the trunk. He pulled a snow shovel out of the trunk; a wide, thin shovel seldom seen in the south. He sat quietly while Uncle Elbert shoveled snow to free the car door and continued making a path to the front door.

He moved behind the steering wheel, stuck his head out the window and saw curtains open in two windows. Two kids were looking through the window to the left of the door, and a woman was looking through the window to the right of the door. The shape of the woman's face did not suggest that she had contributed to the condition of the springs in the car seat. He waved and the kids waved back.

13 – A Large Carnivorous Bird

Uncle Elbert had started on the bottom of three steps leading up to the front door. Snow had drifted and covered half of the front door. He finished shoveling the last of the door snow, and the door opened to hugs from a boy and girl and the sound of "Daddy." It was not a word that he had ever used, but it had a warm tone to it. His aunt hugged and kissed his uncle. His uncle left the three and returned to the car and opened the door. "Come meet your aunt and cousins."

He took a deep breath and stepped out of the car. He began walking to the open door and thought this is the third next. He tried not to look at his shoes when he approached the door. The kids were smiling, and Aunt Sue was looking. He stuck his hand out and said, "Aunt Sue, I'm your nephew, Jim."

His aunt moved the children in front of her and said, "This is Debbie, and this is Tommy."

"Hi, I'm Jim."

They both shook his hand and pulled him inside. "Mom made cookies; we've been waiting to eat them." Both pulled him to the table, and they pointed at the cookies. They were the same cookies and same plate he saw in the filmy images that poured over the surface of his eyes before his uncle pushed the snow from the window. They were Blue and Daisy's staring cookies. Tommy handed him one and both cousins grabbed one. The three stood at the table and ate cookies—more than one.

Uncle Elbert came in with the suitcases. Aunt Sue looked at them and said, "Well, we'll have to find a place for them; there's not a lot of room. I'll unpack them later." He knew she wasn't talking about the suitcases, and he didn't want his aunt touching the few constant things in his life.

"You're going to share my room. Come on, I'll show you." He picked up his suitcases and followed Tommy. He didn't look at his aunt. This was going to be complicated. The room was on the left at the end of a short hallway. It had the front window that was to the far left, the second window from the front door. "This is your bed."

"Thanks." He looked under the bed to see if the suitcases would fit; they did, and he slid them in quickly. He was relieved that Tommy wanted to go back to the kitchen. He knew he somehow had to ease the tension he had felt between him and his aunt.

"Aunt Sue, you have a pretty home."

The response was a thin smile and "It's small, but it's ours." He tried to smile more than thinly.

He could see Uncle Elbert shoveling snow away from the front of the car. He guessed his uncle would work last on the snow ridge where the back tires were sitting. His uncle would probably shovel the ridge between the back tires and then the snow at the outer edges of the tires. If he just dug out the tires the frame of the car would fall on the packed snow, and the tires would hang in midair. He didn't know anything about digging cars out of snow, but it was easier thinking about how he would do it rather than talking to his aunt and feeling like he was taking up too much space.

Tommy and Debbie seemed nice, and the three ate two more cookies each. His aunt warned, "That's enough; you're going to spoil your appetite for dinner."

Where he came from, it was called "supper." The stone-house eaters ate "dinner" at noon. This was not the stone house, and everyone talked a bit differently and Aunt Sue wasn't Aunt Eunice, and this was the third next.

Aunt Sue was preparing "dinner" in a new kitchen with new appliances. The house was new and the furniture as well. The house was wedged between two other houses, in front and back of other wedged houses, all the same. He figured that late at night, people must have made some embarrassing mistakes when they came home and sat down in the wrong house with the wrong family. He wondered if some stayed longer than they should. He knew these were adult situations and none of his concern. He had a sense that the large scales of outward sameness meant differences were subtle or well hidden, revealed by circumstance or the observant eye.

Uncle Elbert had finished digging the car out of its bowl of frozen snow and was removing an additional four inches from the path to the front door. His aunt left the stove and placed a large rug to the right of the door where his uncle placed his boots. He turned and said, "We'll get another ten inches tonight." His uncle's face was red, and snot swung from his nose and joined other frozen streaks on the front of his coat. He didn't know how his uncle was still awake; the best he could tell it had been twenty-four hours, with the last two shoveling.

"Get your father a towel from the closet. Dinner is almost ready. Kids, wash your hands for dinner." He followed the "kids" to the bathroom across from what he guessed was Debbie's room.

Blue and Daisy were probably watching the washing-of-the-hands ritual at the pump and the line marching out of the back door, with no one to not look at on their return to the supper table. He knew Blue and Daisy would not be pleased with the snow, but it would be nice to have them here.

He followed the kids to the table. His uncle sat on one end of the rectangular table with his back to the front window, the one that was to the right of the front door where his aunt's face had been after the car had made its under-the-snow stop. His aunt sat at the other end with her back to the kitchen. "Jim, you sit next to Debbie." His aunt was pointing to the chair to the left of his uncle. Debbie sat to the right of her mother and across from an empty chair, with Tommy sitting to the right of his father. He felt more comfortable with a human between him and his aunt. He was accustomed to sitting to the right of his uncle in the car but was equally comfortable sitting to the left of his uncle. The chance of his uncle speaking to him was remote, so "comfortable" was a good word.

He knew it was a mistake to believe he and his uncle were similar just because both rarely spoke. There had to be some kind of silent bond after the spinning descent of the city hill and the butt-clinching slide through the intersection, but Uncle Elbert was not the decision maker of the family. He was the worker bee, and he served at the queen's pleasure. He knew his uncle had physical stamina that was likely accompanied by the partner of a steady mind to bear the weight of heavy shelves of unspoken opinions and independent thoughts. He was thankful for what he had learned about white-tablecloth living at the stone house, but this table had a blue-checkered oilcloth covering. The house and table were smaller, and the shorter distances allowed subtleties to arrive quickly and be felt before seen.

The meal was tomato soup with two grilled cheese sandwiches cut diagonally. The right side of his face was comfortable, but his left cheek and part of his nose sensed heaviness at the other end of the table. It was a pulling sensation, like the downward slant of a table with uneven legs. He moved back in the chair…it eased but was felt again when he leaned forward to move his spoon up from the bowl.

He felt admiration for his uncle and caught a glimpse of the heavy shelves. He understood the silence and the possible cost of verbally sharing from the countless shelved manuscripts. He knew that the weight of the stored thoughts and opinions eventually would overcome the shelves, and that would be a day long remembered by those who witnessed it.

He looked across at Tommy and crossed his eyes—that brought an easy laugh. He saw Tommy look at both sides of his own nose at the same time; they both smiled. Debbie's giggle brought reminders of proper manners from the slanted end of the table.

The part of his mind that reasoned by symbols conjured up the image of a large carnivorous bird perched on the seat of the chair with its back to the kitchen. The bird's trunk and wings were without flesh or feathers, and atop its spine was an exposed brain with a surface that moved. Each of the two piercing eyes were connected to the brain by twelve string-like muscles that moved the eyes up and down and controlled the beak, a fleshy beak with lipstick painted on the sharp edges that separated the top from the bottom. The bird stood as tall as an adult male, and a judge's robe was draped around its featherless structure. Tips of fan-like bones protruded out of the sleeves and made scraping sounds on the table covering.

Once again, he had wandered off in the maze of dimly lit pathways in the back of his mind. His mind was strong enough to travel the pathways, but his resistive nature had caused him to lose focus and gaze too long at the ancient symbols that stood, unmoving, where the failing light met the darkness.

A more practical use of his energy would be gathering information as to the length of his stay beyond "dinner" at the "wedge house." He knew there had been a discussion before his uncle had begun the twenty-plus-hour journey to the south and back. The discussion most likely began shortly after Aunt Eunice's call on…he had lost track of the days again. The newspaper announcement was on Thursday evening after supper, and the call was later Thursday night; Uncle Elbert's arrival was early Saturday morning. This was Saturday night after "dinner." The discussion would resume tonight after the "kids" fell asleep. He wasn't sure his uncle could stay awake for a lengthy monologue, but his stamina had been impressive thus far.

He realized that redirecting his attention had allowed the left side of his face and nose to feel less vulnerable to the slanting table—although he also must have gained some relief by leaning away from the slanted end of the table during the visitation of the man-sized carnivorous bird. He would continue to focus on more practical and social matters.

A practical and social moment was approaching—the end of a meal. Groups of people who resided under the same roof had rituals that had been shaped on the anvil of time and were used to determine the acceptable from the unacceptable. He had become adept at learning rituals after being cast unwillingly in the role of tribal traveler.

His adeptness had little to do with his length of stay around the communal fire. Length of stay had been determined behind a wall that moved from hospital, to hotel, to shack, to stone house, and now to wedge house. The wall had moved with him, but its other side had become less important. His side of the wall was what he attended to until he was old enough to choose a wall whose other side he could adapt.

Tommy was picking up his plate and silverware and was moving to the kitchen; he did the same. He stood behind Tommy and watched him rinse the bowl, plate, and silverware and place them next to the porcelain sink. Debbie stood behind him as he repeated Tommy's routine. He placed his rinsed plate under Tommy's bowl and his bowl in Tommy's bowl and both sets of silverware on top. He had learned this from the silent woman when she stacked dishes and iron skillets on the low stool during her trips to and from the pump.

He went back to the table to get his glass and napkin and offered to remove his uncle's dishes. Aunt Sue announced she would remove her husband's dishes, and this was her table and her kitchen. He responded with "Yes, ma'am." His uncle moved his index finger along the blue and white checkered table covering, and he could see the muscles in his uncle's jaw tighten. Most likely another document had been placed on the shelves.

He wanted to share with his uncle how he dealt with his own shelved documents. He used quiet times—and there were many—to organize the unspoken. Aunt Sue's last comment would be placed in the section labeled: "Unnecessarily Unkind." He spent each evening straightening the shelved documents and would double check that reasonable rebuttals had been placed in each folder that protected each document. A reasonable rebuttal to "my table and my kitchen" would be: "The table and kitchen belong to the family. It's your turn to be the adult, parent, and wife. It's not about you; it's about the family." A reasonable rebuttal silently read in braille from the subtle bumps on the blue-checkered table covering under his uncle's index finger. He had watched his uncle's finger move across five horizontal lines of small squares of alternating blue and white.

His uncle had moved his finger across the same lines five times before he put the palms of his hands on the corners of the table and stood up. His movement caused his wife to turn her head from the sink, and there were a few uncomfortable seconds as they looked at each other. He was glad he had moved away from the table and had stopped watching his uncle's one-fingered rebuttal.

He followed Tommy to his room. He sat on the bed while Tommy pulled a large tin bucket from the self at the end of his bed and dumped the contents on the floor. The label on the bucket read "Lincoln Logs." He spread out the brown wooden pieces and began connecting them with notches at the ends of each piece.

He was tired from the long car ride but began to organize his thoughts. He guessed there would be another hour and a half to two hours before bedtime. All the houses were too close together to make use of the six river rocks in his right pocket. He didn't want his aunt to know he had a knife in his left pocket. He slid his original suitcase from under the bed. He opened it and placed the rocks in a pouch attached to the inside edge of the suitcase. He put the fingernail and toenail clippers with the rocks. He would keep the knife in his pocket. He had been looking forward to using part of the winter to review the collection of coins to see if any matched the empty holes in the four cardboard folders. He would bring them out when he knew he would be staying at the wedge house for more than a few days. So far, it did not look promising for a lengthy stay.

He took pajamas out of the suitcase and tucked them under the pillow and slid the suitcase back under the bed. He stepped to the edge of the door, where he couldn't be seen in the hallway. The best he could tell, his uncle and aunt's room was across the short hallway. If he stepped into the hallway and faced the kitchen, the adult's room would be the first on his left, followed by the bathroom door. Once again, if he were caught in the hallway after bedtime, he would have the ready-made excuse of having to use the bathroom.

He knew that his aunt had been waiting for his uncle's return to express her thoughts regarding having a third child in the house, and tonight would be the best time to gather the information he needed to plan for his immediate future. He could listen with fewer risks if his aunt gave her monologue in the bedroom rather than at the table next to the kitchen. There was a clear view of the table from the hallway.

There were other possible complications like the light in the hallway. It wasn't in the ceiling; it was attached to the wall between the bathroom and the adult's room. The fixture was hourglass shaped and cast a light up and down in fan-like patterns. The light shone up the wall and bent backward where the wall met the ceiling. The open base of the hourglass fixture cast a diagonal light over the bottom third of the adults' bedroom door. He knew his uncle and aunt's bedroom door would be closed, *but did Debbie and Tommy close their doors when they slept? Did the doors squeak when moved, and there were hardwood floors throughout the house, and did they make noise when stepped on?* He was glad that Debbie was still in the living area so his aunt could not comment on his arrival.

It was less than hour before bedtime, and he listened carefully for floor sounds from movement at the other end of the hallway. The house was small enough that secrets would be difficult to keep around a listening ear. Especially a practiced ear that was accustomed to different tones and words bearing a familiar message. Pain and emotion were pushed away from the familiar message, propelled by repetition—like saying the same phrase over and over until it lost its meaning. The familiar message no longer caused harm; instead, it enhanced preparation for the once unexpected. The familiar message became friend, not foe, and its arrival to the practiced ear brought expectation without fear. The fast-moving frozen clock had condensed time to provide years of experience within weeks; he considered this a gift, unwanted by many and treasured by few.

He heard the sound of his aunt's house slippers moving toward the hallway. The slippers made a popping sound when she lifted each foot. He backed away from the doorway and sat on the bed. The popping stopped, and a voice came through the open doorway. "Tommy, go say good night to your father and get ready for bed."

Tommy dismantled the cabin and slid the logs into the container and snapped on the lid. He followed Tommy through the doorway and down the hall. They passed Debbie's door to the right and made a wide turn around the corner past an end table and lamp next to a couch against the wall. Uncle Elbert sat in a chair just beyond the couch. There was another end table and lamp next to the right side of the chair. The chair was at an angle, pointed at the front door.

Debbie came around the corner and slipped between the couch and the coffee table and walked on her knees on the couch and kissed her mother. Uncle Elbert leaned over and hugged Tommy. Debbie kissed her father.

He stepped forward and shook his uncle's hand and nodded a thank you; Uncle Elbert nodded back. He saw tiredness in his uncle's eyes that had been there long before the fatigue of the sleepless road trip. This room was where the monologue would begin, a stream of words and emotions pouring from the couch onto the angled chair. The volume and weight of the words would cause the chair to sink slowly into the floor, and his uncle would be on the bare wood with the upper part of his body at an angle, supported only by his elbows.

"Thank you for dinner, Aunt Sue." Debbie and Tommy passed between him and the coffee table. He did not see his aunt's response—his attention was focused on any possible changes in light as Debbie and Tommy rounded the corner and moved down the hallway. The corner was where he would need to stand to hear the monologue. The brightness of the lamp on the hallway-end of the couch prevented shadows from moving into the sitting room, but a subtle dimness moved over the tip of the arm of the couch when Debbie and Tommy passed in front of the hallway light. The dimness did not extend to the floor.

He returned to Tommy's room and looked for a toothbrush in his suitcase. "Debbie uses the bathroom first, then me, and then you." He looked in his coat for the salve and waited till Tommy's turn in the bathroom to change into his pajamas. Most of the sores had closed up, but a few had dried blood where his blue jeans had rubbed them during the ten-hour road trip.

He found a plastic pouch with a zipper and clear plastic sleeves that held a toothbrush, toothpaste, and soap. There were empty plastic sleeves, and he put the clippers in one. The suitcase had a towel and a washcloth; he didn't want to use his aunt's stuff.

It was his turn. He started by washing his hands and putting salve on the sores. He brushed his teeth and checked his fingernails. He finished and returned to the room.

The two beds had dark blue bedspreads that were thick and heavy. The room felt cold, and he decided to sleep in his socks. The ceiling light was on, and Tommy was in bed on his left side looking at a comic book. Tommy's bed was against the front wall of the house and the lower bedposts on the footboard were even with the left side of the window. Tommy's bed faced the kitchen and was in a direct line through the inside of the house to the back of the chair where Uncle Elbert sat in during "dinner." His bed was against the opposite wall, with a small window behind the headboard. A tall bookshelf stood between the foot of his bed and the bedroom door.

"Are you and Debbie going to play in the snow tomorrow?"

"Mom said everything was going to turn to ice, and it's going to be below zero in the morning."

"Below zero? How cold is that?"

"Cold enough to freeze parts of your skin if they're not covered up."

He couldn't figure why people live in a place where their skin freezes. This was a frozen-skin place, a place with nonverbal spinning cars, a place of a giant carnivorous bird disguised as an aunt, a place of repeating houses. He had been in stranger places, and Debbie and Tommy seemed pretty normal.

He needed to stay awake to, once again, gather information. He tried to remember the turns the car made on the way to the wedge house. The sum of the turns meant the morning sun would come through Tommy's window, but the house was in the bend of a curve. The morning sun would probably come at an angle through the small window over the kitchen sink.

He heard the popping of the house slippers. He decided he would pretend to be asleep. The slippers stopped at Debbie's door with a muffled "good night." A few seconds of popping and "good night." One second later the ceiling light went out. The hallway light, framed by the partially open bedroom door, made a triangle on the ceiling. It looked like enough space to squeeze through without touching the door. The popping house slippers faded away and stopped. The hallway light was still on. He listened to Tommy's breathing until it slowed and was steady. He started to get out of bed but heard the refrigerator door open.

He had grown tired of hiding and listening. Again, this would be one of the many times spread out over, now, three locations. Listening at the shack had been motivated by survival; listening at the stone house had been motivated by preparedness. He knew listening at the wedge house would come with a strong invitation to feel bad. He was prepared to move again. *So why listen and fight the urge to feel insignificant?* He had to know. He was his own parent.

He slipped out of bed and squeezed between the bookshelf and the door. He walked along the opposite wall past the adult's bedroom door and stopped at the bathroom door. He had passed Debbie's door without being seen. He knelt down opposite the bathroom door and put his palms on the hallway floor. He walked his palms forward until his chest touched the floor, and he lowered the rest of his body against the floor. There was no change in the light on the arm of the couch or on the sitting room floor in front of the couch.

He could see the two outside legs of the end table and the edge of the lampshade. "Elbert, turn that hallway light off." He looked up and the hallway light switch was directly above his head. He heard movement from the angled chair and felt the footsteps in his chest. He tucked his arms and hands under his chest and put the tip of his nose on the floor. His pajamas were dark, and the only skin showing was the top of his heels. The footsteps came closer and stopped. He rolled his eyes up and saw the side of Uncle Elbert's sock with his toes pointed at the back outside leg of the end table. Uncle Elbert's hand moved around on the wall, and the light went out. His uncle didn't look at the switch or see him. The angled chair made another noise.

"Why did you bring that boy here? I don't want him around our children. His father is a drunken gypsy, and his mother is dead."

He had heard it all before, and his aunt's voice began to sound like the clicking beak of a large bird. He had learned to screen out the old information and listen carefully for new details, especially details regarding length of stay and direction of departure. His aunt had stepped into the long line of "deciders" whose opinions meant nothing more to him than the displaced air in front of their moving lips. He wasn't lying on the floor for opinions; he was lying on the floor for useful information.

"Elbert, you have a choice." *Uncle Elbert having a choice—now that was some new information!* He grinned at the floor. "If you don't put that boy on a bus heading south before you go to work on Monday, don't come home."

He felt like standing up and walking into the sitting room and telling his uncle that it was a chance for a new start for both of them, and he would be ready early in the morning. He did not. He scooted backward on his hands and knees and slipped through the door and into bed. He had learned what he needed to know but was certain the beak chattering would continue for some time. He had been on his knees and soon his uncle would be on his elbows; he was the more fortunate of the two.

His mind was quiet. A peaceful sleep came gently without invitation.

Hensen March

14 - Southbound

The bed was warm, and a reflective glow lit the curtains next to Tommy's bed. His arms and hands were under the covers, but his face felt cool and the tip of his nose was cold to the touch.

The sound of a large truck was approaching, and he went to the left side of the curtain to look. Ice crystals covered the surface of the snow, and a large truck with a snowplow was coming around the bend to his right. The plow left a four-foot-high ridge of snow at the end of each driveway across the street. He knew the truck eventually would come around from the left and lay a snow ridge across the driveways on his side of the street. He saw two men come out of their front doors with snow shovels and begin to make breaks in the unbroken ridge from the plow. He hoped that his uncle would do the same before the snow started to settle and freeze.

He stuck his head out the doorway and saw his uncle sitting at the table drinking coffee. There were no other sounds in the kitchen, and he thought this would be a good time to speak to his uncle. He returned to the bed and pulled out the canvas suitcase and removed the jar of coins from the tin pail. He wrapped his blue jeans and shirt from the car trip around the jar and put it back into the bag. He walked down the hallway with the pail in his left hand. His uncle turned just as he passed the bathroom door.

"Uncle Elbert, when does the bus leave?"

"Ten this morning."

"I don't have any money, but I have this pail. Can you put some food in it for the bus ride?"

"Yes. I'll ask your aunt to find something."

"Do you need help shoveling snow?"

"No."

"How much time do we have before we leave?"

"Thirty minutes."

"I'll be ready."

His uncle stood up from the table and put on his coat, wrapped a scarf around his neck and covered his nose and mouth. He opened the door and put on heavy gloves and grabbed the shovel to the left of the door. He didn't think his uncle could shovel all of the snow that was coming from the plow, so he stepped to the window behind the chair and watched. His uncle leaned the shovel against the car and sat down behind the steering wheel. The starter groaned twice, and the engine started pushing clouds out the tailpipe. His uncle began removing the icy snow from the front, back, and side windows. The snow came off in large slabs of ice and snow. Uncle Elbert walked around the car and pushed the slabs away from the vehicle.

He left the window and returned to the bedroom. He put the suitcase on the bed and took out clothes for the bus ride. He peed, used the soap to wash important areas, put on more salve and got dressed. He put the used underwear and socks in the canvas suitcase along with his shoes. He would wear the new boots with clean socks. He set the suitcases on the floor and carefully made the bed. He didn't look around the room—he hadn't been there long enough to feel any attachment. Tommy was sleeping. "See you again, someday."

He heard his aunt's door close. He carried his suitcases down the hall without scraping the walls to avoid causing his aunt's door to open. The tin pail was sitting next to the door. He put the suitcases next to the pail and returned to the window behind the chair at the end of the table.

His uncle had shoveled the top portion of the snow ridge from last night. The shovel went back into the trunk, and his uncle backed the car over the ridge and turned the steering wheel to the right. The car moved forward and stopped on the other side of the street next to the new ridge from the plow. He heard the snowplow coming down the street to his left. His uncle had gotten the car out of the driveway before the plow had passed to block the driveway with snow.

Now it was his turn to get to the car before the plow. He secured the coat and hood and then wrapped the fingers of his left hand around the pail's wire handle and the leather handle of the canvas suitcase. He pulled the door open with his right hand and placed his original suitcase on the top step. He turned and grabbed the door handle with his right hand and stepped out with his left foot and pulled the door shut. As he turned to face the street, the canvas suitcase swung around and hit the blond suitcase. The suitcase slid down the stairs and across the sloping yard to the base of the snow ridge next to the street.

The snowplow was six houses away, heading in his direction. He put the canvas suitcase in his right hand and left the pail in his left hand for balance and made his way down the steps to the driveway. He went down the driveway in a half-run-half-skate motion and over last's night ridge. He continued the awkward motion down the street side of the ridge and stopped where the suitcase had landed on the yard side of the ridge. He shifted the canvas suitcase to his left hand to free his right. He put his left foot halfway up the ridge and reached for the suitcase. He couldn't find the handle at first but kept turning the edges of the suitcase around until he grabbed the handle and pulled it over the ridge.

He stood up with both hands full and started moving across the road to the car. He fell on his back, looked to the left and saw the plow pass his uncle's driveway. He froze and sucked cold air through his mouth; his lungs burned. He knew the plow could not stop in time. He closed his eyes and waited for it to happen.

He had a death grip on the pail, canvas suitcase, and his blond suitcase. He felt it happen. The front of his coat lifted, and his body was moving forward violently. He heard the blast of an air horn and the fading sound of a man yelling, "Get out of the road, you stupid kid!"

He knew he wasn't dead because his lungs hurt, and he was coughing. He opened his eyes to Uncle Elbert's face. His feet were off the ground, and his uncle's hands were dug deep into the front of his coat. He was still holding onto the pail, canvas suitcase, and his blond suitcase. His feet touched the ground, and Uncle Elbert had to pry the items from his hands before he could place them in the trunk and close it. His uncle was behind the steering wheel, and he was still standing next to the car, watching the snowplow in the distance as it rounded the last of the curve and disappeared.

His uncle opened the passenger door. "Are you standing or riding?"

He coughed up a wad of phlegm and spit it into the street and looked at his uncle. "Riding."

The car was warmer than lying on his back in the street. His emotions hovered between child and man and waited at the bottom of his throat for permission to enter his mouth. He swallowed hard, and they fell like a stone to his stomach. The zero-degree springs rose up and pressed against his jeans, and his body shivered once and again. He swallowed, and he felt the stone move in his stomach. The car followed the curve through the repeating houses, and he stared through the windshield.

The dark shadow visitor from the woods moved along with the car and whispered in his right ear. "Release the stone." He began to hum, and the vibrations moved through the bones in his face and quieted the whispers. The imagined shadow left his ears and presented before his eyes the image of the stone shooting up his throat, breaking his teeth and crashing through the windshield causing the car to flip upside down and burst into flames, sliding and spinning on its roof, burning. He coughed up a large amount of phlegm, rolled down his window and blew it out of his mouth. The phlegm came out in a long string with chunks on both ends and began to spin counterclockwise. There was no shadow visitor and no stone in his stomach. It was a choice—to be broken forever or to continue on to the next next. He chose to remain unbroken.

There was a long bus ride ahead, and he would relax and sleep. He thought about his uncle pulling him away from the snowplow and turned to him and said, "Thank you." His uncle didn't turn but gave two slight nods that would have been missed by a less observant eye. He turned back and looked through the windshield and smiled. *His uncle was a brave man that had learned to live with a man-sized carnivorous bird and had faced the fear of his eyeballs being plucked out in the dead of night.*

His lungs were recovering from breathing in the brittle, cold air. The plow wove through the abandoned streets, and the car followed. The replica houses differed only by the patterns on their roofs, carved by the wind into sharp edges with points. The plow and the car were moving around and between small squares of white cake with white icing on a giant flat surface, deep with powdered sugar. The plow and car reached the end of the flat surface and turned right onto the mile-long road that ended between "Tastee Twist" and "A&W." The ice cream place was approaching on the right; the outside round tables had become free standing cone-shaped monuments covered in sequined ice. It was not a busy time for "Tastee Twist."

He heard the sound of a large engine behind the car, and the front grill of a dump truck stopped next to the back bumper. The grill extended beyond the top of the car's back window. The brakes made a loud forced-air sound. He was sitting in a toy car between two large machines with multiple tires. The plow turned left and headed back toward the city. Uncle Elbert moved right to allow the dump truck to pass. The dump truck passed, throwing a hard spray of salt over the car. The car turned left and followed the plow and salt truck toward the city.

His uncle stayed back from the salt spray, but occasionally the wind would blow salt from the bed of the truck. Large grains would ping against the front grill, dance across the hood and ricochet off the windshield. He was thankful the car had not gone into a butt-clinching spin; the likelihood of their reaching the bus station was better than poor.

* * * * * * *

He knew he would be in for a long ride on a southbound bus that left the city at ten. The clock in the dashboard remained secretive. He resisted the urge to ask his uncle for details. Long ago he had chosen to focus his energy on the art of "nexting." The fourth next was approaching from the south. It would drift forward until the bus stopped inside it and the first of its details would present itself. Uncle Elbert was a non-resident of the fourth next, and his information would be secondhand at best. His uncle's imprint on the vast land of verbiage was small, faint, and seldom. The art of nexting was best done in person.

The salt continued to dance on the hood. The snow and ice on the road were the color and consistency of a root beer float. The tires from the trucks and the car had splashed the brown soda on the snowbanks that crowded the edges of the road. He hoped they would not have to go up the hill that they had spun down the night before. They turned right at the base of the hill and stopped at the first red-eyed Cyclops. He could see two more twelve-eyed, hanging sentinels. Just beyond the second set of swinging glass eyes and to the right was a three-story building with a vertical sign, "BUS," attached to the corner of the building. Just below the two-and-a-half-story sign were two sets of double doors facing the street. The doors were mostly glass trimmed in chrome, with door handles attached to large chrome plates. A steady stream of hatted and scarfed people passed in and out of both sets of doors.

The car went under the second hanging light, past the doors to the end of the building and turned right into an open parking lot. He buttoned up his coat and put up the hood. He reminded himself to breathe through his nose to avoid another spinning phlegm-fest. The car stopped, and he opened his door at the same time as his uncle. The air coming up his nose was bitter cold and felt like breathing in shards of glass.

The trunk was open; he grabbed the pail and his uncle the two suitcases. They walked to the parking attendant's shack, and his uncle gave the man a dime. He followed his uncle through the parking lot to the sidewalk and turned left. They stopped at the edge of a wide drive adjacent to the building. A long silver bus passed in front of them. His uncle did not wear a hat when it snowed, and he saw the familiar steam rising off the back of his ears. They crossed the drive and entered the first set of double doors.

He stuck close to the back of his uncle's coat until his eyes adjusted to the change in light from the snow-reflected sunlight outside to the dimmer interior light of the building. The lobby of the bus station was two stories high, with round metal light shades that hung from long chains attached to the ceiling. Directly ahead were six lines of people standing in front of ticket windows where men wearing clear green visors sat on tall swivel chairs.

He knew this was a time to pay attention. He had noticed that his uncle had not looked back to see if he was there since the parking lot. *A person could grow up fast around his uncle.* He had already grown up faster than he preferred and looked forward to the day when experiences came at a more manageable speed. Until that time, the task at hand was to get on the right bus at the right time going to wherever south he was going. It was his uncle's turn at the window. Then came an announcement: the name of a city he didn't recognize "and all points south, leaving in fifteen minutes at number four." His uncle had given the green-visor man money and was handed a ticket.

His uncle was moving again, headed for the double doors to the right of the men in green visors; he followed. He went through the door and shards of glass climbed up his nose again; he walked faster. His uncle stopped at number four and stood in another line moving slowly to the door of the bus. A man in a gray uniform wearing a gray, policeman-looking hat with a dog emblem stood beside the door. He punched a hole in each ticket and tied colored strips with numbers on the suitcases. Another man was loading the suitcases in storage areas under the bus.

Uncle Elbert handed the uniformed man the ticket, and the man tied strips on the two suitcases and punched the ticket. The man in the uniform looked very tall. He saw his uncle speak to the man and hand the man two dollars. Then his uncle stepped to the side of the line. He turned to the right and looked at his uncle. Uncle Elbert handed him the ticket and nodded twice and turned and walked away.

He reminded himself to breathe through his nose. The man in the uniform looked down at him and said, "Sit in the front seat by the steps." Halfway up the steps he realized he had forgotten to breathe. He grabbed the pole with his left hand and swung around and sat, then moved to the seat next to the window. He looked for his uncle; he was not there.

He looked down at the last of the boarding passengers and the man loading the suitcases. The last suitcase was loaded, and the last passenger was coming up the steps. He heard the doors to the storage areas close and lock. The man in the uniform checked the doors and disappeared behind the bus, then the top of his hat reappeared in the large windshield. He came up the steps, sat down behind the steering wheel and pulled the lever to his left; the door closed.

Once again, he was on a bus with a shining pole. This time he was alone.

* * * * * * *

He was the only child on the bus. The driver was writing on a paper attached to a clipboard. He remembered the bus ticket. He looked at his left thumb and saw it pressed against the ticket. His hands were tense, and the bones in his knuckles were pushing the blood away from the skin that covered the center of his fingers. His plan to relax and sleep was off to a poor start. His fingernails were dug into the palms of both hands. He took a deep breath and stretched his fingers out, and the bus ticket fell to the floor. He leaned over to pick up the ticket with his left hand, and as the bus backed up, his head bounced off the metal panel that separated the two seats from the steps. He felt a brief wave of nausea. The ticket was lying face down; he picked it up and slowly sat up in the seat. The nausea passed, and the ticket was back in his left hand.

He decided not to turn it over to see the printed destination on the other side. He needed to get organized and settled in and stop bouncing his head off of metal objects. He put the ticket between his teeth, unbuttoned the top two buttons of his coat and placed the ticket in the front pocket of his shirt. He put the tin pail in the empty seat to his left, took off his coat and folded it over the pail.

He was hungry. He didn't want to explore the contents of the tin pail until he was sure he could manage to keep the head bouncing to a minimum. He did wonder what was in the pail. He knew who placed the contents. *The contents could fall into two basic categories: something Aunt Sue liked or something he could eat. If it were something his aunt liked, it would likely be a generous portion of birdseed sprinkled over raw rodent flesh. The depth of the snow on Vanilla Acres made rodent flesh hard to find. Perhaps the raw meat would have come from a missing pet or a neighbor that came to the door once too often. It was a true mystery that would be easy to solve.* He had spent enough time with his aunt to know that the late brunch in a pail should be approached with caution, and the possibility of it being truly disgusting was, sadly, more than remote. He looked out the window and knew curiosity would soon get the better of him.

He was relieved to be heading south, away from the broken-glass air of Vanilla Acres. The bus was moving through the downtown area with the fancy hotels. It was the same street, different day, different direction but for the same reason. Home remained within; he was merely traveling to occupy space in another location. The emotions of the station and boarding the bus invited rest to come and sit with him. He put his right elbow on the armrest and rested his chin in his palm. He watched the sun race along the surfaces of the storefront windows. He looked at the face of sleep with his eyes closed, and they peacefully sat together for a silent visit.

He was accustomed to silent visits and wordless conversations. The masters of silence were his uncle, who walked away without a word, and the silent woman from the shack. Circumstance had reached down their throats and removed language by the fists full, leaving only small words clinging to the inside walls of their voices.

Above, thoughts whirled around looking for an opening to pass through the silence.

Sleep touched its forehead to his, and he moved through the unopened door of the room with typewriters. Those within had prepared for his arrival. It had been some time since his last visit. Blue and Daisy met him at the door. He hugged and petted both; their tails wagged. They were pleased to be in the room and away from the harshness of the shack. The tapping of the typewriters remained in the background.

Aunt Eunice and Miss Betty hugged him and pointed out improvements to the room. The man with the kind and gentle face had built a fireplace in the wall behind Blue's and Daisy's beds; it held a warm fire. It was the dogs' favorite place to nap. Miss Betty had brought in fancy-hotel Persian rugs, and soft couches circled around the fireplace. The windows were spotless, and he stood with Blue and Daisy and watched his mother walking.

He followed Blue and Daisy to the couch closest to the fire. The dogs sat on each end, and he sat in the center and lay down. He thought of his mother fishing on the banks of the wide river; his head moved up and down on a breathing pillow. The typewriters tapped and the fire crackled. He dreamed inside a dream of a no-lonesome place where the seldom-noticed heart felt the warmth of another.

Chin in hand, he passed through the door and heard the ticket being punched and the door closing. He felt the cold air fall off the man's coat as he passed. The sun against the shining pole told his stomach that it was midafternoon. His hunger would open the pail and eat, regardless of claw, fur, or feather. He put the pail between his legs and touched the lid and stopped. His mind was sound, but his imagination often wandered about unsupervised. He touched the bus ticket in his pocket. The ticket would allow him to continue his journey after recovering from injuries should the contents of the pail crawl or fly out and attack him.

His imagination watched as his hunger opened the pail…no movement. Two glass bottles with wire clasps and clear liquid. Two packs of gum. The second container held five peanut butter and jelly sandwiches on bread cut diagonally and wrapped in wax paper. The bottom container was lined with a blue and white checkered cloth with its corners folded over peanut butter and saltine sandwiches; he counted ten. Imagination returned with an apology but reminded hunger that the length of the journey was unknown and there was no money to purchase more. Hunger negotiated quickly, and his hands chose two peanut butter crackers, one triangle of peanut butter and jelly, one glass bottle, and one stick of gum. He refolded the corners of the cloth, replaced the lids and put the pail under his coat. He settled in for an early supper. Hunger was pleased and imagination rested. He was thankful that the man-sized carnivorous bird had allowed his aunt to provide the food. It was a fine, slow, early supper.

The sun was low and to the right, and on both sides of the road the doors that waited next to the driveways raced backward to make room for the motels with closed swimming pools. Soon the bus would pass the hamburger joints, and subtle whiffs of cooking meat would make their way into the bus. He would eat more slowly to distract a fickle stomach. After the meat smells would come the town and a possible stop at another bus station. Until he looked at the other side of the ticket, he would remain the only passenger without a destination.

He looked forward to seeing the south again with its brown grass of early winter. The first buildings of the town were in the windshield. He closed the clasp on the half-full bottle and put it back in the top container of the pail. He had made his world small in the bus by not looking at the faces of the other passengers. He saw the right side of the driver's face, the windshields, and the front side windows. He did not want to know how many passengers sat behind him or look at their faces. The boundary of his world ended at the armrests. He was the only resident. He knew activity would increase when the bus stopped in the town. Until then he would enjoy his space inside the metal and aluminum tube with tires and glass.

The bus was moving through the downtown. The buildings to his right blocked the sun. The sunlight would race down the cross streets and light up the intersections. The bus passed under the green-eyed Cyclopes and through wide ribbons of light. On the right past the third ribbon of light was the bus station, smaller than the first but flanked by the same wide drives. To his right, the sun flashed three times, and the bus turned into the first drive. The bus stopped at an angle next to a wide sidewalk that led from the back of the building. The bus was facing an identical bus on the other side of the walkway.

He heard voices and activity behind him. The driver announced the town. He didn't pay attention to the name. There would be many towns with names. He would listen for only one name—the secret name printed on the other side of the ticket in his pocket. He looked at the right elbows of the exiting passengers as they passed the armrest to his left. He counted four men and three women.

The cold air tried to climb the steps but was too heavy. The coats and bags of the passengers pushed the cold air down and along the sides and front of the bus. The driver went down the steps behind the last passenger and supervised the removal of bags from the storage areas under the bus.

He counted eleven people in line to board the bus—four more than left the bus. He wondered if one of the eleven would sit down next to him. He left the coat and pail in the seat next to him in hopes that each of the eleven would assume an adult was traveling with him. Adults tended to avoid children they didn't know, especially in confined places.

The driver was punching the tickets, and the bags were being loaded. All eleven passed the armrest; he did not look at their faces. The storage doors closed and locked, and the driver walked around the bus and up the stairs and sat. The door closed; the bus pulled away, turned right and continued south.

The ribbons of light crossing the intersections were dimmer. Distant neon would respond to switches, and the gases would begin their evening shift, then sleep again at sunrise. He touched the ticket in his pocket and wondered if the secret destination would hide in the darkness or wait until the earth turned and reveal itself in the new light of tomorrow.

Knowing the next would not be the last made the destination less important. He would arrive at the new next and faces from the last next would disappear; new-next faces would be seen until the next new next arrived. New faces that would look at his face, and he would look at theirs. Until then, he watched the elbows pass by the armrest boundary of his home within.

Hunger and imagination were discussing the contents of the tin pail under the coat and the bus ticket in his pocket. One wanted to eat the contents and the other wanted to look at the destination. They would have to negotiate; he needed to pee. He started down the aisle, only looking at the arms on the armrests. He counted twelve before the bathroom door to his left. He would make a more accurate count on his way back. He slid the inside lock to the left; he was in a speeding outhouse. He finished quickly and made a back-of-the-head count on his way to his seat. Twenty-one.

He sat down and checked back with hunger and imagination's negotiation.

He took three sips of water and put the stick of gum in his mouth, Clark's Teaberry. The sugars brightened his mood, and he waited to see the neon show begin, starting with the motel signs: "vacancy," "no vacancy," "air conditioned," "pool." Hunger paused and imagination was ready for the light show. So far, he saw only porch and window lights and deep, old snow that had frozen. The seat was comfortable, and the motor hummed in the background.

He chewed the gum and reviewed his three fundamentals: polite, respectful, and quiet. There were others that were only used when absolutely necessary. He practiced two types of fundamentals: the first three were what he did, and the rest were what he thought. Sometimes he knew things that others didn't notice. The "knowings" were not generated by him but passed by him at a recognizable speed. The ones he had recognized came through sights or feelings that instantly were translated into thoughts. He paid close attention when they passed by and carefully remembered them. They were always useful, either immediately or later but always before he needed them. It was not a magical gift; it flowed from senses heightened by necessity and undisturbed by the vibrations of one's own voice.

He knew why he was reviewing the fundamentals that did not need to be reviewed. The earth had turned away from the sun and it was dark. Dark was when he would feel the loss of his mother more deeply. Next would come images and feelings from the strangeness of life without her, followed by the invitation to feel like the inconvenience that someone should attend to but didn't. Someone needed to attend to it; the volunteers were few and the interest low. He had refused the invitation and knew thoughts of one's inconvenience came from minds that served as poor company. It was dark and he missed his mother. It was a pure feeling, second only to the love he felt for her. Hunger and imagination had agreed. It was time to eat.

The choices were the same as before; he replaced the lids and returned the pail to the covering coat. The second supper was slow and comforting. Trees made the distant neon blink. Soon the trees would stand back, and motel neon would decorate the darkness and pour colored light over the frozen snow. Miles and time would unfold before he would read the destination on the ticket. He had decided to look at the other side of the ticket at first light or after the count of two thousand after he passed the last strip of snow. He would begin counting when the grass lay uncovered.

The jelly was blueberry, and the peanut butter was smooth. Outside the window, trees without leaves raced north, scraping the moon. The moon weaved through the speeding branches and behind buildings to keep its spot in the window. Red neon "no vacancy" signs waved the bus past motels, with cars pointed at rows of doors painted sea-foam green and peach pink.

He thought about the whispered contract between his uncle and the bus driver and the two dollars that exchanged hands. His uncle had whispered just a few words to the bus driver. Imagination was eager to guess. "Make sure the kid gets off at the right place." "Make sure the kid doesn't die." "Make sure the kid doesn't fall and split his skull open, and if his brain falls out, don't let it get stepped on." Imagination nervously traveled on the edge of the herd and saw things inside every shadow. *"Watch the kid" would be the best his uncle could whisper.* He wondered how much kid watching you could get for two dollars. He had been watching the bus driver. *There had not been a nickel's worth of kid watching from the driver.*

The bus had passed the hamburger joints and most of the small downtown. This was a town where the bus did not stop; he considered it a bonus. The bus left the commercial area and began to pass through the long stretch of lighted windows and porches. He closed his eyes and would wait for bright lights and the sound of brakes. His shoulders drifted to the right, and his head rested against the window. He began to feel the vibrations from the window in his skull, brain, and eyeballs. He moved his head and shoulders down and lay on his right side with his knees bent around the center armrest and the bottom of his boots next to the tin pail. He pulled the coat up close to his shoulders. His brain was lying on its side, and a memory came before a dream.

It was the memory of the iceman. It was an early memory from when he lived with his mother and father in three rooms at the top of a long wooden stairway that led to the street. He sat at the kitchen table with his father. The back of his chair was against the wall, and he faced the other wall, with two windows to the left and right of a small stove and a tall sink with legs. His father sat to his left in a chair that was turned halfway toward the sink where his mother stood. His mother and father were talking, and his mother would turn from the sink as they spoke. A folded newspaper and a cup of coffee on a white saucer sat on the table. His father's hair was shiny black, and his mother wore a white dress with tiny blue flowers. She stepped away from the sink and looked through the window to the left of the stove. "Iceman's here."

He slipped out of the chair and looked down through the window and saw the ice truck parked just past the door that led to the stairs. His father went down the stairs, and he could see him at the back of the truck, talking to the iceman. The man wore a long black rubber apron and black rubber gloves and held large black metal tongs in his right hand. The iceman reached into the truck and brought out a perfect, see-through rectangle. He had spread out the tongs so that four spikes dug in on two sides of the ice block; he swung it out and carried it on his right side.

He heard his father and the iceman talking and their footsteps up the stairs. He went back to the table to watch them enter the kitchen. The icebox was against the wall to his left, just beyond the kitchen door that swung to the left. His father came in first and opened the lid on top of the icebox. The iceman put the block at an angle across the opening. He opened the tongs and repositioned the four spikes to the top edge of the two long sides. Then he lowered the block into the tin-lined box and closed the lid.

He remembered four things about the day the iceman came: It was morning, the sun was shining, looking at the size of the block of ice with its sharp edges and clear, bluish color, and the warm feeling sitting at the table, watching and listening to his mother and father playfully talking and smiling at each other. He felt fortunate to have remembered every detail. He felt privileged to have been there for such a fine morning, the morning when the iceman came. *It was a most excellent memory.*

He hoped he could have a dreamless sleep with his brain on its side and his boots against the pail. Imagination pictured the brain maintenance man walking the thought factory floor, oiling gears and slowing down machines to a quiet hum, sweeping the day's debris from the floor and standing quietly until shift's end. The factory lights dimmed, and sleep arrived, staying longer than expected. This had been the third time brain maintenance and sleep had been called to the factory floor in the past ten hours. This time they would be able to complete their duties without interruption.

The windshields pushed against the dark, still air and hours passed by the windows. Sleep stood at the exit door and turned and looked with unfocused eyes…he heard the sound of gears. Sleep had left the building. His eyes were looking at the metal panel that separated the two seats from the steps that led to the door of the bus. He heard the forced air of the brakes and saw the movement of light through the windows. He felt the bus turn left and then right. Again, he heard the sound of forced air as the bus stopped.

He sat up and looked down at the window and saw another driver standing outside the bus. Passengers passed by the armrest and down the stairs. He did not count this time. The sidewalk coming out of the station was half the length of sidewalk at the previous station, and there were no other buses. The driver behind the steering wheel looked at his watch and wrote on his clipboard. The driver tore off a piece of paper and wrote something on it, folded it and placed it under the metal clip. The driver went down the stairs with his clipboard. He looked down through the window at the two drivers talking. The first driver handed the second the piece of paper, and they both turned and looked at him.

Imagination tried to control itself until the first driver gave the second driver two dollars. He paid attention to his breathing because imagination was convinced the two men were fugitives disguised as bus drivers. The "G" men were hot on the trail, and he would be buried alive in the darkness of some forgotten patch of trees. Imagination was seldom accurate but always entertaining.

He had survived far worse than mysterious looks and money changing hands. He decided not to close his eyes until the bus reached his destination. The lights of the station and the town made it difficult to judge the length of time until dawn. Life on the couch had made him an expert at anticipating the arrival of dawn. He could sense the east-moving light when it was traveling across the ocean. He would wait until the bus left the town and was deep in the countryside—then he would eat and judge when the eastern edge of darkness would begin to move to the west. The town was small, and the country came quickly.

He planned his meal. He would eat three triangles of peanut butter and jelly and four saltine sandwiches and drink the last half of the first glass bottle of water. He could manage two more meals after this one, and he had lots of gum left. The sugar from the gum could last after the food was gone.

The best he could tell, there were two more hours of darkness. The holes in the snow cover were getting larger. He would look at the destination on the ticket in less than two hours. He ate the food slowly and watched the new driver. The new driver was the only one to board the bus at the last station. He did not count the number of passengers who left and had no idea how many passengers were seated behind him. It made little difference. He knew his destination was not far.

Porch lights were up to half a mile apart. The land was flat, and the moonlight was dim on the stubble in the fields. He drank the last of the water in the first bottle and took out two sticks of gum for later. He looked past his reflection in the window for anything familiar. The land was moving fast next to the bus and slower in the distant fields. It was a time to be more alert and attend to the senses honed by the woods and the couch. Relaxing in the seat would soon come to an end, and scattered, gray light would bring new situations.

The snow cover faded into brown grass and dirt. The snow was in long, narrow strips that traveled along tree lines and on the north side of barns and ditches. The strips became broken lines and disappeared. He began to count. Headlights had stopped approaching. The road silently stretched forward, flat and beyond the lights of the bus...two hundred thirty-seven, two hundred thirty-eight. He reached into his left pocket and pulled out the knife. He opened the blade and checked its edge. He hoped it would be enough—this was the deep country. He also had the six river rocks in his suitcase: nine hundred fifty-nine. He folded the blade back into the handle and put it in his pocket. He reached for the knife again and opened the blade. He did it a third time but faster. He didn't care that the bus driver was watching him—practice made skill; one thousand seventy-two.

He checked the lid on the pail and made sure all of the outside pockets of his coat were buttoned. He checked the laces in his boots and tied a second knot at the top of each. He tucked his shirt in his pants and tightened his belt one notch. It had been some time since he had seen a porch light. He saw a coyote slink across the road just beyond the headlights. This was still better than living in a tiny box in Vanilla Acres, with its broken glass air blowing over frozen snow. He wasn't sure where "this" would be; one thousand nine hundred eighty-two.

He counted a little faster; one thousand nine hundred ninety-eight, ninety-nine, two thousand. He reached for the ticket and turned it over.

He knew the place. It was a little beyond nowhere. He didn't realize the air had left his lungs and he had forgotten to fill them again. He sucked air in through his mouth and coughed. He concentrated on breathing in through his nose and out his mouth. His head began to clear. He didn't know anyone that lived there, and he knew the bus would not be able to get there. He was not going to tell imagination what was about to happen. It would go screaming into a field and grab the dirt and try to hold on to the earth before being flung off into space.

The bus began to slow, and he saw the small white sign about fifty yards to the right on the far edge of a gravel road. The bus stopped, with the door even with the far edge of the gravel road. He put on his coat and buttoned it. He grabbed the tin pail with his left hand and the shining pole with his right. The outside lights above the headlights began to flash, turning the sign from white to amber, back and forth. To the right of the name on the sign was the number "2," with an arrow below the name that pointed to the right, down the gravel road.

The door opened and he followed the driver down the steps. He stood while the driver opened one of the storage doors. He looked up and saw faces in the windows. Some were leaning over from the aisle. He counted ten, all with worried looks. The driver shined a flashlight into the container, and he pointed at the two suitcases. The driver put them on the ground in front of him and closed the door. He asked the driver to shine the light on the blond suitcase. He opened it, pulled out the throwing rocks and closed it. He put the rocks in his right pocket and put the tin pail in the canvas suitcase.

The driver handed him the two dollars. "Your uncle wanted you to have this. Son, I'm sorry the bus won't fit down this road and I'm not allowed to try. Are you going to be OK?"

"Yes sir, I've seen worse."

They both gave a nod, and the driver went up the stairs and closed the door. He stood back as the bus drove off, heading south. He closed his eyes to avoid looking at the lights so his eyes could adjust to the low light. He knew, once the bus was out of sight, there would only be dim moonlight and two miles of dark road ahead.

15 - Coyotes

He stood still with his eyes closed until the sounds of the bus faded. He kept his eyes closed and listened for the night sounds. He heard sounds of cattle off to his right about a mile away. Just to the left of the cattle were horses. Something was disturbing them. If he made the road twelve o'clock, then something was moving from his three o'clock to his two o'clock. This part of the night still belonged to the predators and scavengers. His ears were brushing against the inside of the hood on his coat, making an artificial sound that was distracting. He opened his eyes and the two top buttons of his coat. He folded the hood inside his coat and buttoned his coat. He would be able to see and hear better.

He looked behind him. Across the concrete road was a large field that had soybeans, with a winding line of trees less than a quarter of a mile from where he stood and water beyond the trees. Locals called it a bayou, a long body of water that barely moved during the dry season but drained into larger rivers during the rainy season. Bayous were full of snakes and other reptiles. *Not a place to put a bare toe.*

He turned and faced the road. To the right was a large field of corn stubble with a straight line of trees bordering a man-made ditch a hundred yards from the road. To the left he saw another cornfield with a winding tree-lined bayou two hundred yards away. Nighttime and corn stubble meant nighttime rodents, which meant predators with wings and predators with four legs. He had two legs, six rocks, a pocketknife, and a two-mile walk in the dark. A gravel road meant lots of ammunition. It was time to start.

His estimation of the arrival of dawn was off a bit. It was still at least two hours away. Walking was slow with the suitcases in tow. The moonlight was dim but helpful. A quarter-moon shining a quarter above the horizon at two-thirty made long shadows in the field to the right. The dark shadows from the trees covered fifty of the field's hundred yards. To his left the shadows stretched away from the road, and the field was easier to see. Listening was not limited by direction; seeing was. He knew to watch in order of priority: the road ahead, the field to the right, the field to the left, and behind him.

The road was elevated about four feet. He knew the fields flooded every few years and the road was the only way in and out. He could smell the river.

He had made it an eighth of a mile. He had seen wings drop out of the trees on both sides of the road and grab rodents. Some stayed in the field to eat; some attacked and flew with legs and tails flailing and high-pitch screams. He stopped for a moment and sat on the blond suitcase.

There were eye reflections in all directions. He preferred the small ones to the large, fast-moving ones. He picked up the suitcases and started again. He hoped the fast-moving eye reflections stayed busy with the rodents. Two sets of eyes were behind him about thirty yards back. He could tell they were moving in his direction. He put down the suitcases and gathered rocks from the road and took his best aim; he heard one yelp. The eyes moved into the shadows of the field to the right.

He was about a fourth of the way there—going was slower than he preferred. Imagination was trembling. He walked on, watching the field to the right.

This was a remote place. Nights with cloud cover and no moonlight turned darkness into blackness. He was thankful for the low quarter moon; without it he would not see beyond his own face. He knew he needed to keep moving. Stopping too long would invite night things to come to him. He would need to stop if more than one four-legged night thing got too close. He planned to fill his left hand with as many loose rocks as possible and feed them one by one to his throwing hand.

The canvas suitcase was easy to carry, but his original suitcase was taller than wide so that distance from his hand to the ground was shorter than the height of the suitcase. A growing pain was developing in his right shoulder from keeping the suitcase above the gravel. His right shoulder connected to his throwing arm, and he knew he would need his throwing arm.

Wings continued to drop from the trees, but the sound of his boots on the loose gravel had drawn attention. Four sets of eyes were moving in a line at his five o'clock, and three sets of eyes were moving fifty yards out at his nine o'clock. He hated coyotes. They were cowardly opportunists.

He felt his heart pounding in his neck. He needed a plan, but first he needed to breathe. He breathed in through his nose and out his mouth. He resisted the urge to run. If he ran, he would be chased like prey. *I am not prey; I'm an outstanding rock thrower that knows how to breathe.* He swung the suitcases in front of him and changed hands without stopping. His right shoulder felt better carrying the canvas suitcase.

He had made a bargain with imagination before he left the bus. Imagination was to stand back and remain silent for two miles. Upon arrival at the destination, he would allow it to stretch its legs and ponder why no one met him at the bus and why he was going to a place where he didn't know anyone.

He had lost focus, and the followers to the left had moved closer to the road, and the ones on the right had moved up and had emerged from the shadows of the tree line. Another three sets of eyes were moving fast from the winding tree line to his left. There were six on his left and four on his right. He would wait until the followers were within twenty yards, and then he would do what he had done every day in the woods—throw well and often.

He began to survey the quality of the rocks in the road. Because the road led to the river, there were acceptable rocks that had gathered in long ridges between the tire tracks. The second group of three that had been moving fast from the winding tree line to the left had reached the original three. The six on the left and the four on the right were in single file, moving parallel to the road. Three from the left and two from the right ran ahead twenty yards and stood watching him. The remaining five were moving along at his three and his nine o'clock.

The followers hunted in packs and they were flanking him. They didn't know what was possible, but they were interested. He didn't know what was possible, but he was interested.

When he was even with the followers that had run ahead, they ran ahead again. Each time they ran ahead they inched closer to the road. The three on his immediate left and the two on his immediate right continued to move along at his pace, but then the last follower on both sides began to fall back. If the ten followers were going to do something, it would be soon.

He spotted a pile of rocks ten paces ahead and memorized in his mind every move he would make when he reached the tenth pace. Five paces. In his mind, he had chosen eight individual rocks. They were river rocks similar to the six rocks in his right pocket. Nine paces. His left foot was even with the right side of the rocks. He took the tenth pace with his right foot and pivoted. He put the suitcases down on either side of the rocks and picked up the eight rocks while facing backward down the road. He held seven rocks in his left hand and one in his right.

The two followers that had fallen back were now on the road, slinking toward him with their heads down. They were at the practiced distance: fifteen yards. He lifted the upper part of his left leg until it was parallel to the ground and threw, aiming at the right eye of the follower on the right. The throw was low but hit a bone in the follower's left front leg. There was yelping, and the animal hopped on three legs and bumped into the side of the animal next to it. The follower to the left turned its head toward the other animal and the second rock hit it in the side of the head; it sat down without a sound.

He turned to the left and hit in the ribs the one follower that had flanked to his right. He pivoted left one hundred eighty degrees and hit the two that had been in the left field. He turned and faced forward. Twenty yards ahead three followers were moving down the road toward him. Down four feet on the edges of the left field and the right field were the remaining two, moving faster. The followers were no longer following—they were coming.

He knew the two comers would go up the banks of the road at an angle at his two o'clock and ten o'clock. He had two rocks in his left hand and one in his right. The comer on the right was just short of a dead run, and he aimed in front of the nose; the rock passed in front of the animal and curved to the left. He threw again and the rock struck at the base of the throat, just above the chest. It went back on its haunches and turned left, heaving. The animal on the left had made it up the bank and was coming at an angle. He threw the last rock and hit the animal in the ribs; it ran down the bank.

He knelt and gathered a handful of rocks without looking at them. He was watching the three moving in the road ahead. He stared at them and sorted the rocks in his hands without looking; he had five. The animals were together and walking slowly with their heads down. He would have no problem hitting at least one of them but throwing all five rocks as fast as possible was critical.

The first followers that turned comers were now leavers. Just the three remained. He would try to hit the one on the right first, then the one on the left. He would throw the last five rocks side armed so the rocks would start low and then rise. Side armed was faster than overhand—fewer leg movements. He would throw the rocks just inches off the ground and they would rise, curving left and, he hoped, would hit the underbelly or deliver a rising blow to the jaw and teeth.

He took a deep breath, let half of it out and began. He was able to release the second rock before the first hit its target. The last three rocks were not as fast but accurate. There were sounds of rock hitting teeth and bone and repeated yelps. All three ran off into the shadows. He picked up more rocks and filled the two side pockets of his coat. He stood up straight. He looked behind him and to both sides. A primal sound began gathering in his gut and came out as a long, unchanging yell that made the hairs on the back of his neck rise.

He backed up two steps and grabbed the suitcases and began walking again toward the river. This time he didn't walk quietly. Even imagination stood a little taller. He felt much older and less afraid, less fragile. He stopped looking behind him or to the sides. He looked straight ahead.

He began to see the faint outline of structures sitting high on stilts. It was still a little over an hour before dawn. The morning would cross the concrete road behind him and travel over the rocks and cross the river. He knew where he would be sitting when the light began to move. He was on the edge of the stilted pocket town. Sixteen stilted structures had gathered together to support a common name. His resting place would be the biggest structure, the last on the right before the road went down to the water's edge.

The structure stood quiet and dark. He reached the steps and climbed eight of them and sat. He rested quietly and listened to the edge of the river flapping against the sand. He heard the howls of the followers, comers, and leavers. The cottonwood trees made crooked shadows on the river's edge; the water swirled under the quarter moon. He stared at the top edge of a roof across the road and saw the last of the night stars slowly disappear above its edge. The earth was turning to look at the new sun.

Hunger spoke to him, and his hands reached for the canvas suitcase. He took out the glass bottle, two triangles of peanut butter and jelly, and two of the four saltine sandwiches. Two large sips of water and then food.

Imagination was gathering a story where it was the master of the blackness of night but realized it could be more elaborately grandiose if hunger was allowed to eat. He finished the food and a third sip of water. He put the pail in the canvas suitcase. He moved the tall suitcase on the step below his feet and leaned it in and placed his hands, palms down, on the top. He rested the right side of his head on his hands. The sun would begin to warm his face in less than an hour.

Imagination had abandoned its elaborate story and knew that if it had been in charge, it would have run into the field and been attacked. Imagination had been bored by the endless days of practice in the clearing behind the shack but realized the successful two-mile walk was not by chance. It was a practiced skill gained from months of throwing rocks through a hole in a rotten tree. He, imagination, and hunger were fortunate to be resting on the eighth step at the end of the stilted pocket town next to the river.

16 – The Great Fish

Beyond the concrete road the gaps between the winding trees were beginning to fill with a light orange. The color climbed the trunks and lingered. The orange deepened and left the woods; it rolled over the ridges of the field and slid across the concrete road. The orange flowed around and over the gravel and poured down the rows of stubble. Waves of thick colored light entered the edge of town and cast long, narrow shadows as they crashed against the legs of the structures.

He closed his eyes and felt the wave of warm orange light on his face and eyelids. He rested and remembered his mother's words: "The sky is always red when you look at the sun with your eyes closed." It had been a long time since he had sat with her on the banks of the wide river. The first of the wave of light had passed his face and had rolled down the banks and spread flat across the water. He rested in the orange and fell asleep.

Above him he heard the lock turn and the spring stretch on the screen door. The sounds of a broom and the brittle scratching of dead leaves moved across wood. He turned and saw a man with gray hair sweeping leaves off the porch and down the steps. The man stopped sweeping and looked at him. "You know the cottonwood is a fine-looking tree, but their leaves are as big as a dinner plate. What's your name, son?"

"Jim, sir."

"Jim sir is an unusual name."

"Guess when you put it that way, does sound a bit strange." They both recognized a streak of clever.

"Jim, bring your suitcases up here on the porch while I finish pushing these dinner plates down the steps."

"Be pleased to, sir." He brought his suitcases up the twenty-four stairs and sat in a rocking chair with wide armrests. It took some time to get the dinner plates off the porch and down thirty-two wide steps.

Nothing was said until the man finished and returned to the porch. "Since you're here, might as well have some breakfast with me and the missus. Have you eaten anything?"

"Ate some before sun came up." Since he wasn't in the north anymore, he could leave out a word or two and still be understood perfectly.

"Hold the door and we'll get your gear." They went inside and the man put the suitcases beside the door. "We're in the back, here."

He followed. The man was thin and wore tan pants and a tan shirt, same as most farmers but different. His pants and shirt were starched and ironed. His boots had a high shine—looked like he even polished his belt.

He followed the man through two curtains that covered a doorway. They walked into a large kitchen, where a woman was standing in front of a stove. She turned and smiled. "Well, who do we have here?"

"Said his name was Jimsir."

"Well, that's an unusual name." She smiled. "He does that to everybody that's got any manners. My name is Grace, and this skinny old man is Albert. Bet he didn't introduce himself. Why didn't you introduce yourself to Jim?"

"He didn't ask."

"Found Albert in the woods; been with him near forty years. He's pleasant enough, but don't take well to direction."

"Most of her time is took up with directing; does iron good." Mr. Albert and Miss Grace smiled at each other. They both moved around the kitchen and put quite a spread on the table. Mr. Albert put a large white plate in front of him. Steam was coming off the biscuits and white gravy. Slab of country ham and grits were next to a small bowl of red-eye gravy. He kept his hands in his lap and waited for them to sit. "Mighty kind of you to share breakfast with a stranger."

Mr. Albert looked at him. "Look familiar to me."

Miss Grace poured a glass of milk and set it next to his plate. "It's been a while since we've had a proper guest, one that knows polite pleasantries."

Miss Grace was a gifted cook and of the same stripe as Miss Betty. He thought of the grand feast of conversation and food that would come forth should they ever meet.

All at the table ate quietly for a few moments. About a third of the way through each plate, a warm conversation began with Miss Grace complimenting him on his manners, and she asked where he learned them. Comfortably tucked into the visiting were questions that were difficult to answer. The gentle questions fell within groups of who, what, where, and how.

"Did someone drop you off at our steps?"

"No ma'am, I walked from the concrete road."

"In the dark?"

"Yes, ma'am."

"Did the coyotes come after you?"

"Yes, ma'am."

"Coyotes killed every dog in town. We all decided not to get any more dogs. How did you manage?"

He pulled out a rock from his coat pocket. "These."

Mr. Albert leaned forward. "Grown men don't walk on that road after dark unless they have a shotgun. This is a bad time of year with all the loose corn in the fields. Lucky you made it."

"Yes sir. Got crowded a might some."

He knew more questions were coming. He decided to introduce himself in a different way. He told them he was born in the boot section of their store. Eating, conversation, and questions stopped; an uncomfortable silence seemed to last longer than a moment. They were looking at him without expression, and then the light flickered in their eyes, followed by big smiles. He had heard every detail of his birth and the fact that his mother and Miss Grace really didn't need the doctor.

They told him more about his mother, and he hung on to every word. Miss Grace said that she and Mr. Albert were upset when they found out that his father had left him "at that shack with that awful man. You had been there two and a half years before we found out. Albert called your Aunt Eunice, and she went and got you."

He knew his mother had "gone away" in the hot part of last summer and he had been at the shack until the first edge of winter. It didn't seem right to correct; he listened.

Mr. Albert began talking about his mother. "Your mother was well thought of in this part of the county. She had a smile and a kind word that she gave out freely and often. People up and down the river came to see her off. It was August twenty-six of nineteen and fifty-one—over three years now. It was a Sunday about midafternoon."

He looked down at the white plate and couldn't recall the names of the food. There was a trembling inside that spread out to his hands. He put them in his lap. Thoughts were bumping into each other and were distant from his throat.

They both knew something distressful was happening to their guest. "Albert, me and Jim will finish up back here. 'Bout time to open the store."

"Old men talk about past times more than not…meant no harm jabbering about tender subjects."

"No offense taken, Mr. Albert." Mr. Albert went through the curtains.

Miss Grace leaned over and touched his shoulder. "Try to eat the rest of your breakfast. Common things help steady the mind." Miss Grace sat quietly until he finished his plate. "You had a spell. I've had a few—too much stuff in your head and no place to put it. Doin' a chore helps. I'll wash and you dry, and I'll tell you where things go."

There were empty buckets of questions and not enough memory to fill them. They went slowly, and he kept his mind on common things. He didn't think about before or after. He dried each dish as if it were the only one.

After the dishes, Miss Grace came up with one more chore. She handed him a broom. "This is my outside broom. See if you can sweep the leaves off the back porch, and I'll bring us something to drink when you're finished."

Miss Grace was wiping down the table when he went out the back door with the broom. He stepped onto the porch. The task would not be a quick one. The porch extended out fifteen feet and ran the forty-foot width of the structure. There were four-by-four upright posts on the two outside corners that went up four and a half feet above the porch floor. Three additional posts divided the outside edge into ten-foot spaces. A metal pipe an inch-and-a-half in diameter ran in two horizontal rows that passed through round holes in the posts, creating a railing that surrounded the elevated porch. There were six rocking chairs with slatted backs, wide armrests, and curved wooden seats.

He faced the river and watched it flow from his right to his left, heading south. The cottonwood trees were in a line even with the outside wall of the store, which left a clear view, from the porch, of the river in both directions. He knew things about the river and its effect on people. The river smell was familiar, and he knew if he looked at the river for more than a moment it would charm his eyes and dull his mind and he would find himself standing motionless. He looked at the leaves. They were still falling, making dancing shadows on the ground's brittle carpet. They came down in a gentle angle from the north, following the subtle breeze of air pulled along by the southward flow of the river.

He started sweeping just to the left of the door where the leaves were ankle deep and pushed them under the railing on the south end of the porch. He turned and faced the north and swept to his left, moving to the front edge of the porch. He returned to the outside wall and walked sideways to the edge behind the broom…back to the wall and back to the edge. He reached the rocking chairs and put them on the swept floor behind him. The north side of the porch went faster, and he had pushed the last of the leaves over the edge when Miss Grace came out on the porch.

"You did a proper job. Good to see a young man that can put in a steady lick."

Miss Grace put two large cups with handles on the floor next to the edge at the side of the porch. He leaned the broom next to the back door and put four of the rocking chairs back in the center of the porch. Miss Grace moved one of the two remaining chairs next to one of the cups. He did the same. They were sitting five feet from the edge, facing the river. He picked up the cup and smelled the steam—hot apple cider. His hands were warm around the cup. They rocked slowly and watched the river. He could hear the hollow scraping sound of leaves landing on the wood floor behind him. He didn't want to look but counted up to thirty seconds between sounds. This was a two-times-a-day job.

Miss Grace drank her cider and he his. The river was fascinating to watch and was a good reward for a chore completed. Across from where they sat, the river was three quarters of a mile wide. The color remained the same: coffee with a lot of cream. The water flowed and swirled in eddies, causing branches and debris to change direction as they passed by the funnels.

The fronts of coal barges appeared around a bend to the south, along with a large white tugboat heading north, pushing the barges against the current. He counted fifteen with three abreast. The fronts of the lead barges churned and pushed the light brown water to white, with trails of foam passing down their sides in a steady wave. Coal barges were giant rectangular hollow hunks of metal that sank nine to twelve feet below the surface, depending on the height of the pile of black cargo. He and Miss Grace watched, rocked and drank. The barges pushed past slowly. The sun reflected off the smooth black surfaces of the coal piles. A man in a long white apron came out a side door of the boat, threw potato peelings from a large metal bowl and disappeared inside the boat.

The propellers dug through the river and pushed water out the back of the tugboat. Each turn of the blades pushed water four feet above the surface. Spinning barrels of water shot up and rolled, crashing on the surface.

He wanted to stay with Miss Grace and Mr. Albert in the structure where he was born but sensed he would learn about the fourth next before the coal barges were out of sight. He thought about offering his services as a leaf sweeper for room and board. He could be courteous and helpful to the customers and keep dust off the items on the shelves.

It would not be up to him like so many times before. He would have made wiser choices than the previous decision makers. Each next had a beginning and an end. The beginning was "where" and the end was "how long." Between the two, parades of faces and personalities moved through events ranging from nothingness to heart-pounding terror. He drank the last of the cider and waited for Miss Grace to speak. He watched the river and the falling leaves.

"Mr. Albert called your Uncle Elbert's house." He appreciated the wonderful breakfast and didn't mind the chores but had difficulty focusing on Miss Grace's words—Uncle Elbert was at work…Aunt Sue had the day of the week mixed up…He was expected late tonight. He didn't hear who was expecting him or their connection to him.

"Miss Grace, the breakfast was a fine one." He handed her the cup with the large handle. "Like to finish up with the porch."

He pulled the rocking chair in line with the other four and made a quick estimate of the number of dead dinner plates on the porch floor. There were too many to pick up by hand and not enough to use the broom. He decided not to use the broom and would use the extra time to gather his thoughts. He used the long stems to hold ten leaves at a time and dropped them over the north side rail. He counted each leaf and, when he reached ten, he would drop them over the rail and start again. Counting provided structure for the unknown, a frame to place new information and a reminder to imagination not to run ahead. Forty and drop. Forty-one.

"I'll leave you to your work." Miss Grace went inside with the two cups with large handles.

He guessed he had enough time to finish the porch, put the broom away and gather the two suitcases. It would start again. The vehicle would arrive, driven by an unknown face. He would get in and look out the back window and watch the last next fade in the distance. Thinking about it made him feel tired and numb. He remembered the resignation in the face of the watcher and the vacuum of the silent woman's face. Their journey had likely begun from an uncaring fatigue. It was difficult to resist the mind-numbing repetition that filled the space between "where" and "how long."

He finished the leaves and brought the outside broom back into the kitchen and put it in its place. He heard Miss Grace's voice beyond the curtain door; she was helping a customer in the store. His suitcases were sitting to the right of the curtained doorway. He opened the canvas suitcase to check the contents of the tin pail. The items had been replaced with two candy bars and an assortment of stick candy; he counted eleven sticks. Miss Grace had been generous.

He took a deep breath and looked around the empty kitchen. *Would this qualify as a next? If this were a next, then others would need to be included in the count and by nightfall how many would that be?* The kitchen felt safe, and he was avoiding picking up the suitcases and passing through the curtained door to the start of the newest next. *This would not be the last next, and nothing could be worse than the shack.* With those two thoughts, he passed through the curtains with the suitcases in hand.

He saw Miss Grace to his left, helping a lady with thin brown pouches that held dress patterns. Mr. Albert was to the right at the cash register, pushing down on large keys and pulling down the handle on the right side of the machine. His customer laid a white cloth pouch of tobacco and a long twist of chewing tobacco on the counter. He was wearing gumboots that went up to just below his knees—a fisherman he guessed.

Miss Grace came over to him. "Are you ready? You're pretty much an expert at this by now."

"Yes ma'am, more than most. None of my choosing. Thank you for the candy, the breakfast, and the company."

"You are most welcome and thank you for helping with the chores."

Mr. Albert finished with the customer and came around the counter. "Jimsir, you're a wayfaring pilgrim in a strange land." He shook Mr. Albert's hand and they smiled. He picked up the suitcases and headed for the front porch. He didn't ask for a name or description—it would be a stranger.

He put the suitcases out of sight on the far end of the porch. He sat in the same rocking chair as before, the one just to the left of the door. He looked to the right at the suitcases. He could tell imagination was beginning to spin a yarn involving the circus, the bearded lady, and cleaning elephant poop. Left unattended, imagination tended to end up running into the darkness, screaming. An agreement was reached: imagination would participate in the screening process limited to those who came up the thirty-two steps.

The first of the possible candidates passed by in trucks pulling empty boat trailers. They were heading toward the river to retrieve their boats after fishing through the night. Most had been fishing for bottom feeders, primarily catfish. Night fisherman had what looked like three-sided outhouses built up in their boats; each wall had a window. They sat in a chair inside the structure to stay out of the wind. Most of the night fishermen carried pistols or hammers to kill the catfish, which ranged from thirty to one hundred pounds. All but two-night fishermen had pulled out of town, and the other two had pulled their boats under two separate houses standing side by side on stilts. He watched them carry the fish to a wooden table behind the structures and begin gutting the fish.

Three more trucks pulling boats were coming down the gravel road into town. The day fishermen were arriving. Two trucks with boats passed the store; the last truck stopped in front of the steps to the porch. Behind the truck was a green, flat-bottom metal boat with a black motor hanging on the back. The truck was red, and the body sat up more than a foot above large tires. A fifth tire was secured to the outside of the truck bed, just behind the right door. The side of the hood had large chrome letters: "POWER WAGON."

The engine was running, and two men were sitting in the truck. The man in the passenger side had a long, unkempt beard and a large tear in the right shoulder of his coat. The driver leaned down and looked up through the passenger window at the porch. The driver wore a light-colored, wide-brimmed felt hat with white sweat stains above the brim. These were large men, but the driver was bigger than the passenger. The driver's right hand was the size of a small ham.

He felt uneasy sitting on the porch. He stood up and stepped inside the store and stood looking through the large plate glass door. The truck door opened, and the man with the beard got out and closed the door. The man's hands were flat against the truck door as he leaned in the open window, talking to the driver. The man's hands were dirty, with blackness under his fingernails, and his pants had black and brown stains. The bearded man turned and looked up at the steps and door. *This was not Aunt Eunice.* The man began walking toward the river.

He saw the small ham hand move the gearshift lever that came out of the floor of the truck. The top edge of the driver's door swung forward, and the man's hat began to rise above the cab of the truck. The hat turned, and he saw the man's face, neck, and the upper part of his chest above the cab of the truck. The man looked to be over six-and-a-half-feet tall, with wide shoulders and a barrel chest. An angled shadow across the man's eyes moved with the felt hat. The door closed on the truck, and the man came around the back of the boat. The man and the hat stood at the bottom of the steps, half-lit vertically by the sun on his right. The man's shadow wrapped around the stair rail and darkened the gravel on the edge of the road leading to the river.

The man with the hat began climbing up the center of the stairs. He was wearing farmer clothes with a matching coat. As the man watched his step on the stairs, the brim of his hat covered his face. He had been staring at the man since he had seen the right, small-ham hand through the passenger window of the truck. He stood motionless, staring out the plate glass door. The man's size and the possible mystery of what would happen next had charmed his eyes and dulled his mind like staring at the river too long.

As the man reached the porch and the brim of his hat rose, he saw the man's eyes. The man's right arm came up; at the end of it was the ham with fingers. The man placed his thumb under the front edge of the hat's brim with his forefinger on top and gave a subtle nod. He moved to his right past the door hinges, and the man opened the door. As the door swung open, the plate glass was between him and the man. The man stepped into the store, turned to the right and closed the door with his right hand. The man did not look at him but walked to the counter where Mr. Albert stood. "Albert."

"Junior." *The giant man with hams on the end of his arms was "Junior."* It made part of his mouth grin. "I've come to collect a small boy that travels about."

"You must be looking for Jimsir."

"That's an unusual name."

"Yes sir, heard it from his own mouth." He had heard clever old men bantering and poking around pot-bellied stoves and ranked these two as slightly above average in clever wit. "You might want to ask that fella over there."

They both turned and looked at him. The man had tilted his hat back on his head and revealed a crease across his forehead above kinder eyes than expected. "Those your suitcases tucked away on the far end of the porch?"

"Yes sir."

"So, you a traveling man?"

"Known to be at times."

"Are you waiting on someone?"

"Mostly waiting to see, sir."

Miss Grace came from the back. "Junior, sorry to hear the missus has the sugar."

The man took his hat off and put it over his heart. "I'll tell her you asked about her, Miss Grace. I was about to ask this young man if he would help find a little boy named Jimsir."

"I see you've fallen in with questionable company. His name is Jim, and he's standing right over there listening to you two showing off. Jim, Junior is the biggest man in the county, but I'm not above calling on his mother should his behavior become troublesome." Miss Grace rolled her eyes toward the men and smiled; the men grinned, and he felt less uneasy.

Mr. Junior came toward him, with his hat in his left hand and the other hand extended. He shook Mr. Junior's hand. His hand, wrist, and part of his forearm disappeared into the ham with fingers. Mr. Junior put on his hat and stood up straight and looked down. "Best be goin'. Miss Ellen will be expecting us. Albert, be in on Thursday for feed. Miss Grace, my mother will look forward to your pending visit." He followed the man to the door, turned and waved. They waved back.

Mr. Junior slung the suitcases over his left shoulder—they looked like shoe boxes with handles. He put them in the bed of the truck behind the fifth tire. They got into the truck and headed down the sloped road to the river. Ten feet before the water's edge Mr. Junior made a tight left turn and backed the boat trailer until the trailer tires were half submerged. To the right, he saw the bearded man's back as he peed. The man turned and walked to the back of the truck. Wet spots were all the way down his left pants leg. *Peeing in a cross breeze was never a good idea.* He heard brief cranking sounds.

"Been in a boat?"

"No, sir."

Mr. Junior got out of the truck and looked at him through the window. "It's time." He got out and walked around the front of the truck, away from the bearded man. Mr. Junior lifted him up into the boat and pointed to a metal bench seat. "Sit there."

The bearded man jumped into the boat and headed toward him. He stepped over the bench seat, lowered the propeller into the water and squeezed a black rubber bulb connected to a black hose that ran into the engine. Then the man got out of the boat.

He began to breathe between heartbeats. He had never been in the water, didn't know how to swim, and this was a big river.

To his right was a white steering wheel on the other end of the bench. The metal boat creaked and shifted when Mr. Junior got in; he sat down behind the steering wheel and pushed a black button on the metal plate that held the wheel. The motor smoked and started. After the bearded man unhooked the front of the boat from the trailer, Mr. Junior turned the steering wheel hard to the right, the front of the boat swung left, and the current pulled the boat out into the river. He shifted the lever forward, and the boat went farther out into the river.

173

Mr. Junior handed him a large blue bandana. "Make a triangle and tie it around your nose and mouth to keep the wind off you."

He put the triangle cloth around his neck and tied it in the back. He pulled it up over his nose. *Now I look like a Wild West outlaw.*

The front of the boat was pointing at the sky. Mr. Junior pushed the lever forward, and as the boat sped up, the front came down level with the water and he could see ahead and feel the breeze against his forehead and eyes. His eyes watered from the breeze. He wiped the tears with his coat sleeves. He turned and looked back at the general store and saw the red truck with the empty trailer moving up the bank into town. He saw his two suitcases in the bed of the truck. This was the first time he had been separated from them, especially the blond one that was taller than wide.

The motor had a high-pitched ring. The wind pushed the front brim of Mr. Junior's hat up against the front of his hat. The boat swung to the right and left in slow turns to avoid floating trees and limbs. He felt like a true river man. He buttoned the top of his coat to keep the air from going down his shirt. His legs were protected from the wind by a rectangular box that extended across the middle of the boat.

The high-pitched sound changed, and the boat slowed. The lever to the right of the steering wheel clicked, and the boat drifted forward toward a white object in the water. Mr. Junior moved to the front of the boat with a paddle in his hand. The boat was inching forward just to the left of a white rubber float with streaks of green slime that showed when the current tilted the top.

Mr. Junior used the paddle to lift a half-inch rope tied to a loop on the bottom of the float. When the rope was in hand, the paddle came back into the boat. The rear of the boat began to swing to the right, with the front pointing north into the current. The float and the boat were a little more than a hundred feet from the east bank of the river. He stood up to watch Mr. Junior lifting the rope and moving his hands along the rope toward the shore. The other end of the rope was tied to a large limb of a cottonwood on the shore. The large hands lifted the rope higher.

A smaller fishing line was connected to the rope with metal parts and a piece of lead halfway down to a large hook. Mr. Junior disconnected the fishing line from the rope and placed it in a small metal bucket with the hook resting on the rim of the bucket. His hands moved down the rope and, one by one, placed three more empty hooks on the bucket's rim. There were two more lines with bare hooks. As the hands moved along the rope, the fifth line began to move away from the rope, and the boat began to lean to the right. Mr. Junior placed his right foot on the side of the boat and pulled the rope over the edge; a giant fish head rose above the surface.

The filmy, dark crab-apple-sized eye looked at him. He felt the shiver down his spine, a dark, wet cold. The silent woman's eye was in a creature that lay on the bottom of the river in the darkness with its mouth open, sucking in anything that came near. He came back from the eye and the woman and heard, "Open the lid. Open the lid!"

The latch to the lid was on the side of the box closest to the fish. As he leaned over the box to unhook the latch, he saw the large hand go into the coat. A pistol came out. The fish eye turned away; the sound of the gun made him jump and let go of the latch.

"Now!"

He watched in slow motion the small hams pulling up and the left shoulder going under the fish and flipping it, with the wide tail coming at his face. He lifted the lid, and the tail came over the edge and struck him in the forehead. He fell over his seat and landed against the red gas container with the black bulb and hose that went to the motor. The two-foot-wide tail fin and three feet of the tail stretched above the top edge of the box.

His eyes felt dry; he had not blinked since the giant fish came out of the water. It was as if his eyelids had folded back into his face.

The giant hands continued to move along the rope. He climbed over the seat and stood behind the box with its open lid. *Men and fish were large in this part of the river.* He touched his forehead, and there was blood on his fingers. He took a deep breath and leaned over to look around the open lid. He chose to look at the end of the box without the tail. It was a wide, thick, powerful fish, and he decided never to swim in the river.

Mr. Junior was releasing fish that were twenty pounds or less. They stayed, motionless, just below the surface, and the large hand would push them; they would swim slowly away and down. The last of the lines had been placed in the metal bucket, with the last hook resting on the rim.

Mr. Junior returned to his seat behind the steering wheel. They looked at each other, the giant right hand rose, touching the brim of the hat, and Mr. Junior gave a slight nod. *Mr. Junior didn't talk much, but he was downright gabby compared to Uncle Elbert.* The lever went forward. The wide tail fin waved in the wind. The sun was in the middle of the sky.

The boat weaved around logs and floats one hundred yards or so off the east bank of the river. The trees rained leaves on the water, and waves from the boat sent ripples through the leaf-covered surface. The boat followed the current flowing between the leaf carpet to the left and a large sandbar to the right. The boat was approaching the southwest bend in the river that he had seen from the elevated porch. The tree line on the west bank jutted out, blocking the view beyond the bend.

The boat made a slow turn to the right. He could see coal barges approaching the bend from the south. Churning water in front of the barges looked different—more violent—than it had looked from the elevated porch of the store. The front of the barges made a wave about three feet higher than the top edge of their boat; the wave was approaching at an angle that would strike a glancing blow to the side of the boat. The wave would hit the right front and curl over the right side at a height just below the tail fin of the huge fish in the box.

His left hand was gripping the left side of the boat. The wave was coming, and he planned to stick the fingers of his right hand in Mr. Junior's left coat pocket and make a steel-claw grip with his thumb on the outside of the pocket.

At the last moment Mr. Junior turned the boat toward the barges and took the wave at a slight angle. The front of the boat pointed at the sky, and he leaned forward, holding onto the front edge of the metal bench with his right hand. The force of the wave rolled the giant catfish in the box until the tail fin was vertical, less than a foot from his face. He flinched, and the front of the boat came down hard. Water came into the boat and ran over the top of his boots. The red gas tank floated and scraped the metal sides of the boat and the back of the metal bench; he watched the water level behind the bench.

The wind pulled slimy fish water off the vertical fin, hitting his face and the front of his coat. He pulled the bandana tight around his nose and mouth. Three smaller waves were coming from the tugboat's propellers. The boat bounced three times and moved into smooth water; the high pitch of the motor returned. The bandana was wet with the smell of dead fish.

The boat continued to make the broad turn to the southwest and the river opened up wide. The sun was making the slow climb over his left shoulder and the sunshine had made its way to the upper part of his left forehead. Behind his shoulder the long shadow of the boat raced over the slow-moving carpet of leaves next to the west bank. The hand pushed the lever forward and flat. The boat skimmed on the tops of waves on the surface. The wind dried the fin and pulled the moisture from the bandana, and the smell lessened.

Large amounts of river sand had not made the full turn to the southwest, leaving pockets of sand beaches on the left bank. Large random-shaped driftwood lay on the sand, barkless and gray. He moved to the left side of the bench to see past the large tail fin that had begun to darken and dry. He saw dark moving shapes just below the surface—some larger than the fish in the box.

He could tell the sun would cross in front of the boat from left to right and disappear behind the trees somewhere between west and southwest. The river stretched straight without turns over the horizon. As the river pushed southwest, the sun caught wave-less lumps of water that briefly rose above the flatness. The lighted lumps made fast-moving thumps on the bottom of the boat. Soon he would step off the liquid moving sidewalk and begin the ground journey to the new next.

He knew the new next would lie off the left bank of the river. Mr. Junior told Mr. Albert that he would be back for feed on Thursday, and he had seen no bridges across the river. More than half a mile ahead, he saw a dark shape in the water, close to the left bank. He wondered if this was where the boat ride would end, or was another fisherman pulling in lines from a half-inch rope? It made little difference; he would ride in the boat until it returned to the trailer.

The dark object next to the left bank was less than half a mile away. He still thought Mr. Junior was a farmer, but the fish in the box was the biggest he had ever seen. His head and shoulders would fit in the mouth of the fish, and it looked to be over one hundred pounds. The sun was moving to midafternoon and was directly in front of the boat. He used his right hand as a visor and could see the dark object just below his little finger. It was another boat. He saw movement behind its motor, and the boat quickly disappeared behind low hanging limbs on the left bank.

Mr. Junior swung wide around the limbs and pulled the lever back; the boat slowed. He turned the boat around, facing the northeast, and adjusted the lever to keep the boat in one spot. The motor pushed against the current. He saw the other boat moving up the ramp on a trailer behind a truck.

Mr. Junior stood up and cupped his right hand next to his mouth and gave a yell that started low and ended higher with a yelp. The man with the beard stepped out of the trees on the top left of the ramp and raised his hand high; then he disappeared beyond the ridge. The back of the trailer came over the ridge with the red truck in front, moving down the ramp until the trailer tires were half submerged. Mr. Junior pushed the lever forward and turned the steering wheel right; the boat ran up on the trailer. The bearded man hooked a wire cable to the front of the boat and hand-cranked the boat until the front of the boat was next to the hand crank. Then the man returned to the truck and pulled the boat twenty feet up the ramp and stopped.

Mr. Junior stepped over the right edge of the boat and motioned in his direction. He was lifted out of the boat before the truck pulled the boat and giant fish to the top of the ramp. He followed the huge man up the ramp and wondered if he would be sitting next to the bearded man with no name.

It had been a long night, and the day was approaching mid to late afternoon when the grayness would drop down from the sky and slink out of the woods from the east. The strip that went up the ramp to the back of the boat was wide, damp at the bottom, and wet as it neared the boat. The bearded man with no name was standing in the boat in front of the open lid, inspecting the fish. Mr. Junior reached inside the boat next to the motor and pulled a plug; water shot out. The round stream was brown, black, and green.

He looked up at the bearded man; the top part of his bottom lip was the only mouth he could see. He saw the whiskers move. "Near hundred twenty or so, I reckon." Mr. Junior walked around the back of the boat and headed for the driver's door.

He walked past the bearded, weight-guesser man, opened the passenger door and climbed up into the seat. As he reached for the door handle, he heard the man's boots hit the ground, and the man appeared next to the open door. The man's eyes were a cloudy, whitish color that made it difficult to know his age. His beard grew high on his cheekbones and was unusually close to his eyes. He knew he had forgotten to blink since the man appeared next to the door. The darkness of the beard and the whiteness of the eyes had caused him to stare longer than politeness allowed. He blinked and scooted to the center of the bench seat.

He was next to the driver; the top of his left shoulder was touching just above Mr. Junior's right elbow. The bearded man got in and closed the door. He was shoulder to shoulder with two large men, one larger than the other. His knees were between two gearshifts that came straight up out of the floor and bent toward the seat two thirds up from the floorboard. The two black rods had black knobs on the tops with numbers in white. Mr. Junior pushed in the clutch and moved the longer bent rod toward the dashboard. The truck rolled backward and then moved forward along a narrow gravel road that had more dirt than gravel. Mr. Junior pushed down on the clutch; he moved when the rod and knob came back toward the inside of his left knee and stopped, uncomfortably close to his lap. The road followed a thick, winding line of trees on the left and a field of corn stubble on the right. The gearshift went forward toward the dashboard.

He looked back through the back window of the cab at the fish tail and fin. He knew the men would start gutting the fish soon, and he wanted to see the fish laid out to its full length. It was better thinking about seeing the fish than thinking about the new next. Nexting was a fluid experience of passing through without colliding. There would be plenty of time to deal with the differently familiar next. A one-hundred-twenty-plus-pound fish was likely to be something he would never see again. *The fish was now; next was later.*

The road and trees made a sharp turn to the right and a slow gradual turn to the left and headed east for two miles. The fish followed the truck on an elbow turn to the south for three miles and followed left on a dirt road that ended at a shack in the center of a field with rows of soybean stubble.

Inside the tear that was forming in his left eye he could see the distorted movement of children appearing to the left and right of a heavyset man in overalls with no shirt. The silent woman was floating behind and moving to the far right of the porch. The tear let go of his eye, and his right index finger pushed the wet spot deep into the fabric of his coat. The truck pulled around the empty porch to the back of the shack.

The truck, the trailer, and the fish had gone around the right side of the shack, past where the liquid image of the silent woman had stood. There was no porch or couch at the back of the shack. The back door was center and high on the wall, with no step. Flat boards had been laid on the ground from the door, angling slightly to the left leading to an outhouse that stood twenty yards beyond a shed at the center back edge of an untended back yard.

His window passed close to the shed, and the fish stopped just to the left of the structure. Both men got out of the truck. The bearded man left the door open; he stepped out and closed the door. The bearded man came out of the shed with a wooden stepladder and stood the ladder next to a thick pipe connected to the corner of the shed. The top of the pipe rose ten feet above the top of the shed. Then the two men went behind the shed and carried out a pipe that had been welded into the shape of an "L." Together they maneuvered the L-shaped pipe until the bearded man could climb the ladder and slip the bottom of the L into the upright pipe connected to the shed.

He knew the men were going to hang the fish from the pole. He had been standing near the front of the truck, watching. He moved around the front and climbed up into the bed on the shack side of the truck.

The man with the beard was pulling the last of the logging chain out of a wooden box. The bottom of the box had a smaller chain in a loop and a rectangular scale with a hook on the top and bottom. The man handed it to Mr. Junior, and he slid the loop of chain over the end of the pipe. Mr. Junior's right hand reached into the fish box and pulled out the fish by its left gill and hooked the scale inside the right gill. Mr. Junior eased the giant fish over the side of the truck. The pole creaked and settled. The man with the beard climbed the stepladder and looked at the scale. "One twenty-four. Near six foot long."

He was proud to have seen such a creature. The bearded man headed down the board path, opened the back door, wrapped both hands around the inside door facing and pulled himself into the shack. Mr. Junior walked to the shack and stood at the door. The man inside was passing items out the door, and Mr. Junior was placing them on the long-matted grass next to the back wall.

He turned and looked at the fish. Its belly was white with a tint of yellow. The head moved down flat from the cavernous mouth. The eyes were no longer hooked to a living brain but remained unchanged in the fading light. He and the fish were motionless. Like the river, he had stared at the fish too long.

He climbed out of the truck bed and helped carry items from the shack. The legs of a kitchen table were being angled out the opening of the door. Then the men stacked items on the table and carried it to the fish. Shadows began to stretch out, and the sun would soon begin to color the air. The bearded man carried an oil lamp up the ladder, tied it to the pipe with baling wire and slid it close to the fish. He lifted the glass and lit the lamp from a box of matches, then dropped the box on the table below. Mr. Junior removed six five-gallon metal buckets from the table and lit two more oil lamps from the box of matches.

The bearded man came down the ladder, and the two men began sharpening two long knives and one meat cleaver. The man went up the ladder with a long, narrow-bladed knife and started on the head. He made a deep circular cut behind the eyes and dropped the first cheek into the bucket closest to the ladder. Mr. Junior took it out of the bucket and placed it on the table, then sliced off the skin and dropped it into a bucket under the table. The second cheek fell, and the skin was removed.

The insides of the fish were cut out and dropped with a liquid thud. Both men turned away before the guts hit the ground. He did not and used most of both coat sleeves to see again; he climbed back into the truck bed to watch from a safer distance. Fins were cut from the body including the fin that ran along the back, now curled and darkened.

Sections were removed from the sides and choice cuts from the white belly. Mr. Junior's large hands moved quickly, removing skin and chopping sections with the cleaver.

The man came down from the ladder with the knife and stood next to the table looking down at the full buckets on the ground. He looked at his table with the blood and gashes from the cleaver. The front of the man's head faced the table just above one of the lamps, and his eyes looked up at the bed of the truck where he stood. The knife was in the man's hand, and his gray pupils were slivers below his upper eyelids. The carcass of the fish with the giant head hung behind him.

The man stuck the knife in the table and picked up two buckets and headed toward the bed of the truck. He moved to the far side of the truck bed before the man put the first bucket in the bed. Both men finished loading the buckets and began rinsing their hands from a hand pump at the right corner of the shack. Mr. Junior moved the handle, and the other man put his beard under the spout; pieces of fish fell out.

Mr. Junior's body was beyond the edge of the shack's shadow. In the field beyond the fish and outhouse, he saw the working shadow of Mr. Junior moving the pump handle up and down. The hanging oil lamp lit the fish head against the fading, flat orange air above the field. Pieces of fish no longer fell from the beard.

Mr. Junior put a blue bandana under the spout and walked to the truck. "Wipe your face and sleeves." He did. They got into the truck and pulled past the wet beard. He looked out the back window for one last glimpse of the hanging creature with the huge lighted head.

He turned and saw through Mr. Junior's window as they passed the pump. The windshield was filled with the last of the orange above the trees. The truck and trailer crossed the stubble ridges at an angle, and both bodies moved left and right with the metal buckets until the truck settled on the dirt road beyond the field. He saw the purple pass over the truck and press hard against the orange. The purple sat on top of the trees. The truck turned left.

He looked out his window and watched the orange sink down through the trees and travel away to other woods to the west. Two white bands of light stretched out in front of the truck, heading south. He felt relieved to be away from the moving rod and knob that came up from the floor. The lighted gages glowed on Mr. Junior's large face. His hat touched the ceiling. His nose was shorter than Uncle Elbert's; their lips moved the same seldom.

Somewhere in the purple blackness beyond the two bands of light lay the next. The biscuits, red-eye gravy, and country ham of breakfast had burned away. Hunger began to speak.

Hunger had learned to shout silently. Life on the couch shaped thoughts of food as a privilege and taught him to wait patiently and to graze quietly. He knew a body as large as Mr. Junior's required fuel to move. There would be food where he lived and water.

The salt-cured ham of breakfast had left his lips dry, and his tongue hunted for moisture in his mouth. He put his right hand in his coat and searched the bottom of the pocket for a round pebble that he hoped had made its way down through the throwing rocks. He pulled out one and wiped away grit and gravel dust with his thumb and forefinger and put it in his mouth. He tasted the dirt and dust, and the pebble stuck to his tongue. Moisture soaked into the pebble and sealed the surface. He began moving it across the roof of his mouth with his tongue and pushed it into his right cheek, resting against the outside of his bottom teeth. Life on the couch had provided a rich education and moisture in his mouth.

His eyelids were heavy. He wiped his finger on his coat and placed it on his tongue and spread the moisture on his top eyelids. He felt more alert. He had done this many times while sitting on the couch, staring at the dark woods when noises woke him in the night.

He felt less fear about the next. Mr. Junior was fiercely huge but had a quiet, kind nature. He knew the man was a farmer. People who worked the land spoke little and worked hard. They were not prone to exaggeration and saw usefulness in things that had lost their shine.

The meat in the buckets needed to be prepared and frozen. Next needed to be soon. He sat quietly with the pebble in his mouth. Imagination had been entertained all day and reclined peacefully. There had been no lights from other cars on the road. Deep woods on the left with a more than quarter moon faintly racing through the trunks. Open fields on the right.

They continued south past the last of the woods on the left and a light at the peak of a barn, followed by a white house. The truck turned left into a drive. They passed a lighted screened porch on the left before the driveway curved around behind and the front-lit barn appeared in the center of the windshield. The truck stopped.

Mr. Junior got out and lifted two buckets from the driver's side of the bed. He followed the man to the back door and opened it for him and then went inside behind him. He followed Mr. Junior through a room with thick overalls hanging above pairs of rubber overshoes. Faint odors traveled behind the strong fish-bucket smells—a hint of dirt and dry cow manure. The next room was a brightly lighted kitchen where the buckets were placed on the floor to the left of a large sink.

He followed Mr. Junior to the truck and went in front of him to the back door and opened it. This time he stayed outside and returned to the truck to get his suitcases. He had them on the ground next to the back right tire when Mr. Junior returned for the last two buckets. After he opened the back door and closed it behind Mr. Junior, he returned to the suitcases. He wasn't sure what to do, so he waited next to the tire. *Probably should go in and introduce myself to Miss Ellen.* He would go in and be polite and smile and the next would begin. He felt strangely more comfortable outside, with the barn light and the soft light from the side screen of the front porch.

He sat on his original suitcase and leaned back on the tire. The smell of fish and guts had wrapped around the hairs in his nose. He could picture the giant fish head and tail that hung in the darkness, separated from its flesh—a fish in two places and none.

No one had come to the door to invite him into the house. Common sense would tell him to go in and offer to help. Hunger had its own opinion, and imagination had become bored and philosophical. *Why here and why them?* He knew he would go in, but he would sit a bit longer.

17 – The Screened Porch House

A bit plus piece of time passed by the lighted porch and down the road into the darkness, leaving moments of age behind. He stood up and stepped over the tongue of the trailer and peed in the grass on the far side of the truck. He headed for the back door with the suitcases. He set them down next to the rubber overshoes. A trail of moisture ran under the door to the kitchen, ending behind him where a large freezer sat. He guessed the flesh from the fish was inside. He opened the door to the kitchen; the room was bright. To the left was the round face of a tall heavyset woman who was placing a large pie on top of the stove; she had a thin smile.

Mr. Junior was washing the last bucket in the sink. "Miss Ellen, this is Jim."

"Miss Ellen." He shook the oven mitten on her right hand. She was almost as tall as Mr. Junior.

"You can wash your hands in the sink. The chair is right there."

There had been no time for an invitation to come in the house. The adults had precious little time to wrap and freeze the fish before it spoiled. The bar of soap on the kitchen sink was rough and gritty and his hands and fingernails were dirty. He finished and sat down with his back against the wall, facing the sink.

Miss Ellen was taking biscuits out of the oven. He noticed she was wearing the same kind of pants as Mr. Junior's pants, with a wide, black leather belt. Her shirt was a faded blue.

Mr. Junior sat down to his left, and Miss Ellen poured glasses of milk at all three plates. She set the pie in the center of the table on top of a folded towel that extended out where she put the tray of biscuits.

"Hand me your plate."

He had never had pie with biscuits for supper. She cut a piece and placed it on the plate, along with two biscuits. He put the plate on the table between the fork on the left and the knife on the right with the blade facing the plate and the spoon on the outside. Some of the insides of the pie oozed out of the triangle. It was a meat and vegetable pie—the first he had seen. He waited until the plates were filled and Miss Ellen sat down and said, "Thank the Lord for supper."

Mr. Junior said, "Amen."

The biscuits were better than the pie. Both were hot. *This was not Miss Betty's cooking.* He ate with interest.

He saw Mr. Junior glance several times at Miss Ellen. They were slow movements of the eyes while facing the plate.

He had learned the art of observation without expectation. He knew the basics before his fork had entered and exited the pie for the third time. Miss Ellen was deciding, and Mr. Junior was watching. Miss Ellen wasn't really deciding—she was rearranging details on top of a decision. Mr. Junior was hoping for participation in a different decision. There was the soft sound of forks on plates, with no words.

He focused on the food. A good biscuit was a thing of beauty. It was an honest food with substance that often-held other foods. It was a third hand that held and steadied. The milk was not bought and likely came from somewhere past the sink and beyond the fence. Guernsey, he guessed. He asked for another biscuit, and Mr. Junior put two on his plate. He made sure he finished all of the not-Miss-Betty's pie.

The glasses of milk were empty, and the dishes were being washed; Mr. Junior was drying. He sat quietly in the chair with his coat on, with pockets of rocks on both sides and dried and curled pieces of fish flesh and guts on the sleeves.

Politeness suggested the lack of conversation stemmed from rudeness and indifference. He believed the "no words" was part of everyday life. Lives focused on completing the endless chores that supported the important activities of tending to crops and cattle. Lengthy conversations were limited to practical matters involving farming. Non-physical, private feelings were expected to remain as such. Physical pain was to be discussed when it related to one's ability to complete daily chores.

The fish Mr. Junior caught was more than likely his largest. He guessed there was no great excitement expressed when the buckets began to arrive on the kitchen floor. Miss Ellen knew it was a big fish; there were six five-gallon buckets. Comments about the obvious were not necessary. The task at hand was to process and freeze the contents before they spoiled.

His connection to Mr. Junior and Miss Ellen remained a mystery. Their titles suggested no family connection. His experience with family had narrowed to bloodlines and titles. He had been invited to think he was a single entity viewed as other. The invitation was a whispering mist floating close, always with audible fingers he brushed away by choice. It was an invitation he had not accepted.

The dishes were done, and Miss Ellen turned and spoke. "Get your suitcases and I'll show you the room." He did. As he passed the table with the suitcases, Mr. Junior touched his shoulder. He looked up at him and smiled.

Miss Ellen wore boots and he watched them move in front of him. They were worn rough, without smoothness or shine. They moved across the room past the front door, which stood between double, porch-lit windows on the right and smaller windows to the left. The room was the first on the right in a hallway that moved through the center of the remaining first floor. He stopped at the open doorway. Miss Ellen continued down the hallway and stopped just past a doorway on the opposite wall. "The bathroom is here."

He nodded and stepped through the doorway into the bedroom. He put the suitcases down and turned and stood in the door, facing the hallway. "Thank you for supper."

"You're welcome. Pie didn't turn out. Clean towel in the chifforobe." As she passed the door, Miss Ellen's face was round and tall with a smile greater than thin. It was a comfort to him.

He turned and faced the porch-lit window. The front screened porch extended across the house from corner to corner. A long bench sat on the porch next to the outside windowsill. He saw the warm shadow of sleep sitting quietly next to the front door. After bedtime chores, he hoped the warmth would sit with him until light.

The last night was long and the day full; bedtime chores were brief. This time he did not memorize the room or the doors. This night he would not review each of the journeys or prepare for the unexpected. The warmth came quickly and sat quietly through the night. There were soft, no-memory dreams with distant movement and faint colors.

His nose moved with breakfast smells. Muffled conversation came through the door along with dim light from the hallway. Darkness pressed flat against the porch-side of the bedroom window. The bed faced north, the window was to his left, and the chifforobe

187

stood tall and dark to his right. To the right of the foot of his bed was the open door that funneled the angled light across the bed. He closed his eyes and drifted off again before countless thoughts stood and began to speak at once.

As he drifted, the images came…the warm shadow of sleep stood and petted the mane of the mare of night. The night horse stomped its hooves on the wooden floor and slung its head. The peaceful warmth stepped back, and the eyes of the mare stared at the bed and the sleeping face. Inside the eyelids, liquid images swirled around…his feet buried in ankle-deep frozen mud, facing the shack. The dead fish stood in front of the couch and watched coyotes sniffing his ankles in the mud. His eyes and lids pushed out the images along with two large tears. He gasped and sat up with a sense of someone dark coming soon.

His eyes were open, and he quickly separated from the bed. Standing, he smoothed the sheets and pulled the spread over the pillow. Both sides of the spread were even with the floor. The house was quiet, and the window remained dark.

He turned right down the hallway and left into the bathroom. He splashed water on his face and avoided looking at the mirror. He peed and washed his hands carefully. There were spots of dried blood under some of his fingernails. Habit and fear fed the nighttime leg-sore scratching. Parts of his pajamas were glued to his legs; he hoped there were no blood spots on the sheets. He would begin to put salve on them tonight before the infection and fever returned. He put on new clothes from the original suitcase and folded the dirty underwear inside yesterday's pants and shirt.

Yesterday was the day of the great fish, and his clothes had yesterday's smell. He decided he would leave them on the floor next to the rubber overshoes. He carried them down the hallway toward the kitchen. He passed through the kitchen filled with lingering breakfast smells but no breakfast or people.

He went back through the kitchen, put on his coat, returned through the kitchen a third time and walked out the back door. He brushed the dried debris off both sleeves. There were lights on in the barn. The red truck and the green boat were gone. A shadow was moving inside the barn, and he heard a long, high-pitched "woooo" sound. The gate to the barn swung open with the shadow following behind it. Faint sounds of slow shuffling hooves on dirt were coming from the south. He turned to his right and saw the first of a long, single-file line of large shadows coming out of the darkness. They moved slowly and turned right into the barn under the outside light at the peak. All that turned right had rusty red bodies with white faces. Miss Ellen was feeding cattle; he counted twenty-seven cows and one bull.

Mr. Junior and Miss Ellen started their day while the chickens were still sleeping. Tomorrow he would do the same. Tomorrow he would have breakfast with the workers rather than deal with a hooved roommate bringing a standing fish and sniffing coyotes.

He went inside and hung his coat in the chifforobe. He put the suitcases on the bed and opened them. He decided he would call this stop the "Screened Porch House" next. He knew not to unpack the suitcases. Everything fit well and had its place. Nexting was never a question of "if." It could be found traveling the road to "when."

He placed his palms and fingers flat on the suitcases. He looked down, then closed his eyes. Powerful emotions rolled up from his feet and fell out of his chest and splashed down on his hands with a moan from another voice—a voice from an ancient before.

His mind spun and shot past the pole in the bus and left his body standing on the left side of the bed in the hospital room. Her hair was brown, damp, and flat against her head, with a curl above her shoulder. Her skin was pale and tight on her face. She turned and raised her arms and hands toward him. She said there was no pain. She looked frightened. He put his cheek next to hers. Her arms stayed open until he was pulled away and out of the room. No one said, but he knew this would be the last time he would see her. The next morning, she left, and the black phone rang.

After the phone spoke and the receiver returned to its cradle, the journey had begun. The man with the kind and gentle face said the journey would be long. With effort, he had been able to account for all of the nexts. Mr. Albert's comment regarding his length of stay at the shack was troublesome. He remembered events at the shack when his senses opened wide and extended beyond alertness. Those were events that he saw before they happened, and when they happened, they were in slow motion and allowed close inspection of every detail. He wasn't sure if a moment became an hour or an hour folded in on itself and became a second. *Between events when my senses steadied, did time return in its original form?*

There had been the brief seconds with his cheek next to hers. She had begun to leave before he reached the bed, and her eyes followed him for less than a second as he was pulled away. He wanted her eyes to follow his exit. They did not. At that moment he had felt unimportant and alone. The feeling held tight and remained long.

Standing with his hands flat against the open suitcases, the fist around his mind loosened and the answer came. The hospital room was her world, and the bed was her home. The hours were short, and little was left. She was alone. He would put his cheek next to hers often and she would not be alone, and he would feel less unimportant.

He grabbed the two brushes and the paste and went into the bathroom. He brushed his teeth and hair. He remembered Miss Grace's words: "Common things help steady the mind." The back door closed, and the kitchen door opened. He closed the suitcases and put them on the floor between the window and bed.

He headed for the kitchen and saw Miss Ellen pulling her arms and legs out of a pair of heavy, one-piece overalls. She had on an extra pair of heavy socks that were fastened to the outside cuff of her pants with two large safety pins. She undid the safety pins and put the socks inside a pair of rubber overshoes. He thought he should say something. "Counted twenty-seven cows and one bull."

She closed the kitchen door. "Feeder cattle; another fifty head in the back pasture. Bring them up when we sell the feeders. You missed breakfast."

"Yes ma'am."

"Are you a city boy?"

"No ma'am."

Miss Ellen was washing her hands in the sink without looking back. "If I fix something, could you eat?"

"Be pleased to, Miss Ellen."

"No need standing there. Get you a glass out of that cabinet. Pitcher of milk in the icebox."

He knew it wasn't a real icebox. It had an electric motor and a cord. The glass of milk was on the table, and things were frying in three skillets. He figured the conversation was over, so he sipped the milk and watched the steam float up from the skillets. One of the smells from the stove was hard to identify.

The flames from the burners were out, and the steam hovered just above the rims of the skillets. The contents of the pans were scooped up onto a white plate that came toward him with Miss Ellen's hand and body attached. There was a sliding thud, and the face of the plate looked at him. He tried not to look at one of the items—the one with the smell. There were two round fried mashed potato patties and the two faces of a biscuit with brown, watery gravy on top. The third item was the leg and hip of an animal that was not chicken. It was the size of a small cat or large rodent.

His brain and stomach were discussing how to proceed. He started with a mashed potato patty. The gravy on the biscuit had lumps of flour surrounded by brown grease. Grease dripped off the bone at the end of the leg, just above where the animal's paw had been. He could see through the upper left of his eyelashes that Miss Ellen was standing between him and the stove. He could see her belt buckle.

"This sure is good, Miss Ellen." He wasn't going to ask. He picked up the leg and bit through the tight skin. His teeth hurt. He pulled three lead pellets from his mouth and put them on the edge of the plate. The animal was shot and killed with a shotgun.

"Might want to watch for buckshot."

"Yes ma'am." He still wasn't going to ask. Thirteen lead pellets later, he had finished the meat. He had saved one mashed potato patty to leave a familiar taste in his mouth. After eating the shotgun-murdered leg, finishing the not-Miss-Betty's pie from last night seemed less of an accomplishment.

He thanked Miss Ellen for the breakfast. He went to the bathroom and rinsed his mouth out, then he returned to help dry breakfast dishes. The sun was coming up in the bottom center of the window over the sink. The wire pasture fence ran left and right some fifty yards beyond the window.

The barn was to the left at an angle. The last of the cattle were walking slowly away from the barn down a cow path that led to the pasture on the right. Straight out the window beyond the second wire fence was a deep wood of large trunks and bare limbs, with a sprinkle of green from small cedars. It would take the sun a half hour before it topped the tree line and made the first fence shadows. He handed the last skillet to Miss Ellen, and she put it inside a cabinet below the counter and left of the sink.

He recognized whining gears and the truck motor before both sounds stopped and doors opened and closed. Three men walked in the back yard directly between the window and the barn; Mr. Junior was one of them. Miss Ellen left the kitchen, took her coat off the hook next to the overalls and joined the men.

There was standing, talking, and pointing. Next came pacing off a distance and measuring. All four disappeared from the window and came back with six concrete footings and a wheelbarrow filled with large gravel. The footings were shaped like pyramids with flat tops and foot-long sides. The man with the beard who had cut the fish had one shovel, and a second man had the other. They dug six square holes and filled them with gravel and placed the footings on top. They worked quickly.

He stood at the sink for hours and watched the floor, walls, and roof appear. They wrapped the outside walls with black tar paper and cut a hole in the roof for a metal stove chimney. They finished the inside walls and ceiling and covered the roof with tin. They framed and hinged a door in the front. All of the tools and scrap lumber were picked up, and all four disappeared from the window. He heard the truck start and drive away. The back door didn't open.

He stood at the sink for a long time before he saw Miss Ellen pushing a wheelbarrow along the second fence line. The sun was directly overhead, and there were no fence shadows. Miss Ellen was nailing large metal staples to connect the wire to the wooden fence posts. Over time the wire would rust, and cattle would rub against the posts and barbed wire to relieve itches. Farmers either fixed fences or spent time chasing cows. He watched Miss Ellen work her way down the fence to the edge of the window and disappear.

He got his coat out of the chifforobe and went out the back door to inspect the shed. He could smell the fresh-cut wood and tar paper. Most sheds didn't have chimneys. *Was it a storage shed, or people shed?*

He hoped the man with the beard would not live in the back yard; the man with the beard was scary. He had seen scary before. The man with the beard was "keep your eye on him" scary. The man with the beard was not "keep your eye on him before he kills you" scary. He knew the difference. He had lived it. The bearded man had his own shack. He bet the bony fish still hung from the scale, weighing less but waiting. Waiting for the last buzzard and the dark wind to play a mournful tune through its carcass.

A person was going to live in the shed. He woke this morning with a gasp and the sense of someone dark coming soon. He opened the new door and stepped up into the empty shed. It was built well but felt bad. He got out of the shed and closed the door, hoping his scent left with him.

He would stay out of the back yard. His connection with the shed would be limited to the view from the window above the sink. He would be a front-yard-screened-porch dweller.

He walked away from the shed, around the house and through the screened porch door and sat on the long bench next to the bedroom window. He looked across the road at the empty field. The corner of the pasture fence was to the left, next to the ditch that separated the road from the pasture. He looked straight ahead again and realized he had been looking at the field separated in two by a large oak tree in the front yard. His focus needed to be closer in and away from the horizon line of the next summer and fall. His thoughts were often far away, and his eyes would follow, but they were limited by sight.

It was just past the near edge of winter when objects were colder, and life began to huddle and cover. Soon his time on the screened porch and in the front yard would be in shorter visits. The air would become brittle. He needed something to do for the winter before his body began to live in his mind.

Hensen March

18 – Chicken Hawks

He heard the motor from the north. He turned to his right and saw the red truck through the side screen, traveling south toward the house. It slowed and stopped just past the drive and backed in, even with the back of the house. Mr. Junior came around the corner of the screened porch and through the door. He had two small paper sacks and handed one over. Mr. Junior sat down on the bench, and they ate bologna and cheese sandwiches with two bottles of Coke. There were two thick slices of bologna with cheese in between. The bottom of the sack had a large round chocolate sandwich with the words "Moon Pie" on the wrapper.

"Did the sandwiches come from Miss Grace and Mr. Albert's store?"

"They asked about you. Brought back a bed frame, wood stove, piping, and lumber for shelves."

"Is it for the shed?"

"Yep, Miss Ellen will tell you about the shed." Mr. Junior touched his shoulder and left the porch.

He watched him round the corner and pass by the side screen. He looked at the field, ate the sandwich and pie and sipped the drink. He would be interested in what Miss Ellen had to say.

The bottle was empty, and the sack contained a Moon Pie wrapper and the butcher paper that had held the sandwich. This was the first morning at the new next and he didn't know where the trash went. Most farmers burned their trash in a burn barrel. He left the porch in search of one. He guessed Miss Ellen was still in the pasture fixing fences. Around the corner, Mr. Junior and the other two men were carrying a small, flat-topped wood stove into the shed. He looked at the men's feet and not at the open shed door. He passed by the back of the truck and walked north, looking for the burn barrel. He walked by another truck parked in a small building without doors. Just beyond the building was a rusted fuel drum with burnt grass at the base. He threw the sack over the fence into the barrel.

He felt Miss Ellen would have little additional information about the shed. He knew there was a shed spirit that had been temporarily contained behind its door. The spirit's vapors had seeped into the fibers of the fresh-cut walls and ceiling; he had felt it when he stepped inside, before his rapid exit. Now it would have a bed and a stove and soon, a human resident.

On rare occasions, he had seen long, string-like vapors in the corner of his eye. He knew not to turn and look at them. They drifted in the air and were immediately present to those who turned and looked directly. They were disturbances in the air without wind—a subtle distortion of light that turned to a gray haze around the looker. He had seen the looker's fear and anger feed freely off the vaporous haze. Those who remained near suffered waves of individualized pain.

His own shadow visitor first noticed him when he sat stiff on the couch and had stared too long at one patch of darkness in the night woods behind the shack. He knew the visitor was still hovering about, disguised as a heavy sadness. He had chosen not to look. Each day he had put on the heavy coat of sadness and allowed it to melt away during sleep. There were times when common chores, sunlight, and an escaped smile lightened the weight.

The last few nexts had not required thoughts to be focused on personal safety and basic survival. After the appearance of the shed, the screened-porch-house next now required a new level of caution.

He wasn't sure if the long, finger-like vapors and the grayish haze were real. He had grown to trust his sense of impending danger more than visual distortions. There may not be a shed spirit living in the fresh wood. The dark feeling inside the shed may have been anticipation of the coming shed person. Miss Ellen would not need to tell him to stay away from the shed; he had made that decision when he first entered the door.

On his way back from the burn barrel he saw the red truck pull away, turning right and heading north. The shed had a new chimney and a step outside its door. Miss Ellen was carrying a narrow mattress and bed linens. He stood at the back corner of the house and watched through the open shed door while she made the bed. New shelves were on three of the inside walls, and a small table and two chairs stood in front of the bed, which was against the back wall. The bed was made, and Miss Ellen was inspecting the inside of the shed. She turned and faced the open door, and he could see her mouth was the shape of displeasure.

He wiped his feet on the outside mat and stepped through the back door. He put the empty bottle on the counter next to the sink and sat at the kitchen table. Miss Ellen came in and hung her coat next to the overalls. He watched her routine of safety pins and socks following the removal of the rubber overshoes. She brought her boots into the kitchen and sat at the table to put them on; she laced the boots and wrapped the end of the laces around hooks at the top of each boot.

Miss Ellen turned her chair around square with the table and looked at him. He had learned to watch faces, eyes, and hands when people spoke. He knew Miss Ellen had no children and little experience talking with children. She spoke directly, with purpose; she had little interest in casual conversation. She would tell him to stay away from the shed. She began. "There's a man coming to live in the shed. Stay away from the man and stay away from the shed. Do you understand?"

He nodded yes. She continued to look directly at him; he looked directly at her. He had questions. He did not ask them. He would figure it out himself. There had been animal-leg-and-hip-mystery breakfast meat questions. He had eaten the meat without asking. He would stay away from the shed and the shed man without asking. Answers would unfold before him if he watched carefully. This had become a new next inside the now next.

Once again, he was sitting at the table with his coat on, and the conversation was over. Miss Ellen was gathering cans of food and stacking them on the counter. She put the cans, along with a loaf of bread, in a cardboard box and went out the back door. He stood by the sink and watched the cans and bread move from the box to the shelves. She came back with the box and filled it with three pots with lids and a frying pan. She left the box in the shed and disappeared to the left of the window.

He continued to stand at the window looking at the shed. A white chicken walked past the shed door. Four more chickens followed, all white. He left the window and went out the back door to watch the chickens. Chickens were coming out of a wire-covered pen with a wire-covered roof connected to a small white building. The chickens rushed out of the gate, and after a few feet, slowed and scratched the ground with their feet, took a step back and pecked the grass and dirt. All were very busy, with more chickens in the front yard than around the shed in the back. Miss Ellen was coming out of the small white building with several brown eggs in a basket. She passed him on her way to the back door.

Before she reached the door, three fast-moving shadows went over his shoulder heading for three chickens that had left the front yard and were standing in the edge of the ditch just beyond the corner of the pasture fence. He saw three sets of medium charcoal wings with small white stripes at the tips of the feathers, five to six wide, brownish-red tail feathers, off-white breasts, white legs with black talons.

Miss Ellen came around the back corner of the house with a shotgun and past him to the front yard. "Get back! Chicken Hawks!"

The first hawk dove on the chicken closest to him. The talons were spread wide and sank into the chicken. The next two hawks landed on the grass just beyond the first chicken and short of the other two chickens. The first hawk had its left talon over the chicken's head, pushing it down, and the right talon sunk deep into the chicken's breast. The hawk stood on the chicken with its beak pointing to the left, guarding its prize from the other two hawks. The head turned and looked at him and Miss Ellen's movement.

The chicken made long death screams with less than a second between screams. The hawk began tearing flesh and feathers from the breast. The death screams continued. The time between screams stayed the same, but the length of each scream became shorter. A large section of the breast was gone, and the chicken continued to scream. Miss Ellen steadied the shotgun against the road side of the oak tree and fired. The smoke went past the trunk, and the hawk was blown off the chicken; both lay still in the grass. She fired again and hit one leg of the next hawk. It flopped twice and began to fly with one leg hanging low. Both hawks were flying south along the ditch, out of range.

He heard sounds behind him and saw a flow of white-feathered bodies moving fast through the gate to the chicken pen and into the small white building. He looked back; Miss Ellen was walking toward the dead chicken and its dead killer. The two unharmed chickens were agitated but afraid to walk past the hawk's body. Miss Ellen carried the shotgun in her left hand and picked up the two dead birds by the legs with her right hand. The two chickens followed her, pecking at the blood trail dripping from the dead birds. She walked past him and stopped at the gate to the pen. The chickens rushed through the gate into the building, and she closed and latched the gate.

She continued down past the building with the truck and threw the two bodies in the burn barrel. She leaned the gun against the fence, and she went in the building with the truck and came out with a large metal can with a spout. A dark liquid flowed out of the spout into the barrel. She threw a lighted stick match into the barrel and stepped back with the shotgun. Flames and black smoke shot out of the opening at the top of the barrel. *Miss Ellen was cooking again.* This time he could identify the meat.

He was thankful that the casualties would not be waiting on his supper plate.

Miss Ellen looked like a pioneer woman standing, watching the fire, her face glowing from the flames and her shotgun cradled in her left arm. *Not much of a conversationalist but a true chicken-hawk hater.*

There were lots of conversations in the chicken house from those that saw and those that heard. Chicken brains retelling the event with wordless tales of the day when the great birds appeared in the sky and all were spared but one. The screams of the dying chicken and the shapes of the shadows racing over the grass would forever be connected to the rapid waves of generations to come. Soon the sounds from the coup would slow, and the layers would leave the communal roost and settle in their nesting boxes. The sun would begin to touch the field beyond the oak tree, and chicken eyes would begin to close and open and close. Tomorrow would be another adventure of scratching dirt and pecking the ground.

Miss Ellen was walking away from the barrel toward the house, and the smoke was following her. He stepped to the side and she passed him; he began to smell the burnt feathers. In the front yard, there had been predator birds in the sky with wide wingspans; they had stood over two feet high. The mystery shed was in the back yard. Being outside at the screened porch house had become more complicated.

He went to the front porch and sat on the long bench. He thought about the events of the last hour, and his body briefly shuttered with the image of a flying predator standing on his chest with talons deep in his flesh. He did not want to live or die like a chicken. Tomorrow he would look for a straight limb and make a spear. When winter set in hard, he would work on putting the jar of dimes and pennies in the cardboard folders.

The back door closed. The long, high-pitched "woo" sound followed. He left the porch and walked by the muffled sounds of the chicken house to look for an ax in the building with the truck. The burn barrel smoked and smelled.

The truck was older than Mr. Junior's red truck. The fenders were round and the hubcaps small, with the same three letters in red where his foot had slipped and dangled outside the bed of the same kind of truck on the street around the corner from the dime store. It had been part of a lifetime ago.

He put his foot on the left rear hubcap and swung his body into the bed in one motion and landed on his feet. He stood up straight, just below the rafters. The bucket sat on the ground in the back left corner of the building, with three wooden handles sticking out of the top. He wrapped his left hand around the edge of the bed, swung his legs out of the bed and landed on both feet with his back to the bucket. He turned and walked to the bucket.

He chose the short, curved handle and pulled it out of the bucket filled with sand. The ax was sharp, shiny, without rust. He pulled out the two long handles as well—a spade and a shovel; they were equally shiny, with no rust. The sand cleaned and the oil prevented rust. Something he would remember. He reburied all three.

Tomorrow he would start making a spear. He left the building, turned toward the house and climbed the fence just past the chicken yard. The last of the cattle had turned right into the barn. He headed toward the edge of the woods just beyond the second fence where he had seen the sun come up above the trees. He crossed over the cattle road, a path less than two feet wide and more than three inches deep. The heavy hooves had packed the dirt hard and smooth. The path was carved through the grass in a meandering line that passed through the center of an opening to a large pasture some one hundred yards to the south. The gate to the opening had been swung to the right and tied to the fence. Beyond the opening the path branched into three.

He turned back, facing the woods, and walked to the second fence. He walked looking down through the fence for walnuts on the ground. It was the time of year when many of the walnuts were still covered with a round, oily green shell slightly smaller than a baseball. It was the season when the first to fall from the trees had already turned black and dry; the rest would be combinations of oily green and dried-dead black.

He passed two patches of fallen walnuts. The first tree had straight limbs that were too high to reach, and the second patch was below a tree with no suitable limbs. He continued down the fence heading south. A few yards before the second fence met the east-west pasture fence he saw the third patch of walnuts from a tree with a suitable, reachable limb. He climbed the fence, found a dead branch and wove it into the wire fence so that the top of the branch was a foot or more above the nearest post. He would look for it tomorrow when he came for the limb.

The cattle had turned left out of the barn and were moving down the path to the pasture. He climbed over the fence and walked at an angle toward the opening to the pasture. The first few cows had stopped and were watching; the rest of the line began to stop. He moved through the opening and walked west along the pasture side of the fence toward the road. He looked over his right shoulder. All of the cows and one bull had stopped with their heads turned right, looking at him. This was the first time they had seen him. He was a different face and body, and they were studying him with their cow brains. He looked and walked differently than Miss Ellen or Mr. Junior or the man with the beard.

He knew to walk naturally without jerky movements that would cause them to run. Scaring feeder cattle and causing them to run meant they would lose weight and waste two to three days of feed. They lost interest, turned and continued down the path.

He walked the ditch bank next to the fence with the sun low and to his left; the front porch screen door faced the sun. He looked over his right shoulder again and saw the head of his long shadow pass through the opening to the pasture, moving toward the cattle. He blocked the sun in the moving shape of himself across the sides of the cattle. His boot slipped and his shadow stopped; the cattle walked through it to the pasture. He had stepped in blood, tissue, and red-stained feathers. The grass and dirt held a thick, burnt-sugar scent of death. He scooted his boots through the grass to clean the soles and sides.

He walked past the corner post of the pasture fence. His shadow slid up from the pasture and angled across the right front corner of the house and roof. He walked the front yard, with the shadow passing him and through the front porch screen. He passed the porch, and the shadow raced across the grass to the second fence to the right of the barn. He saw Miss Ellen adjusting the wire fencing covering the top of the chicken yard. Once chicken hawks tasted blood in a place, they returned.

He turned to look at the field just to the right of the oak tree where corn stubble lay before a half sun. Darkness was coming. He would try to go to sleep early so he could be up for breakfast served in the blackness of morning. The first full day of light at the screened porch house had been eventful. Activities and events were more numerous than words heard or spoken.

He stepped closer to watch Miss Ellen hammer thick staples into the tops of posts connecting the wire roof to the wire walls of the chicken pen. She used baling wire to weave the top edges together. He could see the backyard shed out of the corner of his right eye.

There was no shed spirit. The only feelings in the shed were brought by ones who entered through its door. No spirit had traveled from tree to sawmill to truck. A tree had become a box, a container for a person, with the long, thin, rough faces of the knots in each board left to watch the other knots become gray, cracked, and dried…to age without living. *There was no shed spirit.*

The back door closed. Miss Ellen had passed by him without speaking. His mind had been far away among the trees, looking down on where the tree-box container had once lived. He walked away from the house and stood in the gravel road. The air had begun to color itself. The road was made of river rock; he chose a few good rocks and threw the first handful at the corner post of the pasture fence. Most went through the wire fence; a very few hit the post with a knock, followed by the hum of vibrating wire. Sometime tomorrow after he started on the spear, he would find a better place to practice where the rocks didn't bounce into the yard. The air was purple, and howling had begun in the deep woods behind the house. *Inside seemed like a good idea.*

19 – The Shed Dweller

On his way back to the house, he walked past where Mr. Junior parked his truck. It had been good to see him earlier in the day. He and the truck had not returned. He went through the back door and decided to hang his coat on one of the hooks with Miss Ellen's coat and the overalls. The hint of dry cow manure might soften the hint of dead fish. The fast approaching not-Miss Betty's-supper would more than likely overpower smells classified as hints.

He opened the kitchen door with mixed feelings. He and Miss Ellen would be in the same room with conversation sitting on the edge of silent tongues. Too tall to step over and too wide to pass without touching, he heard the question. "Who's going to live in the shed?" It was an unformed thought carried by the sound of his voice. His ears pulled the answer from Miss Ellen's mouth.

"Your father."

His brain lost reference. His mind raced forward. It would snow three times that winter. The third snow would be up to his waist. He would ride in the truck two more times, once to see Mr. Junior's parents, pleasant people with white hair who lived in a remote part of the woods.

Their house was the same color as the woods and was near to invisible if not for smoke coming out of the stone chimney or someone coming out of the front door. In front of the house, an oblong board fence held several cows.

They presented him with a toy double-barreled shotgun that was two feet long. He was so pleased to receive it. It was larger and grander than the one on top of the pile in the dime store in a not forgotten before life. He asked to see the cattle, and they bet him he wouldn't get into the pen. He climbed the board fence with the shotgun and leaned it against one of the posts. He stepped toward the cattle and scratched the underside of their necks. He moved through the pen scratching and rubbing each cow. He returned to the fence and climbed outside the pen and reached through the boards for the shotgun. It wasn't there.

He looked back and saw disgusted faces. Mr. Junior's father pointed a crooked finger toward the center of the pen. The shotgun lay in two pieces. The wooden stock was broken off the barrels, and the barrels were bent sideways. Four cows had their heads down examining the broken gun. Their noses were just above the outside steam coming up from fresh cow manure that covered the pieces. The loss of the toy was of little significance compared to the embarrassment of his disrespect for a fine gift that was well given. He sat in the truck, and they left shortly for a silent ride back.

A few seconds had passed, and he was still sitting at the table looking at Miss Ellen. He knew his mind had retreated to a well-defended place, but now it was back.

"When will he start living in the shed?"

"Your father?"

"Yes."

"Tomorrow."

He and Miss Ellen were having a conversation. He had asked hard questions and received harder answers. He had more. "Why is he going to live in the shed?"

"We gave him a job."

"Where has he been?"

"He had to leave."

"Why?"

"He got into some trouble."

"What kind of trouble?"

"Law trouble."

"What kind of law trouble?"

"The kind where you go to jail for a long time."

"What did he do?"

"He got into a fight in a bar."

"What happened?"

"Be careful what you ask."

"What happened?"

"Your father killed a man."

The last time he would ride in the truck would be with Mr. Junior. It would be a short time after this conversation he was having with Miss Ellen—the conversation where his mind would receive an answer, retreat, digest, and return. They rode in the red truck through field after field without leaving Mr. Junior's land. He asked how many acres. Mr. Junior told him eleven thousand. He commented on the size of the farm. Mr. Junior said that portions of the land would flood when the river rose over its banks from heavy snows in the north and weeks of heavy rain in the south.

It was a special ride where he felt older. He knew that Mr. Junior had taken time from work to show him the land. He felt important. Mr. Junior showed him where he worked from dark to dark. The soil in the fields had a dark, sticky, rich texture that transitioned to dark silt as it approached the cottonwoods next to the river. Countless generations of floods had deposited a thick layer of topsoil of rich river sediment. He liked Mr. Junior, and he could tell Mr. Junior liked him. This would be their last ride together.

His mind came back to the kitchen. "Did he go to jail?"

"No, he left the state and moved. Followed the harvest season."

"Did he ask about me?"

"Don't know. He only talked to your Aunt Eunice once a year."

He would not need to leave the conversation again. His father had been a black-haired ghost even before he disappeared. He did not leave the conversation. The conversation left the room, and he sat at the table. He was comforted by familiar smells from the stove. He had been told he took after his mother, which provided a steady comfort. There were no more questions, just a plan to eat, look at the coins, and sleep. A dark breakfast would come early.

The spirit of Miss Betty's hand had passed over the stove, and his plate was left with only a thin streak missed by the last swipe of the last biscuit. He thanked Miss Ellen for a fine supper. She fixed a large plate for Mr. Junior and placed it on top of the stove under a pot lid that covered the plate and rested on the surface of the stove. He sat and watched Miss Ellen at the sink. He didn't think to grab the towel and dry what was washed. Each item occupied the next placed in front, with all standing at a slight angle in the drainer. He didn't offer and she said nothing.

His mind drifted passively without direction, by salve, sores, and the last time he had a bath. The house had one bathroom, and he was too new to the next to use their bathtub. He had noticed Miss Ellen used the room often. It was a house of sparse conversation that required fewer face-to-face encounters. It would be some time before anyone would notice his lack of bathing. Unlike the stone house, it was a level of hygiene that was familiar.

He was accustomed to moving about unnoticed. Unnoticed from lack of interest and his own finely honed skill. He thanked Miss Ellen again for supper and left the table. He headed to the bedroom with the sound of Miss Ellen's boots behind him. He looked back, and she turned toward the front door. He entered the bedroom and heard a switch click; the bedroom window glowed from the front porch light. He heard her boots again. He guessed she was heading to the back door to turn on the outside light for Mr. Junior.

There was no need to keep track of Miss Ellen's movements—it was a habit. Attention to whereabouts and movements had proven to be necessary in the past, and the pending arrival of his father, the shed dweller, would make it necessary again.

He sat on the bed to take off his boots. It was a comfort to know his pajamas were folded neatly under the pillow and he had made his bed with the covers smooth and straight. It made him feel more human, and the care of the contents of his suitcases allowed him to have a home that was limited but constant. These were routine activities he had learned at the stone house, along with learning to take a proper bath. Miss Betty had taught him how to clip his nails and the importance of keeping them clean. The frequency of bathing differed greatly from next to next. He would wait to see what was routine for the screened porch house.

He took the pajamas into the bathroom and peed. He didn't flush. His plan was to clean the wounds on his legs with wet toilet paper and drop it in the toilet before flushing. He began to clean the wounds and used dry toilet paper to put salve on each of the sores. The toilet water was yellow with small wads of white paper stained with dried blood. The pieces of dried blood floated just below the surface with their edges dissolving into red vines that reached down through the liquid to the darkness where things left the room for the outside. He flushed and watched the colors spin and disappear.

He wore the pajamas and carried his clothes to the bedroom. He folded the clothes and put them on the floor next to the bed. He had decided not to look at the coins. It would be a special activity he would save for a special time—a time when winter pressed against the outside doors, a time when winter became harsh to the touch. Tonight, was for thinking and then sleep.

The conversation with Miss Ellen had caused his mind to run ahead, then stop and catch its breath. His mind had seen three snows and the last two rides in the red truck—brief moments of seeing beyond the horizon line. He had traveled in his mind before but never beyond the present. The events would unfold in their time, unchanged, and he would participate in them with the nagging sense of the familiar.

Tomorrow his father would arrive and step into the shed. It would not be a reunion with smiles, hugs, and warm words of fondness. It would be a reminder of his connection by blood and bone to a man who had made him an orphan by choice. He wondered if the death of the man in the bar was before or after he was left to be a couch dweller behind the shack. *I am a couch dweller fathered by a shed dweller*. It was not his couch, nor was the shed his father's. Both were squatters in other people's lives and spaces.

He had had little time with his mother before she left. In the short time they had together, she had smoothed the fabric of his identity. He alone had carefully hemmed its edges and held it close. His travels through the nexts had been filled with invitations to lay down his fabric as a rug, left to look up at the darkness of the soles of foot, shoe, and boot. He had held it close, and he would do the same tomorrow, the day of his father's arrival.

He was on his left side, looking at the glowing window. He would go to the room with the typewriters and lie on the couch before the fire. Those within would welcome him, and they would hang his fabric on the wall with theirs. All would gaze at each beautiful tapestry. He would hear the low hum of fondness from warm voices. Daisy's belly as a pillow and Blue's body around his feet. All three would watch the fire dancing around the wood, and eyes would close. His eyes opened to a dark window and closed again with a warm face and a breathing pillow.

Miss Betty touched his shoulder. "Time for breakfast." He opened his eyes to a dark window, with light coming from the kitchen and a large shadow passing the doorway. He dressed quickly and walked to the kitchen and heard the last of a sentence regarding Miss Ellen's sugar and limiting desserts.

A third plate at breakfast was a surprise and met with "Morning glory" from Mr. Junior. "You have business to attend to at this early hour?"

"Yes, sir. Several things that need attention."

"Good you got an early start." Mr. Junior talked while getting a plate, putting four biscuit haves face up and pouring white milk gravy with sausage chunks on top. Miss Ellen got a fork and a glass and poured milk from the pitcher on the table. Miss Ellen had the look of irritation. He guessed it had something to do with Mr. Junior's comment regarding sugar and desserts.

Both continued their conversation regarding activities for the day. Mr. Junior planned to keep two combines going along with three grain trucks. This would be an attempt to harvest as many soybeans as possible from the fields closest to the river before the next rains came and equipment would be unable to move through the fields without getting stuck in the sticky, dark "gumbo" mud.

Miss Ellen discussed plans to keep the cattle in the pasture near the barn to feed them more grain when winter set in and the snow would cover the larger pastures. He ate the biscuits and gravy quietly and listened. Miss Ellen commented that the cattle took little time, and she was sorry she would not be able to help with the harvest. He felt her eyes on him.

Miss Ellen's comment had been quietly tucked in among plans for the day and explained Mr. Junior's glances at Miss Ellen during the not-Miss-Betty's-pie supper from the first night. Aside from Miss Ellen's basic non-conversational nature, his presence required her presence. She had been demoted from an equal harvester of grain to a tender of cattle and kid. She would rather be in the fields operating equipment and managing field workers than be in the house babysitting.

There was a slight, unnoticed grin on his face. *Paying attention had provided useful information.* Miss Ellen was a farmer who wasn't able to farm due to his arrival. Miss Ellen had not been rude to him; she had moved about in his presence with a subtle distance. She had no personal issues with him other than his presence. He had no personal issues with her.

This was not his first next. At each next, his arrival and his non-adult status had required each next to provide additional space, with the added responsibility of attending to his basic needs. There had been significant differences among the nexts in terms of available space and services provided. He had slowly learned that the significant differences had little to do with him but were reflections of others' perceptions as he passed through groups of faces gathered together in each of the nexts.

It was a moonlit morning. Breakfast was finished. Mr. Junior had left for the fields, and he had dried the last dish. He felt warmth for Miss Ellen. She had tentatively agreed to support Mr. Junior's wish to raise a boy. She was unable to help with harvest, and now she had the boy's father arriving to live in her back yard. He and Miss Ellen had two things in common: mouths that were seldom full of unnecessary words and concerns regarding the arrival of his father.

He stood at the sink and watched Miss Ellen open the door to the kitchen and get the extra pair of socks. She turned Mr. Junior's chair to face the sink and sat down. She folded the cuffs of her pants tight around her ankles, pulled the second pair of socks up and ran the safety pin through the first sock, the cuff, and the second sock. She repeated the same for her right foot. She stood in front of the hooks and put on the overalls and tucked the pants legs into the tops of the rubber overshoes. She went out the back door without a word. Before he put on his coat, he waited for the "woo" sound. It came and he stepped out the back door.

A three-quarter moon was bright over the large pasture to the south. He saw the cattle coming up their path toward the barn. He stepped back behind the corner of the house where they couldn't see him. No one was in the shed, and he waited for the last cow to turn right into the barn before he walked to the building with the truck. A gray moon shadow stretched in front of him; he walked on the feet of the shadow. He grabbed the ax, and the shadow followed him through the front yard and along the ditch next to the road. He walked around feathers stuck to grass with blood that had lost its smell.

He continued south along the ditch past the west end of the east-west pasture fence. He climbed over the fence and walked east along the pasture side of the fence. He went through the opening and found the dead branch sticking in the fence. He climbed over the fence, stood on a stump and swung the ax. It sunk into the limb at an angle, and he heard the echo of the ax bounce off the south end of the barn.

He made several half-swings that were quieter until the V-shaped notch in the limb was deep enough to cause the limb to fall from the tree. He trimmed the smaller branches off the limb and threw it and the ax over the fence. He climbed over the fence and carried the limb in his left hand and the ax with his right hand wrapped around the handle where it entered the metal. He walked quickly through the opening and headed for the fence next to the ditch.

His goal was to walk past the chicken house to the building with the truck before the cattle began leaving the barn. When he passed the shadow line of the house, his moon shadow slid forward from the bottom of his feet and disappeared in front of the screened porch. The lights were still on in the barn.

He stood the limb up in front of the building with the truck and trimmed the knots where the branches had been. He stepped beyond the edge of the drive where it entered the building and stood in the grass next to the limb and stretched his left hand above his head just short of one foot. He laid the limb down, chopped off the end and stood it up again, point down, and began making a sharper point with the ax. He moved up from the point and began shaving off the bark while slowly rotating the limb. He had learned from the first spear that the bark would dry and become too loose to throw the spear. After he'd removed the bark as high as his waist, he flipped the limb and began shaving the bark off the rest of the limb.

He wondered when a limb could be called a spear. He stopped for a moment and looked around the edge of the building at the barn. The lights were off, and the cattle were gone. He looked at the chicken house and the shed and the house. He didn't see Miss Ellen. He went back to shaving bark off the limb. He was freeing a spear from a limb. *At what point would it be free? Would the limb be a spear when its shape was the same as a spear, or would it have to be used as a spear before it became one?* He stopped again and turned around; Miss Ellen had been standing behind him.

"Did you ask to use my ax?"

The question had come out of a short fat man wearing overalls with no shirt whose name he did not use. He heard the air rush through his mouth and dump down his throat. The figure grew taller and became female. "No ma'am."

"Hand me the stick." She looked at the tip. "You'll need to blacken it." She pointed her finger at him. She rested the stick on her finger. "Needs to be balanced at the midpoint and smooth with no ridges." She handed it back to him. "When you're finished, put the ax back where you found it."

He nodded. He had begun to breathe through his nose again. She walked to the chicken house to gather eggs. He stood still for a long moment.

He finished with the bark and began to plane the ridges until the surface was smooth and round. He used his coat to wipe the moisture off the ax. He laid the wood on the ground; *never lean a straight stick—always lay it flat to prevent warping*. He buried the ax in the sand bucket. Above the wooden handles, a canning jar full of large stick matches sat on a triangular shelf wedged into the corner of the building. He stepped out of the building and looked for a safe place to build a fire to blacken the tip of the stick. A large tree stood in the corner of the barnyard. The tree was surrounded by grassless dirt where cattle stood in the summer for shade. He gathered twigs, sticks, and branches for a fire. He went back into the building, unscrewed the lid, took two stick matches and tightened the lid.

He took the stick with him. *It wasn't a stick. It was a spear.* It was a spear because he said it was. Its name was not dependent on a mysterious stage of its creation. It was a spear when he saw it on the tree. He named it before it was.

The fire went well, and the tip was black and stronger. He used his boot to scrape dirt onto the last of the embers. He would wait until daylight to find a place to practice. He would keep the spear under the long bench on the front screened porch just like the first spear he made that he kept under the couch at the shack. He picked up all the bark and wood shavings in front of the building with the truck and threw them in the burn barrel on top of the bones of yesterday's birds.

The spear was in its place. He left the screened porch and walked around the house to the back door. He saw no signs of anyone in the shed. He decided this would be the last time he used the back door. He did not intend to step out of the back door and be surprised by his father's presence. He would use the front door and sit on the bench or stand by the oak tree in the front yard. Always with his spear in case of coyotes, chicken hawks, or black-haired ghost fathers that may move about unheard.

Hensen March

20 – A Shed Supper

The day of his father's arrival passed, and another day came. The sun slid under the field beyond the oak tree and appeared again above the trees in the deep woods outside the kitchen window. The sun went under the farm and came out the other side. He had seen smoke from the shed coming up out of the metal pipe in the roof.

He began to plan. During the last hours of night, he would be up for breakfast. He would wait for the smoke to slow from the shed and the sun to be well above the trees before he practiced with the spear in the loft of the barn. He would set rectangular hay bales on end in different parts and at different distances in the loft. He would eat the noonday meal and spend the afternoon down the road past the burn barrel and the cow shade tree, throwing rocks at fence posts. He would make sure he was out of the barn when the cows came to eat. He would stay away from the shed in the back yard.

He did not see the shed door open or close. At night the light from the kitchen window shone on the smoke that rose from the pipe in the roof of the shed.

The visit with Mr. Junior's parents came and went. It remained unchanged, with more than a hint of the familiar. The last ride in the red truck happened, with the same words and the same fields he had pictured. He and Miss Ellen lived with a comfortable silence and spoke when necessary. He practiced and his skills improved.

Miss Ellen began to use the bathroom more often and started wearing loose fitting dresses. She baked more pies and cakes and ate most of them. Mr. Junior began to feed the cows more often. He would overhear Mr. Junior's concerns regarding Miss Ellen not attending to her sugar. He believed Miss Ellen had lost farming and cared less about her health. He was willing to go to another next so she could return to the fields, but there were no offers and no place to go.

The first snow came, and he could see boot tracks leading to the shed. The second snow came, and in the light from the kitchen window, he saw fresh tracks. The boot tracks filled in during the day and were cut fresh again sometime after supper.

He continued to make his way to the barn loft to practice with the spear. The cattle stayed in the barn during snow-covered days and had become familiar with his movements in the loft. The third snow came and made it impossible for him to reach the barn. Mr. Junior's red truck made it through each of the snowfalls; deep gouges in the snow led to the shed. Miss Ellen sat at the kitchen table eating meringue pie.

He began to count the coins in the jar. There were eighty-seven in the jar: fifty-one were pennies, thirty-six dimes. His plan was to make the coins last through the winter. Each night he would pour out the coins on the bedspread and separate the pennies from the dimes. One night he would line up the pennies in eleven rows. The first ten rows had five pennies; the eleventh had one penny. The next night he lined up the dimes in six rows with six dimes in each row. Some nights he would mix the coins and place all of them in nine rows with ten coins in the first eight rows and seven coins in the ninth row.

In the next part of his coin plan, he would choose one coin from the jar each night and put it in a round hole in one of the cardboard coin folders. He would choose a random coin and find the year printed below the hole and place the coin in the hole. The coin plan would last until the snows melted and the trees began to bud, and it would be spring. Spring with warmer temperatures and sunlit days. Rocks would thaw on the road and be ready to throw.

Until then he watched the kitchen light shine on the smoke from the shed's chimney. He watched for fresh tracks from the door of the shed, always appearing to the left of the door heading north toward the chicken house. The temperature dropped and the snow froze. He followed the foot tracks past the chicken house where they turned left at the building with the truck. The tracks disappeared at the road just short of fresh tire marks. He looked to the left and saw that the tracks came from where Mr. Junior parked his truck next to the house.

Over the weeks and months, he would look out the kitchen window for glimpses of his father. There were none.

He continued to fold his dirty clothes and put them on the floor next to the rubber overshoes. He sat at the kitchen table with his back to the wall, facing the sink. Miss Ellen would open the kitchen door, and he would look to the left and his clothes would be gone.

His original suitcase was down to the last pair of jeans and underwear.

He began to notice his body had an odor. He cleaned the leg sores and used the salve every third night. He found a washrag and began using it with soap to clean the body parts with the most noticeable odor. He used the soap to hand-wash the washrag after he finished. He washed his feet in the sink twice a week. One day he had decided to use Mr. Junior and Miss Ellen's bathtub for the first time. He planned to take a bath and put on the last set of clothes from his suitcase. He walked into the bathroom, and the room was full of moisture. He told Miss Ellen about the moisture, and she told him she had taken a bath. Using her bathtub seemed intrusive. He would use it some other day.

Miss Ellen was in the bathroom again, and he used the time to look around the house for his clothes. He opened the chifforobe and his clothes were there. The shelf at the top had underwear and socks folded neatly. The shirts and pants were on hangers. He opened the suitcase on the bed and moved everything from the chifforobe to his suitcase. He was thankful for the clean clothes, and he would thank Miss Ellen.

He felt uncomfortable when his possessions were not in the suitcases or in his pockets. He and the items in the suitcases were his world. More clothes were added at the stone house. The other items had remained the same. He knew he was the same but different. He hoped he had not become so distant that he would not be able to find his sense of humor. He had smiled a few times at the screened porch house. He couldn't remember the last time he laughed. He was concerned about Miss Ellen—she had become more withdrawn during the winter. He had a sense that something would happen when spring arrived.

The snow became rain, with a thin layer of ice over mud. The cow path had lost its smoothness, and he could see chunks of mud fly off cow hooves when they lifted to take another step. A low cloud of slung mud moved down the line of cattle, twenty-seven cows and one bull with four hooves each. Each hoof pressing into the mud and lifting with a snap, with hoof-shaped mud chunks flying up and back onto the cow behind—white legs turning into brown and black and drying to gray. Hoof-shaped pieces of mud rested on either side of the path. It was a messy part of the season when mud clung to everything.

He knew that when the mud dried and slowly became dust and the sun became brighter, something different would happen. He guessed he would be carrying his suitcases again and looking out of the rear window of another vehicle for the last look at the screened porch house, the now next. It would be spring, and everyone would be needed to plant new crops.

The everyday cold, brittle air did begin to soften and seldom lingered past midmorning. A brighter light came through the back windows of the house in the morning, and bright, warm light came through the front screened porch in the afternoon. Miss Ellen stopped baking cakes and pies and began to wear pants again. Her step was lighter, and she fed the cows more often. A light green hue grew in the woods behind the house. The mud in the barn lot and fields had dried. The sound of tractors began to fill the air.

He sat on the long bench in front of the bedroom window and watched black smoke come out the stack of a large tractor pulling a two-bottom plow through the field. Black, caked soil curled up and out from the plow blades. The tractor moved slowly with a strain that caused the front wheels to bounce lightly on the ground. The speed of the tractor and the size of the field meant that he would fall asleep in bed to the sound of its motor. Miss Ellen spent less time in the house, and he spent more time on the porch and in the barn loft. The rocks in the road past the cow shade tree had loosened, and he began to ease into throwing rocks again.

This day he had finished practicing with the spear and left the barn loft for the noonday meal. After washing his hands in the kitchen sink, he turned to use the dishtowel to dry his hands. He caught a glimpse of blue work pants and a left boot stepping on the outside step of the shed, a left hand opening the shed door to the right, and a body disappearing behind the closed door. It happened in less than two seconds.

The back door opened, and Mr. Junior came through the kitchen door. He watched Mr. Junior wash his hands in the sink. He could tell Miss Ellen was surprised to see him at midday. The two of them were hovering over the stove, fixing Mr. Junior's plate. He could tell Miss Ellen was pleased to see him. It was good to see Mr. Junior, and it was good to see Miss Ellen pleased and wearing pants again.

Mr. Junior said, "How's the practicing going?"

"Good. Starting to get my eye back."

"Reckon we'll have rocks in the road when you finish?" Both grinned. "Your father asked me if you'd have an early supper with him tomorrow. It's up to you."

"Where?"

"In the shed."

Miss Ellen looked concerned. "Junior, do you think it's a good idea? Is it safe?"

Mr. Junior said, "I'll be here. What do you think? Do you want to do it?"

He nodded in a slightly angular way that suggested yes. There were no sounds to make words to really answer the question. The question passed over ears...its deep roots sunk into dark shapes moving about in fuzzy grays and blacks. The question could not be answered by sound or voice. It was a passive answer, floating without pole or paddle. He answered without speaking. He said nothing.

Mr. Junior and Miss Ellen were discussing cattle and farming. He thought about his acceptance of the invitation from his father to have an early shed supper. The last he had seen of his father was the back of his head disappearing into the trees, shiny hair with no face. How long ago had become a deeper mystery after Mr. Albert's comments regarding the length of his stay at the shack. He didn't accept the invitation because he cared. It was more of a grayish, dark curiosity coupled with fear of his father's reaction if he said no.

He expected his father to allow him to leave the shack unharmed, but he had countless questions about being left alone. He knew the fact that he had these questions meant the answers would be inadequate because the answers would come from the person who had left him. He would not ask the questions. He would eat and listen.

Mr. Junior touched his shoulder. "Don't worry about tomorrow. I'll be home before dark." Mr. Junior's and Miss Ellen's concern regarding tomorrow's engagement was worrisome.

He helped Miss Ellen with the dishes. Mr. Junior left. He tried to keep his eye on the shed door but didn't see if his father had left. He stood at the sink with his eyes unfocused, aware of the light green hue from the tree buds in the woods and the undefined shape of the shed. Later he ended up on the long bench watching the tractor pulling hard, making solid dirt waves that stopped moving when the plow moved past. He closed his eyes and listened to the tractor motor.

He let his mind drift through before-seen images. All the images were moving but one—a strip of moonlight on his shoes from the window in the kitchen door of the shack. He was lying on the linoleum floor, curled around the back of the small wood stove. He was on his right side looking up through the glass at falling snow. Behind the image were other images of him moving about the kitchen and eating food in the darkness, with the man with no name snoring in the next room.

He went back to the sound of the motor pulling the tractor and the two-bladed plow. He was tired. Tired of the images, tired of tomorrow's invitation, and tired of being human driftwood. Floating driftwood that waited to see if it made it around the next bend. *At least I'm not at the shack, but I'm going into the shed tomorrow.*

He left the porch carrying the spear and walked down the road past the cow shade tree and threw rocks at the fence posts. Throwing rocks against the memory wall. Some rocks passed through invisible holes in the wall and stopped with the sound of rock against wooden post. Tomorrow he would see what his father had to say. It would make little difference. He would be polite and expect nothing.

He walked in the road toward the house, stepping through slow time and stopping to watch the tractor. The sound of the motor had vibrated in his ears since morning. There were moments when the sound would fade, and he would hear birds in the woods beyond the second fence. As the sound of the motor returned, he walked slowly and stopped and watched. Soon the "woo" sound would come, and the sun would color and later fold under the field and disappear.

He made it to the screened porch and sat on the bench to wait for the tractor to cross the sun and the shadow of the wheels to roll over the screen. He had spent much of his time throwing things at things. They were times when thoughts rested, and movement was familiar. They were times with open-eyed rest, where his mind reclined with small, smooth, simple thoughts.

He was asleep before Mr. Junior came home from the fields. Dreams raced about in the past, with blurred faces and tilted shapes undefined by edge or place. The nexts swirled around in a pot stirred by wooden spoon with changing hands. He stood at the bottom of the hole in the center of the swirl with hands cupped and pressed against the outside glass of the shack's kitchen door, looking at six heads sleeping against the right wall. He turned and Miss Betty stood on the porch, with snow falling behind her. She wore an apron and held the spoon and said, "Wake up. It's time for breakfast."

He got up quickly and had a heavy, before-light breakfast with Miss Ellen and Mr. Junior. Today would be an early supper with his father.

The day began like the others before. He threw the spear faster, and it sunk deeper into the bale. There were sandwiches for dinner, followed by louder knocks from posts with whines that traveled farther down the wire.

He reached the screened porch before Mr. Junior's truck turned into the drive. Ancient feelings climbed up his pores and spread over his skin. He kicked each leg and snapped his wrists away from his arms and threw off the feeling. Even so, the old feeling followed him through the door to the kitchen.

He washed his hands and stood in the kitchen. Mr. Junior and Miss Ellen sat at the table without plates. Miss Ellen got up and wiped his face with a wet cloth. This was the first time she had touched him. He knew she knew that this was something he would do without reward or reason. A response to a request that if not heeded would go poorly. He would walk through the door of the shed into the past, and his journeys would not be acknowledged.

Miss Ellen remained standing. Mr. Junior stood up, and he watched him rise just short of the ceiling. Both were standing close and facing him. No one wanted him to go; things would be difficult if he didn't.

Mr. Junior touched his shoulder. "We'll be here if you need us."

Miss Ellen said, "If things go poorly, get out of the shed fast."

He stepped out the back door and walked to the shed. He looked back over his right shoulder and saw their faces in the kitchen window. He stood in front of the outside step of the shed. His history with the man behind the door was brief and long ago—how many nexts ago? He had been there for each moment; the man behind the door had not. He leaned over and knocked twice.

The voice behind the door said, "It's open." He stepped up with both feet on the step and turned the knob.

He watched his right-hand push on the knob, and the door opened slowly to the right. To his left he saw two shelves attached to the wall, the back of a chair, and the left edge of the table. Past the chair and edge of the table was the metal headboard of the bed, with a smoothed pillow below. He stepped inside and saw his father sitting in the second chair to his right. His father pointed at the other chair and he sat down. His father turned to the right and stirred a pot on a small camp stove with a blue flame underneath. The pot and stove sat on a small table at the foot of the bed. The second burner had a second flame under a skillet.

He watched his father break four eggs in a bowl and use a metal spoon to break the yokes and pour them into the skillet. He used the spoon to scramble the eggs. He turned off the flame under the pot, turned to his left and picked up two spoons on the shelf behind him. One spoon was old and tarnished and one was new. The new spoon was placed in front of him at an angle, and his father put the old spoon on the other end of the table and returned to the eggs. A coffee cup was dipped twice into the pot and its contents dumped into a bowl that was slid across the table next to the new spoon. His father eased the eggs onto a plate.

He had been watching his father and looking around the inside of the shed. He saw no dust and there was no odor, only the smell of beef gravy and scrambled eggs. Canned food lined the shelves. The cans with red labels caught his eye. Every can was spaced evenly with the labels facing the table. He counted twenty-nine cans.

His father was well groomed, with oil in his black hair. He wore a light-colored shirt with an open collar with wide, rounded tips that hung close to the upper part of his chest. He was clean-shaven and had clean fingernails. The ends of the first two fingers of his right hand were yellow-orange from hand-rolled cigarettes.

The contents of the bowl looked to be beef stew. He thought this would be the time his father would speak. Instead, he watched his father open a jar of grape jelly and put six large globs on the eggs. He chopped the jelly into small pieces and mixed it with the eggs. The spoon went through the jelly and eggs at a rate that bordered on intense and caused him to stare. His father's left elbow was on the table and his arm wrapped around the front of the plate, and he began scooping up the jelly and eggs at a pace that caused his cheeks to puff with food waiting to be swallowed. His father had not looked directly at him, but he heard the word "Eat."

He realized that he had been staring with his mouth open—putting the first spoonful of beef stew in his mouth required little effort. The jelly eggs were gone and the plate was sitting on the pot before he had finished half of the beef stew.

His father leaned forward and began rolling a cigarette. He kept his eyes on the bowl. "Sonny said he didn't like you and he was glad you left."

He continued to look at the bowl and nodded twice.

His senses heightened. He was aware that the doorknob was closer to him than to his father. The front edge of his chair was far enough away from the table that he could move quickly to the right without moving the chair. His face was down toward the bowl, but his eyes were on the center of the table where he could see his father's hands.

A rolled cigarette was in his father's left hand, and a stick match rested in the second joint of the index finger of his right hand, with the thumb balancing it so that the red end with the white tip pointed at the ceiling. The thumbnail scratched across the white tip and the end of the stick flared. There were smells of sulfa and beef gravy. He lit the cigarette, then reached to drop the stick match in the jelly-egg plate. His father leaned back on the back legs of the chair.

He could tell his father was looking at him. He continued to eat the stew and watch the center of the table.

"You moved around a lot. Have you been trouble for folks?"

"No, sir."

"Your Momma was a good woman, then she up and died and that's all she wrote. Do you miss her?"

He looked across the table and slowly up his father's shirt and directly into his eyes.

"Yes."

His mother was tall, and his father was shorter, with a thin, wiry frame. His eyes were an unusual brown—they were a deep mixture of sad-like impulsiveness with fear that oozed up around the rims of the pupils. They were troubled eyes, prone to anger.

The shed supper had been meandering around sharp edges. He finished the stew. "Thank you for supper. The stew was good." His father nodded, and he noticed he had Uncle Elbert's nose. Nothing else was said.

He slipped through the space between the table and chair and was on the outside of the closed door with the hope that a second invitation would not be extended. It was the orange part of the day when the shed stood in the long shadow of the house. He nodded to the faces in the kitchen window and made his way to the long bench and saw the tiny tractor cross the sun. He knew the flat bottle was in his father's hand.

21 – Leaving Soon

Four days later the sharp edge of the shed supper came calling. It was midafternoon. Miss Ellen was sitting in her chair with her back to the sink—her presence required due to his presence. He was standing to her left in the wide opening between the kitchen and the sitting room. He was facing the kitchen door. The door opened.

A dark figure stood in the doorway; the face and hands were the same darkness as the clothes. He knew the figure but couldn't make out the face. He could see the whites of the eyes in two oval bands. The voice from his father's body mumbled something about "the boy." Usually, Miss Ellen slowly sat down and got up from her chair. This time she rose quickly and walked around the back of her chair and stood between him and his father. She said two words. "Get out!"

Miss Ellen was a head taller and forty pounds heavier than the figure. She stood tall. All three stood at the sharp edge for tense, slow moments. His father left, slamming both doors. Miss Ellen locked the doors, and they stood in the kitchen for what seemed a long time.

Mr. Junior came home after supper and said that he had found one of his tractors sitting in the field still running and the shed was empty. Miss Ellen asked him to leave the room so she could talk to Mr. Junior. He closed the bedroom door. Miss Ellen's voice was loud; the door muffled the sound so that the words ran together.

He opened the suitcases on the bed and moved the last of the clean clothes from the chifforobe. His father had worn out his welcome and had moved on. He would be next. He was grateful that Miss Ellen had stood tall in the kitchen. His father's dark anger had erupted out of the cap-less mouth of multiple flat bottles. Miss Ellen was right—her presence was required.

The voices stopped. He knew the cattle were hanging around the barn; he could hear them calling for their supper. He guessed Mr. Junior had gone out to feed them. He did the nightly chores and went to bed. He made an effort to have small, smooth, simple thoughts. He would wait till daylight to digest this day. He kept the bedroom door closed. Sleep raced by with an occasional touch.

Miss Betty did not come to him, and there was morning light on his face. After completing his morning preparations, he headed for the kitchen.

Miss Ellen had heated up biscuits and gravy. "Your Aunt Eunice will be here in an hour."

"Am I leaving today?"

"No. She's coming to see you and have a talk with me."

"About me leaving?" Miss Ellen didn't answer.

Aunt Eunice's big car pulled into the driveway with two of his cousins, the fart master and the royal sleeper. The cousins were bigger, and Aunt Eunice was beautiful. There was a big hug and a kiss, and his shoulders got punched more than once. The stone house crew was from three nexts ago.

Aunt Eunice had brought him a new bicycle. The cousins took turns riding it. He had never ridden a bicycle; the cousins were better at it. He ran into a stump. Everybody laughed, including him.

Miss Ellen brought a cardboard box from the chicken house with six baby chicks. A white towel lined the bottom of the box, and the chicks were bright yellow with fuzzy feathers and high-pitched peeps. He and the two cousins were leaning over the box touching the chicks.

The next moment everything changed. The fart master picked up an empty soda bottle and smashed one of the chicks in the center of the box and broke its left leg.

Jim said, "You broke its leg!"

The fart master dropped the bottle and both cousins jumped away from the box. The fart master yelled, "He did it!"

He was still looking at the chick hopping to the side of the box with a break above its knee and the leg sticking out to the left. He stared at the chick's left eye for a sign of pain. Its face was covered in yellow fuzz; the eye didn't blink. He felt nauseated.

Miss Ellen was angry, and Aunt Eunice was sad and disappointed. Both adults believed he did it. He thought Miss Ellen believed this was the final sign that he needed to live elsewhere. He guessed Aunt Eunice thought he had something wrong with him.

He was still looking at the chick while the adults were talking to him. He was kneeling next to the box and turned to look at the cousins. One had lied and the other was silent. *It was easy to get blamed for stuff when you're a family of one with a highly suspect, absent father.*

He stopped listening and walked around the house and sat on the long bench. The tractor was gone, and the field was full of silent, still waves. The stone house crew stayed for another hour. The cousins played in the back yard and the adults were inside. Later Aunt Eunice's car backed out of the drive and headed north.

He was ready to leave. He would go to the next next with a reputation for harming small, helpless creatures. He was angry with his cousins.

He took the spear and walked to the shed. He looked back at the kitchen window; Miss Ellen was looking at him. He looked back, directly at her face...no expression on his face and none on hers. He went into the shed and closed the door. He put the spear on the bed with the point away from the pillow and sat in his father's chair. He counted the cans on the shelves: two green beans, five corns, seven soups, five white beans, three beef stews...twenty-two cans with tight paper sleeves with labels on the front. He counted twenty cigarettes smoked and put out in the jelly-egg plate and seven empty flat bottles on the floor behind the small table with the camp stove. He sat in the chair, with undefined thoughts that drifted without image.

The sun traveled away, and the red truck's motor came and stopped. He sat. Later he lay on the bed next to the spear. He slept without dreams.

He opened his eyes to a thin glow above the door. He sat up and left the shed, carrying the spear. He walked past the kitchen light and returned the spear to its place below the long bench. He came through the front door and washed his hands and face in the bathroom sink. He looked in the mirror and felt embarrassed for sleeping in the shed. It made him look small and guilty.

There was food on his plate when he entered the kitchen. Mr. Junior asked, "How was the shed last night?"

"Dark. Miss Ellen, you're wrong about who hurt the baby chicken." They looked at each other, and she looked down at her plate.

He had said it and that was it. He knew his time with Miss Ellen and Mr. Junior would end soon. He and his two cousins knew the truth. While he was in the shed, he had stopped being angry with them. The truth about who broke the baby chicken's leg would remain an unshared truth. He knew he would think of the incident more often than his cousins would think of it.

Mr. Junior stayed after breakfast. Now he knew this would be his last day at the screened porch house. Miss Ellen began telling him what would happen shortly after daylight and who would come. He didn't listen. The words ran together into a loud mumble. He looked at Mr. Junior's giant hands resting on the table. Mr. Junior was looking down at the same hands, with moisture filling his lower eyelids. The moisture in the eyes above the giant hands sparkled from the light reflected from the lamp that hung over the table.

Miss Ellen had finished talking. She had ended by asking, "Do you have any questions?"

He put his left hand on top of Mr. Junior's folded hands and left the table. The moisture in his eyes left two drops on the suitcases when he bent over to pick them up. He set them down to open the front door, then set them down again on the screened porch floor just to the right of the screen door. The back door closed, and the motor started. The red truck backed out of the drive and into the road. The truck sat for several moments with the motor running and the headlights pointed north. It was his and Mr. Junior's goodbye. The truck pulled off, followed by the "woo" sound. Miss Ellen was calling the cattle. No one was in the house. He sat on the long bench and cried with only one mournful moan that stayed mostly inside.

He sat on the bench until the shadow of the corner fence post began to shrink, pulling back across the road and growing darker. He waited until the shadow left the far side of the road and rested in the center. The shadow became crisp and divided half of the road in dark squares with two lines of dark barbed wire running south through the center of the road.

It would not be long before the people of the next would arrive. They would be people he didn't know, and he would learn to move about in their world without losing his. He carried portions of each of the nexts, but his time at each had faded for those who resided there. Each of the nexts became a period of waiting to move to the next. Never back, always forward.

The sun had climbed to the top branches of the trees behind the house. The shadow of the house covered most of the front yard. He stepped forward to the front of the screen and looked up at the oak tree. The highest tips of the branches were lit. He stood still and watched one branch stretch up through the light. He estimated that the light would slide down the branches less than a foot before the others arrived.

The moisture in Mr. Junior's eyes explained why he left before the others arrived. Mr. Junior would have his farming partner back but lose his hopes of raising a son. He liked Mr. Junior and would have been proud to be his son. He thought about watching Mr. Junior catch another giant fish and riding in the red truck with the big tires.

The branch had stretched a few more inches above the shadow coming from the top of the roof. The others would likely come from the north traveling south down the gravel road to his right. He had been at the screened porch house since late fall and had not seen a vehicle traveling from the south.

The moisture on the surface of the still dirt waves had dried and lost its shine. The tractor and plow had left for another field beyond sight or sound. The field lay wavy, still, and quiet. The waves waited for discs to slice them into a smooth sea of black dirt. The tractor would return again to pull inch-wide spikes across the surface to break up the wave slices. Planting would begin soon after. He would not be there to see it. He would stand on another porch and see another field.

The roof shadow was coming toward the screen, and the lower branches were lighting up. Faint sounds of motor and tires on gravel drifted through the screen on the north side of the porch.

He walked toward the sound and looked out the side screen at smoky-gray dust rising across light green tree buds on the side of the road. East of the road and beyond the cow shade tree deep woods hid the vehicle. He stepped through the screen door and stood next to the oak tree. He saw a black car moving south on the front edge of clouds of gravel dust shooting out from the backs of tires on both sides of the car.

He needed something to do while he watched every detail of the other's arrival. He returned to the porch and stood inside, left of the screen door near the front screen. The motor slowed and the dust lowered. The car stopped on the edge of the road in front of the house. He stepped to the left to see past the oak tree and found five rocks in his left pocket. He put them on the narrow ledge next to the front screen and began moving them around. His hands were watching the rocks while he eyed the car and passengers. A man in a hat sat behind the steering wheel; on the far side of the seat, he saw a dress with a white-gloved hand resting on a black patent leather purse. The car had one door on each side with the back window set high on a long sloping rear end that joined a chrome bumper. A thin layer of light gray dust covered the black paint.

The long door swung open, and the man in the hat stepped out onto the yard. He wore a black suit with a heavily starched white shirt and a perfectly tied black tie. His shoes were polished to a high black shine; a dress hat sat atop red hair, and gray eyes looked out from below the brim. He closed the car door, adjusted the cuffs of his shirt and buttoned the top button of his coat. He pushed his glasses up on his nose and opened the other door to help the woman with white gloves out of the car. They walked around the back of the car, arm in arm, toward the screen door. He was looking at them just below his top eyelids while moving the rocks around on the narrow ledge.

The man opened the screen door for the woman, and she stepped through first, followed by the man. They stopped halfway between the screen door and the front door and turned their faces to the right, and he turned a quarter turn toward them. The woman smiled and said, "Hello." The man smiled. He smiled at both of them and said nothing. This was their first time. It was not his.

The man knocked on the front door and it opened. They went inside without looking back. They were strangers and would be asking questions about him. He would rather have Mr. Junior answer. During their discussions at the kitchen table, opinions regarding his father and opinions regarding the baby chicken's broken leg may affect his value as a hand-me-down kid.

It was an odd and familiar feeling standing next to the screen while adults discussed where he would go next. The discussion was lengthy. The back door opened and closed, and he saw the man in the suit carrying the bicycle around the corner of the porch. He took off the front wheel and tucked the bicycle behind the back seat next to the inside of the back window. He put the wheel in the trunk. The lady with the gloves stepped out of the front door, with Miss Ellen standing in the doorway.

He picked up his suitcases. The woman was holding the screen door open. He walked past Miss Ellen and leaned over and whispered to her that she was wrong about who broke the baby chicken's leg. He walked past the woman with the gloves, across the yard and put the suitcases behind the car. He ran around to the back door while the man was putting the suitcases in the trunk. He stepped into the room with the hanging overalls and the rubber overshoes and took his coat off the hook and returned to the car.

The man was behind the steering wheel with the door closed. The woman was standing in the road with the door open and the back of her car seat leaning forward. He got into the back seat and the door closed. He turned and looked over the bicycle through the back window at the screened porch house. Miss Ellen closed the door, and he watched the porch become smaller and disappear behind deep woods.

The adults were more excited than he was. They used his name and told him theirs. He didn't listen beyond the names. The woman's name was Elizabeth and the man's name was Joseph. Miss Elizabeth kept using the name "Jimmy" when talking to him. The man corrected her and said, "The boy's name is Jim or James." He was relieved to keep his name. Casual would not have been a good word to describe Mr. Joseph. His suit, shirt, and tie were too perfect, and there was too much tension in his jaw for him to be called "Joe."

The car continued south until the sun began shining through his side of the car. The car turned right into the sun and down a one-lane sand road. He could see cottonwood trees ahead—the car was getting close to the river. The car went around a bend to the right and stopped in a flat sandy area that sloped down to the river.

Mr. Joseph got out of the car and walked to the left of the flat area to a large wooden structure. He stepped up on the base of the structure and pulled down a ten-foot-by-ten-foot flat platform that was painted white. The platform had steel brackets attached to the back so it could swing down on a steel bar. The platform now faced the river. Miss Elizabeth told him it was a signal for the ferry to come to take them across the river. She did not call him "Jimmy."

He stood by the car and watched the river. It looked to be a mile across to the other side. He knew there were big fish in the river. He had seen one. After a few minutes he began to see the ferry—a small flat barge with a wire fence on the sides, pushed by a small tugboat.

The barge was fully loaded with four cars. The tug pushed up the river at an angle against the current flowing to his left.

It took just short of thirty minutes for the barge to reach the bank. A ramp came down in the front and banged hard on a long thick layer of boards just above the waterline. The cars pulled off one by one. Mr. Joseph flipped the wooden platform back up, with the white painted side facing away from the river. The tugboat continued to push hard against the current to keep the barge from drifting away from the bank. The barge stayed in place for another fifteen minutes to see if another car arrived. The deckhand motioned for Mr. Joseph to drive down and onto the barge. The car bounced, the lumber rumbled, and the car stopped in the center of the barge.

He stood next to the wire fence on the ride across the river. He stared at the river, and for a time, forgot about the now next. The river was big and wide; those that stared at it felt drawn to it. The river was powerful and ancient. It was the home where things began but had been forgotten over time and distance. Once returned one felt the draw of an ancient home. Miss Elizabeth called him back to the car.

The distant reality of the now next crept into the back seat. The car pulled off the barge and up the bank. Cars were waiting. Then came another sandy road, followed by a turn south on gravel, another turn to the west and later, south again. After the last turn to the south, they drove on pavement for half an hour before turning to the north for five miles.

Around a small curve to the right, the car pulled into a gravel drive by a small house on his side of the road. He counted three sheds and a large barn. The front door faced west, and the road continued past the door running north and south. South of the house was the large barn, and the outbuildings were slightly to the right of the south-facing side door of the house where the drive ended. He got out of the car facing the side door. The outbuildings were to his right and the barn behind him.

Two long-haired collies ran from the barn and stuck their noses in the palms of his hands. He knelt down and petted both of them. Miss Elizabeth told him their names. The male was "Prince"; he didn't hear the female's name. He looked deep into their eyes for the spirits of his old friends. They looked away but sat close. He would be their friend.

He followed the two adults through the side door. Mr. Joseph carried his suitcases. He had done this before—it had always been a strange experience. There were new people, new objects, and new rooms with different beds. He maintained his separateness when he entered each environment. He protected himself from being pulled into a new place where he became another object that blended in with other objects placed there long before his arrival. At each next, those in charge of routine and custom had a predetermined place for him. He had maintained a quiet resistance against patterns forming on his skin that too closely resembled the wallpaper chosen by those in charge of each next. He had to pee. He saw the toilet and began using it.

Miss Elizabeth leaned through the open door. "We close the door when we use the bathroom." She pulled the doorknob and the door closed.

This was a teaching place that would require his attention. He had been lost in his own thoughts and had forgotten what he had learned at the stone house. There were no doors to close in the woods. He had peed outside more times than inside. He did wash his hands and apologize to Miss Elizabeth.

She showed him the room where he would sleep, which contained a wide bed with an iron frame like the one the silent woman slept in. It had a solid red bedspread. Miss Elizabeth said she had gotten it for him because the original one was pink with flowers.

The house had four main rooms. The side door facing the barn opened to the kitchen. A large picture window in the kitchen looked out at the barn, the drive, and the north-south road. The sitting room was in the front of the house next to the kitchen; the front door was in the right corner. Miss Elizabeth showed off the piano that sat in the far-left corner, facing the center of the room. She called it a "baby grand" piano. The top lid of the piano was propped open with a stick. Between the front door and the piano was a couch with fancy pillows. Sitting just off the south-facing wall were two chairs with a floor lamp between them.

He followed Miss Elizabeth to the kitchen and stood at the large window, watching Mr. Joseph put the front wheel on the bicycle. He had ridden it once. The generous gift was connected to Aunt Eunice's belief and disappointment about his harming the baby chicken.

Mr. Joseph motioned for him to come out. "Keep the bicycle here. It will be out of the weather, and we don't leave things lying around in the yard." Mr. Joseph opened one side of a double door to a shed just off the drive. "Use the kickstand. Don't leave it in the dirt."

The shed was painted a dark green with a dirt floor, and these were not suggestions. He put down the kickstand and left the shed. He wasn't sure he would ride the bike anytime soon. Mr. Joseph carried a lot of tension in his jaw.

Mr. Joseph took a pair of overalls off a hook and put them on over his suit and tie. He took his shoes off and put on rubber overshoes lined with leather house shoes and headed to the barn.

He walked around the house and sat on the concrete steps leading to a small front porch. Across the north-south road was an abandoned general store with two large windows and a door between them. The screen door in front of the wooden door had a narrow tin sign across the center with a picture of a rabbit head with tall ears with the words "Bunny Bread." Two burnt-red lines began at two rusty screws on the ends of the sign. The building stood behind a wire pasture fence surrounded by tall, dead, matted grass.

The sound was somewhere between "woo" and "whoa." It was deeper and longer than at the screened porch house. It sounded more ancient. A sound passed down by wrinkled, cupped hands that opened before the sound passed by the last finger. The cattle were coming from his right, headed south through the pasture and around the back of the outbuildings into the east side of the barn.

He looked at the bread sign. The sun was making longer shadows and warmed his face between his left eye and ear. The land was as flat the north-south road, with thin lines of trees in the distance. All land without a house, barn, building, or pasture was used for row crops. The wind whipped around empty space, slowed briefly by narrow lines of leafless trees. It was a place of dirt and wind. And there were rules. Next would come the confined space of the supper table.

The first table meal at each of the nexts had revealed much about its residents. A drifting mind at the eating table would be unwise. He knew the now next was a teaching place. He had felt like a feral cat being taught to use the litter box when Miss Elizabeth's hand pulled the bathroom door closed. The time for washing hands was fast approaching. He left the front of the house and went around to the side door. The bicycle-shed door was open. He turned left and went through the side kitchen door.

"Time to wash your hands. Use the kitchen sink."

He wasn't sure why he didn't say, "Yes ma'am." The soap was smooth without the grit of the last next. He dried his hands and looked out the large window. Mr. Joseph, no longer in overalls and overshoes, was closing the shed door. He turned toward the house, straightened his tie and buttoned the top button of his suit. The sun flashed off his shoes when he walked.

He left the window and stood to the left of the stove. He watched Miss Elizabeth move about the stove with the smooth movements of experienced hands. He knew he was distracting himself from memories of adult men passing through kitchen doors. The door opened and he did not look. He could see Mr. Joseph washing his hands in the sink. He had never seen a man wash his hands without rolling up his sleeves. Mr. Joseph's coat was still buttoned, and his pressed shirt cuffs were tight and dry around his wrists.

The table was set, and large bowls traveled from counter to table. Like at the screened porch house, he was offered the chair facing the sink with wall behind him. Mr. Joseph was to his left and Miss Elizabeth was facing him with her back to the sink. The sitting was the same. He was the same. The faces and place were different. He would stick to the basics: polite, quiet, and respectful.

"Our Heavenly Father…" He watched their eyes close and their heads bow. Miss Elizabeth opened one eye and saw him looking. This was a ritual he had not seen before. This was prayer about the food. He looked down. He had learned to watch for quick movements when people were near. Muscles in the upper chest and lower arms moved a half second before the hands. He would bow his head next time, but he wouldn't close his eyes.

The food had a rich, heavy smoothness. It was the best he had ever tasted. *Sorry, Miss Betty had met her match.* Both were experts but different.

He responded when he was asked. He remained silent after answering. Mr. Joseph explained to him that Miss Ellen felt she needed to be in the fields to help Mr. Junior, and he was a fine boy who had been through a lot and needed someone who had the time to teach him about proper living. He nodded as if Mr. Joseph had revealed information that explained everything that he was too young to discover himself. His ability to read people and situations would be a secret that he would keep close.

He already knew a great deal about Mr. Joseph. The attention to detail of his clothing, the level of formalness, and the tension in his jaw suggested little tolerance for mistakes. He saw a quick temper behind gray eyes. Mr. Joseph would be a hard master. He would hold the fabric of his identity closer than before.

He was tense, and his stomach was moving. He finished his plate and complimented Miss Elizabeth on her cooking. She was pleased, and Mr. Joseph's jaw eased a bit. He was thankful that he had not lost his manners or the desire to offer them.

Supper was finished. Miss Elizabeth was washing the dishes, and Mr. Joseph was drying. He sat and watched Mr. Joseph dry the silverware without touching it with his hands. He used one end of the towel to pick it up and the other end of the towel to dry it. He dropped each one into the drawer without touching it with his hands.

Steam came out of the sink where the dishes were being washed. It was different than watching the silent woman stand in mud to wash spoons and skillets at the pump. The kitchen chores were finished. Mr. Joseph left the room while Miss Elizabeth wiped the last of the counter. She washed the cloth and draped it over the faucet. The wire edges of the dish drainer pushed up the center of the dish towel left open to dry.

Miss Elizabeth turned and smiled. "Let's put your things away."

He followed her into the room with the wide bed. He saw her bedroom to the left, which shared a common wall with his room. A four-drawer dresser sat to the left along the shared wall. To the right of the door was a smaller door—a narrow door with shiny white paint that matched tall baseboards that rose from the floor. The ceiling was tall and the floor wooden, with a window to the left of the bed. The bed was pushed into the northeast corner with the iron headboard against the north wall and the footboard pointed at the narrow, shiny white door.

Miss Elizabeth put his suitcases on the bed and opened them without asking. "We'll keep your socks in the top drawer, underwear and T-shirts in the second drawer." It reminded him of Aunt Eunice and Miss Betty talking over the same suitcase—this will fit here and that will go there. His things separated from the suitcases caused the same discomfort.

"Pick out a shirt and pants for tomorrow and I'll iron them." He had seen Miss Betty iron one of Aunt Eunice's dresses, but he had never worn a piece of ironed clothing.

"Looks like all of your shirts and pants need pressing." He wondered if his clothes would look like Mr. Albert's, straight creased from iron pressed on fabric. "I'm going to change into a housedress before I start on your shirts and pants. You can wait here or sit in the living room."

He nodded. He would stay in the bedroom. Miss Elizabeth left the room, and her door closed. His shirts and pants were in two stacks next to the open suitcases. He found his coat hanging on a wooden hanger behind the narrow, shiny door. He removed the fingernail clippers from the left pocket and felt the last of the rocks in the right pocket. He removed some of the items in the suitcases and put them in the top drawer. The clear plastic sleeves with toothbrush, paste, and comb were on the left and underwear and socks to the right. He kept the pocketknife in his left pocket and the last of the rocks in his right.

He had left the spear under the long bench. He wished he had it under the wide bed, but he doubted there would have been room for it inside the car, and it was too long for the trunk. He hadn't been bold enough to carry it to the car. Before he left the front screened porch, he had been aware of Mr. Joseph's and Miss Elizabeth's possible discomfort with an unknown kid with a spear riding in the back seat.

The original suitcase lay open with the top unfolded to the right. Inside the top was the cloth pocket with the picture of his mother when she was eighteen years old. He touched the right edge of the picture and slid it out of the cloth pouch.

"Did you get unpacked?" He slid the picture back into its place. Mr. Joseph stood in the doorway wearing light-colored pants and long sleeve shirt—the clothes of a farmer. The shirt and pants were ironed with a sharp crease down the front of the pants and the outside of the sleeves.

"Yes sir." He felt protective of the picture with Mr. Joseph standing in the doorway. Miss Elizabeth's door opened, and she stood with Mr. Joseph. Both were smiling. He wondered if the window behind him was hard to open.

He followed his pants and shirts and the two adults to the kitchen. Miss Elizabeth set up the ironing board and plugged the iron into a brown extension cord plugged in below the large window that overlooked the barn.

Mr. Joseph set a large pitcher on the table with two glasses and a plate of cornbread. "Do you like buttermilk?"

He didn't know how to answer the question. His face said maybe. Large clumps slid over the edge of the wide-mouthed pitcher and floated in the glass on top of thick milk. Mr. Joseph broke off pieces of cornbread and dropped them in the glass and pushed them down with a spoon. He did the same. Mr. Joseph tipped the glass, and he watched the clumps and cornbread slide over the edge and disappear. Mr. Joseph put the glass down and waited for him to take the first drink. He lifted the glass with his left eye looking down the side of the glass at Mr. Joseph.

It was not the drink of his choice. It was hard to describe. It resembled the taste of gritty clumps of butter the size of small raccoon turds floating in heavy milk that was moments from turning sour. He swallowed the gritty butter turds and put an empty glass on the table. He had seen men do the same with glasses of whiskey, and the man watching would fill the glass again.

"Want some more?"

"It was good. Still full of supper." He watched Mr. Joseph grin. He looked straight into Mr. Joseph's eyes. He knew it wasn't smart. He did it anyway.

Most of his shirts were waded into balls and sat damp in a large, polished metal bowl. Two of his shirts were on wooden hangers that hung from a metal bar at the end of the wide part of the ironing board. The sleeves had sharp creases like Mr. Joseph's shirt. A Pepsi bottle filled with a clear liquid sat on the ironing board. A cork was stuck in the mouth of the bottle with a small metal sprinkle head coming out of its center. Miss Elizabeth would sprinkle, and iron and another shirt would hang low at the end of the ironing board.

He wondered who would win an ironing contest. Mr. Albert said Miss Grace "ironed good." He did look sharp for someone that had been found in the woods forty years ago. The shirts at the end of the ironing board had creases that could cut. It would be a close contest. Mr. Joseph poured another glass. He didn't look.

Mr. Joseph and Miss Elizabeth took turns telling him about themselves. They were both older than the adults he had stayed with before. They told him they had been schoolteachers who started teaching in one-room schoolhouses. Mr. Joseph had stopped teaching to farm. Miss Elizabeth said she had stopped teaching for a while and planned to go back when he was settled in his new home.

He had seen a school before with children playing outside the building; he had not been to a school. His reading was limited to road signs and labels on cans and flat bottles. Arithmetic was a vague concept of counting things in his surroundings and the number of times open bottles touched lips before violence began. He knew the schoolteachers would expect him to go to school. He would start late and know less. He would be older.

This new next was closed in tighter. It was an organized house that was clean, with every object resting in its own place and, once moved to be used, returned to rest in the same place. He had learned to move about in each of the nexts without touching or moving objects, leaving no trail or sign of his passing presence. This next was different than the before nexts. Mr. Joseph and Miss Elizabeth seemed of like mind that he live with them. This was a large difference.

Living with those who welcomed his presence did not change his having one true parent. Before he was pulled from her bed, he had seen his mother travel away from him. She did not return. Each memory and image of her had a soft glow. He had gently separated the living from the leaving. He visited more often the floating, soft glows of the living memories and images. He tended to the dimmer glows of leaving less often and from some sense of duty and at some distance.

The voice came from the ironing board. "Tell us about yourself."

He looked at Miss Elizabeth. "Been called a wayfaring pilgrim in a strange land." Both adults were amused.

Mr. Joseph added, "You are our son, and this is your home." The grip of Mr. Joseph's mind had tightened; the room seemed smaller. This had not been a suggestion. His mind stepped to the side, and the closed hand of Mr. Joseph's mind went past and gripped empty air. The noise of the words was distant. He moved no object and left no sign. He moved his head to acknowledge the words. His resistive nature remained private.

Mr. Joseph washed the glasses and spoons and left the room. He heard the sound of a newspaper opening. The buttons slid inside the grooves near the point of the iron.

He watched Miss Elizabeth move the iron across the fabric. The blue jeans were hung on the wooden hangers with straight, sharp creases down the front and back of each leg. He walked behind Miss Elizabeth carrying jeans on hangers past Mr. Joseph sitting behind an open newspaper. He hung the jeans to the right of the shirts and closed the narrow door.

"Time to wash up and get ready for bed." Miss Elizabeth left the room. He closed the door and found his pajamas in the bottom drawer. He folded his clothes with the underwear inside the jeans and stacked them on the floor under the window.

He was washing his hands when Miss Elizabeth came in with a soapy rag and washed his face and neck. He couldn't recall anyone washing his face and neck with soap. It was different and a bit strange. He guessed there would be more soap in his immediate future.

"Go in and say good night. We have an early day tomorrow." He knew about early. Each next had its early. He stood in the doorway opposite the front door. Across the room and to the left were creased pants and gray socks with light blue tips below an open newspaper. He wasn't sure what to call Mr. Joseph. "Good night" came out.

The paper lowered. "Good night, sweet prince. Sleep well." The paper went up.

He closed his mouth and left the room. He closed the bathroom door, peed and washed his hands. He got into bed with his clean neck and the sense of the house getting smaller. The now next felt confined. Miss Elizabeth came in and did what she called "tucking in." His thoughts smelled of damp caution. Tonight, he would sleep in the first wide bed. He pushed away thoughts and hoped to sleep well.

Next

First night at the past nexts had been filled with watching the residents before, during, and after supper. The loss of sight from closed eyes and the lack of protection in deep sleep fed the invitation to stay awake. The repetition of leaving and of arriving drained the spaces around awake. He tried to sleep after the sun fell out of the trees and buried itself in the dirt. Daytime thinking and nighttime sleeping seldom spoke but nodded in passing. The sun would come up on the outside wall of the house. His mind saw breakfast cow shadows moving across the east side of the house just after dawn. A dreamless sleep came.

22 – The Edge of a New Darkness

The door creaked; Miss Elizabeth was standing in the opening. "Time to get up. We have a big day."

He got up and made the bed and looked out the north window and saw the slow parade of cows coming. Early was later at the now next. Breakfast cow shadows rubbed across the east wall while he completed closed-door bathroom chores. He changed clothes and put the folded pajamas under the pillow. He stopped at the big window in the kitchen and looked up at a clear sky. It would be a nice day.

He turned and walked across the room and stood to the left of the stove with his back to the wall. Miss Elizabeth asked him if he slept well. He said he did. The door opened to the left of the big window. Mr. Joseph stood next to the back of Miss Elizabeth's chair. They were facing each other four feet apart. "Did you sleep well?"

"Yes sir." A skillet made a sound, and he turned his head to the left to look at the stove. "Miss Elizabeth, what are you going to put in the skillet?"

"You call her mother!"

The words pushed against the side of his face. His head snapped away from the stove. The word was in his mouth, and it slung out of his left cheek past his teeth. "Elizabeth."

Mr. Joseph was two feet from his face. Miss Elizabeth's hands stopped moving. He felt the back of his head against the wall. Mr. Joseph's fingers had folded into his palms, and he could see brown freckles on the top of his hands.

"Joseph, you have to give him time." She spoke the words to the top of the stove.

There was no movement in the room. Mr. Joseph was deciding. He knew about deciding. Deciding was when grown men prone to anger stood rigid while blood pumped away from their brains to their limbs, and red stains in their heads raced about screaming. The air was thick and still. He could feel each hair pressed against the wall.

There were two pockets on the front of Mr. Joseph's shirt. He watched for movement above the pockets and on the insides of Mr. Joseph's forearms. He stood in the small space between the stove and the corner of the room. Mr. Joseph would decide, and that was what would happen. He had stood before violent men before. Each time his heart beat a little less fast. Mr. Joseph turned and closed the kitchen door behind him.

He had made a mistake. His head had turned fast, and the word had slung out before he could catch it. He had had a mother. She had left. He was the head of his family of one. The loyalty to his mother had formed the word, but his resistive nature had failed to catch it before it slung past his teeth. Miss Elizabeth was standing at the big window looking at the barn.

He left the kitchen and went out the front door and sat on the concrete steps. He had not thought of a name for this next. The sun had lit up the matted grass around the general store building. Large splotches of the tin roof had dried to a sunken burnt red surrounded by tin with a flat shine. A pleasant breakfast would have been nice. He sat on the steps for a long time and tried not to think of what would come next at the now next.

Miss Elizabeth came through the door and handed him two sausage biscuits and a glass of milk. She looked down at him and said, "It's been two hours. He hasn't come back from the barn. He's mad. Eat your breakfast. We have to leave in ten minutes."

Leaving sounded good to him. He finished the food and milk and put the plate and glass in the sink. Miss Elizabeth had changed clothes, and he followed her to the car. She backed the car away from the big window and pulled forward, facing the road. "Need to tell Joseph we're leaving." She walked toward the barn. She called his name, and he saw them talking over a board fence. He tried not to look.

The car pulled out and turned left and headed south on the north-south road and right heading west. The car turned right in the center of a small town and headed north for about an hour.

Miss Elizabeth liked to talk. He listened. He didn't ask where they were going. His suitcases were not in the car—he had been relocated for less than not calling a stranger "Mother." He learned about Miss Elizabeth's family who lived in the hills. One of her uncles had carried a pistol, and another was a hermit who lived on top of a mountain. She spoke well of her father and of her mother who had passed away.

The car pulled into a parking lot next to a building with three rows of windows. They went up a wide set of stairs, turned right at a landing and went up a second stairway. The leather heels on Miss

Elizabeth's shoes clomped on the wooden steps, and her purse swung on her arm in front of her left elbow. The woods had taught him not to step down flat. His feet rolled forward lightly off the back of his heels onto the balls of his feet without making a sound.

At the top of the stairs, they turned left down a hallway of wooden doors with frosted glass and gold letters. "Dr. Stanley Buford" was painted in gold on frosted glass above a doorknob at the end of the hallway. They turned right through the doorway. The last time he had seen a doctor was shortly after Miss Grace had scooped him up off the tarp and put him on his mother's chest. He was told the doctor wasn't needed then, and he wasn't sure Dr. Buford was needed now. Nevertheless, he would submit to an examination if called upon to do so. He wondered if Dr. Buford would write his findings on the flap of an envelope.

He followed Miss Elizabeth to a second room behind the gold letters. They waited in the small room with a narrow table and a large window. Dr. Stanley Buford, wearing a white, pressed coat and name tag, entered the room. Introductions were made. The examination began with ears, nose, and throat. "Swollen tonsils will need to come out." Things began to go poorly after he was asked to take off his shirt. The sores were examined with stern looks at Miss Elizabeth. He was asked to take off his pants. The doctor was visibly angry. He sat on the narrow table in his underwear. He hoped Stanley Buford would not ask him to remove his underwear. He was asked and he did.

"How did you allow this boy to get in this condition?"

"I just got this child yesterday."

The adults were angry, and he was ashamed. Before the anger, the adults had the same expression on their faces as the kids at the shack watching him standing in the washtub. Dr. Stanley Buford's gold letters made no difference. The feeling was the same.

"This child needs to be bathed once a day. Use this medicine on the sores, and this one on the penis." The adults turned their backs to him and spoke quietly. He heard three words: husband, penis, clean.

Miss Elizabeth's heels hit hard on the stairs. She was still angry. It was unlikely he would step behind Dr. Stanley Buford's gold letters again. The car pulled away from the building without stories of pistol-carrying hermit relatives. The car was quiet.

He listened to his thoughts. The car left an angry adult heading south to a second angry adult with a third angry adult in tow. He wondered if Miss Elizabeth thought less of him after the examination. *Would my presence become an inconvenience requiring relocation?* It was an old question that had been posed and repeated and answered often. The first answers arrived in heavy containers without handles—difficult to move and burdensome to carry. Along the way he had learned to drop a container and roll it down a bank of indifference and watch it sink below the surface of a no-care pond.

"You have a lot of cousins that are your age." Miss Elizabeth had spoken and looked less angry.

He had little to say after the examination. He wondered if he had more holes in his skin than the average kid his age. He knew he did. He would be glad when they all closed up and healed. He had great difficulty staying away from the scabs that covered the sores. The tops of the scabs were hard and ranged in color from dark burnt red to black. He pulled them off; connected to the bottom of the scabs were cone-shaped tissues that ended in a point that sunk deep below the skin. The front of his legs below the knee had sores that reached bone.

He had many secrets. The sores and the condition of his penis were the ones he hid most often. The others were ones he didn't share. He didn't offer, and no one asked. Skeletal reports from each now next to the next next seldom described the rawness that grew smaller in the rear windows set atop the tires that rolled forward over the dust to each coming next.

Miss Elizabeth had been talking. Something about doctoring the sores and his learning to keep his body clean. He looked at her and smiled. He had spent little time examining his skin. Those who had seen it reacted to it—Miss Elizabeth had been shocked. She had defended herself well against the doctor's comments and had shifted into correcting the situation. There was a sense that much was coming his way. He would ride the wave and hope not to be injured.

He saw the north side of barns and sheds on the return trip. The car passed the morning pastures a second time. Many of the cattle were grazing on new spring grass and had moved little. He had wondered why cattle often faced the same direction whether they were eating or just standing. It was a question he had not asked, and he had heard no one mention it.

Next

Cattle tended to face the same direction, and each herd had at least one crazy cow. Crazy cows became a problem when farmers moved herds from old pastures to new ones with more grass. Crazy cows moved just behind the lead cow when the herd would approach the gate to the new pasture. The crazy cow would run ahead and stop at the opening and turn with their weight on the back hooves and lurch forward with their front hooves in the air, then go left or right in a dead run. The herd would startle, and most would follow the crazy cow at a full run. A few of the cows would go in the opposite direction. The process of moving the herd to the new pasture would begin again.

Most cattle farmers sold their crazy cows at a bargain, and they often ended up in a herd of crazy cows bought by the beginning cattle farmer who appreciated the bargain but later learned to hate each and every cow. Crazy cows would break fences and spend half their time in the road. They ran about in short bursts and rarely gained weight. It was a hard lesson for the new cattle farmer.

He had been in cow land with the humming words of Miss Elizabeth in the distance. The car pulled in the drive. Mr. Joseph stood in the large kitchen window. He felt tension in his jaw and stomach; unpleasant things were coming his way. He followed Miss Elizabeth into the house. Mr. Joseph seemed less angry.

Miss Elizabeth turned on the bathtub faucet, and the white rubber stopper blocked the water from running down the drain. Miss Elizabeth whispered to Mr. Joseph. She turned and told him to take off his clothes, and she would help him take "a good clean bath." She said, "We'll put medicine on those spots." Mr. Joseph stood in the doorway.

He sat quietly in the water and Miss Elizabeth washed his hair and body with white soap with no grit. "There, that's good. Your father will help you clean your private parts." Miss Elizabeth stepped away from the tub.

The messenger of fear, humiliation, and pain knelt down next to the tub and pulled the chain connected to the white stopper, and the dark gray water flowed down the drain until two inches of gray water remained in the tub. His hands were smaller than the freckled hands that began pulling the skin away from the end of his penis. There was blood and pain in the water, and his hands pulled at the larger wrists.

"Hold still!"

Miss Elizabeth called Mr. Joseph's name. Mr. Joseph's voice was loud against his left ear. "This will get done. If you need to leave the room, you may! Hold still!"

A portion of the pain left with his mind; he was no longer a part of the event. He and Miss Betty were sitting at the table in the room with typewriters discussing Miss Elizabeth's cooking. Miss Betty asked about the amount of butter used, and he reported that it was significant. He saw his mother standing on the opposite curb, smiling, and watched the blue fabric of her dress move across her legs when she turned and disappeared around the corner.

A portion of the pain returned when he left the visit with Miss Betty, and he stood in the bathroom with Miss Elizabeth kneeling in front of him putting medicine on the sores. He had on new underwear with three faint red spots in the front.

He was relieved that he had not attended the entire event. Mr. Joseph's "This will get done" was uncomfortably close to the sentiment one would expect before completing the chore of shooting a dog after it had killed chickens. Kindness and respect had not arrived before his departure to visit with Miss Betty. Mr. Joseph's morning kitchen anger and afternoon bathroom disregard fueled a distanced resolve to protect the essence of his being.

He was dressed and sat quietly on the high stool in the kitchen. His body was under a patterned plastic garment with his head sticking out an opening in the top. Miss Elizabeth took the lid off an old flat box. Inside were two long combs, two long, pointed scissors, and a large metal object with teeth on one end and two handles on the other end. She removed the large object and stood over the sink and blew on the teeth. It was to be a kitchen haircut.

He asked to see how the object in Miss Elizabeth's hand worked. She held it front of him and squeezed the two handles together and blades filled the space between the teeth. The handles moved together and apart, and hair slid down the patterned plastic. The object returned to the box, and long scissors moved around his ears and neck. More hair lay in the folds of the patterned plastic and on the floor than remained on his head. The scissors returned to the box, replaced by a wooden-handled brush with long, soft bristles. Cut hair was brushed off his face and neck; the plastic came off and his shoulders were brushed. He wondered if he was up to the now-next standards.

Next came another car ride to see Mr. Joseph's mother. He had not seen Mr. Joseph since the bathroom. The car turned left for five miles and right for three and entered the southwest side of the small town. Mr. Joseph's mother lived in a large two-story white house with a black iron fence and concrete carriage steps facing the street. White columns held a wide porch that stretched around three of the outside walls. A new aunt stood at the top of the steps with a movie camera and filmed the first cousin he met.

The car returned to the house across the road from the abandoned general store. The windshield faced the kitchen window, and there was pain in his underwear when he got out of the car. The dogs ran to him, and he heard Miss Elizabeth call their names. The female was "Queen."

"Next week you'll go to school. I'll help you get caught up with the others." Miss Elizabeth stopped in the kitchen.

He passed her on his way to the front door and sat on the concrete steps. Spring was coming up and out of dirt, limb, and stem. He had grown unaccustomed to close supervision. He had learned to tend to his own business and maintain a suitable distance from the waves of unpredictable behavior that swelled up from gathered faces in the places where he had stood in the shadows watching. His wide bed stood in a small house of supervision. He watched them watch him.

Two heavy weights strained each top line of the daily numbered calendar squares that represented each day of spring where a bath was required: the bath given by Miss Elizabeth and the ritual cleaning of the penis by Mr. Joseph. The events were large, rusty ball bearings that rolled slowly and heavily across the top line of the seven days of the first hard-pressed week. There was no physical privacy. Dignity was a faint fluttering held within and fiercely protected.

At the end of seven days, he was able to negotiate the privilege of taking his own bath and cleaning his own penis. He bathed with a proper carefulness. He put medicine on the sores and medicine on the underside of the foreskin. He put on the pajamas and combed his hair. He put everything back the way it was in the bathroom and went to the sitting room to say good night. Miss Elizabeth was sitting and reading. "My, you're a handsome young man. Did you get everything doctored up?"

He nodded and said, "Good night."

"Good night."

He walked into his bedroom with the red bedspread and saw Mr. Joseph lying on the side of the bed next to the window. Mr. Joseph's head was propped up with two pillows. He motioned for him to come closer. "Let's see if you got everything clean." His hand kept motioning for him to come closer.

He felt small, weak, and scared. The top of his pajamas was off, and Mr. Joseph was examining the sores. He was turned several times.

"Take the bottoms off." He stood naked in front of the man with the gray eyes. "Give me your leg." He stood on his left foot and Mr. Joseph held his right ankle and examined the sores on the front of his leg. "Turn." He turned his left foot with the toes pointing away from the man, and sores on the back of his leg were examined. Then he stood on his right leg while his left leg was examined.

"Come closer." The examination of his penis lasted longer than his legs. He was relieved to step back and put on the pajamas. Mr. Joseph's voice was matter of fact during the examination. Mr. Joseph's breathing had been forced and unsettled and betrayed a notion of pleasure that demanded privacy. Mr. Joseph left the room.

He brushed off the pillows and turned them. They still had the scent of sweat from unwashed hair. He lay in the wide bed and looked at the ceiling. Each place he had been left had its own cost and caution. He had learned to use caution to reduce the daily cost of residing in each of the past nexts. He had just experienced the edge of a new darkness that had crossed his path for the first time. He had most likely crossed its path where it lay in wait for a chosen one that had strayed beyond the reach of its kin by hide and herd and was left undefended. It had a taste and would return.

23 – Birth Certificate

Morning came with the creak of the door and Miss Elizabeth's voice. He did the waking chores of pee, hands, hair, and clothes. Miss Elizabeth stood at the stove. He said good morning and was asked how he slept. He did not stand in the small space at the left of the stove in the corner of the room. He stood in the doorway leading to the sitting room. He had decided that he would live his life with an available exit. He would do his best not to be hemmed in by wall or headboard.

Mr. Joseph came in the kitchen door with mail in his hand. Mr. Joseph spoke to him and he to Mr. Joseph. He was afraid of the man. He looked down and tried not to run.

Breakfast began with prayer and a comment about receiving a letter from the judge. Mr. Joseph opened it and unfolded the paper. He showed it to Miss Elizabeth. She smiled and said, "It's your birth certificate." He left the chair and stood to the left of Miss Elizabeth. She read it. "Certificate of Live Birth, Father Joseph, Mother Elizabeth, Length of Pregnancy Nine Months."

He pointed at the "Length of Pregnancy" and the handwritten number "nine" with "months" written after the number. "You weren't pregnant with me."

"Yes, we know that. It's just simpler this way."

Mr. Joseph was angry. He didn't care. The judge and the paper had erased his parents. The paper had tried to push his mother beyond the outer edge of his memory. He sat down and finished his breakfast. He would sort it out later. Miss Elizabeth was disappointed in his reaction. He didn't look at Mr. Joseph.

After breakfast he went to the concrete steps. It was his responsibility to remember his mother. Those who knew her would fade, and he would be the last to remember. The record of their connection was gone. His mother walked along the far sidewalk and turned the corner. His mother sat on the bank of the wide river with his head in her lap. The sound of her voice, the kindness of her nature, and the gifts she passed to him would remain close and held with great care. One day he, too, would pass by the outer edge of memory, and another would take his place.

He unfolded the facts of the now next and laid them on the dead, matted grass on both sides of the abandoned general store building. He sat on the concrete steps and watched the facts across the road. There was no place to go. The facts remained. The judge's paper had built a fence around the now next, and he could not leave without one of his new paper parents.

Known events began to approach from the front, and unknown events began to approach from the side. Miss Elizabeth spent time helping him with reading. She taught him how to tell time from a clock. Time had been measured by the sun and adjusted by season. He had seen and felt the earth turn inside the sky. The turning into and away from the sun and the appearance of the moon gave time, direction, season, and temperature. Clocks seemed more confined and less accurate. Each clock had a slightly different interpretation of the unchanged push of the earth against the moving sky. These were concrete-step thoughts. School would require clocks, reading, and arithmetic. The movement of the sun pulled the days closer. He prepared with Miss Elizabeth.

Church arrived before school. The clock face supervised the collection of polished shoes, pressed shirt, and pants with jacket. The ride in the back seat was followed by bone pressed on flesh above wooden pews and words stopped by song. Upon completion of the rituals, he was introduced to many smiling faces with pleasant words said, and he shook hands and smiled. Mr. Joseph and Miss Elizabeth knew every name. There were special names with faces that smiled wider and were introduced as cousins. He smiled wider, too, and hoped he would see them again away from polished shoes hanging below wooden pews among the rituals of words and songs.

Instead, he rode in the back seat to the house with the big window by the door to the kitchen where the table filled with beef roast with potatoes and carrots. Ritual clothes were put away. Mr. Joseph and Miss Elizabeth took naps while he explored the sheds and barn.

He would attend school tomorrow. It would be the first time.

24 – First Day of School

The chair had chrome legs that stood straight in the front and sloped back in a curve behind the seat. It was the fourth and empty chair whose seat rested below the table to the right of where he sat for meals. The chair stood tall with a new purpose and title. It had moved from the table; it stood and looked south out the big window. It had become the sit-and-watch-for-the-school-bus chair.

He sat in the chair and faced the road. His hands were folded over a vinyl briefcase with leather straps balanced on his upper legs. He stared at the road without moving, and his eyes became unfocused, his mind drifted. The school bus would come out of the trees in a slight curve heading to the north. His eyes centered on the outside tree that stood closest to the curve. He saw the yellow appear around the tree. He looked hard and it disappeared. It happened again before the real bus drifted around the curve and he saw the man in the big windshield.

He was out the door without a word. He turned at the drive and raised his right hand at Miss Elizabeth in the big window. She raised hers. The bus turned into the drive between the fence and south side of the yard. He walked around the front of the bus and up the metal steps.

Brown vinyl slots had faces wedged between. Larger faces rose higher above the slots. He chose the third seat to his right behind the driver. The driver's side of the bus allowed his throwing hand and arm to be available should any of the slotted faces choose to participate in some unforeseen event. The bus backed out of the drive and headed back to the tree-lined curve.

The bus stopped one mile from the concrete steps at a small opening in the edge of the woods. A heavier-set boy one head taller than he was came up the steps and sat in the seat in front of him. He saw the boy's head turn and his right elbow and forearm rest on the top of the back of the seat. "You're the new kid down the road." A big smile rose up from a round face. "I'm Ray."

He shook Ray's hand and felt the smile rise to the surface of his own face. Ray was OK.

The bus slowed and stopped at a dirt road leading to an unpainted house with a tin roof. Two smaller girls came up the steps followed by a tall, older girl. Their mended clothes were faded; their faces showed no dirt. He recognized the color of unwashed skin—he had seen it in the mirror. They lived in an unpainted house with no running water and an outhouse downwind from a back porch that had a metal washtub hanging on the back wall. He smiled at the faces that looked down the way he often did.

Ray knew all three and spoke to them as a group. The tall girl looked at Ray and spoke. The girls had a quiet sadness that came from faded clothes and dulled emotions. It was familiar.

The bus turned right onto the three-mile road that led to town. He was glad he had met Ray. Ray had a ready smile and a kind nature that eased the tension of a first day. The bus went into town and stopped at the edge of a large square of land bordered by sidewalks. A wide sidewalk led to double doors of a two-story brick cube with tall windows.

He followed Ray off the bus and waited on the sidewalk. The door closed, and the bus pulled away with four older kids still on board. One was the tall girl who had spoken to Ray. The two younger girls from the unpainted house stood at the edge of a group of twenty kids that began to flow up the wide sidewalk. He lost sight of Ray after passing through the double doors and walking up fourteen steps.

Several women stood in the hallways with clipboards, asking for names and directing kids to rooms. He stood in the hallway to the right of the fourteen steps. A thin woman in a gray dress and heavy black shoes asked his name. He looked up at short black hair and a nose that stuck out uncomfortably far from a severe, angular face. The nose was unusually thin and long with two round, shiny bumps at the end where the skin was pulled tight. He gave his name quickly and was directed to an open door five steps to his right. He looked back to watch the nose slice through the air racing to keep in the center of the face when the head spun to look down on another small, frightened face. He knew the room would have a clock.

He stepped into a room of desks, with tall walls and windows. A short, round woman greeted him and asked him to choose a seat. He sat in the middle of the room with two large windows behind him and two large windows to his left. The teacher's desk sat in front of black slate and white chalk. "Mrs. Bass" in cursive chalk stretched across slate beside the last small faces entering the room. Mrs. Bass was pleasant and kind, and the first of the morning was slow and easy.

Recess was announced and a line filed out and to the right, down another fourteen steps, and through double doors at the side of the building. A dirt basketball court with a smooth, brown surface lay twenty yards from the edge of the building. Beyond the court, grass extended out another fifty yards to a sidewalk, curb, and street.

He walked across the edge of the brown surface into the grass and stood some twenty plus yards from the street. He watched the cars and trucks moving left and right. The cars were long, with chrome and colors from yellow to light blue. Some trucks had flat beds with no sides, and others had metal beds with wheel wells that bulged out the sides. He watched for a while, then turned toward the building and walked around the basketball court where a wad of kids and a ball were moving to his end of the court.

"Jim." He looked up at short black hair and the knife-like nose with the two bumps at the end. He was a small fish spotted by the crane. He looked down at sticks falling out of the end of the dress and rising up out of giant black shoes. The beak nose came down close enough to pluck out an eyeball, and a small thin slit below the nose parted. "Was that you out by the street?"

"No ma'am." It was a poor answer. There were technical issues. The definition of "by." He had been separated from the street by twenty yards. There were the curb, the sidewalk, and the grass to consider. The shiny bumps came closer and the eyes narrowed to two black pebbles; the slit parted, and the question came again. His second answer was equally poor.

The basketball rested in a low spot in the smooth, brown surface. He could hear faint laughter. It was in the distance; there was silence around him. The corpse of the game stood on the smooth surface, and all of the players had the back of their throats exposed in open mouths from dropped jaws on frozen faces.

His left arm moved forward from bony fingers wrapped around and pulling above his elbow. He followed his arm through the double doors on the side of the building. His feet touched eight of the fourteen steps. He moved with the gray dress past the front fourteen steps to his left. The floor was divided by narrow strips of honey-colored glows where dust floated through thin walls of angled light and disappeared over shoe paths worn through clear varnish. The nose and bones and gray dress belonged to the principal.

His left arm entered the office first, and the door closed behind him. He faced the principal, with her desk to his right holding a wooden nameplate: "Miss Horn, Principal." In a hair's width sliver of time, a thin, flat, crystal thought shot through the closing space before the finger would rise and the value of truth would be laid out before him in a true life-changing speech. *She was "Miss Hornnose!"*

What followed was unpleasantly long, filled with stern-faced words and a large wooden paddle. He basked in the warmth of his cleverness. Before Miss Hornnose's last wooden, two-handed swing hit its mark, he realized he could tell time upside down. He was bent over, and the clock was behind him. The clock was briefly fuzzy from shaken eyeballs when wood met fabric at the end of the last swing. The bell rang.

He walked away from parting warnings, out the door, and through dusty, thin walls of light and sat down carefully in the center of Mrs. Bass's room. He had left the principal's office with her secret name and the ability to tell upside down time. He looked above Mrs. Bass's chalked name. It was ten o'clock.

The rest of the day was less eventful.

Ray said, "You're famous! You got a whippin' on your first day of school." The bus turned north on the five-mile road that went past the unpainted house and the small opening at the edge of the woods where Ray lived. "Do you think you'll get another beatin' when you get home?"

The bus stopped at the dirt road and the three girls walked past. The tall girl touched his shoulder with her left hand when she passed. Ray continued talking about famous beatings. He thought about the act of kindness from someone who lived under tin held up by outside walls of unpainted, decayed wood still damp from the last rainfall. Kindness was a seldom visitor to stark structures where clothes and bodies were cleaned in the same metal container that hung on a wall or sat in mud. There was a whipping at school, a beating to come, and he was and would be present for both in clean, pressed clothes.

"See ya tomorrow." He nodded. Ray went down the steps and around the front of the bus. He watched through the window as Ray walked to the small gap at the edge of the woods and disappeared behind leaves and limbs.

He turned from the window and looked beyond the driver. There were no rolls, ridges, or high spots on the land. The road lay flat with the land. He could see the black car and the big window next to the side door; it would be one mile to the concrete steps. The bus pushed through thick thoughts that rose up and then settled just below his nose. The bus turned, backed up and returned to town.

He stood with his back to the house and watched the bus travel south on the five-mile road, shrinking past Ray's gap and the unpainted house and disappearing behind the tree closest to the tree curve. He stood and watched the empty road. The bus was gone, and in a moment, he would turn and face the house and the rest of the day.

Today he met Ray, the principal, and felt the kindness of the tall girl. He saw cars and trucks and sat in a room and watched slow-moving electric hands climb up the left side of a face and grind down the right side of the same. He had not paid the full price for the day. Ahead would be words, belt, bath, and examination of his body that involved touching. He fought a growing fear that the price of each day would increase beyond his ability to pay. He turned and went through the side door.

The first part of the night went as he thought. He spent the rest of the night on his back staring at the ceiling, with Mr. Joseph's right leg draped over his. Darkness had come back for more of a taste.

* * * * * * *

"Did you get a beatin'?" Ray had come out of the woods, with his round face and his big smile. Ray's brain filled his mouth with edgeless words that bathed listening faces with a warm summer mist. Ray made people smile.

The plan for today was to travel with the herd and to watch for horn-nosed cranes with wooden-paddle wings. The bus stopped for the three girls. He and Ray spoke to them when they passed by with the scent of no running water. He looked back and to his right to smile at the tall, older girl who had been kind to him. She sat two seats back on the other side of the bus. She smiled. He knew she went to the older kid's school. Other kids sat behind her, and he knew kids sat behind him. He didn't look at their faces the first day on the bus; he didn't look at them today. Everyone knew about him. The principal had gotten him the first day.

Ray told him it had been twelve years since someone got a whippin' on their first day at the school. He said he had asked his parents about it last night. It was a kid named David that was sent to live with the local preacher. The story was that the kid lived up north and got kicked out of school for breaking another kid's nose and arm. Ray said some older kids told him the kid was over six feet tall and weighed three hundred pounds.

Ray's parents said his uncle was standing in the hallway and saw the kid run out of a classroom heading to the side doors next to the basketball court. The door to the principal's office opened halfway and a long, thin arm shot out and grabbed the kid's shirt, and he disappeared behind the closed door.

Ray was talking louder for a growing group of ears in the back of the bus. The story had a feel of one passed down by more than one uncle. He turned sideways in the seat with his back against the metal panel below the window. Ray was to his left, and the rest of the gathering covey of ears was to his right. Ray continued the story, with some faces nodding at parts they had heard before.

The new kid, David, had disappeared behind the principal's door when each class had sat down after standing and reciting, with hand over heart, the Pledge of Allegiance "for which we stand." The flag and the reciting were the first thing each day. When kids were opening their paper-sack lunches, the principal's door was still closed. Ray's eyes got bigger. "The kid was in the office with Principal Horn for hours!" Some of the ear-covey eyes widened, and some faces nodded. "And then…the door opened and closed and the new kid, David, was standing there in the hall."

Ray said his uncle told him that the recess bell rang, and all the kids on that side of the building walked past the new kid. He didn't look up, and he didn't move. Mr. Hilbert Shot, the janitor, helped David down the front stairs and out the double doors and stood with him until the local preacher arrived. David came back to school the next day. He was better, but he didn't speak.

A few days later three men came to school. The man in charge wore a suit and a bow tie. He had round wire-rimmed glasses that he would take off and clean with a white handkerchief. Ray's uncle said the man in charge cleaned his glasses four times while he was talking to the principal in the hallway. Ray's uncle and the others that saw said the man in charge was afraid to look Miss Horn directly in the eye.

Ray continued with relish, "Everybody was outside for recess when the man with the bow tie came out the double doors. Behind him was David with two big men in short white coats. They walked across the basketball court to the street and put the kid in the back of a white panel truck. My uncle saw the whole thing. They say the preacher goes to see David every month up north in the crazy people hospital."

The bus had stopped, and everyone was on the sidewalk. The bell rang and Ray shouted at the four older kids when the bus pulled away. "Nobody has seen the kid in twelve years!" He could see the tall, older girl grin at Ray and the audience through the window.

He turned with the group and headed for the double doors and up the fourteen steps. It would be his second day, and he would move with the herd. He did not intend to be visited once a month at the crazy people hospital up north. It was a good story and Ray told it well.

Miss Elizabeth's food agreed with his body. He could tell he was getting stronger. At school, each age group went to a different room to eat the noonday meal, sitting at wooden desks with small paper sacks. He followed the class out the door and right to the last door before the steps that led to the basketball court. It was Miss Cramer's room; Miss Cramer ate her lunch at her desk. He reached in the sack and pulled out the food and used the sack as a plate. The apple sat on the brown bag waiting its turn after the sandwich.

The kid behind him tapped his shoulder and motioned with his eyes toward Miss Cramer. He looked around at Miss Cramer and saw a structurally improbable sight—a nude, wrapper less Hershey bar perched at Miss Cramer's lips. It was there and then it wasn't. Her jaws didn't move. The flat sheet, scored, chocolate envelope sailed through the mail slot and was officially delivered. He was told it was a highlight of the sacked-food period. Many theories had been offered. None proven.

He stayed with the herd during the afternoon and made it to the bus with only brief glimpses of partial sticks coming out of big black shoes.

"Did she get you today?"

"Nope." He had listened carefully, and the best he could tell, if the principal got you, it was best not to get got again.

The bus had turned north on the five-mile road to the concrete steps. The familiar heaviness quickly returned. It was the next with no name where Miss Elizabeth saw to his every need and Mr. Joseph was secretly cruel and different than other dismissive men. The next had rigid routine with waves of anxious unpredictability.

More nights than not he was required to sleep with an adult male with body hair where he had none. There was no one to call out to who would come. Slowly each week, he was touched longer and pushed farther into the corner of the bed where the two walls met. He had become skilled at avoiding and seasoned in absorbing massive blows to his selfhood. He had passed through and stayed in nexts that offered little other than caution and violence. The indifference of the before nexts had allowed movement without being seen. The next with no name had eyes peeled and keen. After dark, an apple was an orange and black became white.

The next with no name was a shiny apple with a rotten core. He lived in the space between core and surface. He lived in a quick-slow time and watched sunken rot reach for shine and surface. It was an unspoken-thought language from a mind that floated and made small corrections to avoid large objects.

Ray smiled, "See ya tomorrow."

"See ya." He watched Ray step into the woods and disappear behind leaf and limb.

Darkness with double snoring from the other room meant a night of peace and rest. The bed and the room were not his, and he stayed away from both as much as he could. He had grown to dislike the red bedspread. The other—the thief of memory—lived beneath the spread, and he lived in someplace upright and away.

Sunday brought church in a different building and town with no cousins. Mr. Joseph moved from pew to pulpit, and Miss Elizabeth was up front at the piano. Church rituals increased to three a week. He sat in the pew and memorized every curve and tile and wondered if he could hit each with a spear thrown from ten to sixteen pews away. There were stories and reports of Preacher Joseph's good deeds and quiet kindnesses to others.

Another week went by with the school bus stopping and turning, Ray's smiling face, the fourteen steps, and lazy clock hands pushed by gears attached to tiny electric motors, each with its own quiet hum. Hands spun around in the center of identical faces—identical faces that watched the movement of big and small, followed by still when the sun warmed the empty desks and painted their likenesses on the opposite wall. Later the clocks prepared their time for the arrival of the first movement of the next day. It continued for five days.

On Saturday at first light, he rode in the front seat of the black car to the hills to see Miss Elizabeth's father. She had told Mr. Joseph that she planned to check on her hermit uncle if he would allow her to come up the mountain. He didn't ask how high the mountain was or if it had snow on the top. He sat in the front seat and watched the land change from flat and smooth to wavy and wrinkled, with large gouges filled with moving water.

The car followed the road up and around land that had pushed up from the surface. The motor pulled harder. Miss Elizabeth told him what to do to deal with the discomfort inside his ears. The road went from hill to taller hill, with zigzags up and around where land disappeared, and empty air waited at the edge of the road. The air was cooler, with a crispness that pulled in unfamiliar scents. He knew mud, sand, and river. He did not know when a hill became a mountain. The road had climbed for more than an hour. Breaks in the tree canopy revealed how far down it was from up.

Miss Elizabeth pushed the accelerator down, and the car sped around a curve and left the road. He saw sky in the windshield and his back pressed against the seat. The car had left the road and moved up a dirt hill with deep, water-carved gashes. The car stopped in a flat area the size of four cars, with tall dead grass and thin saplings with big leaves. The mountain continued up just outside Miss Elizabeth's window. He looked out his side window and saw nothing but sky and clouds.

He waited for Miss Elizabeth to get out and retrieve a large basket from the back seat. He got out through her door and closed it. He walked past the trunk and looked out and down the mountain. He felt the pull of the deepness; he grabbed a sapling to steady himself. Miss Elizabeth put the basket down. It sat at an angle.

She cupped her hands and never-heard-before sounds came out of her lungs. It was a combination of calling cows and singing. "It's to let him know we're on the mountain, and we plan to come see him. He may still shoot at us."

He'd been shot at before. It wasn't pleasant. "Maybe you could do the thing again in case he didn't hear you."

"I'll do it when we get closer."

Miss Elizabeth zigzagged up the mountain and he followed. There was no path to suggest movement up or down the mountain, and there were no animal paths other than the occasional partial deer track. The ground was hard, and the rocks were large, white, and flat. He looked back once and felt dizzy and the pull came again. The grass was over his head. It was white and had recorded its last wind before it died and became stiff and motionless.

It had been an hour of climbing. Miss Elizabeth had continued her angular approach up the mountain without stopping. He followed without stopping. He had been thinking for some time that it was past due for another cow-calling-song thing from Miss Elizabeth.

He jumped from the sound. It was a gunshot—a shotgun loud enough to be a twelve gauge. The loud sound was followed shortly by a gentle rain of lead pellets that rolled off leaves and bounced lightly off flat rocks. Miss Elizabeth gave a shorter version of the cow song. Two long, deeply southern syllables rolled down from the top of the mountain. The first was lower than the second. "Awwwwright." He guessed this meant no more shooting.

He followed Miss Elizabeth's zigzagging for another twenty minutes. He stepped off the last of the incline onto level ground and into deep woods. It had been a mountain meadow rudely interrupted by big trees with flat tops from heavy winds that swirled more than blew. Three or four steps into the woods Miss Elizabeth gave a low "Woop, woop." All around him the trees were large, with trunks less than twenty feet apart. The silver bottoms of the leaves twisted and pointed as the wind entered the woods from different directions, running through the trunks and leaving faint whispers and rubbing moans.

Miss Elizabeth's great uncle stood tall and thin in front of a cabin built from trees whose stumps rested below hand-hewn floors. The single-barrel gun grew out of the man's hands—both gun and hands were old, familiar, and without shine. Man, and gun were steady and purposeful. He followed Miss Elizabeth into a brown, earth-toned world where thin shafts of light splashed on brown dirt.

"Elizabeth."

"Wilton."

"Have your partner step out where he can be seen." He stepped out.

"Great Uncle Wilton, this is your great, great nephew, Jimmy." He preferred Jim. Miss Elizabeth liked to add letters to people's names, especially the ones who were not graced with two first names like "Jim Bob" or "Bobby Jim." Amid the drifting names, all three and the gun had made it inside the cabin.

The inside was one large room. To the left was a rounded-stone fireplace with a large opening fitted with two swinging iron arms that held two iron pots with lids. Daylight shone through horizontal cracks in the logs where the wall met the pitch of the roof. To his right was a chair that faced the door and, just beyond, was a narrow iron bed. It was a large cabin made bigger by being one room and larger, still, by its limited furnishings.

Miss Elizabeth was offered the chair and he the end of the bed. Miss Elizabeth put the basket on the floor to the right of the chair. He looked at the walls; there were no pictures or windows. Animal skins of different sizes and colors were stretched tight, attached to the walls with handmade square nails.

Miss Elizabeth did the talking and addressed her great uncle with a respectful fondness. Her great uncle responded with head movements and single-syllable words. Miss Elizabeth listed the items in the basket in her hopes of sparing her elder a trip down the mountain for supplies unavailable in the wilderness.

Miss Elizabeth's great uncle reached under the bed and pulled out a flat, round, lidded tin. Underneath splotches of rust was the picture of a heavyset man, with a very large cigar sitting in an ornate chair. The lid was pulled off and snapped back on, with the hint of something shiny covered by the man's right hand. "This is from the Great War." It was a large gold-colored coin imprinted with the same lady he had seen on silver dollars. "It's for you in honor of your visit."

The coin had a metal ring at the top so it could be used as a necklace. The bottom of the coin had the date "1918." He stared at it too long before he said, "Thank you."

He saw the reflection of the coin in the man's eyes and, behind the reflected coin, a sadness he guessed came from war. He smiled, and the quiet man nodded with the knowledge of a gift well received. He looked at the coin, and Miss Elizabeth began to report the family news and that she would be visiting her father. The report finished, brief parting pleasantries passed through the door, and he followed Miss Elizabeth into the whisper-moan trees. He looked back, and the man and the gun had faded into the color of the cabin, there standing unseen.

He learned quickly to avoid the draw of the deepness of the distance that pulled down on the up. It worked better if he didn't look out or down. Going down the mountain was different than going up. He watched Miss Elizabeth's boots and where he placed his own.

He felt the coin in his pocket. It had been a generous gift that was well given. He wondered if he would see the fading hermit man again, the man who lived on top of the mountain in the center of the whisper-moan trees. He saw brief glimpses of the top of the car while moving sideways down the slope.

His mind was still in the cabin and with the trees that made the cabin and those left that surrounded and hid it. The cabin used only the trees it needed, and the rest stood upright and close. He had heard the trees speak in whispers, creaks, and moans. The roots below the scalp held hands silently, and the trunks were hairs on a giant head above the face of the mountain. They walked down the face to the car that rested on the mountain's left shoulder. It had been a visit that would stay large and long.

The car moved down from mountain to hills and stopped next to the front-yard well. Miss Elizabeth's childhood home rested in the shade of the afternoon, cooled by tall pecan trees. Light breeze and leaves painted moving shadow spots on house, ground, and well. A wide, lazy porch sat high on steps with a curved rail that traveled across the front and turned right at the left front corner of the house. A tall, straight man with a full head of white hair stood at the top of the porch steps. He looked at the man and felt calm. The man's stance and his face were strong and kind. He had seen the great difference in men from loudly less to quietly more. This was Miss Elizabeth's father, and he would spend the night in Miss Elizabeth's childhood home. It would be a welcome relief from the red bedspread.

He climbed to the top step and was introduced. He reached high to shake hands. The white-haired man did not lean over to make it easier. He'd had cause to shake a number of adult hands, and all the adults had bent forward and reached down. Miss Elizabeth's father did not. He would wait to see what it meant; it was unusual and would require thought.

He soon learned that the front parlor of the house was heated by coal burning in a tall cylinder stove and the kitchen had a low, flat wood stove for cooking. The doors were closed to the rest of the rooms; they were unheated. One was used for eating, with a long table with twelve chairs. The rest were for sleeping and had deep feather beds with blue-striped ticking.

He entered the door across the porch from the front steps and stepped into the front parlor. The stove stood tall in the center of the room, with a mantelpiece for an unused fireplace on the left wall and a single iron bed carefully covered with unfolded newspapers to the immediate right. The bed lay across the front wall with the foot just to the right of the front door. The chairs, five in all, were on rockers with woven straw seats and backs. They looked to be very old. In between Miss Elizabeth's questions and her father's brief answers, the wind-up clock on the mantelpiece ticked, and the rockers made dry-straw sounds and squeaked from wooden joints that rubbed.

He learned how to take the shells off of pecans and peanuts. He took the meat from the pecans, put them in an empty tin can, set the can on the curved top of the stove and ate poached pecans. He learned to look for the navel-looking end of the peanut shell where it had been connected to the plant's stem and to turn it face down in his palm and push his thumb into the middle of the shell below the folded-over-nipple end of the shell.

Miss Elizabeth's father was a peanut farmer and also raised Indian corn. The best he could tell, the corn was used for looking, not eating. The ears were much smaller than field corn and had multi-colored kernels that people used for decoration.

The air was colder, and the sun was a faint glow behind the nearest of many tall hills. He had lost track of the sun, and the hills had hidden its true direction. He believed it would turn up again in the morning above one of the hills behind the house.

Nighttime chores at Miss Elizabeth's childhood home were different. Running water was in the kitchen in the form of an outside pump that rose above a hammered tin sink. The bathroom was manual and outside at the end of a winding path down a small slope. Drinking water came from the well in the front yard.

He negotiated the differences and stood next to the parlor stove waiting for the brick to heat. He wrapped the hot brick in a towel and carried it to bed. He put the brick under the covers next to his feet. He sank down into the feather mattress with only ceiling visible—he looked to the left and right and saw only mattress. He could hear the back and forth of the rocking chairs, the clock, and soft voices. He would not have to submit to an examination or be touched. He could sleep alone and in peace. And he did.

He woke to light and biscuits. Miss Elizabeth had told him that her father believed each day should include the Bible, a fried sweet potato, and biscuits with a preponderance of flour. It was breakfast. He bit into the biscuit and white dust shot out the sides. His hand looked like he had completed a lengthy arithmetic problem at the chalkboard. He ate the egg and finished the fried strip of sweet potato. He had slept well.

Miss Elizabeth had a broom and dustpan and was lifting rugs to find carefully swept dirt piles that had begun to grow shortly after her last visit. She said nothing. She and her father would smile at each other. She would return to move them again—same pile, different dirt, same smiles.

He watched Miss Elizabeth's father turn the handle on the wheel that pulled the round metal cylinder up from the well. Near the bottom of the cylinder a door was opened, and cold water poured into a shiny metal ladle. The water tasted good and had a hint of sweetness.

He reached high and shook hands; the man stood erect. It would remain a mystery as to why. He was thankful for the bed, the sleep, and the things he learned. He sat in the front seat while Miss Elizabeth spoke softly to her father and hugged him. The car backed out of the yard, with the tall man standing next to the front-yard well. The sun was climbing the back side of the hills behind the house. They headed down out of the hills where the ancient hand of time had passed over and smoothed the land in front of the car.

He heard his ears pop, and the air began to gain weight. A clear, thin, wavy line hung close to the road at the horizon. The road passed by the edges of farms with livestock where the air smelled brown and leaves hung low with a midday droop. The car had moved down through crisp and clear to waves of soft and haze.

He asked about the unfolded newspapers on the narrow bed next to the front wall. He learned that Miss Elizabeth's father lay on the bed to digest the noonday meal before returning to the field. The paper kept the surface cooler and protected the fabric from dirt and dust from the field. He moved on to the high handshake and learned it was due to back problems.

He said little after that. His mind wandered through the whisper-moan trees. He felt the coin in his pocket and saw the sad eyes of the hermit. He asked Miss Elizabeth about her great uncle. She told him she was five years old when her great uncle came back from the Great War. He didn't speak and sat on the porch where the curved railing turned right at the left corner of the house. He sat in the rocking chair from daylight till dark. He wouldn't speak again until Miss Elizabeth was ten years old—she remembered the day. It was midafternoon in the late summer. Her great uncle stood up from the rocking chair and began to talk. He thanked everyone for the care he had received, put his belongings in a large canvas bag, walked down the road and over the hill and never returned.

Miss Elizabeth said she had used portions of the visits with her father to look for her great uncle. She drove through the hills and down into the small valleys and hollers and asked around about a man who lived away and apart. She had an old picture of her great uncle from back in the day when cars had small wagon wheels with wooden spokes and solid rubber strips that covered the rims. The picture showed him clean-shaven and standing next to his older brother who was seated. Both wore three-piece suits with pocket watches. His older brother had long white hair and a full white mustache and was known to carry a pearl-handled pistol and reportedly had been in a number of situations where it had been necessary to draw and fire.

The brothers had seen changes in the country during the trailing years of the nineteenth century and the preteen years of the twentieth. It had been years since an armed altercation. During the last days of the century, the pistol was pulled and fired in close situations with poisonous snakes and to practice with tin cans and the occasional whiskey bottle.

The twentieth century brought killing sanctioned by the government and carried out by soldiers. Soldiering had taken the younger brother's voice and began Miss Elizabeth's belated search for a man who lived away and apart. Miss Elizabeth's story had carried the car out of the hills onto flat land with afternoon sun. She began to finish the story of the search for her great uncle, recalling the day she had entered a single street carved out of the high side of a mountain. He listened with his mind's eye and saw the black car on a narrow, carved-out road making a slow left turn around the upper edge of the mountain, with the mountain on the left side of the car and hundreds of feet of air on the right side of the car.

The story described a day seven months ago, and his mind placed him in the front right seat as the story continued. He saw it through the windshield. The view shifted left around the curve, and the car continued left into a deep fold in the mountain where eleven houses appeared in the windshield. Seven houses backed up to the mountain and faced away from vertical back yards. The houses on the right side of the road had back yards filled with downward-facing heavy air and no back doors or windows. The right side of the road had suffered trauma, and only four perched houses remained. The jagged remains of the unfortunate had poured down hundreds of feet of dark coal dirt. The car had turned left, and the windshield had been greeted by the rotten-tooth smile of a forgotten mountain-perch town.

The last of the town was close to the end of the single street. Money and interest in coal had been lost. The missing-house town sat in front of a wide, dead-end turnaround where the car stopped at a porch marked "General." The porch had rocking chairs that were occupied by opinions and stories from the last of those who carried the dark images of the blackness that waited in the deepest part of the mine. The mine was closed; the elevator down was turned off. The last mark from the last machine lay open in the blackness, undisturbed.

Clever tall stories poured over and through porch railings of buildings marked "General." The same was true in the perch town. The best stories and tellers were often found inside. Around pot-bellied stoves slunk a creature that appeared as a twinkle in eye, face, and mouth during the telling of tall stories with rhythm where listeners participated in movement, expression, and comment—an understated theater that entertained all. The sitting and standing circle around the stove was where Miss Elizabeth said she was told that a tall, slim man who lived away and apart could be found two mountains to the east and on top of the next mountain to the north. He saw the car pull out of the perch town, turn right into the fold and out again, and right around the last turn. The story was finished, and he remained in the front seat on flat land passing before-seen barns.

Hensen March

25 - Slaughterhouse

On the way home from visiting Miss Elizabeth's relatives, the car continued east through the small town and straight across the main street. He rode the three-mile road where the car turned left on the five-mile road heading north past the concrete steps. He looked through the side window behind Miss Elizabeth and saw the tall girl at the pump behind the unpainted house. He watched for the wide gap in the trees where Ray would come out of the woods to catch the bus. It was Sunday, and dark was trying to sit on the sun; the best it could manage was a hint of pastels climbing over the back side of a dusky gray.

Miss Elizabeth said Mr. Joseph was at church for an evening service. It seemed church with no cousins had moved into the house and planned for a long stay. Three times a week brought polished-pressed travel to a designated building to conduct rituals that were listed in paper bulletins.

He had been to a night church in a before next. The memory was stronger than memories of the next itself. It stood alone, with when and where in a slow circling fog. There were sounds with pieces of visual movement. The pews had three-board seats and two-board, straight backs. Flat hands could pass through the spaces between boards. The boards were new lumber untouched by plane or paint. The pulpit stood in front of the pacing preacher. Words tumbled out of the preacher, rolling end over end, slowing then speeding with repeating rhythms and movements. Hands stretched up and out, and he fell, Bible in hand, with both knees striking the planks of the altar.

Heads went down with closed eyes, except for his two wide eyes watching women run through the aisles, screaming and falling in front of the altar and shaking. Some flailed about, and others lay stiff with arms tight against their sides. Some men rose from the three-board pews and knelt next to the flailing women while other men picked up the frozen women, balanced them on their shoulders and carried them out the front door. A shiny material with small print contained a stiff woman, face up, balanced at the small of the back on the left shoulder of a large man. She passed over, above, and to the left of where he sat. He saw the stiff legs, with large black shoes pressed together and a triangle of material hanging down just above the ankles. It lived in his mind on the edge of before and after, somewhere beyond when and where. He heard it, saw it, and he had been there. He'd been to night church.

Night church at the now next was quieter. The aisles were empty, and the floor in front of the altar was clear. No bodies were carried out of the room. His soft mind and unfocused eyes waited their turn to leave the building unassisted. He'd been to night church.

The car was pointing at the big window next to the side door to the kitchen. The motor stopped, and feet on the ends of stiff legs stepped out of open doors. They had just returned from the trip to the hills to visit Miss Elizabeth's family. Tomorrow would be school with Ray coming out of the woods and the three girls from the unpainted house.

Soon it would be dark, the difficult time when he was expected to allow things to be done to him. He had been told it was a special secret and he was not to tell anyone. He knew there would be violence if he told. He knew no one would believe him or do anything; it was his word against the preacher's. It continued, but not that night. He slept alone. There had been no shared bed and no night church. He'd been to night church.

The next morning, he finished breakfast and heard Miss Elizabeth ask Mr. Joseph to bring meat home from the frozen meat drawer at the slaughterhouse. Mr. Joseph told him not to take the bus home after school. "I'll take you to get meat, and you can see where it comes from."

He'd rather come home on the bus and talk to Ray. He nodded. Time alone with Mr. Joseph was a risk at best and usually turned out poorly for him. Mr. Joseph's skin was pulled tight over bones filled with old anger. It was well disguised from others. He could see it, and Mr. Joseph knew he could see it.

He moved to the chair facing the big window and looked for the bus. He knew the day was coming when he would have to call Miss Elizabeth "Mother" and Mr. Joseph "Father." Now they were his new paper parents. He was the last of his family. He stood at the front of an invisible line. His mind often looked behind his body, and no one was there.

On the bus Ray was smiling and talking about television. Mr. Joseph and Miss Elizabeth did not have a television. He had heard them discuss television; they said people would stop talking to each other and stop reading. Mr. Joseph and Miss Elizabeth were readers.

Instead of television, they had an electric radio that sat on the kitchen counter in the far corner to the right of the stove. The glass dial with the numbers had broken and was held up by tape. The dial moved one inch to the left and right of "1400." It was the station in the small town at the end of the three-mile road.

On those first few days of school when he got off the bus, Miss Elizabeth had the radio on. He listened to two radio programs before doing homework: "The Lone Ranger" and "Sargent Preston of the Yukon and his Wonder Dog, Yukon King." Radio stories in color and detail. King had found an injured man in a blizzard and Sargent Preston took the man to a remote trading post. A glancing blow from a grizzly bear's paw temporarily blinded the man. A meal was prepared for him, and Sargent Preston told the man to imagine the plate was a clock face. The meat was at five o'clock, fried potatoes at eleven, and biscuit at one o'clock. The livestock report followed, citing hog futures and price per pound for feeder cattle.

On the way to school, he and Ray devised a plan—he would go to Ray's house to look at his television. Ray didn't like schoolwork and planned to join the army when he grew up. He had similar thoughts about school but not the army. He seemed to get along with most of the kids at school. He had little interest in school and did what was necessary as seldom as possible. He carefully coasted between he could do better and the bottom part of average. For their plan, he and Ray had come up with Wednesday night at eight to see Ray's favorite show. They walked through the double doors and the school day began with bells and pencils.

He had continued to assist the principal in becoming convinced he was a changed student, a young man that had discovered the value of truth and spoke it often when called upon. He made no eye contact with the principal. He did, however, know the sound of her large shoes and often followed the shadow of her nose across the walls and floors. The nose and its many shadows were impressive. The shadowy movements across the hallway walls were crane-like on the good days. On other days the nosed-head shadow made shorter, jerkier movements seen in birds of prey that were on the hunt. He walked easier on the days when the nose and head made shadows that moved forward and back from the gait of long, skinny, bony legs that lifted and dropped heavy shoes with thick heals on wooden floors.

The bell rang; he walked down the fourteen steps, out the double doors, and toward the buses. He turned left at the first bus and walked down the sidewalk past two more buses until he saw the farm truck. He could see Mr. Joseph's face above the steering wheel. The other side of the divided windshield had a deep diagonal crack that began low on the door side and went up to the top center corner. Mr. Joseph's face remained unchanged when he saw Jim.

The round fenders of the truck and the face over the steering wheel brought lighted-up pictures of the shack truck behind the dime store, the image of the shack truck wrapped around the farm truck. The images blurred and cleared, blurred and cleared. Each time the image came into focus a different face was above the steering wheel. The headlights would glow, and the face of the short violent man whose name he didn't use came into focus, then blurred, followed by the preacher's face, Mr. Joseph.

Both were bullies—one louder than the other and one smarter than the other. One was then and one was now. Mr. Joseph saved his smiles for those who cared about his position in the community. It was Mr. Joseph and the farm truck.

A less-than-shadow change in light flowed out of the bottom of the crack in the windshield, poured onto the sidewalk and passed between his right foot and the curb, leaving bumps on his skin. It was the same shadow that passed over people when a predator was near. It left a sense of uneasiness for those who could not see it. The paper-parent predator's face hung low and severe off the front of a brain that performed well publicly but touched freely when young skin was available, and witnesses were not. He looked behind him and saw innocent feet wading ankle deep through the less-than-shadow change in light, pairs of feet splashing below small faces uneasy from ancient senses. He guessed he was the only one that knew the lessening of light moving down the sidewalk belonged to the preacher.

He got into the truck, closed the door and looked forward through the crack in the glass. The wheel turned left and then straight. Something was said, and he turned and smiled with a nod, his eyes focusing one inch above where Mr. Joseph's nose came out of his face—slightly above the area between the two gray eyes. He turned toward the side and saw Ray wave through the bus window. He waved back.

The truck turned left at the first cross street. Two blocks down it turned left again and went straight for three blocks. After another turn to the left, the truck went east half a block and slowed in front of a one-story concrete block building. The building had been painted white some years before, but the lack of gutters had allowed rain to pour off the roof and splash mud up the outside walls. There was a brown and whitish door in the center of the front wall. The truck went past the front of the building and turned right into a drive. The dirt road along the side of the building had deep, dried, hard ruts from large livestock trucks. The trucks had thrown mud up to the roofline. Mud had dried on parts of the wall; some of it had fallen away in large thick sheets that lay broken at the base of the wall.

The truck passed the back corner of the building and slowed. The back wall of the building faced a large dirt area for trucks to unload and load. He saw three openings in the back wall. The unloading chute where livestock walked down a ramp from the truck was tucked in just past the corner of the building next to the dirt road. At the far side of the back wall a tall garage door was connected to an elevated loading dock. The center of the wall had a brown and whitish door like the one in the front of the building.

The wheels of the truck struggled across deep ruts where trucks had loaded and unloaded in the rain. The hood of the truck stopped under a low branch at the far corner of the empty space. He could feel his senses widen; his eyes and time glanced back to the sound of a door closing. The seat behind the steering wheel was empty. His head turned, and his eyes took in every detail on the dashboard; he saw his hand on the inside handle. Sixty yards away Mr. Joseph looked back from the brown and whitish door. He got out of the truck and started across the empty space. He looked up and saw Mr. Joseph saying something he couldn't hear. There was silence.

The bent bumper of a truck came around the corner of the building pulling a trailer with a large animal inside round bars. There was silence. He could hear dirt crumble under his boots when he stepped on the edges of the dried ruts.

He looked up again and saw Mr. Joseph yelling and pointing at the truck and the animal following it. "Stay out of the way! Hurry up!"

Crumbling-dirt sounds faded as noise from Mr. Joseph's face began to match the movements of his mouth. He moved faster. He could hear the trailer pushing and pulling against the truck. There were sounds from the large animal inside. He didn't look and pushed through the noise and advice coming out of the severe face standing next to the door.

This was an adult place where unattended manners and business-like somberness mixed with deepened voices with short words, where male boots struck the ground harder. It was a place of death. The building held the last moments of hair, fur, and hoof. Death smells sucked away the thoughtless contentment of the snap of grass pulled from sunlit pastures and the calm of cow-path following to the breakfast-supper barn. Those not in charge—those with too many legs—entered, died and left in pieces. Somewhere another animal would stand under the favorite tree, and the animal behind followed a new tail down the path to the breakfast-supper barn.

He didn't bother to look up at Mr. Joseph. Stern disapproval looked the same on all faces. Mr. Joseph said things once. Unlike Mr. Joseph, Miss Elizabeth believed every subject should be discussed with each sentence blessed with a bounty of words. She began on the outer most edges of a thought and traveled around the concept, lightly touching the surface of related subjects. Occasionally, she would veer off and come within sight of the point, and the listener would lean forward. The point would lose its footing and roll to the back of Miss Elizabeth's brain and hang by one syllable on the lower part of her brain stem. Listeners knew it would take great effort to hoist the point up to within sight, and they would smile and ride the surface of the spoken word.

Mr. Joseph did not repeat himself unless he stood behind the pulpit. He had yelled and pointed once. If the truck hit the boy, he had been warned.

He followed Mr. Joseph through the brown and whitish door. They turned left and walked along the inside of the back wall. The room was large, with concrete walls and a floor with a slight angle beginning at the walls and sloping down to the center of the room where a heavy metal grate covered a drain the size of a washtub. A large sledgehammer sat to the left of the drain. They turned right at the corner of the room and walked along the far wall.

A half-turn to his right the loading chute door opened, and he heard the animal walk down the ramp. The cow walked ten feet into the room and looked at them. A large man walked to the center of the room, with the drain between him and the cow. The cow looked at him and walked toward the man and stopped just short of the drain. The man leaned to his left and picked up the sledgehammer, so it hung just off the floor. The cow put its head down. The man faced the back wall and swung the sledgehammer backward and low next to his legs, then forward over his head and struck the cow in the forehead. The cow fell on its left side. The man put down the hammer and pulled out a large knife and cut the cow's throat; a wide stream of dark blood rose up from the floor and flowed down the drain.

He stared at the cow and asked Mr. Joseph why the cow didn't run or fight. He turned; Mr. Joseph had left the room. The man was bent over the cow cutting its flesh with the knife. The man stopped. He stood up, turned and pointed the knife toward a door to the left. "Preacher went through there." The sight had sucked him in, and it was difficult to pull away and walk left to the door. He reached the door. The gravity of the life and death scene pulled his face around for one more look.

He stepped through the doorway, and steam went up his nose and down his throat. He was standing next to the snout end of a dead hog, chest high in a machine full of hot water, steam, and moving rollers wrapped with sharp blades. The hog was on its right side with a crescent, gelatin eye jiggling beneath a thick, half-closed eyelid with blond eyelashes. He walked past other machines doing other things to other bodies. He chose not to look. His afternoon memory had seen enough.

He passed through another door and was in the front lobby. To his right was another door and beyond that was a window with a woman sitting at a high counter.

"Lookin' for the preacher?" He nodded. "He left the building. You can go back through the building through this door."

He nodded again and went out the front door. He did not intend to stroll through other parts of the building where metal met flesh after breathing became meat. He turned right out the door and walked across the front of the building toward the side road. A soft rain had begun, something easy and slightly heavier than mist.

He heard the forced air and chirps of air brakes out on the road. A tractor-trailer rig turned left into the dirt road that ran down the left side of the building. It was a mixture of forced air, chirps, squeals, lights, and eighteen wheels with a trailer leaning at a severe angle to the right after the two sets of tandem tires on the back left of the trailer ran up and over the street curb.

The trailer carried hogs on two levels. The sides of the trailer had slotted openings where portions of each hog on both levels could be seen along with excrement in the form of liquid and solids shot out or rolled down the side of the trailer. The big death party was about to be hammered down from two levels, and each of the hogs knew it. The sounds became louder and more frantic.

He stepped back out of reach of an arching stream of hog urine that came across the edge of the grass and melted mud in a dripping curve on the front corner of the building. He waited for the last of the trailer to pass. The activities of death in the building had caused time to glance back as it moved forward. He believed the farm truck was probably still behind the building, but he had little sense of how long he'd been inside. He stepped toward the side road and looked around the corner. The air brakes and taillights were active, with hooves shifting to stay upright. The truck stopped, and he saw the driver step down out of the cab.

He heard oxygen rush up snouts and down into lungs. The oxygen reached down to the bottom of lungs and picked up screams marked last and pushed them out with a bone-chilling sound recognized by all living beings.

The rain had passed heavier than mist. The drops were bigger and struck the top of his head harder and more often. He started down the side road, stepping over muddy ruts with soft sides. On the side wall of the building, mud chunks turned into globs and fell into weeds at the base of the wall. He moved away from the wall and walked on the far side of the road.

He could see the driver next to the back corner of the building. The man was connecting a metal chute to the upper level of the trailer. The side road ruts had filled, and he walked through water with mud hidden below. He reached the back corner of the building.

"Got no business here, boy! Stand clear!" The head inside the baseball cap was even with the top of the trailer, with a right hand holding the corner of the trailer and the left hand resting on top of the metal chute.

He kept walking, giving the trailer lots of room. His brain was becoming familiar with the screaming, but the eyes through the slats were full of terror, and he could feel them press against his skin. He reached the front of the trailer and looked through the space between the truck and trailer. No farm truck.

He walked around the front of the truck. Mr. Joseph had left. He stood and let the rain wash the surprise off his face. He turned and started back toward the side road. The slatted eye wall tried again to pull him closer—two levels of slatted eyes with fear chewing on the gelatin back of each. Something was moving through the trailer, and he walked just beyond its reach. He heard the metal door slide open on the upper level of the trailer, and the sounds in the trailer changed. He passed the end of the trailer in a dead run. Through the doorway, he saw the one-handed heavy hammer rise high and blur down in a fluid-filled crack. He reached the street as the trailer erupted with screams.

The farm truck sat across and up the street. The driver's side window faced the street. Mr. Joseph continued to look forward through the windshield. He crossed the street and walked around the back of the truck. He got into the truck and sat down and looked through the crack in the windshield. The steering wheel turned hard left and the truck swung away from the curb making a "U" turn; the building and the side road slid across the windshield and disappeared behind his right shoulder. The truck wove through town and headed east on the three-mile road. The upper level of the hog trailer was empty.

He had anger in a small space. He didn't ask why he had been left at the slaughterhouse. It was most likely one of Mr. Joseph's hard lessons about keeping up and paying attention or getting left behind. It was not a lesson. It was a reminder that he lived with a hard master who often engaged in the unnecessary and the unkind.

Unnecessary and unkind darted by turned heads and were rarely seen in public beyond partial glimpses. They lived in Mr. Joseph's mind and did not bother to hide from the less powerful or those who lived under his own roof. He less powerfully lived under Mr. Joseph's roof and was a witness-victim graced with experience and nature to stand steady on the far edge of unnecessary and unkind.

The dog jumped the ditch next to his window and ran fast enough across the road. Mr. Joseph turned the wheel to the left to hit the dog forward of the left haunch. The dog's spine broke, and its limp back legs and head spun twice before it went over the edge of the ditch.

"Why did you do that?"

"It was in my way."

"You hit the dog because you wanted to!" Mr. Joseph did not respond. The truck turned north on the five-mile road

He had big anger in a small space. This was a thing that, once seen, changed the looker. It was a dark energy that ground light to ash, and those who touched it lost their way back to before they had touched it. He had seen beyond unnecessary and unkind. The essence of him retreated to high ground and watched for the darkness. He had drifted away. His eyes grabbed the crack in the windshield, and he pulled himself back.

The truck was half past Ray's gap and almost to the concrete steps. The truck would stop, but the sameness would elude him. He would step out of the truck and walk toward sameness without reaching it or touching it. Sameness lay cuddled close to the last belly movements of the dog in the ditch. Sameness shared its last breath with the dog. Both would not be seen again.

"Take this to the kitchen." Mr. Joseph headed to the barn to feed and he to the door to the right of the big window. The two packages were thick, flat, and frozen. Both were wrapped tightly in butcher paper secured with masking tape. He went through the door and heard Yukon King barking on the radio and Miss Elizabeth asking about the day and the ride home. He stepped back from the abyss beyond unnecessary and unkind and chose "OK." He sat down at the table and let the radio words paint over what he had seen Mr. Joseph do.

26 – A Shed Full of Hoes

It was nearing the end of the school year and he had done a fair job of catching up with his classmates. School was little more than an escape from the farm and chores that continued to increase. He had been told he would be working in the fields when school let out for the summer. A few precious days lay between now and his introduction to the wooden end of a hoe and long hours of work in the fields. He was told that he would be working in the barn feeding cattle and on the edge of pastures fixing fences. He knew cows and fences were before and after fields. The kids at school talked about family vacations and spending the summer at the city swimming pool or with their grandparents.

The last bell rang on the last day; kids ran down the fourteen steps and out the double doors to the buses and down the streets. Ray stepped back into the woods, the bus turned around, and he watched it disappear behind the tree curve. He went in the side door to a silent radio. There was no bark from Yukon King, and the Sargent's duties had taken him elsewhere. He changed out of his school clothes.

He walked out the side door and saw Miss Elizabeth step slowly and lightly in the front yard. She had on white gloves and held an oval object with a large spoon. He turned away to the sound of Mr. Joseph approaching with two hoes. He was taught how to sharpen a hoe correctly. The value of a sharp hoe would continue to reveal itself down rowed fields of hidden weeds where he had stepped the year before.

An old hoe is better than a new hoe. A new hoe's long wooden handle is fat and slick with varnish. New hoes have painted metal and are slower to take an edge. With a new hoe, the distance from the bend of the neck to the edge of the blade is greater, making the metal end of the hoe heavier. With an old hoe, the distance from neck to edge is shorter from repeated sharpening. The metal has learned the file and lines up well for a sharp edge. An old hoe has a worn handle that fits the palm; the wood is gray, dried light, and easy to grip. An old hoe with familiar hands responds well to the touch. An old hoe is better than a new hoe.

He was handed a new hoe with green painted metal. He laid the varnished handle flat on the ground and steadied the metal end on a flat rock. He knelt down and placed his right knee less than a foot above where the handle was fastened to the metal collar of the bent neck that held the blade. The flat rock raised the blade high enough to be able to push the two-inch wide file down the length of the blade without pushing the file into the dirt. He pushed the file down the metal edge with the heels of both hands. The green paint curled up and dropped off the edge of the blade. Small shiny metal curls climbed over the file and rolled over the top of his right hand and disappeared in the grass. He picked up the handle and held it straight up with his left hand, with the front of the blade resting on the rock. His right hand moved the file in tight left circles on the back side of the blade. Mr. Joseph touched the edge and said the blade was sharp enough.

He followed Mr. Joseph to a small shed behind the larger shed next to the drive, the larger shed where the bicycle stood at an angle on its kickstand. The small shed was painted the same as all the outbuildings including the barn; all were a dark green. Behind the door of the small shed were more hoes leaning against the walls. His new hoe rested next to the two walls of old hoes—it was always easy to spot a new hoe in a crowd of old hoes. Files rested on top of boards nailed across the inside walls. Each hoe had a file. The shed was mostly full of hoes.

Mr. Joseph handed him a pair of worn gloves. "You'll need these tomorrow."

He had seen, heard and avoided a lot in his few years. He knew he could adapt to work in the fields. He had been unable to avoid Mr. Joseph's hands during the dark space between Miss Elizabeth's snoring and the sounds of bird chatter in the predawn hours. He felt the heaviness of what lay ahead. Tomorrow he would rise early and spend the day with the man who came for him in the night. He hoped Mr. Joseph's daytime hands stayed full of work.

Miss Elizabeth was still in the front yard, acting strangely. Her white gloves were still on, and she moved very slowly in light, tiptoe movements. The white-gloved fingers of her left hand were wrapped around the spoon, with the brown ball resting in it. Her right white-gloved hand held the butcher knife. Miss Elizabeth's feet would slowly rise high and quietly go down like a cat stalking a bird. The sun flashed off the butcher knife, and the brown ball rolled around the inside edge of the spoon. Miss Elizabeth's feet and legs raised and lowered.

He stood a safe distance away. He whispered, "What are you doing?"

The answer came back in whispered parts. "Moles...poison. They can smell your hands on the poison, and they can feel you walking." Miss Elizabeth put the second foot on the ground and bent over and cut a slit in the mole tunnel. She gently placed the brown ball inside and closed the opening.

His body startled from the cow call, and he felt heavier than when he was watching Miss Elizabeth's mole dance. Miss Elizabeth, the butcher-knife-flashing spoon dancer. He headed for the barn for his first lesson in feeding cattle. The first lesson would be like all the ones to follow in which Mr. Joseph's presence and eye made mastery of the simple impossible, and the plain became complex and beyond the understanding of those viewed as less than.

Upon his arrival at the barn, Mr. Joseph presented him with his new title of gatekeeper. As gatekeeper duties were explained, he felt his mind tense and begin to fog. The gatekeeper needed a working knowledge of Mr. Joseph's feeding system, which included different feed for different cows in different areas reached by moving combinations of large gates. The cattle began to arrive at the gate. They did not introduce themselves or request a menu, and they were not waiting to be seated.

It was his first shift as a gatekeeper, and the soon-to-be-familiar stern disapproval and volume of Mr. Joseph's voice pumped more fog into his brain until all cows looked the same. All cows look the same until you know them. Cows have cowlicks. Most are found on their foreheads in the space between their eyes. Some cowlicks on foreheads swirl left and some swirl right. Some have a large one in the center of their forehead, and some have up to four in different swirls between their eyes.

Cows have friends—at least they tend to hang out with the same group of one or two other cows that stand closer than the rest of the group. Different cow friends hang out in different parts of the pasture.

Slow gazes through wavy glass windows and fast glances from moving trucks find cow friends in five areas of pastures. One group of cow friends likes the shade of trees that grow at the bottom of easy slopes that lead to water. Some cows require entertainment and are found close to the fence, some eating grass and some stretching their necks over the top strand of barbed wire. The road is the entertainment, and they line up next to the fence and turn their heads together, blankly staring at passing trucks and cars. Some cow friends are private and like to be small spots on green grass at the most distant part of the pasture.

High-ranking cows are often found in the center part of the pasture with the bull, and they notify the bull if any cows need to be serviced. He had seen cows mount other cows and walk on their hind legs behind the mounted cow. The bull would follow and wait for the mounted cow to pee. The bull would stick its nose in the urine stream and rear its head, wrinkling its nose and snorting. If the cow passed the pee test the bull would mount and, in one push, service the cow. It was an event that caught attention in pastures and barn lots. It was a powerful image for first timers.

He had watched and been around cows for as long as he could remember. He had seen that cows have basic natures. Some cows are calm, and some are not. Cows respond poorly to people who make jerky, fast movements, especially cows that are not graced with a calm nature. He had noticed people do not respond well to people who make jerky, fast movements. Most calm creatures have an even, oval band of white that surrounds the colored portion of the eye. Cows and people avoid creatures that have pupils that dart and make the white oval uneven, with large flashes of white. Calm-natured cows have eyes that are mostly chocolate brown, and if white is seen, something is wrong.

Cows like to do the same thing every day—cows like to do the same thing every day. Today was different. The gatekeeper did not open or close the inside gates correctly. The cows were in the barn but could not reach the trough they were accustomed to—none were pleased. Tension and chaos wrapped the cattle into a tight mass that pushed against the front gate and forced it open. He stepped up on the inside of the gate and rode it as it swung wide to his left and bounced off the front right side of the barn. Cattle came out of the barn in a dead run and turned a sharp left. He stepped up two rungs.

Left-turning cattle bounced the gate several times against the barn. The barn was empty, with Mr. Joseph standing in the opening that faced south where the latched gate had been. The speed of the hooves hitting the ground stayed the same until the cattle became small against the far north fence.

"Ran off two weeks of feed. Go to the house. We'll start early in the morning." He didn't bother to look. He knew the face. He stepped off the gate and walked away.

The four-board fence was straight ahead. It marked the northern boundary of the barnyard, running left to right and ending at an outbuilding where the cattle had pounded past. He knew the gate would be simple to fix. The latch was made of two-inch oak that had been cut in a sawmill and planed by hand back when plows were pulled by mules. The sliding-board latch was four feet long with a hand-hewed peg coming out of the front side approximately a foot from one end. The oak had aged to concrete and dried to a familiar gray.

He put his right foot on the bottom rail of the fence near the post and his left foot on the second rail. He swung his right leg over the fourth rail. He held the top of the post and swung his left leg over and, on his way down, glanced at the barn and knew Mr. Joseph was fixing the latch.

He turned and walked to the house. He shuffled his feet back and forth in the side yard to let the grass clean the cow manure off his boots. Gum boots were required for cattle feeding. Next time he would get one of the extra pairs from the small shed where the hoes stayed.

Through late-day purple air, the light from the kitchen lay golden on green grass. He tried not to think of what lay ahead. He knew if somehow he were to be told half of what lay ahead, he would run into the woods and disappear forever. If he knew everything that lay ahead, he would lose the ability to speak. Thought would cease. He would be unable to move and would stand motionless in the side yard. The earth would spin and pull the sun behind it. Light would begin where hoes leaned against inside walls, and it would chase the earth across the sky and disappear behind the abandoned general store. And he would remain standing. He didn't know what lay ahead.

He walked through the kitchen door to find Miss Elizabeth frying okra in a large iron skillet. He stood next to Miss Elizabeth and watched the grease bubble around the okra. The okra had been cut in round slices and stood the height of six nickels with a width just shy of a quarter. Miss Elizabeth turned each breaded coin using an ancient fork with the remains of a wooden handle. Miss Elizabeth said it had been her great grandmother's. She said her great grandmother was easy to find because she sang more than talked. As a child, Miss Elizabeth would visit and her great grandmother made cookies in the oven of a wood cook stove and they sang together. He counted one hundred and three breaded, brown, round okra. He said nothing about the cattle stampede.

He guessed Mr. Joseph would leave him alone in the night. He knew Mr. Joseph was still angry and would not have the patience to go through the empty gestures that helped disguise dark, wrongful, adult movements on too-young skin. Tonight, he would be cautious of jerky, fast movements at supper. Mr. Joseph ate quietly with a shiny film of anger on the surface of clinched jaw muscles. He remained cautious and ate without flaw.

His mind drifted across the line of persons he had avoided. The line began at just after his mother left and ended at just before Mr. Joseph. Following the predawn bird chatter, any relief from Mr. Joseph's presence would be handed out in small, thin wafers of time. Tomorrow would be a long day.

27 – Cat / Rat Fight

Mr. Joseph's shadow stood in the doorway. Was it day or night? He hoped for light followed by work. A soft light pushed against the south wall behind Mr. Joseph. "Ten minutes. Barn. Overshoes on kitchen steps."

The shadow was gone, followed by a made bed and a pass through the bathroom on his way to the kitchen. The ceiling light was on, and Miss Elizabeth was moving about the kitchen in a housedress and long apron. She spoke.

The overshoes were too tight over his boots. There were leather-soled house shoes inside the overshoes with wadded paper stuffed inside. His socked feet fit inside with more than extra room on the sides. He closed the four metal clasps on each black overshoe and walked heavily toward the barn.

The car windshield pulled wet drops out of the air. He turned to the right and saw low-hanging mist on the matted grass to the left of the abandoned general store. Ahead were two dim lights inside the barn.

He climbed over the four-board fence and walked down the east side of the barn. He turned right around the corner and saw Mr. Joseph had repaired the latch to the gate. Their eyes met. He looked down. Mr. Joseph let him in through the gate. To his left twin Guernsey's waited at double gates on the south side of the barn.

The twins were let in, and he was handed a pail. "Stool over there. Watch and do what I do."

He did and he began. His hands cramped and fingers ached, and the cow head turned back and looked at unsteady hands. The cow looked back over its left shoulder and watched the tail sweep the hands' face with mustard brown streaks. Tomorrow he would tuck his head into the lower left flank and pull the milk out of the tit in long pulls, letting the milk drop down from the bag in an uninterrupted flow…left hand first and then right. Each hand around and pulling down until the tit sides lost their firm curve and hung flat and rested. Mr. Joseph moved in with another three-legged stool and finished with fast, long pulls; white foam climbed the walls of the pail.

The twin Guernseys were fed behind a gate separate from the soon-to-arrive feeder cattle. He had last seen the feeder cattle with tails up heading fast to the north pasture. They would arrive after the feed had been mixed.

The layout of the barn was similar to the stone house barn. Two twenty-foot troughs on wooden skids lined both sides of the central hallway, butted lengthwise along a wall thirty-six inches high made of two by twelves. A two-foot horizontal slot ran along both sides of the hallway; another five feet of board above the slots met the floor joists of the loft. The far end of the hallway had two doors on the left. Four bulbs lighted the barn: two in the large room just inside the front gate that he had ridden the night before, one bulb in the hallway, and one connected to an ancient brown switch at the foot of the stairs to the loft.

The bulb in the hallway was wrapped in cobwebs. Bundles of folded baling wire hung from inside the floor joists, their looped ends resting on square nails. The hallway had shadows and cats jumping down from higher places and moving along the floor, a before-dawn-furry shadow floor that slowed when the first door opened.

The first room had no ceiling. The walls ended in a square hole in the floor of the loft. A no-angle cone pyramid of gray and white cotton hulls filled most of the room. At the edge of the pile sat a deep, unpainted wheelbarrow with a scoop shovel lying face down inside.

"Fill the troughs with a half foot of hulls."

The bottom of the shovel made a scraping sound on the concrete floor. The hulls were light and slipped too easily over the edge of the shovel. The hulls fell into the wheelbarrow with muffled scratching sounds. The threshold of the door was raised with a concrete strip; a board leaned at an angle served as a ramp. The wheelbarrow was old, with a metal wheel and four round spokes. The metal wheel made gritty sounds on the concrete floor.

Hours ago, when his mind approached the grayish haze of sleep and just before eyelids closed on eyes that had seen more than wanted, he had made a decision. He would find his way through the day from the now dark to the night dark when feelings could be attended to before eyes that had seen enough closed.

The wheel creaked up the ramp and dropped on the hallway floor, made a gritty, quarter turn to the right and faced the hallway, with the front gate beyond. Thirty-six eyes in the front of eighteen faces watched from the bottom lip of the two-foot-high horizontal slots where feed passed from hallway to trough. Ten cats on the left and eight cats on the right, tails twitching, waiting. The wheel creaked and lumped along to the far trough on the left. He would learn to ease the metal wheel over the concrete strip, with hulls piled high…two high loads per trough, four troughs—eight times easy over the concrete strip.

This was the first load, and the aim of the shovel was poor with new hands. A third of the first trough held six inches of hulls. He stepped back and walked to the right with handles in hand and wheel angled left…then stopped. Eighteen cats low against the floor, tails rigid, flat, with tips up and twitching. There were no eyes, only heads with the backs of ears.

Although his legs were new behind the creaking wheel, his presence was not the focus of whiskered face or ear. It was the door with Mr. Joseph's hand approaching the latch. It was the door that opened once in the graying darkness of morning and once again in the thin, pink light just before dusk. Their focus was the door to the concrete-walled room with its visitors whose images were seen inside slit pupils when catnap slowed into dream. Rodent flesh and bone did not appear every twice-opened door. The image of the last to rush out of the room—hard, fast, and low—remained in memory and dream. They waited. He waited. The door opened.

The rat was nearly one foot long with as much again in tail. It emerged as a shadow, low and fast, from the crack of the door. It ran into the light and rolled out of a pile of cats, belly to belly with one cat. It was the first giant corn-fed rat he had seen, and it was rolling fast toward him with its front claws dug deep into the cat's armpits. The rat was screaming and biting at the cat's neck. The cat's scream was high then lower, holding the rat teeth just out of reach and trying to pin the rat belly down and snap the rat's neck with larger teeth.

The rolling and screaming continued past the metal wheel and ended just left of his left foot. The rat's chin bobbed off its chest, with cat teeth deep into the back of its neck and the dead body being dragged under the cat closer to the cat's right legs. The cat's head dipped low and jerked to the right when its rear paw stepped on the dead body's tail. The cat paw had stepped on the tail just behind the fat muscle part before the tail turned into a skin–covered string.

At the other end of the hallway the pile of cats had flattened and walked away casually. Two of the larger cats watched sideways at the cat dragging the heavy dead body. Cats with no chance of breakfast rat worked hard to act otherwise occupied; all watched.

Dragging nearly one-fourth of its weight in rat, the cat stepped heavily away from the wheel and ran fast through watchers and past the two large cats. With a low growl, the cat stopped halfway up the loft stairs and watched through the open back of the steps. The two large cats moved to the bottom of the stairs.

The wheel creaked again, and he followed the wheelbarrow back to the cotton hull room, over the concrete strip, and back to the scraping of the shovel and the soft scratching of hulls. There were more trips up and down the hallway, followed by carrying heavy bags of bonemeal with gritty floating dust. Next came ground corn from the rat room behind the opened-twice-a-day door.

The three ingredients were mixed by hand in the troughs using three pairs of gloves. First, he put on the brown cotton gloves, followed by rough leather gloves with wide cuffs. The third pair was engineer gloves with gray leather up to his forearm and cuffs above his elbows. He leaned through the two-foot opening and spread his arms wide, palms up and fingers apart. As he pulled his hands together under the feed, hulls, bonemeal, and ground corn fell between his gloved fingers. Each spot in the trough required four passes with the wide-fingered, gloved scoops. He became aware of the muscles in the areas where his arms met his shoulders.

On the way to the cotton-hull room, he pushed the wheelbarrow past three cats eating the last of a rat leg connected to the gnawed remains of a tail just as Mr. Joseph walked through the front gate and made the "woo" sound.

He stepped out and closed the door to the hull room, turned and saw forty feet of cow heads appear over the troughs. There were sounds of giant blunt molars grinding corn. Heads evenly spaced over each of the four troughs showed side views of muscles and thick tongues guiding feed toward dark throat shadows. Large nostrils snorted bone dust and cotton hulls onto adjacent heads. Snorts traveled down rows of heads, followed by large lungs sucking air down throats while nostrils cleared. Each animal weighed over a thousand pounds and drank twelve to twenty gallons of water a day. Thick necks and heavy bodies pushed against troughs and wore oak sides down to smooth, wavy neck rests.

Mules had stood at the same troughs, ate and left and did not return, replaced by bellowing tractors with wide spiked-metal wheels. Rubber-wheeled tractor mules came, followed by years of streaming cattle with hooves buried in manure and chests and necks pressed against the sides of the oak troughs where mules once stood. The barn was between old and ancient, and Mr. Joseph remembered the mules and how teams of them pulled the four troughs on their skids along with belongings and people right before the river came and rested at the peak of the roof. It was an old barn, and many had passed through it.

He stood and watched the heads pushing sounds through the thick manure air. Tongues licked under the chins on either side. Tongues ran along oak seams and corners. Heads began to turn away, with tongues sliding along the smooth, wet, oak insides of skid-footed feeders. Each head turned away first, with the body that always followed. The last of the cattle left the barn, and Mr. Joseph motioned. He passed through the front gate and walked behind the milk pails and his new father.

He had walked behind men before. They were connected to families but not to him. The one he followed now was not the one he would have chosen.

He stepped over the board fence and put his overshoes on the side steps next to the kitchen door. The sky had moved from light pink to see-through orange with wide stripes of clear light. The kitchen was bright, and the table was full. The milk was poured through cheesecloth into a three-gallon glass jug with a wide bottom and a large mouth. Chunks of white butter with hints of yellow that sat heavy in the cheesecloth were removed with a wooden spoon and placed inside openings in the sides of hot biscuits. There were three kinds of meat and eggs fried in butter. Coffee-colored grease from salt-cured ham was poured on open-faced biscuits sitting with pools of spoon-fed butter.

It was an early feast. One, most would consider, fit for a celebration. He would find there was no celebration. It was an introduction; it was the first meal to fuel a body to work in the fields without stopping until it was time to eat again. He didn't hear the introduction. He didn't know about the fuel. It was a most excellent breakfast, and his mind saw steam from biscuits rise through angled light from the window over the sink.

Miss Elizabeth had kitchen skills. She had helped her mother prepare noonday meals for thrashing crews of twenty to thirty men. It was just past the time when steam-powered tractors pulled giant thrashing machines, and under tall shade trees food was laid out on long tables of thin lumber atop wooden sawhorses that were covered with tablecloths. Miss Elizabeth had cooked for working men. She was a worker known for her gardening and strawberry picking. She had picked one hundred twenty quarts without stopping. She had some pride in the story, and it was retold often in the community. She was careful not to mention it herself but allowed others the pleasure of weaving the feat into one of their own stories.

He finished the celebratory meal and commented on its virtues. Miss Elizabeth seemed pleased with the compliments and handed him a wide-brimmed straw hat. "This is your choppin' hat. Keep it on all the time." The straw was flat, wide, and woven more loosely than the hats he had seen in store windows.

He followed Mr. Joseph to the shed where the hoes stayed. The first time he had touched a hoe was the day before, sometime before he stampeded the cattle. He grabbed two hoes just below their necks and headed for the truck. The hat sat low on his ears.

28 – Choppin' Cotton

Mr. Joseph filled his arms with hoes and laid them in the truck bed, neck first, with the handles spread out like so many wooden legs. The truck turned right and traveled north on the north-south road. Long cow shadows with forty-foot legs and small heads passed through the gate to the north pasture and poured over the grass, walking flat to the left of hooved creatures that passed by low sun and early light.

North and east of the north pasture, the cotton fields stood flat and green. All moved outside the open window just above his resting arm. He sensed the approach of heat and sameness.

He looked at Mr. Joseph. The man's jaw was set, and the burden of heavy lessons would begin again—this time in the cotton fields. The lessons would come like large hands that pushed down on his shoulders. The sun would heat the straw in his hat, and the wooden handle would become heavy but not yet. He sat balanced and easy and rested his mind.

The pasture left the window just before the last fence post passed across his arm. The truck turned right onto a dirt lane that ran along the outside of the fence that marked the north end of the pasture. Thirty-eight fence posts passed by his window. The truck left the last post that marked the northeast corner of the north pasture. The dirt lane ran parallel to rows of cotton that ran down the left side of the truck coming from the north-south road and continuing east toward a tree line some thousand yards beyond the windshield. Rows of cotton began on the right of the truck just past the last pasture post.

It was another early morning when the new sun ran through the woods bright and crisp and then slowed to a walk when tree leaves began to push back and make shadow spots on edges of sharp light. Cotton plants stood thick and straight, with thin brown stalks that turned to green and branched out to broad pointed leaves covered in sparkle dew that flashed and fell. The plants stood just shy of one foot, with stems jammed together that had begun to compete for what fed them—roots eating fast in the dark.

The dirt lane ended with a second lane that ran north and south. The truck turned right and crept along in an idled first gear. He looked over his arm and down the rows to the pasture posts in the distance. The spaces between rows closest to his window were wider and moved faster than the spaces one hundred, two hundred, and four hundred yards out. The spaces moved toward the pasture fence and became thin brown lines.

The line of posts moved straight and slow, and the wire between them hid in the distance. Each post stood with both sides covered in wood-knot faces that watched pasture and field. Each day pasture faces watched lines of cows that spread and ate. Field faces watched hoes with flesh arms, bent backs, and faces down behind straw hats.

The truck stopped, and the first cotton choppin' lesson began. He remembered an old hoe was better than a new hoe. He chose a middle-aged hoe and put a nice edge on the blade. Cotton choppers were expected to chop two rows at a time. The two rows were on one side of the chopper, usually the left. City people said, "hoe the garden." Country people said, "choppin' weeds," and if people were "choppin' weeds" in a cotton field they were "choppin' cotton." First day, first lesson; he would be responsible for one row at a time.

Choppin' cotton involved two activities. Although of equal importance, one was considered primary and the other a prominent secondary. At times the secondary was done first and the primary second. It depended on the chopper's preference. Most choppers did the primary and secondary simultaneously and went back over the same area and did the primary followed by the secondary. However, when they did the secondary the second time, they once again did the primary at the same time. Fog rolled over his brain while Mr. Joseph's explanation droned on.

The first row was longer than the first lesson, and Mr. Joseph left in the truck to pick up the choppin' crew in town. He was left with his lesson and a long row that ended at the edge of the woods. He did the primary and prominent secondary in various orders with his back to the pasture and his face down behind the straw hat. He found the primary required skill and the prominent secondary judgment. He walked back to the beginning of the row where Mr. Joseph had chopped. This was where the lesson had begun. He compared his skill and judgment to the beginning of the row. He knew this was the part of the lesson where the teacher was not present but would reappear to continue instruction.

He returned to the spot where he had stopped. There were sounds in the woods. He kept his head down and moved his eyes to just below the hat brim and saw a dark shape that moved from left to right, stopped and faded away; prominent secondary and primary, prominent secondary and primary. He knew if he looked up and turned in a full circle, he would see no moving vehicle or human. He held his hoe tight and worked on his skill and judgment.

Midway down the row were moments when his body and hoe stepped and swung together—strings of moments when his mind traveled, and his body stepped into the flow of those who had swung and stepped on the same brown spaces in a time before. He shifted his weight forward and back in half steps and watched the hoe move through the plants.

He chopped the weeds and thinned the plants, primary and prominent secondary. There were half steps and stops, with head turned and ear pealed. He finished the row and faced the pasture with his back to sounds in the trees. Behind him a truck motor hummed far beyond the woods. The distant motor sound traveled through the trees and over the cracks of dead branches pushed down by no-see shadows that walked in the woods. The hum began behind his left ear and moved forward to just short of his left eye. The truck appeared as a metallic bump that moved north on the north-south road, a metal-shelled beetle that moved past the spaces between distant rust-colored cows. The idled first gear approached and stopped with the truck.

Ten dark-skinned adults stepped down from the bed, and an older, black-skinned woman stepped out of the cab. He had another fifty yards to chop before he reached the truck. Those who had arrived were bent forward on one knee to put an edge on metal using large files. As he chopped his way to the truck, those who had arrived stood up, spread out and began the rhythm of metal through dirt.

He turned without stopping and began his single-row half step to the woods. The pace was faster, smoother, and with less effort. Occasionally he stepped into the rhythm but sadly, often remained at the edge with awkward movements.

The hoes moved through like razors, scissors, and combs, and the plants that filed out behind those who had arrived were cleaned, shaped, and thinned. It was a sound difficult to describe. It arrived. It stayed. He would find that the sound would sit quietly in the moment but would stand and respond clearly when recalled.

Mr. Joseph faced the choppers. He stayed two steps back and to the right of Mr. Joseph's back. He maintained an angle that required Mr. Joseph to make more than a half turn to the right to see him. He watched the wet dots on the man's shirt grow to circles and large ovals and join into a solid, darker, no color.

This was his third single row. He smelled the warm straw in his hat and felt the sweatband leak down the top part of his jaw just in front of each ear. The metal at the end of the handle weighed more, and the wood felt thick and heavy. The sun climbed the trees, and shadows walked to the woods; the heat sat down on his head.

In the space between the back of his eyes and the front of his brain, dark birds circled—slow, circling, black dots. They were floating. They were waiting. They were waiting for him to look at one of them for a moment too long. And he did. The bird pulled its wings in close to its body and came down fast and hard, leveled out and shot across the back of his eyeballs, making him flinch. He had seen them before with legs and arms silhouetted in the shadows of trees and standing in corners of empty rooms. They were changing shadows that fed off the carrion of fatigue and fear. His mind glanced up and saw broad wings and red, featherless heads with white curved beaks. His mind looked away from black eyes and focused on light green weeds between dark green stalks. He had been in the field for three rows' worth.

Each row was two hundred sixty yards shy of one mile. It took considerable effort to stay up with the experienced choppers who chopped two rows at a time and could finish each set of two in thirty minutes. He counted five thousand half steps per row and nearly as many times that the metal moved through the cotton. The equal swings and half steps were six days a week. And at the end of eighty days, he will have chopped his way through each field twice. But this was the first day, and there were ten more hours.

The chopping crew would quit for the day, load up in the truck and return to town. He would stay in the field till just before sunset then walk to the barn and begin mixing the feed for the troughs and familiar cow faces.

The wood twisted in his hand, and the metal end rolled out of the plants with four black eyes set between protective head plates. Twenty pounds of snakes, six-foot bodies rolling up the hoe handle and sliding down to a hot metal blade and back up the handle toward his hands. Tops of the heads were brown and the bottoms cream-colored atop deep black, thick bodies. They were full-grown, venomous water moccasins. His hands and the snakes were wrapped around the handle, his mind mesmerized by the twirling and shining blackness.

"Drop the hoe! Drop the hoe!"

His eyes were using massive amounts of brain energy that caused the shouts to sound faint and tin like. He saw the metal end of Mr. Joseph's hoe strike the wood just below his hands. He felt the wood sting when the handle left his hands. He saw the handle move fast, away and down. The snakes slid down the handle and piled up on the flat, inside surface of the blade. The metal came out of the dirt slowly, with the snakes' blunt snouts touching. Very slowly, dirt fell away from the blade. Snake heads turned and black eyes looked. Wet fangs in front of white mouths lurched and left quickly. Muscles stood hard and still; sounds remained faintly shallow and distant.

The sounds of the hoes returned. A staggered line of backs and elbows moved straight ahead to his left. He retrieved his hoe from three chopped rows to his right. He saw the last of the snakes moving over and around dry dirt clods, heading at an angle to the woods. He saw a dent in the handle just below where his hands held the hoe. The dent would be a reminder that fields of hoes often attract visitors.

The day continued with the sun in his face up the rows and, down the rows, hot light on wet hair drawn in dark lines down his neck. Midday the shadows disappeared, and he could feel the sun push down on the top of his hat. His scalp sat in dim golden light and whispered to his hand to remove the covering for breath.

After bologna sandwiches, the afternoon continued. He felt heaviness in his limbs. He stumbled over dirt clods that, earlier, he stepped over and through. Requests to leave, stop, or rest had never been spoken in the field. He chose not to look up at the black dots circling above his mind's eye. He focused on the rhythm of metal through dirt. He watched the hoes rise in a staggered wave and come down with a long sound full of short metal parts.

He began to move the blade through the plants faster, and half steps widened to nearly full. He moved out of Mr. Joseph's blind spot. He saw the man's gray eyes slide sideways. He moved up and past Mr. Joseph and then was called back for a missed weed. The weed grew in cotton and soybeans. It hid next to stalks with similar color and leaves, and it was missed most often when weed and plant were the same height. It was his turn to be called back and introduced to the "careless weed." He returned to cut the weed out and be told to chop with the crew.

He had planned to put distance between him and the crew. The rhythm of the hoes had continued for hours, unchanged. The body heat of the crew made the air still and damp. Mr. Joseph's nearness was draining—draining because of the energy used to be cautiously unnoticed.

An hour had passed, and he had inched ahead of the crew and stopped and stretched. The pain was in his spine five bumps down from his neck. The pain was intense, sudden, and came from outside. Mr. Joseph swung his hoe a second time, and the metal neck struck him in the spine. His back arched in and his arms out and up.

He turned and looked at Mr. Joseph. The hoes had stopped moving; the crew was watching. He had been made aware of his place. He was embarrassed and wondered if those who stared had an opinion. He didn't say anything. They didn't say anything. Mr. Joseph didn't say anything.

The rhythm started again, blade through plant and metal through dirt. He stepped into the rhythm, and a great sadness came like a hard rain. He had been hit before with a boot sunk into his chest that had sent him flying. The sadness was not from pain or embarrassment. It was a hard rain of sadness from unnecessary unkindnesses that grieved the spirit.

Midafternoon brought heat from the ground that rolled up and stayed under his chin, while hot air wrapped around his face and sat heavy on his shoulders. There were no more plans to separate from the crew or to ask or to speak. He lived in the motion of the handles and the staggered sounds of the blades. He stayed in the rhythm and waited for feet to step on the bottom of long shadows when the sun reclined and removed its gaze. He knew the light would dim and heat would sit closer to the ground, and the sound of the motor would fade as the crew returned to town.

A vapor of a thought passed, paused and stayed. He used the see-through thought as a companion for his mind after his brain had tumbled end over end moments before. His mind's hands held the thought until it stood on its own and could be revisited when the heated hours drudged on and his brain lay flat and unfocused.

It was not a new thought. It lingered, and he recognized it from before. The thought had rested against the middle post that held up the back porch of the shack. The thought had leaned against the post for some time before he was aware of its presence. He had sat on the couch with his mind full of the creaks and cracks of night that were just below the constant buzz and ring of what's-going-to-happen fear. He and the thought and the dogs rested together. The next day he began to carve out something of his own. The thought had been his, and he and the thought had practiced throwing until what was going to happen happened. Now his thought had returned as a reminder to stay busy with something of his own inside somebody else's something.

The light had dimmed, and the crew had finished their last row for the day. The crew gathered around Mr. Joseph. Mr. Joseph handed each person a five-dollar bill for one day's work. The crew headed for the truck.

He turned and started on his single row, headed east toward the woods. His body faced northeast up the row with the truck motor in his left ear. The truck turned left and headed for the north-south road. The sound faded around the back of his head from left ear to right, slowly silenced by trees and distance.

He finished the row, walked with his hoe to the shed and leaned the hoe against the wall across from the hoes from the truck. He walked to the barn and eased full wheelbarrows of cotton hulls over the concrete strip. He poured a thick, wide stripe of bonemeal down the center of each trough and headed for the ground-corn room where rats dined when they could. He was in the room with five-gallon buckets in the corner and cats looking through the opening when the thought came with features and form. The thought was to become stronger, and the plan was to carry buckets of corn until he could defend himself. Every week he would add more corn to each bucket.

He heard the low "woo" sound, followed by the glow of cobwebs from the hidden bulb in the hallway ceiling. He finished emptying the last two buckets and began mixing the feed with the engineer's gloves. He had an early start. He had left the field early and walked directly from the woods without chopping his way toward the pasture fence. He didn't mention the last row and Mr. Joseph didn't ask.

He tried to stay alert around the man. But his mind would fill with fog. Words were hard to understand, and he found it difficult to respond correctly.

The cattle filed in and stood where they always stood and leaned against the same board with the same groove. The cattle filed out, finished. The cobwebs stopped glowing. The gate closed, and he followed the man back to the house.

29 – Growing Stronger

The summer continued with each day the same: house, barn, field, barn, and house. Sundays were religious rituals where Mr. Joseph preached sermons with three points and a hymn, followed by house, barn, and house. Some nights were more unpleasant than others.

The start of school was delayed while crops required cultivating. There was more chopping and hand pulling of Johnson grass, with roots and seeds placed in feed sacks to prevent the grass from spreading and choking out the cotton and soybeans.

The day would come when the barn, house, and fields would take their turn moving away from another back window. Until that day he would grow stronger. He knew he would not walk away unaffected. There would be harm to his spirit from the monotonous days of work and the lurking, unnecessary contact that would whisper non words that moved the tiny hairs on the back of his ears. Years would teach him to turn away and escape with only glancing blows from word and hand. He had walked down the hallway with the buckets. Each was half full.

School started six weeks late when the water in the air eased and breezes were pleasant, before the leaves colored and air had edges. School brought recent friends and cousins. The hours of school offered a childhood lightness that lifted and came with easy smiles and girls with long, brushed hair. Boys' shirts were ironed and buttoned over white, round-necked T-shirts.

The bus stopped next to the gap in the woods, and his smiling friend stepped out of the trees, with tall tales of summer with relatives out West. The bus went past the three girls' house. A brown dog slept on the porch to the right of the open door. The screen door was off the top hinges and lay at an angle across the opening. He guessed the girls had left, struggling with more and arriving to less. He remembered the oldest girl's kindness.

School lasted a few short weeks then harvest began. The cotton had grown to four feet. He had watched the fields grow white. It began with dots and splotches of wet off-white and grew to a dry, fluffy, pure white. He noticed that the ends of the rows next to the ditch were dusty brown from the road. The cotton plants had turned a brittle gray covered with bright white cotton puffs just shy of a large man's fist. The cotton sat in its pod, once green and sealed but now open. Cotton sat in its place from bloom to pod to dead hull.

The hull was hard and ended in four to five knifepoint tips. The cotton sat inside, behind the points. When hands reached for the cotton, the points jabbed and scratched from middle knuckles to nails. Fingers bled for the first week and hands were sore.

A tan canvas bag was folded six times, with a sash that went over his left shoulder and across his chest. The bag had a wide mouth and rested on his right hip just under his right arm; it stretched ten feet behind him. The air was pleasant and lay easy on his face.

The wagon sat at the brown-cotton end of the rows where the edge of the north-south road lay beyond the ditch. The wagon had eight-foot side boards, front to back, held together with three brackets on each corner. The wooden wagon sat on its metal bones and stretched behind its tongue some twenty feet. The wagon moved on old truck tires wrapped around rust-filled wheels. An angled two by four rose out of the back right sideboard; a rectangular scale hung from the board.

Cotton pickers were able to rest for a moment when their sacks were weighed and marked in a ledger next to their name…High Speed Jones 114 lbs. It was an unspoken rule that pickers would not approach the scale with less than one hundred pounds in their sacks. Each sack had a sash on the mouth end and a canvas loop on the bottom. Sacks with one hundred pounds or more were stuffed round, making it difficult to bend to attach sash and loop to the scale.

He had been a cotton chopper and now a cotton picker. He had the sack, and his mind was willing. His hands pulled back just short of the knifepoint hulls. The pickers moved ahead while his brain pushed his hands into the hulls and cotton into the sack. The rhythm of metal blade through dirt had become short drags of canvas over dry clods, a scooting sound where sack pushed picker through the cotton. He learned to drag near his weight to the scale.

* * * * * * *

Fall fell into Christmas with cousins and short months with cold that froze cow pee into crystals that hit the ground with shallow crackles. His hands had grown into the feed gloves. He carried full buckets of ground corn, two in each hand. He was stronger and resisted more of Mr. Joseph's advances.

At neighboring farms, the winter had brought sickness to cattle. Mr. Joseph brought boxes filled with huge vials of medicine. There were two metal syringes with needles the thickness of straw. Men came, and the cattle were pushed through a chute that closed around their necks. The thick needles pulled clear syrup from the vials. Queen and Prince barked and helped move the cattle toward the chute. The thick needles slammed through cowhide high and behind the left hipbone of each cow. When it was finished, the men left, and cattle were fed.

Queen and Prince sat by the board fence while Mr. Joseph walked toward them. He ran to catch up. Mr. Joseph had the syringe in his right hand. The dogs sat close together with Prince on the right and Queen on the left. He caught up with Mr. Joseph as the man put his right knee on the ground and brought up the syringe.

He touched the man's right forearm. "The needle is too big."

"Dogs need to be vaccinated. Cattle can make them sick. If they don't get vaccinated, they may get pneumonia."

"The needle is too big."

The syringe was parallel to the ground, and he could see the tip of the needle had been cut at a forty-five-degree angle. The tip was face up with the hole showing. The needle disappeared into Prince's chest without a sound. Prince looked at the man, turned and watched the needle go into Queen's chest. Prince fell hard on his right side and was eyes-open dead. Mr. Joseph had turned and was a few steps away when Queen fell. Her eyes were half open, with her jaws opening and closing over and over.

He called out for Mr. Joseph. "She's still alive!"

Mr. Joseph came and grabbed Queen's back paws and swung her one-half turn, smashing her skull against the outside wall of the hoe shed.

Mr. Joseph walked away quickly. He hoped it was out of grief for the death of his two dogs. *Did Mr. Joseph think he was protecting the dogs from sickness? Did he make a terrible error in judgment?* Queen and Prince loved him and trusted him enough to let a too-large needle be stuck into their chests without defending themselves. He guessed the man felt bad. He didn't know. He sat with Queen and Prince's bodies until it was dark, and Miss Elizabeth began calling for him. He knew it was something that would never go away. He would carry it forever.

The winter he lost Queen and Prince passed. Some mornings still had an edge to the air. They were mornings when cattle came early and knelt down, and barn cats sat on cows for warmth and kneaded their paws on itchy cowhides—a cat-like arrangement mutually beneficial and peculiar in nature. He guessed it started with a dozing cow and passing cat. It was a morning with cats and cows that his fingers laced around wire handles and he carried six full buckets of ground corn. His hands were big, and his back was strong.

* * * * * * *

Mid-August found him standing in formation, wearing white shirt, black pants, and a narrow, white belt. Miss Elizabeth felt strongly that he should have house shoes—they were the only civilian shoes he had. He stood at attention with the heels of the house shoes touching. His red-beaded, white moccasin house shoes stood out in a battalion of Weejun penny loafers—each polished to a high burgundy shine.

It was a military school—strict, hard, and sparse. He found it much easier than the farm. He was told that he would receive "a better education." He was told that his morals were incongruent with the way he was raised. He was told that he would attend the out-of-state military school, and upon graduation he could not return to the family home.

He stayed at the military school for a fall, winter, spring, summer, fall, winter, spring, and summer. There he used his practiced eye for targets to earn a stint as captain of the rifle team. He was given a diploma, and he left the school.

Seven summers later he visited the farm and left shortly after his arrival.

He carried memories that sat heavy in his gut. Sonny's words, "He's simple ya know," hovered in the distance joined by the words of others over the years. Mr. Joseph had explained, in a direct way, that it had been necessary to speak in a simplified manner to the boy. This had been a courtesy, according to Mr. Joseph, in light of the boy's poor breeding and previous circumstance. "You came from trash" stood tall next to Sonny's "He's simple ya know."

Hensen March

30 – The Call

He drove the car after the call. Aunt Eunice said what had happened, and the time was short. The car went straight past twenty-four-cornered blocks. It was a pass-through-quickly part of the city, a flat concrete road with cavity panes hanging loose in the sides of forgotten buildings. He turned right, and the car passed through no-light intersections with forgotten-longer buildings with rusted iron fronts and side walls of failing brick patched with concrete.

Occasional vacant lots sat next to old brick, lots with man-tall weeds and dirt paths that turned sharply for cover. The air came in below his nose. His eyes had opened his mouth at the sight of moving brown from the right. A vacant lot with no grass and pressed-flat dirt with men lying on their backs and sides in rows, twenty across and faded-brown deep. Some moved about the edges. All men down were feet to the street. There were no faces—only dirt, clothes, and men with shades of the same brown. It was a fearsome sight of need and danger. He was relieved to pass.

There were more no-light intersections followed by a mass of parked cars wrapped around half of a gray-stoned square with ten floors and doors on each side. He parked in a gap next to the sidewalk beside the street and walked up wide granite steps through polished metal doors. Four women sat in the middle of the lobby behind four maple wood desks, each facing one of the four entrances. Footed questions had made worn-wood paths to each desk. He walked his question up the path and stood before a portly woman behind horn-rimmed glasses and wrapped in a sweater with brown buttons. He delivered the question, was given the answer, then followed the imaginary line from the tip of a round, short finger to a staircase to his right. He walked halfway up the inside of the building. He stopped at the landing with a long hallway to the left and a short one to the right that had a nurses' station at the end beside double swinging doors. He went down the short hallway.

It was another long walk down a short hallway that may have shaped the tone of the two questions. He gave the name, and the nurse's response was "yes." He asked about prognosis.

"He has brain cancer! How do you think he's doing?"

He felt his shoulders rise, and he looked hard into the woman's eyes. He saw no anger, irritation, or resistance. There was the soft, thin air of casual indifference. It was a proper introduction to the world that lay beyond the double swinging doors.

He used his left shoulder to push through the left door to an open ward with smells that reminded hands not to touch. There were fifteen men in fifteen beds lining the walls; the soles of their feet faced the center of the room.

Fear oozed out the edges of pupils set deep in a gray face last seen for an early shed supper twenty-five plus years before. It lasted less than a moment.

He stood on the sidewalk and heard the air escape from the brakes. The sunlight through the windows of the bus was bright against the pole that steadied the riders as they filed down the steps. It was summertime.

Epilogue

In the years before his father died Jim had walked away from the unnecessary unkindnesses and was graced with a family of his own. He earned four university degrees.

Mr. Joseph and Miss Elizabeth were invited to his graduation, where he received an advanced degree and the title of Doctor. Miss Elizabeth attended. Mr. Joseph did not.

He understood why Mr. Joseph did not attend. He remembered Mr. Joseph's words to him, "It's just a state university. I wouldn't be too proud. Ph.D.'s are a dime a dozen." Remembering the words made him smile—*vintage Mr. Joseph!*

* * * * * * *

Years passed. Miss Elizabeth's health became fragile. Jim took a leave from work and returned to the farm to care for Mr. Joseph who had received a terminal diagnosis. He sat next to Mr. Joseph's bed.

"I was not a good father."

Jim lied and said, "You did OK." He figured dying was hard enough without going through each of Mr. Joseph's unnecessary unkindnesses. There had been times of great generosity when Mr. Joseph had helped with education expenses.

Mr. Joseph described his physical actions toward Jim, as a boy, as "an unnatural relationship." Jim knew about pedophiles and their ability to rationalize their abusive behavior. Still, it was shocking to hear the words come out of his adoptive father's mouth—as if a child had the option of consent. Mr. Joseph felt the need to unburden himself by telling each of the extended family members about his and Jim's "unnatural relationship."

* * * * * * *

It was an hour after dawn at the poor-choice hotel. The officer walked next to Jim, on his right, along a concrete hallway that ended with narrow, metal stairs leading down to another floor. The walls were dark, thick concrete, and the passageway felt like a hole with steps. His throat was thick. A drop of cold sweat dropped from his armpit down his side. He felt it hit his rib and drip on the roll of skin above his waist.

He had been counting the steps down. Counting helped but not this time. He had counted seventeen steps, and there looked to be five more. He was going down a hole where those who came and went watched those who stayed.

Death Row was in the hole. When those who stayed left the hole, they were placed in another hole where they lay flat, still, and forgotten.

One day he would come out of the hole and not return.

Ten years passed.

Jim came out of the hole—officers opened the crash gates with giant brass keys. He walked under the razor wire and through the gates and did not return.

He had served ten years in the poor-choice hotel—without sentence—and retired. Those who came and went and those who stayed had called him the "Nut Doctor."

The End